# Phantom Force

James H. Cobb

SILVERTAIL BOOKS • *London*

Dedicated to the merchant mariners and the merchant fleets of the world, the red corpuscles in the flowing blood of civilization

# Prologue to Conflict

A snowflake falls on a suitable slope, another follows, and then another. The snow pack thickens. The cornices mass. Pressure and instability increase.

A kind of ambience may ensue for a time, the disaster held at bay for another day, another hour. But inevitably, inescapably, there falls that one last snowflake too many.

The great wars of human history frequently begin in the same way. Rarely is there a single cause or triggering event. Rather, like a mountain avalanche, there is an accumulation building to catastrophe.

# Part One

# Initiation of Engagement

There is truth in the belief that things can be "too quiet", especially in the jungle.

Like the sea, the jungle is an all-inclusive environment. Any disruption within it radiates outward among the millions of living organisms that make up its existence. The night birds cease their singing, the animals huddle unmoving in their hides, and the myriad of crawling, creeping, chittering things go silent in the darkness.

Captain Baktiar Rajamala of the Indonesian army knew about such silences. From his position in the main gate watchtower, he swept his night glasses across the forest line a quarter of a kilometer beyond the perimeter fence. He saw nothing, but he knew they were out there, lurking in the shelter of the undergrowth, staring back across the defoliated dead zone that surrounded the colony. The terrorists of the Morning Star Movement were always out there.

Captain Rajamala's lip curled in contempt. Filthy savages! Hadn't Indonesia driven out the damned Dutch, freeing the Papuans from the tyranny of European Colonialism? Hadn't Jakarta taken Irian Jaya and its Stone Age peoples under its wing, seeking to administer its mineral wealth for the betterment of all? Couldn't these black monkeys understand that it was for their own good?

Apparently not, for the ingrates had raised their Morning Star flag, arrogantly demanding a plebiscite on the annexation of their island by Indonesia and calling for independence. As if these Stone Age barbarians were capable of caring for themselves in the modern world.

Totally unaware of the irony of his thoughts, the Javanese-born officer continued his visual sweep around the port facilities, panning his binoculars across the administration complex and the barracks of the security garrison. Beyond the buildings, glowing an evil murky green under the glare of the work arcs, were the settling ponds for the copper slurry brought down by pipeline from the mines deep in the Maoke mountain range.

Farther to seaward, the lights of the loading jetty extended into the bay. Clustered at its shoreside were the dwellings of the two thousand Javanese workers and their families brought in to service the port and the ore handling facilities.

Putting the residential area so near the pier had been a mistake as far as Captain Rajamala was concerned. It caused no end of trouble for the Army security force. The damned lazy *transmigrasi* kept trying to stow away on the ore transports. Those peasants had yet to get it through their heads that Irian Jaya was their home now and this was their new life. Jakarta had made the decision and that was an end to it. Like the Morning Stars, they seemed incapable of understanding that this was for their own good and the betterment of the nation.

The garrison commander lowered his glasses, letting them hang from the strap around his neck. All was as it should be. And why not? Captain Rajamala prided himself on keeping a tight camp. Port Aiduna had been ringed by an eight-foot high electrified and sensor-studded barbed wire fence. Automatic weapons mounted in watchtowers like this one covered every inch of the perimeter and banks of floodlights blasted the darkness with their glare.

True, it was more corporate security than a real military defense, but then the Free Papuan Militia had little more than machetes and shotguns to fight with.

Still, what did the Asmat tribesmen call this place? "The Land of Lapping Death", wasn't it?

Captain Rajamala hesitated for a moment then reached for the tower's field phone. He would declare a "mad minute" and have the duty gunners hose down the tree line, just in case.

But before he could lift the receiver, a series of hollow metallic coughs sounded from somewhere out in the darkness.

The first mortar salvo, precisely targeted, took out the power station transformers. Disrupted electricity arced and blazed, the compound was engulfed in darkness. Swiftly, the Papuan mortarmen swung their

6

tubes to bear on their next pre-registered target. A storm of 81mm rounds rained down on the garrison barracks, blasting and slaying.

At the edge of the forest, orange backflashes silhouetted the areca palms as recoilless rifles barked, their shells sequentially demolishing the spindle-legged perimeter gun towers.

Captain Rajamala's last living action was to stab a thumb down on the alarm button, an act of futility as the power failure had silenced the sirens. Then the platform atop the main gate tower took a direct hit, bursting like a fiery balloon.

Papuan warriors poured out of the forest line, some clad in the black uniform of the Free Papuan Militia, others naked save for their ammunition belts. The majority of them carried modern assault rifles and grenade launchers. Screaming battle cries older than civilization, they charged the collapsing colony defense line.

Bali has been called "the Land of Ten Thousand Temples." This is erroneous, for in truth there were over fifty thousand temples scattered over the island. They could be found in the mountains and on the ocean shores, along the roads and byways, in the cities, towns and villages. Even the smallest and most humble of communities had its shrines to the *Trisaki*, the three primary manifestations of *Sang Hyang Widhi,* the One God who rules all.

For the Balinese did not merely follow or prescribe to their unique form of the Hindu religion, the *Agama Tirta* (the Science of the Holy Water), as much as they lived it. They shared their island with their Gods. They stood ever at one's shoulder and were intertwined into every facet of daily living. Every tree, every stone, every living thing of Bali held its guardian spirit which, in turn, was but a glittering fragment of the One God, a thread in a great, ancient and all-encompassing tapestry.

This was the essential, universal truth of the Balinese people. It had given them the strength to survive as an isolated Hindu island amid a frequently hostile sea of Muslim fundamentalism. It had given them the endurance to live through centuries of European Colonialism and decades of oppressive Javanese administration and yet remain unique.

Each Balinese village had three obligatory temples, each representing one of the primary holy manifestations. Dedicated to Vishnu the Preserver, the *pura puseh*, the "navel temple", was located in the center of the village and served as the shrine around which the community grew.

To the north was the *pura desa*, the "village temple" dedicated to Brahma the Creator. Here, the everyday matters of the village were dealt with and the village's ritual feasts and celebrations were held.

To the south was the *pura dalem*, the temple of Shiva the Destroyer and his consort Durga. In many ways, the Balinese Hindu hold this the most critical of the three. Vishnu and Brahma deal in life, creation and

8

growth, beneficial affairs. Shiva rules on matters involving death, destruction and damnation. The prudent individual assuages him first and earnestly endeavors to stay in his favorable lights.

Taman Karangasem was the *pemangku* of the village of Anak Angung Garong's *pura dalem*, the lay priest who maintained the little temple and who officiated at its routine, day in and day out ceremonies. In marked contrast to the grim visage Shiva presented to his worshippers, Karangasem was a genial, kindly man, deeply involved in the welfare of his village and much admired and respected in return.

Middle-aged, graying and stocky for a Balinese, he strode down the forested path to his temple, savoring the hint of early morning cool. For the moment he was clad in the simple wraparound sarung and sandals of a common villager. He would shift into his more elaborate ceremonial garb later in the morning to deal with his religious duties. For now he had the more plebian tasks of cleaning and maintenance to deal with.

The *pedanda*, the high priests of the Balinese religious cast, sometimes disdainfully referred to the village temple keepers as "sweepers" – but Karangasem took no offense at the name. If the One God could be honorably served by wielding a broom then he was proud to do so. Humming softly to himself, he rounded the corner of the stone temple wall and passed through the open and elaborately carved split gate that led to the outer courtyard.

Abruptly, his tune trailed off. Across the flagstones, the main doors to the inner courtyard, the *Jerone*, the "holy of the holiest" stood open as they should never be, save for when a ritual was in progress.

Sandals slapping, Karangasem raced across the courtyard. Theft from Balinese temples was not unknown. Carvings and art objects were stolen for sale overseas or to the tourist shops. Also villages frequently would invest whatever wealth they might accumulate in gold and silver ornamentation to honor the Gods.

Such crimes were neither undertaken or responded to lightly. For a thief caught stealing from a temple, the sentence was frequently death, with the local police and the court system not being involved.

When he reached the door of the inner courtyard, Karangasem brought himself up short. It was worse than theft. Worse than he could ever have imagined.

The offerings to the gods brought to the temple by the villagers – the flowers, the artworks, the food – had been ruthlessly scattered and trampled across the court. The *padmasana*, the stone throne of the sun-god Surya in the upper right-hand corner of the temple yard had been tipped over. The deer's antlers had been broken from the *Maospait* shrine that commemorated the divine first settlers of Bali. And the *paruman*, the pavilion in the center of the *Jerone* that served as the communal seat of the gods had been smeared with animal excrement.

The Muslim battle cry of "There is no God but Allah and Muhammad is his Prophet" had been spraycanned in garish colors again and again around the walls of the *Jerone*.

In matters of joy or sorrow or passion, the Balinese are an open, exuberant and demonstrative people. Only in anger do they turn inward. Only in rage are they impassive. Karangasem expressed himself by the paling knuckles of his clenched fists. But the words of warning from a seventeenth century factor of the Dutch East India Company whispered down the ages.

"Do not lightly provoke the little brown people."

"Mohammed Sinar."

His name might have been a dreamed murmur in the darkness of the cheap *losman* lodging-house room, yet Sinar's eyes snapped open and his heart stuttered and slammed in his chest. He knew that some night he would wake up to die. It was a fate frequently reserved for losers in the game of power and territory.

As the most recent wave of Islamic radicalism had engulfed Indonesia, a variety of tribal, religious and political factions had become involved in the reviving the Aceh Merdeka (Freedom for Aceh) movement dedicated to the establishment of an independent Muslim fundamentalist state in northwestern Sumatra.

Theoretically these factions were united in a revolutionary cause against western secularism and the Indonesian government. In reality, the movement was wracked by schism and counter schism as warlords struggled bloodily for position and power, the civil war against Jakarta frequently taking second place in their priorities.

Muhammad Sinar was – or at least had been – one such player. Formerly a minor police official in western Sumatra, he had been cashiered from the security forces for misuse of government funds during the last attempt by the Jakarta government to suppress corruption.

Sinar proclaimed that the charges had been trumped up against him and that secularist persecution had been the real reason for his discharge. In reality, he had indeed been an embezzler and a fairly inept one. However, such truths would have gained him little status in the eyes of the mullahs.

With his dreams of power within the establishment disrupted, Sinar sought out the revolutionaries he had once fought. Using the contacts he had gained in his time with the police, Sinar rallied a band of former criminals and disgruntled ex-police officers to his cause. He had impressed the local revolutionaries with a great deal of bombastic rhetoric and a couple of minor coups against the provincial administration and had bullied the leadership of a small number of province villages into half-heartedly supporting his cadre.

After that, things had gone downhill. Muhammad Sinar lacked the monetary and military backing and the political acumen to maneuver himself into a position of real power within the movement. But while hindered by his bush league resources, Sinar still had world series intentions.

He had invited the warlords of two of the other Merdeka factions to a council of war, the stated intention being to merge the three factions into a single united force. Then Sinar had endeavored to bring this to pass by massacring the leadership of the other two groups.

His plot misfired catastrophically. The ambush had failed and now his two fellow warlords were seeking Sinar's head as fervently as they sought independence from Jakarta.

With his disgruntled "Army of God's Sacred Vengeance" scattered and laying low – and with both government security forces and revolutionary assassins on his tail – Muhammad Sinar found himself a man hard on the run.

Accompanied by his last two trustworthy bodyguards, Sinar shifted his name and the place where he slept daily. He'd had no chance to rest or to rally his troops. Even if given the opportunity, he would have few resources to rally. His faction was breaking up. His people were no longer willing to follow a man perceived as a loser. Escape from his predicament could only come through death or a miracle, with the former seeming far more likely than the latter.

And now, apparently, that death was upon him.

"Who are you?" The foolish, instinctive demand rasped from Sinar's lips as he smelled the stink of his own sweat and fear.

"That is irrelevant." The replying voice spoke Bahasa Indonesia, the approved universal tongue of the archipelago, but not with a Javanese or Sumatran accent. It was more the structured formality of the Straits Chinese. In the dim streetlight filtering through the curtains, Sinar became aware of three men standing at the foot of his bed.

12

All three were indeed Chinese. The two who flanked the third were young, powerfully built and clad western style in jeans and dark shirts. Gun steel glinted in their hands, making a grab for the pistol hidden under the mattress seem a very bad idea. Despairingly, Sinar wondered what had happened to his bodyguards.

The central Chinese read his thoughts. "Do not concern yourself with your guards, Mr. Sinar. One is unconscious; the other, regretfully, is dead."

This man was decidedly different from the others: elderly, slightly built, almost frail, his white, short-trimmed hair glowed in the feeble illumination. He wore a dark suit and tie and he seemed to radiate an aura of calm, precision and order.

"What do you want?" Sinar demanded, somehow sensing that death would not be forthcoming, at least not instantly.

"I have come to present you with this."

Sinar started as a heavy manila envelope plopped onto the sheet beside him.

"Enclosed you will find a set of maps and directions to a group of three hidden arms caches located on the northern coast of Sumatra. In each cache you will find weapons, ammunition and other military equipment suitable to your needs and adequate to make you the equal of the local government security forces and the decided superior of your enemies within the Merdeka movement. Also in the envelope you will find an amount of money that no doubt will prove useful. Use both as you will."

Fingering the envelope, Sinar felt the bulge made by a thick sheaf of cash.

This was incredible, impossible. He had feared death – but instead a miracle had come out of the night. Here was all that he would need to restore himself in the eyes of his followers and resume his march to power. One instinctive reaction was to suspect a trap, but if his proclaimed benefactors had wanted him dead why not simply kill him here and now? Why bother with sophistry?

"Who are you? Why do you do this?"

"As I stated, who we are is irrelevant and why we do this is our concern. Good night, Mr. Sinar. Our business is concluded."

The elderly Chinese began to turn away, and then hesitated. "Oh and do not discommode yourself concerning the body of your late guard. We will deal with it. Please offer our regrets to his family."

And then, as silently as they had come, they were gone. They might have been a desperate man's dream, save for the envelope they had left behind.

Sinar lit the room's single small lamp. With his pistol at his side, he eagerly scrabbled through the contents of the envelope, examining the maps and counting the cash. A thousand questions should have plagued him at that moment, a thousand answers demanded for them. But for Muhammad Sinar all such questions had been washed away by thoughts of triumph and revenge.

As the island of Java is the heart of the Indonesian archipelago, Jakarta was the heart of Java. With a population of over ten million, it is the fifteenth largest city in the world, its population density per square mile being one of the highest on the planet. In a distilled form, it possesses all of the mind-boggling contradictions inherent within twenty-first century Indonesia.

Reefs of modern high rises hung above an ocean of shantytowns and shops peddling the cheapest plastic tourist kitsch. The perfume of walled tropical gardens contrasted with the stench of motor exhausts and sewage-polluted canals.

Above all, the inherent, almost instinctive friendliness and amiability of the Javanese people clashed with a growing unease and anger.

In central Jakarta could be found the Lapagang Merdeka (Freedom Square). In colonial times it had been a military parade ground. Now it served as the physical core of the Indonesian Governmental bureaucracy. Encompassing almost a full square kilometer, the Presidential Palace, the Parliament building, Army Headquarters, the National Museum and the Ministry of Finance were spaced around its perimeter. The United States Embassy and a variety of banks, hotels and upscale businesses could also be found there.

The square itself had been decorated with a selection of heroic statuary commemorating great moments in Indonesian national history. Dominating its center was the MONAS, the National Monument. Built by the Soviet Union in 1961 in honor of Indonesian Independence, the gigantic marble obelisk rose one hundred and thirty-seven meters to a tip jacketed in thirty-five kilograms of pure gold.

No longer impressed, the city's inhabitants referred to it as "President Sukarno's last erection."

Freedom Square was a natural locale for a political protest, the logical place for the Indonesian people to rally, provided the government that purported to represent them would permit it.

There had been no single call or spur for this day's demonstration. The people simply started to stream inward toward the Square from the slums and the universities and from the other lesser demonstrations flickering and sputtering around the city. The involved peoples had no single grievance, nor were they of any one faction. They were as many and varied as the cultures of Indonesia itself, which meant they encompassed an incredibly broad spectrum.

They had but one point in common. They wanted things to be better.

They were tired of uncertainty. They were tired of corruption. They were tired of perceived government lies and favoritism and perceived religious and racial persecution. They were tired of political solutions that seemed to solve nothing. In the way that a mob can become like an angry, cranky child, they wanted someone to make their world immediately right, even though they themselves had no valid solutions to offer.

Like rivers growing in the rain, the trickle became a flow and the flow a flood.

The floods were dammed at the edge of the Lapangan Merdeka. The police blocked the demonstrators, keeping them from the square.

The security forces did not dare allow the floods to meet and become an angry ocean of demonstrators. The groups must be kept separated and thus manageable. Should they combine, the outcome could be disastrous for Jakarta and the Indonesian government.

The accumulated anger was not for the government alone. Many of the factions involved held deep animosity against each other. If they met and clashed, the effect might be similar to slamming two chunks of weapons grade uranium together.

Already reports were coming in of factional clashes on the side streets, pro-something versus anti-something else. The police could only hunker behind their clear Lexan riot shields and pray that the dam around the square would hold. If it didn't, water cannons and tear gas wouldn't be adequate.

There would be tanks and machine gun fire in the streets before nightfall.

He was unobtrusive, a slender dark-skinned, dark-haired man in a city of slender dark people. But a skilled ethnologist or an old East Indies hand might have been able to note the hints of facial caste and accent that would mark him as a Bugi.

It was comparatively rare to see a member of this tribal group away from the dock areas of the city, for the Bugi were a people wedded to the sea. They were master mariners, sometimes called the sea gypsies. For centuries, they had ranged the vast Indonesian archipelago from the coasts of Asia to the Philippines, more at home on the waters than upon the land.

Almost every inhabited island in the East Indies had at least one Bugi colony that served as a base for the tribe's vast fleet of sleek Pinisi schooners. They were the maritime glue that tenuously bound the myriad islands of Indonesia together, a proud people with a proud history as sailors, fishermen and traders.

They had also been the most savage and successful pirates in all the sea reaches of South East Asia.

On this particular day, this Bugi did not look exceptionally piratical. Clad in worn jeans, flip-flop sandals and a T-shirt bearing a Thailand sports shoe logo, he worked his way through the crowded upper middle-class neighborhood near Freedom Square, deftly avoiding both the streets gridlocked by the growing demonstrations and the police security checkpoints.

The Bugi had received his insurgency training from a former North Korean Death Commando turned mercenary advisor and had been briefed on police riot doctrine by a bought member of that agency. He had been preparing for this specific mission for over three weeks, finding a suitable strike point near a likely riot site close to the square and scouting his insertion and escape routes. All that was required was for the proper hysteric environment to develop. Two hours before, as the demonstrations had started to build to a critical level, he had received the go order.

The side street he now followed was parallel to one of the major arterials feeding into Freedom Square. The angry rumble of massed voices interspersed with shouts and bursts of chanted slogans flowed over the tops of the building. The security forces were focused on the demonstrators massed on the arterial; consequently, they had no time to waste on a nonpolitical innocent hurrying homeward with a burden of shopping bags.

One block short of the square, the Bugi turned into a narrow doorway between a restaurant and a novelties shop, climbing the narrow stairway beyond. The building he had entered was a comparatively new structure, a combination apartment and business complex, the apartments all being on the second floor, spaced on either side of a corridor that extended the full width of the block.

The corridor was warm, humid and rich with the smell of Indonesian cooking. The Bugi hastened down to its far end, ignoring the murmur of radio music and television chatter leaking from some of the apartments. His destination was the right-hand door at the end of the passage. Pausing, he listened. All seemed quiet in the rooms beyond and the door's cheap lock yielded readily to the silent thrust-and-twist of the heavy-bladed screwdriver he carried.

The apartment belonged to a young, childless married couple, both of whom had day jobs with the Indonesian civil service. That was one of the reasons the Bugi had chosen it, following an extensive reconnaissance. Clean and brightly decorated with inexpensive furnishings and knick-knacks from Thailand and Malaysia, the studio apartment boasted both a personal computer and a DVD equipped television set, the universal symbols of the young and upwardly mobile.

It also boasted a window that looked out over the arterial and the approaches to Freedom Square. This was the other reason the Bugi had selected it.

Setting down his shopping bags, the Bugi removed a gallon plastic jug from one. Filled with a viscous dark red fluid, it had a crude tear strip igniter screwed into its neck. He placed it carefully on the table in the center of the main room. Then he produced a folding stock AK-47 assault rifle and a single thirty round clip of ammunition from the second bag. Extending its wire stock, he expertly snapped the magazine into the weapon and glanced at the gold-finished wall clock, cross-referencing the time it displayed with the wristwatch he had been given for the mission.

Two minutes remained. Perfect.

Setting aside the rifle, the Bugi crossed to the front window. Rolling up the rattan blind, he opened the glass pane to its fullest stop.

Below, the broad street was a solid, jammed mass of milling angry people. At the head of the block, where the arterial entered Freedom Square, a line of riot police backed by a Cadillac Gauge armored car held the human avalanche back.

Here the rumble of voices had turned into a roar. There were swirls and eddies within the crowd, pushing and shoving taking place as rival factions within the demonstration clashed. From somewhere came the crash and splinter of storefront glass. Tension was a physical thing in the air, like a cloud of explosive vapor – but the igniting spark hadn't yet been struck. The protestors had not quite become a mob. Beyond hurled epithets and the occasional bottle, the police line had not been challenged, the demonstrators held at bay by the poised rattan riot batons of the security forces.

The Bugi retrieved his rifle and set its selector to "autofire". Standing far enough back from the window to be invisible in the room's shadows, he aimed at the interface line between the police and the demonstrators. He noted one uniformed individual working his way up and down the line of riot police, obviously the commander of that particular tactical detachment. He would be the logical first target.

The Bugi thumbed off the safety and peered over the AK's sights.

The last seconds ran down. The spit and crackle of gunfire sounded in the distance. On this cue, the Bugi opened fired as well, his first rounds dropping the targeted officer. Alternately lifting and lowering the muzzle of the assault rifle, he raked short, three round bursts indiscriminately into the security line and the front ranks of the demonstrators, the blood of the police and the protestors spraying and mixing as they fell. Chanted slogans turned to screams. The crowd writhed like a wounded living thing and the surviving police instinctively clawed for their sidearms.

The AK's magazine emptied and the Bugi sniper abandoned the weapon, letting it fall to the rice-matting floor. Then he turned to the table and the plastic jug resting upon it. The container had been filled with a mixture of gasoline and oxblood, the blood serving as a gelling agent to produce a crude form of napalm.

The Bugi yanked at the igniter in the neck of the jug, pausing for half an instant to ensure the fuse had sputtered to life. Then he was out of the apartment door and running down the hall, ignoring the other opening doors along the passageway.

He was in the stairwell when the incendiary exploded.

Once in the street, he was just another figure running through a city suddenly gone mad. More gunshots sounded over a growing rage of lifted voices, many more, followed by the savage rip of a heavy machine gun.

The plume of smoke that rose over the burning apartment block was only one of several lifting into the Javanese sky.

The situation briefing was informal only in that it was held in the small Presidential study off the Oval Office, and that it involved a single, select advisor. The matters discussed were of major import, not merely to the United States but to an entire corner of the planet.

President Benton Childress, forty-fourth President of the United States – intent, portly and scowling – lightly buffed the lenses of his glasses with a Kleenex. He was an ex-High School History Teacher, an ex-Mayor of the city of St Louis, an ex-colonel in the Missouri Air National Guard and the first black American to hold the presidency. In all of these incarnations he had not been a man given to wasting time.

"The short form, please, Harry," he said to his Secretary of State, "short and sweet – or bitter as the case may be. We're due to meet with the congressional leadership this afternoon and they'll be expecting direction from this administration."

"As you wish, sir." A graying Caucasian New Englander, Secretary of State Harrison Van Linden was a physical counterpoint to his president, but he too disliked the squandering of time. He aimed a computer access pad at the fifty-two-inch flat screen display set into the far wall of the study. "But I'm afraid there is nothing short or simple about any aspect of this situation."

At the touch of a key the screen filled with a map, a great, crescent shaped archipelago off the northern coast of Australia, extending some three thousand miles from the Philippines to the tip of South East Asia.

"The nation of Indonesia, Mr. President, made up of some thirteen thousand six hundred separate islands, six thousand of which are inhabited. The total population is in excess of two hundred and twenty million, divided among better than one hundred distinct ethnic groups and cultures, speaking over three hundred mutually unintelligible languages and dialects. Forty percent of the world's maritime trade passes through its territorial waters, including one of the primary oil transit lanes from the Persian Gulf. It is the fourth-largest nation on the planet and a major petroleum producer in its own right." Van Linden glanced at his Commander in Chief. "At the moment, it is also dying. If it goes terminal, reverberations from its fall will shake the geopolitical structure of the South East Asia and the Pacific Rim, not to mention the entire global economy. The monetary loss from such a collapse will go into the hundreds of billions. Given the conflict models we've seen during the Indonesian anti-Communist purges in the 1960s and in the East Timor conflict, the loss in human life will also be staggering. We can expect casualty counts that will range well into the six and possibly the seven figures."

The Secretary of State paused for a deliberate breath. He wasn't pleased with having to speak his next sentence. "It is also questionable if anything can be done to check this disaster."

"I'm not a believer in the single-option scenario, Harry," Childress replied firmly. "There is always something that can be done."

Van Linden nodded. "There is one possible corrective measure that I have heard proposed by our people in-theater."

"Let's hear it."

"We have to kill this man."

The image on the plasma screen changed to that of smiling, debonair figure in a well-cut safari suit of the kind that served as business wear in the East Indies.

"This is Makara Harconan, Mr. President, the instigator of Indonesia's current state of anarchy."

"I've seen the name in the security briefings." Childress sat back in his chair, the soft leather creaking. "He's a good-looking devil. What else does he have going for him?"

"Considerable personal wealth for one," Van Lynden continued. "Harconan is, or was, a prominent twenty-first century taipan, a trading magnate and business entrepreneur. His holding company, Makara Limited, was a major economic force in South East Asia, especially within Indonesia. He had links to international cargo brokerage, banking and the shipping industry. This was not a coincidence. All of these factors were critical to his long-term intentions toward his

22

homeland. In fact, it can be safely said that his entire life has been focused on one specific goal."

"Which is?"

"The destruction of the nation of Indonesia."

Childress's frown deepened. "The overthrow of the Indonesian government, you mean?"

Van Linden shook his head. "No, sir. I mean the physical dissolution of the Indonesian State. Harconan seeks a deliberate Balkanization of the archipelago into scores of independent island states."

"For what purpose? Your average revolutionary wants to seize a nation, not destroy it."

"Harconan is not your conventional revolutionary, sir. Nor has he launched a conventional revolution. His point of contention is that the existing Jakarta government is unjustly Java-centric. That is, that the island of Java with its massive population and political and economic power base dominates the other island groups and cultures, economically and politically.

"Speaking frankly, he has good reason to feel so. The stated motto of the Jakarta government is '*Bhinneka tunggal ika*', the 'Many are one.' In reality, the Javanese always seem to end up a little more 'one' than anyone else. In many ways, they've supplanted the Dutch as colonial overlords, dominating the other peoples within the archipelago."

"And what does Harconan propose to replace the existing Indonesian state?" the President inquired.

"Harconan seeks to return Indonesia to the days of the Bone Empire, an idealized golden age that existed before the coming of the Europeans. At that time the archipelago existed as a scattering of independent island nations and kingdoms, each with its own chosen religion, government and culture, loosely bound together by the Indonesian seafaring clans, such as the Bugi.

"Harconan himself is half-Bugi and he is already recognized by many of the tribes as the semi-mythic *Raja Samudra*, the 'King of the Sea.' As the Bugi seafarers would dominate the archipelago, he, in turn, would dominate the Bugi."

Childress snorted. "I have yet to see one of these great revolutionary leaders who didn't have at least a tinge of enlightened self-interest. What's his game plan?"

"There is a grim but elegant simplicity to it, Mr. President. In any nation as fantastically diverse as Indonesia, there will always be discontented minorities and political factions. The Jakarta government's heavy-handed treatment of many of these minorities and factions has only aggravated the situation. Long before Harconan launched his destabilization program, the Indonesians had to deal with any number of sputtering minor insurgencies ranging from the Morning Star separatist movement in New Guinea to Islamic extremism in Sumatra." Van Linden sank deeper into his chair, interlacing his fingers. "Harconan is not seeking to organize or unify these highly diverse elements into one revolutionary army. That would be an act of futility. Many of the involved factions hate each other more than they do the central government. In fact, there is evidence that he is using Bugi agent provocateurs to incite these various political and social factions to greater violence against each other. Then, through a second network of agents, he provides these various inflamed insurgent groups with arms and funding, no questions asked."

"I see." Childress settled his glasses back onto the bridge of his nose. "He's setting up a titanic game of 'let's you and him fight', with the end result being anarchy."

"Exactly, sir. The minor conflicts are flaring into major conflagrations, putting greater and greater stress on the Jakarta government. Eventually, the governmental structure will shatter, and Harconan and his Bugi will be there to pick up the pieces."

Childress processed the information for a moment. "If we go for a direct military intervention to block this Harconan, we could find ourselves committed to a nation-building operation that would make the restructuring of Iraq look like child's play. That will never fly with Congress, Harry, and I'm not too crazy about the notion myself. There has got to be something else."

"I agree, sir," Van Linden replied. "President Kediri's government has its failings but the devil we know is definitely better than the multitude we don't. It's a certainty that some of the islands of a sundered Indonesia will fall under the control of Muslim radicalists, becoming tropical Afghanistans."

The Secretary of State chose his words and emphasis carefully. "The one possible rectification of the situation is to cut the supply lines feeding the insurgencies. Then, with enough economic and military aid and assistance, the Jakarta government just might be able to stabilize the situation."

"You're prevaricating heavily, Harry."

"I'm fully aware of that, sir. To have any chance at all of pulling this thing off, we have to eliminate the primary immediate agent of destabilization. We have to destroy the Harconan organization and the man behind it. If we can accomplish this in the short term, maybe we can use the leverage we'll gain to arm-twist Kediri and his people into some of the policy reforms needed to correct the situation in the long term."

"Assassination is a word that doesn't sit well with the American people," Childress said slowly. "I believe the Politically Correct term used these days is that we must 'sanction' this Harconan individual."

"Yes, sir. Unfortunately, there is another factor we also have to consider, Mr. President."

"And that is?"

"Before we can make rabbit stew, we first have to catch the rabbit."

# Part Two

# Convergence of Forces

He was a profound believer in discipline, especially within himself.

Without exception, he ran and swam a cumulative total of four miles every morning, hardening his body and clearing his mind. Today, as the sun edged above the horizon in a flaming tropic dawn, he alternated quarter mile sprints along the sand with plunges into the strip of azure water that lay between the deserted beach and surf-smothered reef, slashing through the low waves with a powerful Australian crawl.

The regimen of hard-driving exertion had long ago paid off for the man. The body revealed by his swim trunks was tall and broad-shouldered, tapering to a narrow waist and solidly layered with muscle. His skin had been darkened by a tropical tan.

He was Eurasian, his height and bulk coming from his Dutch father while his litheness of movement and the exotic cast to his strong, decisively masculine features stemmed from his Indonesian mother.

She had been a princess of one of the Bugi sea clans – and possibly this connection with an ancient, royal bloodline accounted for a great deal else in this man's makeup. For in an age of kings, he would have been a king, and this was the kind of world he sought to restore.

His four miles completed, he emerged from the sea. Pausing ankle-deep, he bent forward, his hands braced against his knees, inhaling deeply, regaining his breath. In this place, he had the luxury of not being concerned with his personal security. This island and every last man and woman upon it were his, sworn to his cause and chained to his destiny.

The man straightened. Lightly backhanding his pencil-line moustache in a reflexive gesture, he looked out across the waters that would someday be his as well. No other islands could be seen, save in the mounded cloud caps on the shimmering horizon, but he knew they were there, in their thousands. He also knew of the wars that raged upon them, conflicts that he had carefully fanned into a blazing existence.

He was by no means an inherently vicious person, no monster who took joy in death and destruction for its own sake. Nor was he a man driven with any particular lust for power or personal avarice. Wealth, respect and position had all been his, earned via a comparatively peaceful methodology.

But three extremely dangerous factors had converged within this man who would be king. At one and the same time he was an idealist – outraged at what he perceived as injustice and oppression – and a romantic who, as one great American writer had phrased it, "Saw paradise either around the next corner or behind the last." However, in practical matters, he was also a stark realist, one who recognized that blood was frequently the lubricant of history and violence its driving mechanism.

Bind those factors with a focused willpower, an imagination and a dynamic capacity for organization and leadership and a force was created that could shatter nations.

He recognized and regretted the death, destruction and agony that came with his dream, but like so many kings before him, he rationalized this devastation as a price to be paid for something stronger and cleaner beyond the next corner.

But even a king-to-be could find doubts within a dream. Unbidden, Makara Harconan found himself recalling a pair of large, golden hazel eyes with an unnerving capacity to look into his soul. He recalled also the words of their owner: "There are no problems left that can be solved with one bright clean slash of a sword ..."

Some fifteen hundred miles to the southwest, another solitary figure emerged onto another beach, beneath the same flaming sunrise.

She had indulged herself in this moment of solitude, not bothering with the aggravating constrictions of a swimsuit. Nor did she have anything to be ashamed of in her unselfconscious nudity. She had the firmly compact yet gracefully curved body of a trained dancer and there was a disciplined grace in the flow of her movements, an instinctive, natural pride in her bearing. Of only average height for a woman, she was inevitably remembered as being tall.

Her fine-planed features were not classically pretty but they held a striking attractiveness, the beauty of a drawn saber's blade, dominated by a pair of large golden hazel eyes, usually intent on the world around her but for the moment, introspective.

The thick fall of hair bound back at the nape of her neck shone wetly in the dawn light, an unusual combination of brown, red and sun-bleached blonde. There was also the first thin frosting of gray as well. Crow's-feet wrinkles, earned by much horizon scanning, marked the corners of her eyes.

Still, the hand of maturity rested lightly on her shoulder. She was a decidedly desirable woman and likely would remain so for many years to come. The other predominant aspect of her being – her decisiveness, the radiating sense of presence, the air of regal, natural command – would be hers for the rest of her life.

She walked slowly up the beach to a worn blanket spread on the coral sand and her little pile of possessions. She ignored the clothing for the moment, still savoring the cool free brush of the morning's sea breeze against her bare skin, but soon she lifted a hand towel and began to dry her hair, turning to study the vista far across the bay.

The warships of three nations lay at anchor there, readying for battle. Pale wakes streaked the gunmetal surface of the anchorage, trailing behind landing barges, hovercraft and patrol boats. Aircraft strobes flickered in the sky, helicopters and Osprey VTOLs shuttling in supplies from Darwin and lifting troops out to the training grounds. The whine of turbines and the mutter of rotors drifted faintly across the still waters.

The woman paused for a moment, tinged with pride in the knowledge that some of those ships and warriors were hers. But also with a degree of sadness, for she sensed that the conflict they were preparing for might already be lost.

Impatiently she shook her head, casting aside the damp towel. Hopeless or not, she would try to turn the coming tide with all of the skill, focus and fierce cunning she had accrued in her lifetime as a warfighter.

To herself, she acknowledged that she, above all others, might have the best chance. For victory could rest on the defeat of one man, a man, who, for a brief moment, had also been her lover.

She would not have been surprised to learn that Makara Harconan was thinking of her at that same precise instant. She recognized the hot spark that had jumped between the Indonesian "King of the Sea" and herself and the bond that had trailed after it. Like had sought out like. She would be counting on that link in the hunt to come. If the predator could think like her prey, it might give her an advantage in the stalking and the kill.

In addition to her clothing and a webbing belt with its holstered pistol and a sheathed knife, a small active radio transceiver sat propped on the blanket at her feet, voices whispering from its speaker. Now, amid babble on the Task Force command channel, she picked out one specific call sign, her own. She grimaced, then smiled wryly. Sinking down onto the blanket, she unclipped the radio's hand mike.

"This is The Lady. I copy you, *Carlson*. Over."

"Sorry to bust into your downtime, ma'am," the filtered voice came back from her flag ship, "but we just got the word from Strike Group Command. Admiral Sorenson has called for an operations group meeting aboard the Peleliu at 0900 Hours."

"Very good, *Carlson*. Have my gig pick me up."

Captain Amanda Lee Garrett USN reached for her uniform and began her day.

Lake Toba, the largest and deepest lake in South East Asia was born out of fire and thunder. Some seventy-five thousand years ago, the most titanic volcanic explosion in known geologic history blasted a seventeen hundred square mile crater in the mountainous spine of prehistoric Sumatra, the rain of ash darkening the skies of the world and triggering its last Ice Age.

The passing eons had healed the vast wound in the planet's skin, and the water-filled caldera had become a place of cool, verdant peace with steep, pine covered mountain slopes rising above its placid waters.

Centered in the great lake was Samosir island, home of the Batak tribal clans, the legendary "headhunters of Sumatra", who had blended a high native civilization and written language with ritual cannibalism well into the nineteenth century. But Protestant Christianity and a milder form of native animism had claimed the Batak, and now Samosir knew peace. Even so, on the island, moss-sheathed monolithic ruins and cemeteries studded with stone urns and statuary still marked the mystic places where the ancient rajas and gurus had cast their enchantments and debated issues of life and death.

At the western end of the island, a private estate encompassed several hundred acres of forested land between the lake's edge and the central mountain spine. That an entire village had been displaced in its establishment was of no consequence. That this theoretically private estate's perimeters were also guarded by an elite platoon of Indonesian marines was also of no consequence. Its owner was a man of unquestioned and unquestionable power.

The estate's mansion house had been built at the foot of a black basalt cliff, its cantilevered roof inspired by the traditional saddleback design of the Batak clan houses. Done in polished natural wood and glass, it was a most impressive structure.

If one knew of the facilities built into the lava cave concealed behind it, it would be more impressive yet.

34

The mansion's owner paused for a moment in his morning stroll through one of the side gardens to breathe deeply and to gaze out across the lake and craggy crater rim beyond.

Tall and spare for an Indonesian, with angular, almost aesthetic features emphasized by a finely trimmed beard, he was of Batak ancestry, a man who loved the highlands and mountains. This was one of the contradictions inherent to the man, for he was deeply involved in the affairs of the sea.

Indonesia was an island nation, dependent upon the sea. If one wished to control Indonesia, the sea must also be controlled. Thus, he had made himself an Admiral, a master of the sea, albeit one who had strode few decks in his naval career.

The man looked around at the approaching hesitant footsteps of his aid.

"Mullah Amar and his party have arisen and are making ready for the Morning Prayer, sir. He wonders if the Admiral might wish to join them?"

Admiral Merpati Ketalaman, Western Fleet Commander of the Indonesian Navy, tilted his head and smiled a smile that had no meaning behind it. "Please tell the Mullah that I would be honored," he replied softly.

Presently he would join the radical Islamic leader who was his guest, and he would kneel on the prayer rug and bow to distant Mecca and murmur the appropriate words. Ketalaman had been born and raised as a Christian but he had converted to Islam perhaps ten years previously, when he had commenced the preparation of his destiny. Not that religion was of any particular concern to him – but God, like the ocean, was a useful means to an end.

Three time zones to the east and northward beyond the equator, another Admiral sat at his desk and considered the phone call he knew he was about to receive.

A sea-tanned Caucasian with light brown hair streaked by both the blonde of the sun and the gray of maturity, he was square-set, solid and slightly too tall to be considered stocky. His regular, weathered features were marred by adhesive bandages covering recent healing wounds.

In comparison to Merpati Ketalaman, Vice Admiral Elliot Edward MacIntyre was a decidedly different breed of naval warrior. The collection of naval prints and the model of the Arab dhow that decorated the sunlit office marked him as a true seaman, as did the way his eyes drifted toward the gray and black upperworks of the ships rising beyond the dockside warehouses. Likewise, his personal wants, needs and desires had long ago been rendered subservient to the dual concepts of duty and service.

The telephone deck on his desk rasped, and he scooped up the handset. "Yes, Miss Hansen?"

"General Wheeler for you, sir, on Shadowline One."

MacIntyre reached up and punched a series of keys on the communications deck, bringing up the encryption coding and the line and room bug sniffers. "Very well. I'll take it. Hold all other calls and visitors until further notice."

General Maxwell Wheeler, United States Army, was the first four-star snake-eater. He was authorized to wear both the tab of the Ranger battalions and the silver wings of Special Forces. In his thirty years in uniform he had also commanded the 160th Special Operations Aviation Regiment and had served as the Army Chief of Staff to SOCOM.

His current posting was as C-in-C JSOC.

As with all American military professionals, MacIntyre spoke a fluent acronymese. Both SOCOM and JSOC had considerable meaning for him.

The Armed Forces of the United States were a complex, multi-leveled structure, especially in the area of "Special Operations", the martial euphemism for counter-insurgency, counter-terrorism and commando/raider activity.

The overt Special Operations community was gathered under the collective control of the United States Special Operations Command. Staging out of MacDill Air Force Base, Florida, SOCOM served as supreme headquarters for the majority of US Special Mission forces. These included the combined Naval and Marine elements of Naval Special Forces, the Army's Green Berets and 75th Ranger Regiment, and the Air Force's Special Tactics and Air Commando squadrons.

But beyond SOCOM, was JSOC, the Joint Special Operations Command.

JSOC existed as a command inside of a command and a mystery inside of an enigma. It controlled America's "National Assets," the hyper-elite, hyper-secure elements of the defense community, such as the Army's Delta Force and the Navy's SEAL Team Six, combat units that were known publicly to exist, but that were not officially acknowledged by the Department of Defense.

Other elements, drawn from the other armed services and from the "wet" direct action branches of the US Intelligence community, remained a matter of speculation and absolute secrecy. No one, or at least no one without both an extremely high security clearance and a "need to know", had access its entire Table of Organization.

As the Commander and Chief of US Naval Special Forces, Elliot MacIntyre had such a clearance and such a need. His "second hat" was as JSOC's Naval Chief of Staff.

"Hello, Eddie Mac."

"Hello, Max, what can we help you with?"

As MacIntyre expected, Wheeler cut directly to the chase. "As you have been advised, JSOC has been given a tasking notification from the National Command Authority. The President desires a positive outcome to the current Indonesian crisis and he is requesting we provide him with one."

MacIntyre took advantage of his security isolation to tilt his chair back and brace a foot against the edge of his desk. "I gather that means a conventional military response has been ruled out in the archipelago?"

"Yes and no," the general replied. "It depends on what tasking you're talking about. Are we prepared to provide support for the Australian Regional Intervention Force? Yes we are. Are we prepared to extract foreign nationals and embassy personnel from the conflict zone? Yes we are. If you're talking about the maintenance of Freedom of the Seas? Yes, we are. But if you're talking about a meaningful military intervention in support of the Jakarta government and in an active defense of US economic interests in the area, no we are not."

"The Joint Chiefs are projecting it would take everything the Aussies have plus at least a full Marine Expeditionary Force and the designation of a carrier MODLOC in the area to make an appreciable difference. It would mean the assumption of another major nation-building mission. That's not going to happen. Neither Congress nor the President are interested. We've already got too many other fish to fry."

"But they still want that successful resolution," MacIntyre replied with a degree of irony.

"That's correct, Eddie Mac," Wheeler replied, matching ironies. "The State Department and the National Command Authority feel that, if Indonesia comes apart, some of the islands are bound to come under the sway of Islamic radicalism. That is not acceptable. Our orders are to ensure that the Government of President Kediri stands and that an outcome favorable to US interests is produced for the region."

MacIntyre cocked an eyebrow at the empty room. "Anything else?"

"Yes," the voice on the phone replied. "Foggy Bottom is projecting that, at best, we have two months before the Kediri government totally disintegrates. Possibly three at the outside. It all depends on the Indonesian military and how long they keep the faith. If some of the officer cadre come down with coup fever, and they're prone to it down there, it could all go to hell tomorrow."

MacIntyre nodded his agreement. "My people in-theater are saying the same thing. Three months, if we're lucky."

"And what do your people have to say about what to do about it? Your Sea Fighters were the ones who cracked Harconan's piracy and arms smuggling operation. They have the recent hands-on experience. Do you and your theater commanders have any suggestions on how we deal with this mess?"

"Possibly, Max," MacIntyre replied. "The way I see it, we're fighting a swarm of bees in the archipelago. There isn't any one insurgency or revolution to counter – there are dozens of them, the root causes all set in cultural, religious and political conflicts that are beyond our influence.

"At the moment, the one thing all these different factions have in common is that they're all receiving various levels of aid from the Harconan organization in his drive to break up the Indonesian State. If we can take out Harconan and cut the supply lines feeding the insurgencies, maybe – and I emphasize, maybe – the situation, can be re-stabilized.

"The Jakarta government has always been good at juggling fractious minorities. If we can just take some of the heat off of them, maybe they can pick up the balls and get them into the air again."

MacIntyre could hear the scowl in the JSOC Chief of Staff's voice. "Again, State and the National Command Authority agree with you. We have been given the authority to sanction Harconan on sight, but I'm not convinced his elimination will get the job done. It sounds like the same trap we fell into with Bin Laden. One man isn't an entire organization."

"I don't see the scenarios as being comparative, Max," MacIntyre replied, swiveling his chair a few degrees. "Islamic radicalism bred Bin Laden. The Harconan organization is Harconan's alone. He's created it and he's making it work. Knock it down and the whole thing may implode on itself. Beyond that, he's all we've got. He's the only specifically targetable factor we can hit in the region that might prove corrective in the existing scenario. All we can do is kill him and cross our fingers."

"All right, Eddie Mac. I still don't like the concept – but since no one seems to have anything better to suggest, including me, I'll have to say we go with it. How would you propose we set up the ops package?"

MacIntyre applied a final few seconds of mental polish to a problem that had been dominating his thoughts ever since his return from Indonesia. "We're bucking two major problems down there, one being the archipelago is possibly the most totally hellish littoral conflict environment on the planet. There are over thirteen thousand islands down there and Harconan could be holed up on any one of them.

"For the other, I know something of the man. I've met Harconan and I've fought against him. He is brilliant, knowledgeable and intensely cunning. He also possesses a superb intelligence gathering organization of his own – and he is fully cognizant of our special ops capacities and how to evade them. You can be certain he's taking extensive and effective countermeasures. Beyond sheer dumb luck, the only way we're ever going to get close to Harconan is to blindside him. We need to hit him with something he doesn't expect. With something he doesn't know even exists."

"Such as?" Wheeler grunted.

"I think we've only got one unit in the JSOC inventory that could be applicable in this tactical situation and environment. I want to send Phantom Force in after Harconan."

There was a protracted silence on the far end of the circuit. "Wait a minute, Eddie Mac. According to the last Phantom Project update I've seen, most of the hardware is ready to go – but we're at least six months away from initial effective deployability."

"I know all about the Phantom timeline, Max. My people initially projected it. But we don't need her in six months. We need her now."

Riding the thunder of their rotors, the Seawolves came in low across a sky-colored sea. They also came ready for war, the blunt-muzzled grenade launchers in their chin turrets seeking for targets while their door gunners leaned watchfully out of open side hatches.

Flying nose to tail, the skids of the four UH-1Y "Super Huey" gunships almost grazed the golden sands of Turtle Island as they swept across the beach, their pilots pulling up to barely clear the uppermost limbs of the banyan forest beyond.

Their speed and their belly-raking altitude were a mechanism of survival. A hostile shooter firing from the forest floor would see only a momentary blur of dusty low-vis gray flashing past overhead.

Ahead lay their objective, a clearing that materialized amid the darker trees, a patch of swampy green just large enough to serve as auey Huey landing zone for a single aircraft.

The helicopters broke formation, the leader flaring into the LZ in a deft, precise combat approach, its three flight mates going into a race track holding pattern around the clearing, warily guarding their vulnerable sister.

The lead Huey didn't quite touch down but went into a minimum-altitude hover, bobbling a few feet above the rotor-flattened salt grass. Around the perimeter of the clearing, four patches of vegetation wavered and transmuted into four men, their faces, clothing and equipment mottled in shades of green camouflage.

Double-timing through the mud and scrubby undergrowth to the impatient aircraft, they hurled weapons and load-bearing harnesses in through the open side doors, the men heaving themselves over the hatch sills after their gear.

Turbines spooled up and the Super Huey lifted for the sky, making room for the next recovery helo in the LZ and taking its place in the guardian circle.

Aboard the gunship, the fire team of Force Recon Marines, sweat-sodden and mosquito ravaged, were content to sprawl on the aircraft's deck, panting, and dreaming of hot showers, soft bunks and beautiful, wondrous air conditioning.

Then the team leader swore savagely.

Stacked in the forward end of the cargo compartment were fresh rations, ammunition reloads and full hydration bladders for their MOLLE harnesses. This was no recovery. They were merely being transferred to another of the training ranges staked out around the perimeter of Bonaparte Bay. Another simulated combat mission awaited them – and another night to be spent with the mosquitoes and crocodiles.

There was nothing for it but to slouch against the rear bulkhead and curse fate and the grinning helicopter crewmen. The man who commanded them and the woman who commanded that man were both ardent believers in the truism, "The harder you sweat in training, the less you bleed in war."

The second and third helos each scooped up their respective fire teams. But only a single passenger awaited recovery by the fourth and final aircraft.

An M-8 assault carbine with a shotgun module clipped below its primary barrel sailed through the helicopter's open side hatch. Amanda Garrett caught the compound weapon. Passing it on to the gunship's crew chief, she braced a foot against a cleat in the deck of the cargo compartment and grabbed the shoulder straps of Captain Stone Quillain's MOLLE harness, assisting him in his heave through the door.

Over the hammer of the flailing rotor blades, she faintly heard the crew chief yelling to his pilot, "Passenger embarked! Go, go, go!"

The helicopter pitched and swooped like a small boat in heavy seas, lifting out of the Landing Zone. Quillain shucked out of his gear and collapsed into one of the aircraft's aluminum and nylon strap seats. Amanda belted herself in beside him. Before attempting to speak with the commander of her Sea Dragon company. she plunged a hand into an ice chest strapped to the back of the cockpit braces, passing Quillain a can of Coke dripping with condensation. Coca-Cola was the only soft drink the big Georgia-born Marine ever indulged in. It was a matter of patriotism.

She let him drain the first two cans. When he started to sip rather than gulp the third, she knew he had adequately rehydrated and she passed him a cranial helmet with an intercom headset.

"What the hell are you doin' out here, skipper?" Quillain spoke without preamble or obsequiousness into his lip mike. As plank owners of the Sea Fighter Task Force, Stone and Amanda had long ago entered into the unique comfortable comradery and intimacy that exists within a small close-knit fighting unit.

Beyond that, Stone Quillain had become possibly the closest male friend she had ever had, at least with romance left out of the equation. In either instance, Stone was on her list of privileged individuals.

"Partially to see how training is coming," she replied, "and partially to pick up and deliver you. Admiral Sorenson wants another conference with his element commanders this afternoon."

The helicopter had departed from the extraction formation. Proceeding independently, it had broken training protocols and was heading out over the bay at a conventional altitude, returning to its mother ship.

The expression on Quillain's bluntly angular features went from its usual dour to sour and his lip mike caught a muttered "Christ Almighty."

"Sorry to have to drag you out of the field like this, Stone, but that's how our new boss does things. How's the cross-training and unit integration coming?"

"Getting there, skipper." The Marine backhanded the perspiration from his forehead, smearing the pattern of his face paint. "My boys are perfect – but then you knew that. The Anzacs ain't at all bad either, but we figured that'd be the case too. The Aussies and the Kiwis have always had a handle on jungle warfare. And the guys from the Marine Amphibious Unit are all right. They aren't Special Operations Capable, but they're a good solid line outfit and there ain't nothing you can't teach a Marine about fightin'. Mostly it's a matter of getting everybody broken in and used to how the other guy does things. That, and getting the time in the field to get it done."

Amanda recognized the heavy emphasis Quillain placed on certain of his words. "How are you getting on with the MEU's commander?"

"Colonel Dogert is a very capable officer, ma'am."

Amanda grinned at the rough-edged sophistry. "I didn't ask about his capabilities, Stone. I asked how you were getting on with him?"

Quillain killed the last of the third Coke and crushed the can in one massive fist. "Well, I probably won't really kill the tight-assed son of a bitch."

She laughed aloud. "We're spoiled, Stone. That's our problem. We've been our own lords and masters for too long. It'll do us good to be back in the real military for a while."

Amanda was the TACBOSS of the Sea Fighter's and she had to set a good example. Accordingly, she didn't mention the occasions with Admiral Sorenson when she'd had to strangle down a screamed, "Just what in the hell are you thinking of?"

Quillain glanced at her. "Maybe it'll do us good, but how much good will it do for the job? When are they cuttin' us loose again, skipper? We got business to finish up north."

Amanda found herself glad that her sunglasses screened her eyes. Too much truth might have escaped otherwise. "That's for wiser heads than ours to decide, Stone. For now, the job is to help bring the Intervention Force up to speed and ready to move when the time comes."

Quillain didn't reply aloud, but his faintly derisive, faintly sympathetic expression told her that he recognized her militarily correct platitude for what it was.

The Sea Fighters had been the ones who had uncovered the Harconan plan. Amanda also knew how close to final fruition it was, and that the window of opportunity to stop it was closing rapidly. She also recognized the extent of the holocaust about to be unleashed upon the islands to the north.

And here she sat, chained in this bay, unable to do anything about it.

Damn! Damn! Damn! When *was* Admiral MacIntyre going to cut her loose to go after Harconan?

Over the years, MacIntyre had become – in the vernacular of the Fleet – her "Sea Daddy," her sponsor and mentor. First with 2nd Fleet in the Drake's Passage Conflict and then with NAVSPECFORCE off the China Coast and West Africa, the Admiral had always trusted her with freedom of action. He'd selected the targets and pulled the trigger, allowing her to do the job as she'd seen fit.

She could recognize now that she had come to both relish and rather take for granted her role as Eddie MacIntyre's troubleshooter. In return, she had always given a hundred and ten percent of herself to justify his confidence. She had created the Sea Fighter Task Force for him and had forged it into the premier strike element of Naval Special Forces.

Possibly upper echelons had tied MacIntyre's hands. Maybe CinC 7th had insisted that the Sea Fighters be placed under the overall command of the Regional Intervention Force. She knew there were those in the service who considered her a loose cannon, possibly with some justification.

Or maybe MacIntyre was reining her in himself.

If such was the case, she couldn't blame him. In the course of their Indonesian piracy operation, she'd gotten herself taken prisoner by Harconan. The Admiral had been forced to bail her out of that mess personally, putting his career, the Sea Fighters and Indonesian-US relations at risk.

And, of all the people in the Navy, there were only two who knew of the fullest extent of Amanda's past relationship with Harconan. One was her friend and Intelligence officer Christine Rendino. The other was MacIntyre.

He would be fully justified in his loss of trust in her judgment. But still, she had hoped for the chance to prove herself again. To erase the stain.

"You okay, skipper?" She felt a large roughened hand rest on her shoulder for a moment. Startled, Amanda came back into herself. A blunt object in so many ways, Stone Quillain could sometimes surprise you by being amazingly perceptive.

"No, Stone. I'm fine. I'm just thinking."

The Francis Bay anchorage lay below them, along with the ships of the joint US/Australian Regional Intervention Force.

In maritime technology, it spanned generations.

The two ships of the Sea Fighter Task Force, the CLA (Cruiser Littoral Attack) USS *Cunningham* and the LSD (Landing Platform Dock) USS *Evans F. Carlson* were both twenty-first century designs. Built with the geometric, slope-flanked sleekness of stealth ship technology, their deck fittings and weapons systems fared and folded into envelopes of RAM (Radar Absorbent Material) and their radio and radar antenna merged into the "smart skin" of pylon masts and finlike free-standing mast arrays. Swept by a probing radar beam, the two vessels would produce the radar return of a couple of small fishing craft rather than the multi-thousand-ton men of war they were.

The other naval vessels of the Intervention Force – American, Australian and New Zealander – ranged in technology from merely state of the art to Cold War leftovers.

All were configured for the same mission, however: surface combatants and amphibious warfare vessels working together as a team to lift in and support Special Operations Forces at a littoral crisis point.

As they overflew the anchorage, Amanda found herself musing at the evolutionary process of naval warfare.

At the turn of the past century, the dreadnought had been the queen of the seas. It had been the core element of the navy, the "capital ship," that all the other fleet elements were intended to support.

In the aftermath of Pearl Harbor, the cloak of the capital ship had passed from the battlewagon to the aircraft carrier. Then, with the development of the atomic submarine, the Bubbleheads and Airdales had squabbled over the title throughout the Cold War.

But then came 9/11 and things had changed again.

With the coming of the struggle against global terrorism, the amphibious warfare vessel with its capacity to project power into a disintegrating Third World state had become the new Ship of the Line, the ground troops it carried serving as its main battery.

Now, the missile-bristling surface combatant, the lordly flattop, the dark and deadly submarine, all served as handmaidens to the humble "gator freighter".

The Super Huey planed down toward the Sea Fighter's end of the anchorage. Circling the sleek shape of the *Evans F. Carlson*, they lined up on the rectangular helipad that took up the entire aft end of the main weather deck. A few moments more and the helo rasped down on the antiskid.

*

It was after the formal shipboard lunch hour and the *Carlson*'s big wardroom was almost empty. Only a single chair at one of the long central tables was occupied, a small intent figure leaning forward to study the screen of a laptop computer, a pair of glasses shoved up to rest atop her tousled blonde head.

"Morning, Boss Ma'am," Lieutenant Commander Christine Rendino said, without looking up.

"It's the afternoon, Chris," Amanda replied, tossing her salt-stained *Cunningham* baseball cap onto the hat rack beside the entry. The contrast between the air-conditioned coolness of the wardroom, and the humidity-sodden heat beyond was striking. The chill it put in her perspiration-soaked utilities produced a pleasant shiver.

"Details, details," Amanda's closest friend and senior Intelligence officer replied offhand. Without taking her blue-gray eyes from the screen, she reached for the half-consumed plate of nachos at her side.

Amanda moved to Christine's shoulder. "What are you working on?"

"The latest dope from up north. I'm hoping that something useful will jump out at me. So far something hasn't obliged."

Amanda nodded, "I'll be right with you."

At the rear of the compartment, the mess steward leaned out of the pantry door. "Good afternoon, ma'am. Can I get you anything?"

"Definitely, Nick. I missed lunch. Can I get one of my specials?"

"Not a problem, ma'am. Chunky peanut butter and grape jelly on French on the way. You want chips with that?"

"No thanks." Amanda started for the beverage dispensers on the serving board but allowed herself to be diverted for a moment.

Every wardroom, as with every ship and crew, had its own unique personality. The *Carlson's* wardroom, with its deep maroon carpet, dark oak furnishings and framed lithographs of classic naval vessels on the bulkheads radiated an air of cool, military dignity.

With one glaring exception.

The miniature palm tree that dominated one corner of the compartment. An expatriate decoration of the Pearl Harbor Officers club, it had materialized silently one night, complete with a hand lettered "Captain Garrett's property" sign spiked into its redwood planter.

Anyone versed in the literature of the United States Navy would instantly recognize the "in-joke" and Amanda's only dignified counter had been to adopt the tree and insist that it stay. Only to herself would she ever admit that she had actually come to enjoy tending the damn thing.

She checked the grow light mounted over the planter and gave the palm an affectionate squirt or two with a misting bottle before drawing a tall glass of milk for herself. She arrived back at the table at the same moment as her sandwich.

"Thank you, Nick," she said distractedly, sinking down into the chair beside Christine. "Okay, what have we got?"

"Absolutely nothing surprising or out of place, damn it. That's the problem. Our friend Harconan's plan is purring along like clockwork."

The screen on Christine's laptop displayed a map of the Indonesian archipelago, marked with an ominous number of red conflict zones. Christine tapped the largest of these, the eastern end of New Guinea, with the tip of a fingernail. "Over here, the Morning Star Separatists have successfully made the conversion to a second phase insurgency. The Indonesians aren't just fighting scattered guerilla bands any more; they're fighting an army, one that's taking and holding ground, including a number of the island's critical copper mining facilities. Ore production is practically at a standstill."

"What's the status on the foreign workers at those facilities?"

"Apparently it's open season on the Javanese *transmigrasi*. But the Morning Stars seem to be bending over backwards not to harm the out-country workers. They're either being repatriated or are being allowed to stay in their compounds under the protection of the revolutionaries. The Morning Star leadership is also talking with the mining corporations about protecting the facilities from war damage and looting."

"I'll wager that's not all they're talking about," Amanda mused. "I met with one of the senior Morning Star cadre when I was being held at Harconan's base in New Guinea. He was a very canny old gentleman. His people know their copper mines will be a critical national asset if they can get their independent Papuan Republic going."

"Uh huh, they're playing it smart." Christine's fingernail moved across the screen to the western end of the vast island chain. "Not so over here in Aceh Province on Sumatra where an ugly Muslim radicalist insurgency has just gotten uglier."

"What's happened?" Amanda took a bite of her sandwich, her brows knitting together.

"A faction leader called Mohammed Sinar, a loser that both we and the Indonesian security services had discarded as no longer being a factor in the area, has suddenly jumped back into the game. Apparently he's received a massive infusion of funding and weaponry and he's launching a pay-back campaign against both the provincial government and the other radicalists who've been slapping him around. We're seeing convoy ambushes, kidnappings, tribal leadership assassinations and general blood, guts and feathers raining down all over the landscape."

"Is this Sinar a capable leader?"

Christine looked pained. "The man is a tail-wagging idiot who shouldn't be trusted with a burned-out match. But that fits perfectly with Harconan's Chaos Theory strategy. Armed force is essentially a tool. Put a tool in the hands of a skilled carpenter and he can build something with it. Put it in the hands of a dweeb and your front porch falls off."

Amanda set the half-finished sandwich down on the plate, her appetite gone. *Damn you, Makara.* "What else is going on out there?"

Christine's fingertip skipped from flashpoint to flashpoint. "More outbreaks of tribal violence against the *transmigrasi* colonies in Borneo. The Dyaks are apparently starting to take heads again. Over here in Brunei, the Sultanate is trying to hire another battalion of Gurkha mercenaries to counter an increasing number of bandit incursions from Indonesian Territory. In the Ambon group, the Christian Ambonese are starting to talk *loudly* about the good old days under the Dutch. And last, but certainly not least, there is a growing wave of vandalism against Hindu religious shrines in Bali, purportedly by Muslim extremists."

Christine looked up from the laptop screen. "This latter is a very bad idea on somebody's part. The Muslims constitute less than six percent of the island population and the Balinese are getting royally pissed off."

Amanda nodded in grim agreement. "I recognize the potential. Back in 1965, when the Balinese exorcised the Communist 'demons' from their island, there were over fifty thousand religious executions within a matter of days."

She gestured at the laptop screen. "You can see Harconan's strategy developing. He's feeding the insurgencies around the perimeter of the archipelago, drawing the Indonesian forces out of the core islands, making them disperse to these fringe areas where they can be isolated and cut off. What about the Bugi pirate clans? What are they up to?"

"Something very indicative, Boss Ma'am," Christine replied. "Attacks against foreign flag vessels have dropped off to almost nothing. But they're steadily increasing against domestic shipping within the archipelago, focused almost entirely against the PELNI national shipping line and Javanese inter-island coaster and ferry traffic. And get this, the pirates are not just boarding and looting cargo as has been SOP in the past. Now they're sinking the ships."

Amanda nodded. "He's begun the sea control mission. He's started to isolate the islands from each other."

"Uh huh." Christine sat back in her chair and rubbed her eyes. "He's right on the beam and there's still nothing much we can do about it."

"Show me where the bastard is and I'll show you what can be done," Amanda found herself saying, with more vehemence than she had meant.

"I can tell you a lot about where he probably is, Boss Ma'am," Christine went on after a moment. "He won't be in any major military base or installation, like he was in New Guinea. Such sites are too easy to locate now that we know what to look for. He'll be using a Bin Laden defense. He'll be at some pre-existing location, a village or something where the inclusion of a small command staff and security force won't be apparent to aerial reconnaissance. It will also be a pre-selected site, with a hand-picked population sworn to the cause of the *raja sumadra,* probably through clan or cultural ties. Bugi or those Nung Chinese mercenaries Harconan likes to use."

Christine was drifting into her intelligence officer's muse, looking up at the cable clustered overhead with her arms crossed. From long experience, Amanda knew with a 99% certainty that the little blonde would be dead right in every word she was saying.

"There will be sideband radio receivers and a camouflaged satellite mini-dish to access CNN, but no sat phones or Internet access. His field commanders can radio in – but not a single loose electron goes out. All of his feedback to his people will be via courier through off-site communications nodes located some distance away from his hide. Slow, but given his game plan, not critical.

"Other than Harconan's personal security force, there will be no heavy defenses, just a lot of lookouts. At the first hint of a strange ship on the horizon or the sound of a helicopter rotor – or even a stranger poking around in the district – foop! He'll do a fast fade down a prepared escape route."

"Fine!" Amanda found herself fighting frustration. "Points all taken and agreed to, Chris, but where is he?"

"In any one of ten thousand such places, Boss Ma'am, and there's absolutely no way anyone pick any one over another."

Amanda lost the battle. She pushed back from the table and started to pace, her sketchy meal forgotten. Under tension, she had to move. "That's not good enough, Chris! Not nearly good enough."

Christine shrugged. "You've said it yourself more times than I can count, Boss Ma'am. 'Patience is the hunter.' All we can do is wait him out. Harconan is only human. Sooner or later, he's got to make a mistake."

"We don't have the luxury to be that reactive, Chris. By the time Makara makes that mistake, he might already have won the damn war!"

"Then our only option is to force him to make a mistake."

Amanda paused in her pacing. "That's not going to be easy. He doesn't do stupid."

"That's not exactly true, Amanda." Christine softened her voice so it couldn't be heard in the pantry adjoining the wardroom. Christine's rare use of her given name also caught Amanda's attention.

"What do you mean, Chris?"

"We know that Makara Harconan does stupid around you."

*

Upon leaving the wardroom, Amanda had a precious uncommitted hour before having to depart for the Force flagship and a plan to productively put it to use. She'd learned over the years to be careful about her personal maintenance, not out of any kind of self-indulgence but out of the sure and certain knowledge that an over-tired or over-stressed officer was prone to make errors of judgment.

Giving a nod to the young Marine sentry on station outside of the door to her cabin, she entered and crossed to her desk, reported herself in quarters to the Duty Officer in the *Carlson*'s Combat Information Center.

As the Senior Tactical Officer of the Sea Fighters, she had first call on the LSD's Flag officers' quarters. There was a small office, large enough for a desk, a steel tube and leather couch and a single recliner chair. There was also a connected sleeping cabin with a single bunk and a head and shower combination. Beyond the navy blue carpet, the artificial pine paneling and a painting or two on the bulkheads, there was little that could be called luxury. Yet this was home, all she'd had for close to a year, and she was eminently content with it.

She sighed and snapped the rubber band binding her hair back. Chris was right; she must grit her teeth and wait for luck to break her way. There was no other option.

Stripping off her salt and sweat encrusted utilities, she took advantage of flag officer's privileges, taking a long and leisurely Hollywood shower and shampoo. After toweling off vigorously, Amanda donned a fresh bra and briefs and popped the soundtrack from 'Kismet' into her disk player. Stretching out on her bunk, she closed her eyes.

She'd give herself fifteen minutes of unwinding and then she'd rally and rise again.

The world refused to cooperate.

Amanda was just drowsing through 'Night of My Nights' when the phone deck on her desk shrilled, demanding attention. She slapped her hand down on the player's pause button and swore her way out to her desk. "Garrett here!" she snapped, keying the speakerphone.

"Captain, this is communications," a voice replied apologetically, the watch sparks recognizing a POed commanding officer when he heard one. "We have an incoming Milstar link with CINCNAVSPECFORCE. Full encryption. Security Max. TACBOSS access only."

Amanda sank into her desk chair, pique forgotten. "Put me through."

Admiral MacIntyre at long damn last. Maybe with her steaming orders. She waited impatiently for the security prompt and spoke her voice pattern identification key. "This is Captain Amanda Lee Garrett ... Sweetwater ... Tango ... zero ... three ... eight ..."

The circuit cleared. "Good afternoon, Amanda."

53

She smiled a little, both in pleasure at the sound of MacIntyre's voice and at herself for the way her hand instinctively came up to smooth her damp hair. She couldn't help it if Elliot MacIntyre was a well set up man as well as a friend and commander. "Good afternoon, sir."

"That remains to be seen," MacIntyre said cryptically. "I need to speak with you about something."

She frowned. There was an odd tone in Elliot's voice, almost calculating. "Of course, sir. What can I help you with?"

"Something's come up in relation to your Phantom Project."

Phantom? Amanda frowned.

Phantom was something from out of her past, stemming from the days when she'd been attached to the naval stealth program at the David W. Taylor Naval Ship Development and Research Center in Bethesda. She had done a paper on the Q-Ship and Raider doctrines employed during the First and Second World Wars and on the possible application of those doctrines to a twenty-first century conflict situation. She had dubbed this hypothetical application "Phantom Force."

In the years since, Phantom had intermittently bubbled to the surface. The Naval War College had asked her to do an updated and expanded version of her paper shortly after 9/11. And later, when she'd first been attached to NAVSPECFORCE, Admiral MacIntyre had asked her to chair a Special Operations symposium on the subject.

Phantom Force was her concept, but it was only a hypothetical one. For the moment she had a great deal of reality to cope with.

"What about it, sir?"

"Would you be interested in becoming involved in the project again?"

Amanda found herself becoming a little aggravated. What about Harconan and the volcano she was sitting on here in Indonesia?

"Sir, I'm very pleased that somebody finally might be getting interested in my idea, but just now I'm a little too tactical out here to commit time to another paper."

She heard MacIntyre chuckle grimly. "We don't need another paper, Amanda. People are interested enough in Phantom Force as it stands."

Her breath caught in her throat and she sat a little straighter. "You mean they're thinking about building her?"

"I mean she's already been built, Amanda. Her base and support elements have been assembled and we have her cover in place. She's also been taken beyond what you initially envisioned. She's bigger, more sophisticated and considerably more mission capable."

Amanda's chair creaked as she slumped back. To say that MacIntyre's flat statement was stunning was an understatement. It was fully the equivalent of going to the doctor for missing a period and being told that her baby was waiting in the next room. She shook her head, still not believing. "You mean that Phantom is operational? But I haven't heard a word ... not even a rumor ..."

MacIntyre sounded both pleased and amused with springing his surprise on her. "You set the parameters yourself in your paper. 'Absolute operational security must be maintained at all times over all aspects of the project to ensure its successful deployment.'"

She couldn't restrain the explosion. "But, damn it, Phantom's mine! I thought of it!"

MacIntyre chuckled again. "Compartmentalization does not recognize proprietary interest. Actually, the project is not quite fully operational. Our initial deployment capability was projected for another six months down the line, but recent developments have made it necessary to move things up. We're activating Phantom Force now and we're sending it in after Harconan."

A chill beyond bare skin and air conditioning rippled through Amanda. "That's what I designed her for, sir."

"Very true, Captain. Now the only remaining question is, do you want her?"

The chill became a physical shiver. "Am I being offered command of Phantom Force, sir?"

MacIntyre snorted. "Hell, you've been the first and only choice for the plank commander since we started bending metal on the project. You've not only developed the base concept, but between the *Cunningham* and the Sea Fighters you've built a reputation for proving up new weapons systems and doctrine under combat conditions. We want you to do it again."

"Th – thank you, sir."

"We were going to approach you under more controlled circumstances when you'd completed your tour with the Sea Fighters," MacIntyre continued. "But now we've been denied that luxury. It'll be another hair-on-fire transfer with no down time in between, but Phantom Force is yours if you want it."

He hesitated. "If you elect to not accept this particular assignment, it most certainly will not affect your career, nor will it be held against you in any way."

Amanda knew, or at least she strongly suspected, that Elliot MacIntyre was aware of her indiscretion with Makara Harconan. It was a point of some embarrassment to her –and now, Eddie Mac was as much as offering her a way out if she didn't want to take on the assassination of the man who had been her lover. It was an intimacy she never expected and a consideration she didn't deserve.

"Sir, I accept, and I thank you for this opportunity."

She heard what might have been a sigh of relief at the other end of the circuit. "To say I am pleased is an understatement, Amanda. I don't have to tell you that we'll be sending a very raw, untested and speculative outfit into an incredibly unstable situation with a bare minimum of working up time."

"How long will I have, sir?"

"You're closer to the fire than I am at the moment. You tell me."

She hesitated for only a few seconds. In that brief period, she jettisoned the load of the Sea Fighter Task Force like a satellite launch vehicle jettisoning a burned-out stage, her mind leaping ahead to encompass this new mission. She had no details to work with. No exact table of organization beyond the outline she had sketched out, but she knew where her priorities must be.

"I'm not sure myself," she replied. "But one thing I do know. If I'm to get Phantom up to speed fast enough to make a difference, I've got to have the people for it. Specifically, I've got to have my people.

56

Officers I know and who know me and how I work. I'm definitely not going to have the time to break in a new operations staff."

"Understood and concurred with," MacIntyre replied. "I'm already trying to pull in as many of your old hands as I can from other assignments. I think you'll be pleasantly surprised."

"What about the Sea Devil force commander and Intelligence/recon officer? Have those slots been filled?"

"Not yet."

"Then get me Christine Rendino and Stone Quillain."

MacIntyre hesitated. "Hmm, that might not be ... quite so easy to swing."

Amanda frowned. "Why not? They're the best we've got."

"I agree, but we have what you might call it a visibility problem."

"What do you mean, sir?"

"I mean, over the past few years you've developed into something of a media darling, Amanda." She could hear a hint of frustration creeping into MacIntyre's voice. "Thanks to Drake's Passage, China and North Africa, you've become something of a celebrity."

Amanda felt her jaw drop. "A celebrity? Me? Admiral, I have absolutely no idea what you are talking about."

MacIntyre sounded grimly amused once more. "You should. You're a very attractive young woman who also happens to be a world class war hero. You are made for newsbytes. You may not be aware of it, Amanda, but CNN and the other infonets have you red-flagged as a permanent person of interest and they track you wherever you go. That includes the Indonesian archipelago."

"Oh, damn, damn, damn!" Amanda viewed the members of the media in the same way she did strawberries. She was allergic to them both.

"We'd originally intended to ease you over to the Phantom command after cooking up some innocuous and dull on-the-beach assignment for you to disappear into," MacIntyre continued. "As it is, we're going to have to cook up some other justification for detaching you prematurely from your current assignment. Possibly we'll have to fake some health or personal problems. Something that will let us ease you out of sight without too many questions being asked. If some of your current 'Band of Brothers' disappear at the same time, people might start asking questions about where you've all hauled off to. That could compromise the whole project."

Once more, Amanda ran her hand through her damp hair. Elliot was right, of course – but that didn't reduce her need for her people. Again her mind sprang ahead, assessing and adapting.

To convert a negative into a positive. To turn a disadvantage into an advantage. That had been a pet tactic that had served her well many times before.

"Admiral," she said, deep in thought, "I think I might have a way to solve a number of our problems simultaneously."

"Already?"

"I don't have the time to lollygag," she replied wryly. "I have to start being brilliant immediately."

She outlined her resolution to both her visibility and personnel problems and rode out the explosion at the other end of the circuit.

"It's my career to throw away, sir," she said finally. "I've seen you work miracles with the Bureau of Personnel before. I trust in you to cook up something this time. And if it doesn't work out, well, Phantom will be as good a capper for my time in the navy as I could ask for."

"Besides," she mused, tilting her chair back, "it was pointed out to me a little while ago that we aren't going to get at Makara Harconan until he does something stupid. Maybe this will encourage a little stupidity on his part as well."

Reporter Ethan Smart ran a hand through his thinning hair and scowled down at the meager handful of notes scattered across his desktop. For once, the Washington beat was running cold. The single potential lead he'd been dogging all morning, a totally nowhere piece on malfeasance in Midwestern farm subsidies, had just flamed out.

The murmur of telephone conversation and the subdued clatter of word processor keys issuing from the surrounding cubicles in the newsroom only enhanced his sense of frustration, if not desperation. He had a deadline thundering down on him and a very unforgiving editor whose battle cry was, "If you can't find news, then make it!"

His desk phone rang and the reporter scooped up the handset without enthusiasm. "Smart here."

The voice at the other end of the line was feminine, hushed and nervous. "Mr. Smart, my name is ... Well, never mind my name for now. I think I may have something, a story you'll be interested in."

"That depends," Smart replied laconically, wondering if he was dealing with yet another of the nutcases who plagued the media, especially the *Washington Post*. "What do you have?"

"I'm a civilian employee at the Pentagon, attached to the office of the Joint Chiefs of Staff. A big fuss has broken out about something that's happened recently in Indonesia. A senior officer is going before a Board of Inquiry that could lead to a court-martial. Because of who's involved, they're trying to keep it quiet."

Smart came out of his slouch. "Who is involved?" he asked cautiously.

"The commanding officer of the task force we have down there. Captain Amanda Garrett."

Smart's spine went ramrod straight. "Are you sure about this?"

"I am," the voice replied. "I even have copies of some of the memos and documents."

*Oh, those lovely, lovely words.*

"Can you give me some idea what they say?"

"They don't go into a lot of detail but they mention, 'dereliction of duty and conduct unbecoming to an officer.'"

This woman might be a nutcase but she was a nutcase Smart definitely wanted to talk to. "Look, can I meet with you somewhere? I'd like to have a look at those documents and talk with you about this further."

"All right, all right. I left early today. I told them I had a dentist's appointment. I could meet you at the Denny's at exit 29 on the Beltway. Would that all right?"

"Great! I can be there in an hour, Miss ..."

There was a final hesitation. "Dewarshnick, Susan Dewarshnick. I hope you understand that I'm doing this because I really think the truth needs to come out, Mr. Smart – but I've had some family expenses lately ..."

"Not a problem, Miss Dewarshnick," Smart replied, smoothly taking his Post checkbook out of his desk drawer and tucking it in his jacket pocket. "How will I recognize you?"

"I have dark hair and I'll be wearing a red blouse and black skirt. You won't have to use my name, will you? It would cost me my job."

"Of course not, Miss Dewarshnick. You'll just be one of our 'informed sources.' I'll see you shortly."

Smart hung up the phone, his day suddenly brighter. Amanda Lee Garrett of US Naval Special Forces had been one of the premier news figures of the past decade.

Smart checked out of the newsroom, the sweet siren song of the Pulitzer Prize singing in his ears.

Across the Potomac, in an office in the E Ring of the Pentagon, Ensign Terri Calvert, USN ended the call on her cellphone and looked across at her commanding officer. "Now I know how Benedict Arnold must have felt."

"Apparently all this is Captain Garrett's idea, Ensign," Rear Admiral Nick Dunnigan, NAVSPECFORCE's liaison officer to the Joint Chiefs, replied from behind his desk. "Let's just hope she knows what she's doing. Do you have the documentation?"

"Yes, sir." She held up a file folder. "Phony signatures and all. They'll look good but they'll be deniable when the time comes."

"How about your story? Got it down pat?"

"Yes sir, a team from Navy CID mock-grilled me all morning. And Defense Intelligence has provided me with falsified identification."

Dunnigan nodded. "Very well, Ensign. Thank you for your assistance in this matter. It will be noted. Now, you'd better get into your civvies. You've got an appointment to keep."

An open line light was blinking on his desk phone. Lifting the handset to his ear, he accessed the connection. "You may inform Admiral MacIntyre the bomb has been dropped."

One of the peculiarities of twenty-first century California is that wilderness coexists so closely with modern urbanity.

To the northeast, Palm Springs and its satellite communities glitter, turning the floor of the Coachella Valley into a tapestry of diamonds. To the northwest, the glow of the Los Angeles basin drowns out the stars as, to a lesser extent, the lights of San Diego do to the south. But on Thomas Mountain itself, the cougar and the black bear still reign and the only sound is the hissing sigh of wind in the pinon pines.

Then came the intrusion, an edgy, trilling growl that grew swiftly in intensity. Four shadows snaked up one of the seaward canyons of the coastal range, skimming the treetops, hugging the contours of the jagged terrain, flying with the same effortless surety of the night-hunting bats and owls with which they shared the mountain darkness.

The formation broke as it vaulted the mountain ridgeline. The leader continued its climb into the star-strewn sky, while its three flight mates dove, slaloming down the far side of the range toward the desert floor far below.

Lieutenant Colonel Robert Cassin USMC paced behind the row of computer workstations, his eyes warily scanning the glowing topaz screens that dominated the forward wall of the darkened simulation control center.

As an OPFOR commander at the Air-Ground Combat Center, he was fully cognizant this was only an exercise. He and his team of veteran battle management controllers recognized that their job was to teach and to assist their "students" in gaining experience under fire. Winning was not an absolute necessity to accomplish this mission.

Yet Cassin and his controllers were both human and Marine enough to relish the victory whenever a "Blue Force" incursion into their territory was defeated.

When the small cadre of military intellectuals nicknamed the "Jedi Knights" rebuilt the wreckage of the United States Armed Forces in the aftermath of the Vietnam conflict, they integrated a potent and devastating weapon into the revised structure of the American Military.

Training. Vigorous, intensive, and most importantly, highly realistic training, performed under as close to actual battlefield conditions as was possible to simulate.

It was recognized that the soldier was never more vulnerable than during his first ten days on the battle line. Likewise, the military aviator was never more at risk than during his first ten combat missions. If this "bloody ten" could be experienced in an environment where a "death" could be an event assessed and learned from, then one could produce an army of exceptionally capable and survivable warriors.

Using a sophisticated blend of cybernetic simulation and Hollywood special effects, a series of training ranges were outfitted to simulate the modern battlefield environment and OPFOR (Opposition Force) units were organized. Trained and equipped to emulate potential enemy military formations, the OPFOR mission was to challenge the United

63

States Armed Forces to mock battle, the conflicts to be judged by exacting and impartial computer referees.

The prize awarded in the contest were the priceless skills needed to stay alive.

The National Training center at Fort Irwin, California, the Joint Readiness Training Center at Fort Polk Louisiana, the "Red Flag" Air Warfare Center at Nellis Air Force Base and the Naval Strike and Air Warfare Center at Fallon, Nevada, all were dedicated to OPFOR training.

The Marine Air-Ground Combat Center at Twenty-Nine Palms, California was another such facility. Occupying more than 900 square miles of sun-blasted sand and red-rock mountain range in the heart of the Mojave Desert, a steady stream of Marine Expeditionary Units and combat squadrons cycled through the A-GCC, honing their skills and experimenting with new equipment and doctrine.

Tonight, however, a hundred square miles of the Center had been apportioned for another decidedly unusual tasking. Tonight, the OPFOR team didn't know who, or what, they would be opposing.

The basic scenario was a simple one. Cassin and his staff had been ordered to "develop a medium intensity Third World air defense network capable of disrupting and/or providing a one-hundred-second advanced warning of an air strike of undetermined size, nature and capability."

The range controllers and field teams from A-GCC had done so, establishing a hypothetical but effective anti-aircraft zone within the exercises area using a mixed bag of export weaponry and sensors common in the average Third World military.

From a desert mountain peak, an air-search radar tuned to match the frequency and performance characteristics of an older model French Thomson CFM system swept the skies, while low-light television cameras on several other points of high ground simulated sky-watch sentries equipped with NiteBrite binoculars.

Half a dozen point defense emplacements armed with Russian SA-18 man-portable surface-to-air missiles and German Reinmetal 20mm anti-aircraft guns also guarded the center of the exercise range. The actual weapons were not deployed, only fiberglass and inflatable plastic mock-ups. Pyrotechnic devices and strobe lights would simulate missile launches and gunfire and implanted radar and thermal beacons would register the appropriate image on airborne sensors.

As the attacker's aircraft came within range of the defense emplacements, the God computers overseeing events on the range would calculate the detection and hit probability. Should a hit be scored with a SAM or with gunfire, the kill would register on the screens of the range control center, and an electronic impulse would trigger a strobe light pod and an alarm tone aboard the targeted aircraft, announcing its destruction.

In addition, a pair of California Air National Guard F-16E jet interceptors circled above the range at thirty-five thousand feet, playing the role of a Third World Combat Air Patrol.

Located at the center of this half-dome of defenses was the "the villa." A dozen rusty Conex containers had been stacked into a rectangular house-sized pile. More cargo containers had been spaced around the central stack to form a perimeter wall and a couple of junked military trucks had been parked in the created courtyard.

The villa was what the exercise was all about – the villa and whatever might be coming after it. It could be anything, Joint Strike Fighters or F/A-22's, Tactical Tomahawk cruise missiles, even experimental UCAV strike drones. But Cassin and his people had faced all of those threats previously, and they always been told what to expect. It was one of the inherent advantages always given to the OPFOR in a training exercise.

But not tonight.

Then there was the mysterious onlooker in the range control war room, a neutral-featured middle-aged man in casual civilian clothes. He lacked even the usual photo ID security badge issued to the run of the mill op center visitor.

Cassin's immediate superior had escorted this individual to the room and left him there along with a curt set of instructions. "This man is not here. He has never been here. Totally ignore him unless he says something to you. But if he does say something, listen!"

So far, the interloper had kept his peace. He sat silently in the rear of the darkened room, fingering a sports watch.

Cassin glanced back at the man, trying to judge his impassive face. Then the Marine returned his attention to the master display. A video image had been windowed into the lower corner of the central wall screen, a view of the villa registering in the flat, gray tones of a low-light television camera.

Hands clasped behind his back, Cassin stepped to the shoulder of his senior systems controller. "Anything happening, Gunny?"

"Not a thing, sir. Dead as a whorehouse on Monday morning."

Cassin shot a look at the time hack counting down in the upper corner of the display. The scenario was scheduled to run from twenty-two to twenty-four hundred hours; right now, they were an hour and twenty-seven minutes into the run with only a little more than thirty left to go.

"Let's not get cocky," Cassin said. "They still have time."

"Any more word who's coming in on us, sir?"

"I suspect you'll know before I do, Gunny."

\*

High atop Hidalgo Mountain, the scanner head of the air-search radar rotated silently under its fiberglass dome, its beam dominating four thousand square miles of airspace.

The system had been deliberately detuned to match the performance of a less sophisticated technology for tonight's operation, but it was still an effective and reliable early warning system.

So effective, in fact, that the bottom lobe of the scan frequently reacted to ground vehicles moving along Highway 62, beyond the southern border of the A-GCC. The system operators had long ago adjusted the radar's computerized ground clutter filter to erase this distracting and aggravating disturbance.

Likewise, State 62 caused problems for the sky-scanning NiteBrite cameras. Even at a twenty-mile range, the glare of the highway

66

headlights had a tendency to overload the sensitive photomultiplier optics, causing them to lose sensitivity and definition, blinding the visual coverage of the highway corridor.

The big curtain-side semi-truck labored up the long, gradual grade that climbed out of the Yucca Valley. Road traffic on the isolated desert highway was scant, the stars overhead were bright and the ground lights were few and very far between. There was an eeriness to the Joshua tree studded wastes, an otherworldly air that possibly prompted the topic of conversation in the semi's cab.

"Flying saucers, Hank."

"What about flying saucers?" the semi's co-driver muttered back. He slouched in the cab's passenger seat, arms crossed, eyes closed, chin on chest.

"This is good country for flying saucers," the driver replied from behind the big rig's wheel.

"Ervin, how in the hell can country be good for flying saucers?"

"Lots of 'em have been seen around here," the driver insisted. "And there was that guy up at Giant Rock airport who claimed he actually talked with some people from outer space. They had some big old conventions up there with thousands of people from all over the country showing up to tell how they'd seen spaceships. That's got to mean something."

A snort prefixed the response. "Yeah, that there's whole lot of nutcases running around loose without a keeper."

"Oh, yeah? Well there's just a hell of a lot of things in this world you don't know about, Hank." The driver glanced into his side view mirror. Three sets of headlights were coming in fast from behind the semi. Dazzlingly bright and blue-white, they were likely the mercury iodide headlamps of a pack of desert racing tuner cars.

On second consideration, maybe the lights were a little high for sports compacts. A convoy of hijacker 4X4s then.

"One thing I do know, Ervin, is that there ain't no such thing as flying saucers and ... what's that?"

The coffee mugs in the cup holders on the dog box began to dance and chatter with a heavy, tooth-rattling vibration. From somewhere out in the night, a hard-edged vibrant growl intermingled with a piercing metallic trill began to leak into the cab.

"What the ...?"

Silvery illumination spilled past the truck. The three sets of "headlights" overtook the big rig and separated in a bomb burst. One set flared to the right, another to the left.

The third set went straight up.

"Hank?"

Beyond the cab driver's side window, a man – or something like a man – appeared, seemingly sitting in mid-air perhaps twenty feet off the ground. Visible from the waist up and illuminated in an eerie green-gray glow, the entity wore a bulbous helmet and facemask, a heavy, glassy visor covering whatever it used for eyes. That visor turned, looking casually into the truck's cab for a moment. Facing forward again, the otherworldly figure swept on past the semi.

The truck staggered on the roadway, buffeted on all sides by a massive displacement of air. Sleek, multi-finned shapes were hinted at on the outer edges of the headlight fans. And then it was over, the three alien invaders regrouped over the centerline of the highway, skimming the pavement as they pulled swiftly away into the night.

"Hank?"

"Ervin, just drive. I ain't saying nothing and you ain't saying nothing. Just drive!"

"Colonel Cassin, we have acquired a bogie approaching the hot range."

A single air contact hack blipped into existence on the master display, creeping from the southwest. Its course would take it across the southwestern quarter of the A-GCC and through the active exercise zone.

Cassin was at the shoulder of his senior controller in an instant. "What have you got, Gunny?"

"Single target. Clear return, sir. Altitude, twenty-two thousand feet. Airspeed, two hundred and twenty knots. Bogie is displaying a civil aviation traffic transponder."

"Where did he come from?"

"It looks like he's climbing out of Palm Springs, sir. I think we've got a lost civilian out there."

"Maybe," Cassin replied, his voice neutral. "Range traffic control. Warn the bogie he's intruding into military airspace."

"Aye, sir." Two workstations down, a young female Marine adjusted her headset and spoke into her lip mike. "Civil aircraft Echo George Tango, this is Twentynine Palms Air Traffic Control. You are about to enter closed airspace. Alter your course. I say again, alter your course. Over."

Static whispered on an overhead speaker, then a fragmented voice sputtered. "Marine ... Echo ... Ge ... Palm ... Las Vegas ... break up ... say again ..."

The aircraft hack held to its flight path, creeping across the southern boundary of the Combat Center.

The Air Traffic Controller keyed her mike again, her voice more determined. "Echo George Tango, this is Twentynine Palms Air Traffic Control. You are intruding into military airspace. Execute an immediate turn to the south. I repeat, execute an immediate turn to the south."

The target hack on the big screen turned away to the south – but, after only thirty seconds, it conducted a second right-angled turn to the west, drawing a misshapen triangle in the sky.

70

"Mar ... Air ... copy ... heading ... Cannot ... Nav ... Do you cop ..."

The bogie began to repeat its triangular flight pattern over the southeastern corner of the exercise range, the airborne distress signal of an aircraft suffering a communications and navigation failure.

The air traffic controller looked up from her screen. "Sir, I think this guy is in trouble."

"Maybe," Cassin repeated. But civil pilots did blunder into reserved military airspace with frustrating regularity, and anyone could suffer an in-flight systems failure. "Signal Intelligence, assess the target."

"Signal patterns are compatible with a civil air radar transponder and a standard civil air radio transceiver with a signal strength variance compatible with a malfunction, sir."

Cassin considered for a long second and then asked his senior NCO's opinion, always a wise move.

"Gunny, what do you think?"

"He's not a fast mover," the Gunnery Sergeant replied, "and I'm getting a hint of a prop flicker. The flight profile matches with a small turboprop of some kind. He could be as advertised, sir."

"Any chance he could be a helicopter?"

"Unlikely at that altitude and impossible with that airspeed, sir."

Cassin still felt a sense of unease. "Get the CAP in there and get a visual ID of the target. If he's a civilian, escort him out of the range and back to the Springs. If he isn't ... Ladies and Gentlemen, ride those screens. Somebody could be getting sneaky on us."

Cassin didn't notice that the silent observer at the rear of the control center was no longer idly fingering his sportswatch, but was cradling it carefully, his thumb resting on the start button.

Likewise, no one noticed one particular display tucked off in an odd corner of the room.

It was a test circuit, an old fashioned circular PPI scope displaying the raw imaging feed from the air search radar. Had a very good operator been watching that screen very closely, he might have detected three extremely faint intermittent returns creeping northward into the exercise range.

The command center's battle management system had been detecting those returns for some time as they had traveled eastward along Highway 62 at seventy odd miles per hour and had categorized and filtered them as routine ground vehicle clutter.

The system continued to do so now, even as the "ground vehicles" veered off the highway to transit terrain unbroken by any road.

*

"Civil Aircraft Echo George Tango, this is California Air National Guard Butterball Two Five, do you copy? Over. Civil Aircraft Echo George Tango, this is California Air National Guard Butterball Two Five, do you copy? Over."

Captain Brenda Zabreski, tonight known as Butterball Two Five, pulled her throttle back and flared her speed brakes, bleeding off the excess velocity built up by her descent. As the airspeed sank below three hundred knots, she dirtied up the airframe, dialing in fifteen degrees of flap and popping the speed brakes, her elderly F-16 shuddering in protest.

Over her left shoulder, the aircraft of Lieutenant Dennis Ramirez, Butterball Two Six, held station on her as the two fighters dropped from thirty-five thousand feet in a lazy pursuit curve, lining up on the blip in their cockpit intercept displays.

"Ah ... lease repeat ... can't ... system ... position ... Over."

Zabreski sighed and toggled up to the command channel, "Two Five to Two Six. Did you get anything out of that, Denny? Over."

"Negatory on that, Captain, just grass and garbage."

"Roger, Denny, let's come up on his port side, nice and easy at about a hundred-yard separation."

"Acknowledged, ma'am. Wish we could rattle this dork's doors with an afterburner run. We got better things to do out here tonight, Captain."

"Stand easy, Denny. This guy could really be in trouble. Beyond that, the State of California doesn't need a lawsuit from some civil aviation puke claiming we scared him into a permanent sexual dysfunction."

72

Another voice intruded into Zabreski's helmet phones. "Butterball Two Five, this is Twentynine Palms Traffic Control. We have the bogie at your one o'clock at five miles. Do you have a visual? Over."

Zabreski thumbed the transmit button on the top of her side-stick controller. "We have strobes at our one o'clock. They appear to be the running lights of a civil aircraft. Do you wish us to continue the intercept? Over. "

The pulsing strobe flares crept into the cartwheel sight of the F-16's heads up display as the interceptors aligned with it.

"Affirmative, Butterball Two Five," Twenty-nine Palms replied. "Close the range and make skin identification of the target."

"Roger. Will comply." Muttering to herself about pernickety jarheads, Zabreski juggled her flaps, throttle and flight angle. The F-16 was sluggish and sullen as it crept closer to its target, unhappy at this airspeed.

As their range closed, Zabreski reached up with her left hand and flipped down her low light vision visor, trying to see the aircraft behind the lights. The target's strobes were set to bright rapid flash and it wasn't easy.

The bogie wasn't very big, whatever it was. Maybe a Turbo Mooney. But was that a tail boom? Could it be an old Cessna Skymaster flying flat out and balls to the wall?

Abruptly the strobe lights snapped off and Captain Zabreski got a single instant's good look at the target.

It was like nothing she had ever seen before in her life.

In the Range Control Center, the strangled yelp of the interceptor leader sounded from the overhead speakers. On the main screen, the target hack of the unidentified aircraft suddenly and radically decelerated.

Out in the night, the "distressed civilian aircraft" halved its speed in a matter of seconds. Helplessly, the two interceptors overshot the mysterious intruder, the bogie weaving and striking at the trailing jet like an airborne cobra.

The bogie's pilot spoke over the communications link, but this time both his voice and his transmission were clear and cool as he chanted, "Guns! Guns! Guns!"

A red death box snapped into existence around the trailing F-16. "Butterball Two Six has been terminated!" a marine controller yelled. "Twenty millimeter, air to air!"

The range computers had declared the Air Guard jet shredded by a storm of autocannon fire. Cassin crushed down the transmit key on his headset. He had only seconds. "Butterball Two Five! Call your target! What's out there?"

"I don't know!" The air guard pilot's voice was frantic as she tried to clean up her aircraft and regain airspeed. "I've never seen ..."

"Fox three! Fox three!" That cool, masculine voice overrode her words. Out over the range, hypothetical infrared homing missiles were screaming off their launching rails, targeting the exhaust plume of the Air Guard jet. The computers adjudicated and a second death box materialized around Butterball Two Five.

"Butterball Two Five has been destroyed by a Sidewinder X," a controller reported. "Direct hit!"

In the shadowed corner of the command center, the nameless observer thumbed the timer button of his sports watch. One hundred seconds and counting.

In frustration, Cassin stared up at the overhead speaker. By the rules of the game, the interceptor pilots couldn't even describe what had so suddenly killed them. They were dead. But by then the interceptor killer was the least of his problem.

Another trio of hostile aircraft symbols seemed to materialize magically within the radar sweep as the befuddled filtration system belatedly acknowledged that they weren't ground clutter.

"Multiple airborne targets on the range!" the senior controller yelled. "Altitude, nape of the earth, airspeed one hundred and twenty knots and accelerating. Bearing zero degrees true. Convergent on primary target!"

"Gunny, call the incoming! What do we have coming in?"

"Gotta be helicopters, sir."

Gunships, Cassin thought feverishly; it had to be a flight of AH-64 Apaches escorted by ... something else. "Weapons free, all stations! Nape of the earth engagement envelope!"

The OPFORs still had a chance. According to the victory conditions of the scenario, the intruding blue force had to put fire on the villa within one hundred seconds of detection and the choppers had been detected a little too far out. They weren't going to get within range in time.

"Wait! Delay that!" the master controller yelled, all rank protocols forgotten under the stress. "Target airspeed now over two hundred knots and still accelerating. Targets are not, I repeat, not, helos."

"Then what the hell are they?"

"Beats the shit out of me, sir. The airspeed was too low for fixed wing aircraft. Now it's too high for helicopters."

"What about tilt-rotors? Could they be Ospreys?"

"The radar cross section is way too small! The radar signatures and flight profiles don't match with anything in the book!"

It all came clear to Cassin now. The secrecy concerning their attacking force. The nameless observer in the Op Center. This wasn't just another training exercise. He and his people were being used to field test some new, secret and radically different weapons system.

Video windows were snapping open around the perimeter of the main screen, low-light camera feeds from the air defense perimeter gun positions. The range controllers were trying to acquire the invaders visually – but all the cameras picked up were launch flashes in the darkness.

The video relay from the three air defense sites broke to static as the cameras disintegrated. The attackers had been authorized to use real weapons on the simulated ground targets. Death boxes outlined the gun positions guarding the southern approaches to the primary objective.

"Air Defense sites three, four and five destroyed. Hellfire air-to surface missiles."

Hellfires, 20mm cannon and Sidewinders. At least whoever was kicking their ass was using American technology.

All eyes turned to the television image of the villa, save for those of the silent observer at the back of the room. He watched the luminous second hand of his watch sweep around the dial. Fifteen seconds ... Twenty ... Twenty-five ...

In his mind's eye, another sequence of events was unfolding. A wary, cunning, frightened man sleeps in a darkened room. A telephone rings. A warning is shouted over it.

Thirty ... Thirty-five ... Forty ...

Boots hammer up a stairway. Frantic fists pound on a locked door.

Forty-five ... Fifty ... Fifty-five ...

Bodyguards drag a sleeping man from his bed. Explanations and orders are screamed. A mad race back down the hall and stairway.

Sixty ... Sixty-five ... Seventy ...

Limousine engines crank over. An escape convoy stands ready, doors open. Courtyard gates swing wide, making way for a race into the darkness.

Seventy-five ... Eighty ...

On the wall screen, a three-round Hellfire salvo slammed into the front face of the target house; a second salvo followed, a third, a fourth. Riding the beams of their guidance lasers, the missiles caved in and flattened the Conex container building blocks of the structure.

It was a focused rain of firepower, targeted not merely to damage or conventionally destroy the mock villa and its compound, but to obliterate it, to level every possible, survivable corner of the structure.

It succeeded.

Within thirty seconds, nothing remained save a charred and scattered fan of scrap metal sprayed across the desert.

The observer smiled and clicked the stop button.

Nothing remained on the main wall display as well. The position hacks of the three attackers had faded, ghostlike, from the screen at the moment of the last missile launch. The track of the fourth invader, the one that had ambushed the Combat Air Patrol, had disappeared as well, dissipating as it had spiraled down toward the desert.

All that remained in the sky over the A-GCC were the two humiliated Air Guard F-16s, returning to their base.

The observer pocketed his watch, left his corner and walked to where Cassin stared at the master screen. "Thank you, Colonel," he said. "You and your staff have been most helpful. This exercise is concluded. "

Then he turned and left the command center.

The first warning the steaming watch in the wheelhouse had was the appearance of the Marine sentry. Crossing to the portside bridge windows, the Marine tugged on the tapes that bound up the canvas dodger mounted over the windscreen. Unrolling the canvas to block out the view of the big amphib's full length flight deck, he put his back to the windows and went to a watchful parade rest.

The helm and lee helmsman at the wheel and engine controls exchanged glances, but the Officer of the Watch murmured, "Eyes forward, gentlemen. You know the drill."

A few moments later, a voice rolled from the ship's MC-1 loudspeakers. "Stand by to recover aircraft. Stand by to recover aircraft. Set all special security protocols. Secure all topside video cameras. All unauthorized personnel proceed below decks immediately. I say again, all unauthorized personnel proceed below decks immediately."

For the past week, the crew of the Bonne Homme Richard, affectionately referred to by all hands as "The Bonny Dick", had been involved in some very deep mojo indeed.

The Wasp class LHD had been designed and intended to carry the bulk of a Marine Expeditionary Unit and its supporting air elements. On this cruise however, someone else had come aboard and had taken over. Just who was a matter of some conjecture.

The Air One Flight Control Center at the aft end of the LHD's island was manned by a complement of the mysterious strangers. Likewise, the aircraft handling details and fire and crash crews standing to on the flight deck were also numbered among the nameless.

The ship's aviation service spaces had also been declared off limits with the after half of the hangar bay walled off by a tarpaulin barricade, guarded by prowling, pistol packing Marine sentries.

Nor was this security contingent made up of commonplace leathernecks.

These were Fleet Marine Force, the same hand-picked unit that stood guard over the navy's nuclear weapons arsenals.

Shipboard scuttlebutt had naturally run wild, but no concrete conclusions had yet been reached.

The watch officer tilted his head, listening to the voice in his command headset.

"Helmsman, come left to zero nine eight true. Put her across the wind."

"Helm coming left to zero nine eight true, sir."

They were swinging across the wind to recover the VTOL aircraft.

A trilling roar began to filter down from the night. The crew of the Bonny Dick had become very well-acquainted with that sound over these past two weeks. It was very similar to the sound of the conventional helicopters they were accustomed to handling, but not quite the same. Not quite.

Whatever they were, they only flew after dark, launching after sunset and returning before dawn. Daylight would find the flight deck empty.

The shipboard speculators had one more clue to mull over. The airdales and aviators who had come aboard to maintain and fly this mystery air group all wore the same odd little unit patch on their flight and service gear. There was no unit name, number or motto on the simple circular black device, just the horizontal slash of a silver lightning bolt morphing into a red-eyed striking Cobra, its fangs bared.

*

Still wearing his life jacket and survival gear harness over a camo-pattern flight suit, the wiry naval aviator with the movie star's face came to a relaxed parade rest before Captain DeVille's desk.

"How did it go tonight, CAG?" The Bon Homme Richard's commander inquired, using the anachronistic but traditional acronym for 'Commander Air Group.' As the one man of the LHD's compliment authorized to know the nature and intent of the black squadron carried by his vessel, he had the privilege of asking.

"Pretty good, sir," the aviator smiled. "In fact, it couldn't have gone better. I'm damn pleased with how this outfit is dialing in, especially with all of the developmental work we still have to do with the technology. I'd say we're damn near deployable as we stand."

The LHD's skipper replied with an ironic smile of his own. "I'm pleased to hear that, Vince. After you launched this evening, we received a flash red from NAVSPECFORCE headquarters at Pearl."

DeVille unlocked a desk drawer and removed a message flimsy, passing it to the younger officer. "We've been ordered to abort your training cruise two days early. The SPEED Cobras are to be flown off to Edwards Air Force Base tomorrow night and we'll land your support personnel and equipment at Coronado the following morning. I am authorized to inform you that your squadron is to be airlifted out of Edwards to an undisclosed forward staging base within the next seventy-two hours."

Deville handed a second flimsy across the desk. "There was a second communication designated specifically for you."

Commander Vincent Arkady's expression went from amiable enthusiasm to thoughtful neutrality as he considered the flimsy. Its sender was Admiral Elliot MacIntyre and its message was succinct in the extreme.

One word:

NOW.

Arkady looked up from the message. "It says all it needs to, Captain."

"Senator Donovan, you've been a player in our current controversial involvement in the Indonesian crisis from the beginning. Now it appears to be evolving into the Amanda Garrett crisis. Do you have any input for us in this recent turn of events?"

"Firstly, Larry, I'd like to make it clear that both I and my party have stood firmly against the Childress administration's reckless brand of cowboy interventionism, not only in Indonesia but around the world. Having said that, I must also say that a loose cannon spawns loose cannons."

"How do you mean, Senator?"

"I think it's fairly obvious that the President's aggressive foreign policies and blank check treatment of the Armed Forces has spawned a dangerous 'Rambo' attitude among our military leadership. Hyper-aggressive risk-takers such as the Garrett woman are allowed to come to the fore, individuals willing to subvert the will of Congress and the American people in their hunt for personal glory."

"I must point out, Senator, that Captain Garrett is a two-time winner of the Navy Cross and the recipient of a Special United Nations Medal for Peacekeeping."

"I don't mean to belittle this young woman's legitimate accomplishments – but it is also obvious she has now exceeded even the loose mandates of the Childress administration. Justifiably, she must be brought to book."

"The press statement issued by US Naval Special Forces still only mentions a nonspecific Board of Inquiry."

"We are clearly being stonewalled by Admiral Elliot MacIntyre, the NAVSPECFORCE commander. He's using the old bugaboo of National Security in a flagrant attempt to shield Garrett, but I can promise you, Larry, the truth will come out ..."

Diego Garcia was not near anything. It was a desolate flyspeck of coral lost in a vast waste of open sea. The only real value rested in its location. From this particular set of geographic co-ordinates, one could dominate the entire Indian Ocean basin.

Nominally, Diego was a British possession. However, it had been given over to the United States under a long-term lease, the only tenants being the American armed forces. You did not go to Diego unless you'd been invited and you were not invited unless you had specific and approved business there.

A single, huge air base complex took up the bulk of the main island, its runways, parking aprons and servicing facilities capable of handling the largest aircraft in existence. Naval patrol planes, military transports and tankers shuttled through routinely, going about the Pentagon's affairs. The heavy hitters of the Air Combat Command – the B-52 BUFFs, the B-1 "Bones" and the B-2 Spirits – had also staged out of Diego for the conflicts in the Gulf and the 'Stans.

More heavy hitters could be found moored in the island anchorage, the great gray ships of the Military Sealift Command. The Diego Garcia Maritime Pre-positioning Force stood ready to race to any potential hotspot along the Asian or African coast. Its fast transports were packed solid with the equipment kits of an Army Mechanized Expeditionary Force, a Marine Expeditionary Brigade and an Air Force Combat Wing – along with the munitions, fuel and supplies required for a month's worth of war. There, the equipment could be mated with troops airlifted in from the continental United States, vastly reducing the response time to a potential crisis.

The world's military communities readily recognized that Diego Garcia was the linchpin of US military power in Asia. Any stirrings of the giant would be reflected by events on the little island. Accordingly, Diego had become one of the most thoroughly spied upon locales on the planet.

For the past six months, military reconnaissance satellites had noted something new and puzzling added to the facilities at Diego. For lack of any better name, it was referred to as "The Cocoon."

A gigantic floating dry dock, easily large enough to handle an American Nimitz-class aircraft carrier, had been towed to the island and positioned in the anchorage. It was a reasonable addition to the island's naval support facilities. However, this particular dry dock had been roofed over with a white geodetic canopy, obviously intended to conceal whatever it contained from the prying eyes of the fleet of orbital voyeurs.

Of course, using some of the more esoteric forms of infrared photography, it was fully possible to "see" through the walls and ceilings of a building, granting a fair view of the interior. A couple of millimeters of fiberglass construction fabric shouldn't constitute a difficulty.

But what looked like fiberglass construction fabric, wasn't. It was an infrared absorbent stealth material as impermeable as a mountainside.

If infrared wouldn't work, then perhaps passive microwave would. If the cocoon contained a large metallic object, such as a ship, said ship would radiate a minute but detectable electromagnetic emission. When scanned by a properly equipped satellite, the ship would literally draw a radiant picture of itself.

But, when such a satellite was maneuvered into position, it was found that an array of broad-spectrum microwave emitters sprayed the sky above the cocoon, washing out all effective passive imaging.

Grumbling, the orbital reconnaissance specialists withdrew. The United States had developed satellite surveillance and they were still the undisputed masters of the craft.

One foreign power, a theoretical ally of the United States and a fellow member of the North Atlantic Treaty Organization, had not been satisfied. Launching out of a base in the Seychelles, it attempted to sidle an unmanned, instrument-laden reconnaissance drone in close enough to Diego Garcia to get a look at the mysterious dry dock.

The last image transmitted back from the drone was of a Patriot III interceptor missile flaming in for the kill. Treaties that might count for something in the North Atlantic did not necessarily apply in the wastes of the Indian Ocean.

For the past week there had been a massive upsurge of activity around the cocoon, but the outside world was unaware of the development. Diego Garcia's "Captain Kirk", the orbital traffic officer, had been playing a deft and elaborate game of strategic peekaboo. Whenever the skies above Diego were empty, a steady stream of barges, landing craft and cargo lighters shuttled between the shoreside base facilities and the anchored dry dock. But whenever a suspected reconnaissance satellite popped above the horizon, the support craft were either huddled under the shelter of the dock's protective hood or dispersed elsewhere around the anchorage.

On this night, the support craft withdrew for the last time, their tasking complete. Aboard the dock and aboard what it contained, crews stood to their stations, waiting for a gap in the orbital surveillance.

At exactly 23:24 Hours, the Japanese Self-Defense Force Reconsat Shiun 5 sank below the northern horizon. Following a final check with Space Command Headquarters beneath Cheyenne Mountain, "Captain Kirk" gave the final clearance.

Warning klaxons blared within the cocoon. Line handling details flipped down their night-vision visors as bank after bank of the interior work lights blinked out. In the darkness, compressed air hissed and powerful engines cranked into life.

The klaxons blared once more and the mammoth forward gates of the dry dock edged open, displaced waves sucking and swirling around them. Python-thick nylon mooring lines splashed free of mooring bitts and the waters roiled beneath a towering counter as multiple propellers began to turn.

A great angular shadow crept out into the night, tropic phosphorescence burning coldly along its waterline. Running blacked out, it turned with ponderous grace toward the anchorage channel and the open sea beyond, the doors of its secretive home closing on its wake.

Forty-five minutes later, the Canadian Commercial Earth Surveillance Satellite, Red Eagle Alpha, swept over Diego Garcia. On behalf of a number of different governmental and private subscribers, a photo series was taken of the complex. Nothing out of the ordinary was noted.

The air was rich with the scent of cloves, vanilla and the sea. The breakfast table on the lanai of the old East Indies Dutch plantation house had been decorated with a bowl of forest orchids picked by one of the servants. It was an incongruous centerpiece for a war room. Likewise, the chatter of the wild parakeets made an odd background note for the topic of conversation.

"We need to start ramping up the air isolation phase of the campaign, Lo," Harconan said to his factotum. "I want to start the disruption of the inter-island air traffic." The taipan was clad in safari jacket and slacks while the Straits Chinese seated across from him wore his inevitable black business suit.

"We have several vessels available with man-portable surface-to-air missile systems," Lo replied. "They can be positioned in the flight paths of some of the major coastal airfields."

Harconan shook his head, his dark hair still wet from his shower. "We might consider that for the military transports but not for Garuda and the other civilian airlines. I want to use sabotage teams on them. Overt, direct-action sabotage. I want those aircraft taken out on the ground, not in the air."

Lo frowned lightly. "I must point out that the terror factor of mid-air losses would expedite the isolation process."

"True enough, bapak," Harconan replied, using the affectionate Indonesian term for father. "But it will hold down the casualty count a little. God knows it's growing fast enough as it is."

"We recognized the inevitability of this factor when we launched this enterprise, Mr. Harconan." An individual well-acquainted with the Lan Lo might have recognized and understood the slight softening of his voice.

"I know, I know." Harconan took up the silver fruit knife beside his plate. Without much interest, he cut a slice from the mango he had selected. "We went into this thing knowing we must be bastards, but there is no sense in being any bigger a bastard than we have to be."

"I daresay there is wisdom in that position, sir."

The taipan took a bite of the fruit and frowned as a thought caught at him. "In relation to that, what in the hell is going on down in Bali?"

"In respect to what, sir?"

"The religious unrest we've been getting reports on. None of our agents or units are involved, are they?"

Lo shook his head. "No sir. None of our cells are undertaking any operations at all on Bali. As per your instructions, all of our clan chiefs and ship's captains have received orders to maintain a low profile and to perform no provocations of any kind."

"Well, some idiot is starting trouble of a kind even we don't want. I need chaos, but not a Muslim-Hindu blood jihad."

Lo nodded. "Indeed. But it must be recognized that any time of unrest might be viewed as an opportunity by the power hungry. That may be what we are seeing here. We know that there are any number of Islamic racialist factions maneuvering for positions of power within the archipelago. No doubt one of them is seeking to prove his power by provoking a confrontation with the followers of Agama Tirta."

"He picked a damn poor place for it." Harconan slowly chewed a second slice of mango. "If this kind of vandalism and harassment continues, the Balinese Muslim minority could become extinct very abruptly."

The Chinese gave the slightest of shrugs. "One shouldn't expect rational thought from a man who believes that the Gods hold him in extraordinary favor."

"That's exactly what I'm afraid of, Lo. Put Intelligence Group Bali on this. I want to know who's behind these disturbances. Possibly an over-enthusiastic Mullah or two requires an early return to Allah."

"At once, sir." Lo took no notes. He required none. But this morning, he did bear a single hardcopy file with him. "Sir, there is something else I believe you might wish to see."

Lan Lo was an impassive man in the extreme – but Harconan had a great deal of experience at reading his minute leakages of emotion. His factotum was concerned about something and on a personal level.

"What is it, bapak?"

Silently the Straits Chinese passed the file folder across the table. At the front was a news file download photo from CNN, a picture of a soberly attractive red-haired woman in an American "Blue Baker" naval uniform.

Harconan read the first paragraphs of the attached hardcopy and scowled.

## COURTMARTIAL CONSIDERED FOR FAMOUS WOMAN WARRIOR

*Dateline Washington DC: Informed sources within the Pentagon are reporting that America's most decorated female combat officer, Captain Amanda Lee Garrett, has been relieved of command as part of a secret Department of Defense investigation into charges that include 'Dereliction of duty and conduct unbecoming an officer.'*

*In recent weeks, Captain Garrett and her command, the elite Sea Fighter Task Force of US Naval Special Forces, have been deployed to the waters off Indonesia, involved in what have been described as 'anti-piracy operations.' However Congressional critics of the Childress administration have called them a 'flagrant intrusion in the domestic affairs and responsibilities of a foreign power.'*

*Details concerning the investigation have not yet been released and Department of Defense spokesmen have no comment beyond a statement that Captain Garrett is being recalled to NAVSPECFORCE headquarters in Hawaii for "a debriefing on recent events in Indonesia ..."*

"I warned you, Amanda," Harconan spoke aloud to someone not present. "I warned you that, even if you won, you would lose in the end."

He shook his head, musing at the past and at himself. Amanda Garrett was the woman who had shattered his meticulously developed multi-million-dollar piracy cartel and who had placed his plans for the future of Indonesia at risk. She had also come within a hair's breadth of seeing him dead.

Yet he could also recall seeing her walk naked and unashamed on the beaches of his family's island stronghold, and of feeling her arch in piercingly sweet passion beneath him. At one and the same time, she was his enemy – and yet also the one woman he had ever found worthy of the title Radu Samudra, the Queen of the Seas.

Kismet could be both sardonic and perverse.

*What of it, Amanda? Has this betrayal by those you've served broken you? Are you ready to try a new way?*

Harconan paused for a moment, considering. *Or could it be that you are already trying a new way?*

"It would seem that Captain Garrett has fallen in the eyes of her superiors," Lo said with circumspection. "We may take comfort in the nullification of a potent foe."

Harconan had long ago come to accept the fact that Lo could read his thoughts, including those he had concerning Amanda Garrett.

"Possibly, Lo. It is conceivable that the American authorities are indeed this stupid." He slid the folder back across the table. "Then again, possibly they are not. Get on with Intelligence Group Amanda about this. I want everything that can be acquired on this theoretical court-martial. Also I want a real-time track placed on Captain Garrett. I want to know where she is and what she's doing at all times to the limits of our capacity."

"As you wish, sir." There was the briefest instant's hesitation. "May I ask, Mr. Harconan, is this concern in relation to our operations within the archipelago or is it of a more ... personal nature?"

Harconan smiled. "You may ask, but I'm afraid I don't know the answer myself."

She still smelled fresh from the builder's yard, the paint unmarred on her bulkheads, her fittings still tight, polished and new.

Lieutenant Commander Dixon Lovejoy Beltrain worked his way through the empty, echoing holds and compartments, ensuring that every watertight door and access hatch had been wedged securely open. The crew was all off. The main engines were silent. Only a single auxiliary generator maintained the internal lighting. The great ship was adrift in the trough, the roll of the light-riding hull exaggerated, the steel of her frames creaking softly. It was as if she were deep in a sleep from which she would never awaken.

Once more, Beltrain felt the dull ache of regret – and, for the dozenth time, the Alabama-born naval officer brusquely told himself to not be a damn fool.

And yet, you don't usually become a naval officer unless a love of the sea and of ships has been born or bred in you, along with an instinctive sense that ships are more than just mere artifacts, that there is a life there. With it comes a sadness at seeing one die, no matter how necessary.

Beltrain made his way aft, hurrying to have done with it, stepping carefully over the ominous gray cords snaking down the passageway.

Hunching through a final hatch, he emerged onto the second level of the main engine room. Below him, under the shadowless glare of the work lights, the huge diesel generator sets and mammoth electric motors gleamed. There also was a single man. Rangy and tall in his middle age, he was clad in an engineer's coveralls and he knelt beside a partially disassembled coolant pump, the wrench in his hand glinting as he worked over it.

"Hey, chief," Beltrain called, "it's time to go."

The man in the coveralls hesitated, then gave the socket wrench a final tightening twist before setting the tool back into the kit on the deck beside him.

"Coming right up, Mr. Beltrain. I just spotted a lubricant leak down here ... ah, to hell with it."

Beltrain thought it still sounded funny to have Carl Thomson address him as "Mister". When they had served together aboard the USS *Cunningham*, Thomson had been the Duke's senior engineering officer and Beltrain's vast superior in both rank and experience. Now, Beltrain was first mate and the Chief insisted on following the proprieties. His orderly engineer's mind required it.

Thomson clattered up the ladder to the gangway and the two men studied the silent engine room for a long moment more.

"Christ," Thomson said finally. "But it makes you want to weep."

"I hear you, Chief," Beltrain replied, pleased that he wasn't alone in his sentimentality. "They tried to figure it every other way they could, but she's just too dangerous to keep around. Even under another name."

"That's true, I guess," Thomson nodded. "But being sensible is a pain in the ass sometimes."

They went topside.

The sky had started to pale with the coming dawn and the horizon was empty, save for a single cluster of ship's running lights on the horizon. The wind had a bite to it that hinted at the Antarctic. They had come to this specific spot in the wastes of the southernmost Pacific for two reasons – one because it was far from all the frequently traveled sea and air lanes, and the other because the nearest land was four miles away, straight down.

An unmarked Agusta Bell A-109 helicopter sat atop one of the MacGregor hatches amidships. As Beltrain and the Chief emerged from the deckhouse, the pilot spotted them and lit off her turbines, preparing for take-off.

The only other person aboard was clad in army camouflage with a green beret tugged low over one eye. "We're all ready, sir," he yelled to Beltrain over the spool up of the aircraft.

"Very well, Sergeant. Set 'em and let's get out of here."

The Special Forces trooper turned his attention to the end of a wiring cluster that emerged from a nearby hatch. Kneeling, he plugged a series of connector jacks into a small black box. Carefully, he checked the timer settings, then flipped a final set of switches. With his task accomplished, he joined Thomson and Beltrain aboard the waiting helo.

The Agusta Bell lifted off and climbed away, going into an observation orbit above the ship as the seconds ticked off on the LED displays on the little black box.

Alone now, abandoned to her destiny, the vessel drifted, her lights still glowing.

Five minutes passed and the relays closed. Detonator cord flared and the linear explosions streaked away into the bowels of the ship. The decks shuddered.

There were no overt indications of an explosion, no bursts of fire and smoke, but small carefully placed shaped charges cut through the ship's hull in a score of places, admitting a deluge of chill seawater.

The ship's lights went out and, within moments, she began to settle. Five minutes more and the Motor Vessel Galaxy *Shenandoah* lifted her bow, vanishing in the nexus of a boiling fury of foam and spray. She left nothing behind, not even an oil slick, for she had carried only enough fuel to reach her dying ground.

The helicopter circled once more and then angled away towards the cluster of lights in the distance. Shortly thereafter, the Motor Vessel Galaxy *Shenandoah* steamed over her own grave, heading north.

"You're not going to believe this, you preposterous piece of vegetation," Amanda commented aloud to the little palm tree, "but I'm actually going to miss you."

She gave the palm a final farewell squirt from the misting bottle. Setting the sprayer down on the counter, she took a lingering look around the deserted wardroom. Someone – she thought it might have been Marion Hargrove – had once said that leaving home was always sad and a soldier has so many homes. That applied to sailors as well.

She would not be back here again. At least as the TACBOSS of the Sea Fighters. It had been a long road, from the Chesapeake Bay to the savage coasts of West Africa to the pirate stalking grounds of the East Indies to here. Now, this door in her life was closing behind her and she was stepping into the unknown.

When she had stood down from the Captaincy of the *Cunningham*, there had been the solemn litany of the change of command to work through. There would be no such ceremony this time. There was only the helicopter waiting to lift her into Darwin. In theory, she was flying back to NAVSPECFORCE headquarters at Pearl for a board of inquiry.

But she was also leaving under a steadily darkening cloud. The carefully orchestrated campaign of "leaks" and half-truths being fed to the media were making it look as if she had totally fallen on her face here in Indonesia. A number of noteworthy political pundits critical of the Childress administration were already predicting a court-martial and a possible congressional investigation. Other media talking heads were salivating over the titillating phrases "dereliction of duty" and "conduct unbecoming an officer."

*Oh well,* Amanda mused grimly, *if one's career was going to be trashed, one might as well have it trashed spectacularly.*

She wasn't happy with the effect the situation was having on the Sea

Fighters, however. No US Naval Task Force had ever mutinied *en masse* before – but her people were close. She'd done her best to mellow the situation, insisting that it was only a hearing and that things would be straightened out in due course. Still, she was glad she was handing the temporary TACBOSS slot over to Captain Carberry of the *Carlson*. An outsider would likely have had tough sledding for awhile.

The Board of Inquiry was sophistry, of course. It would never convene. Nor would Amanda ever reach Hawaii.

Someone cleared his throat near the passageway entry. Stone Quillain stood in the door, twisting his utility cap in his hands. "Your gear's loaded and ready to go, Skipper."

From the tone of his voice, he might have been inviting her to try on her coffin. In spite of herself, Amanda had to smile. The big marine was positively suffering.

She lifted an eyebrow. "And you came all the way up here just to tell me that they've put my suitcase on the helicopter?"

He grimaced. "Aw hell, it's just that the other officers are gettin' together on the flight deck to see you off and I guess I wanted to get a head start on it."

"Stone, it's just a board of inquiry, not a firing squad."

"I know, I know, Howlin' Mad Smith had a few of those in his time." He hesitated and then exploded. "The thing is, it's a load of crap! The whole damn deal!"

"Of course it is," Amanda nodded. "That's how it goes sometimes. We were bucking a complex situation out here and we had to get extraordinarily unconventional. That never sits well with some people. I've got some actions to justify, that's all."

Quillain's brows knitted together. "I can see how the way we operate might get sideways with some of the brass hats in CONUS, but hittin' you with a dereliction of duty? What kind of drunk 'n constipated son of a bitch came up with that one?"

Amanda found it increasingly difficult to stay in her lie. "No doubt I'll find out when I get back there," she said, straightening from the edge of the table. "Speaking of that, I'd better get going."

She held her hand out to Stone. "You take care of business here and I'll take care of things back in Pearl."

Her hand almost disappeared inside the marine's powerful grasp, but his grip was gentle in its firmness. "You give 'em hell, Skipper, and get back here fast. We got things to do."

"That we have," Amanda hesitated. "Stone, have you seen Commander Rendino around today?"

"I think I saw her up on the superstructure a little while back. She ain't been happy about this situation either."

"I know." She lifted her hand to Quillain's shoulder and let it rest for a moment. "Do me a favor and tell them on the flight deck that I'll be along shortly. I have to take care of something."

She found Christine Rendino at the isolated after end of the *Carlson*'s main deckhouse, the most private place on a ship where privacy was at a premium. The Intel was leaning at the rail, staring out across the Bonaparte Bay anchorage without seeing any of the ships there. Nor did she look around at Amanda's approach.

"Chris, are you all right?" Amanda inquired softly, coming up beside her friend.

"No, I'm not. And I don't think you are either." Christine turned to face her. The Intel's eyes were reddened as if she had been crying recently. "Amanda, please take me with you. Cook the books. Call in favors. Screw it, I'll go AWOL if I have to, but let me go back to Hawaii with you."

Amanda was taken-aback by the sheer desperation in Chris's voice. "That's impossible, Chris, you know that. Why? What's the matter?"

"I think you're going to need someone on your side when you get back there."

"On my side? Chris, what do you mean?"

"I mean, something crazy is going on back at NAVSPECFORCE. I think you're being set up for something."

Amanda felt her eyebrows lift. "What kind of something?"

"Something like you getting your throat cut at a drumhead court-martial."

"Chris, you're not talking sense."

"I am, Amanda, honest I am! Listen to me, please. I've been trying to get to the bottom of the Board of Inquiry business, to find out who and what's behind it all. I figured I could give you an edge going in. But all of my contacts in NAVSPECFORCE HQ and 7th Fleet have been scared dry. Nobody's talking. Nobody! All of a sudden, you're like *persona non grata* back there. Nobody's even willing to say your name out loud. The fix must already be in!"

The penny dropped with a loud, resounding clang.

*Oh Lord, save us from our devoted friends,* Amanda thought feverishly. Of course Chris would be concerned about her apparent situation, of course she would go under the table to try and help – and of course the Intel would slam right into the security wall put up around Amanda's involvement in the Phantom Force project.

For once in her life, Christine Rendino was deducing all of the wrong conclusions.

"That doesn't necessarily mean anything, Chris," Amanda replied, trying to keep her voice casual. "Nobody's supposed to talk about the evidence to be presented at a Board of Enquiry before it convenes."

Christine shook her head vehemently. "No, this is something more than that. I have a real nasty hunch that something else may be going on. It's the only thing that seems to make any sense." She trailed off, fumbling for the right words. "Look, I've developed a pretty close working relationship with Admiral MacIntyre since North Africa. One that's sort of outside the box, like with you. Ever since this Board of Inquiry's cropped up, I've been trying to get in contact with him. I wanted to find out if he knew who was responsible and what we could do about setting up your defense. I figured he'd be on your side. But he's not! I think he's the one selling you out."

"Admiral MacIntyre? Chris, that's frothing-at-the-mouth insane!"

The Intel shook her blonde head. "It's not! If he was on your side, he'd be kicking ass and taking names trying to quash this thing. As it is, he's on the horn all the time with JSOC and the Joint Chiefs – but he's not talking to us. Look, Boss Ma'am, I know he's the admiral and all, but I also think he's setting you up for a court martial."

Amanda put her hands on the younger woman's shoulders. "Chris, this is just a Board of Inquiry, it's not a court-martial."

"Yet!" The word was spat out.

"Chris, believe me – for once, you're making a wrong call. Admiral MacIntyre has no reason to sell me out over anything."

"Maybe he thinks he does." The younger woman insisted.

"Why, for God sake?"

Chris pulled her voice lower. "Because of Makara Harconan."

Amanda let her hands drop to her hips. "Well, I'll admit that wasn't my proudest moment, but I doubt Eddie Mac is going to cut my throat over it."

"He might, Amanda. Believe me. He just might. Jealousy can make people act very strange sometimes."

*Jealousy?* "Chris, Clarify! Bottom-line this for me. Why should Elliot MacIntyre be jealous of ... anything?"

"Oh hell, because fa'sure he's in love with you," the Intel replied impatiently. "Or he was."

For a moment, the *Carlson* seemed to go out of trim, the deck tilting under Amanda's feet. She shook off the effect and shot a fast look around to ensure no one was within hearing range. "Have you gone completely crazy, Chris? How can you say such a thing?"

"Because it's the truth." Christine swiped at her eyes then looked up defiantly. "Like I said, I've worked outside of the box with the Admiral and we've talked about a lot of things. Your name has come up in a lot of those conversations."

"You mean he's actually said to you ..."

Christine shook her head. "No, of course not. For the most part, he's as big a straight edge as you are. But, while the Admiral may be a very cagey individual in a lot of ways, he's as transparent as any other male in others. I saw the way he acted when you were Harconan's prisoner, the way he sounded when he thought you might have sold out. Look, I know what a man who's gone over the edge for a woman looks like and Eddie Mac has been seriously gone over you for a long time."

Had the main pylon mast toppled over the side with no warning,

Amanda could not have been more stunned. This was impossible. Elliot MacIntyre was her commanding officer and a comrade and she liked to think a friend. Yet Amanda was so accustomed to Christine Rendino being totally right about her pronouncements that she couldn't automatically assume she was wrong.

"Your affair with Harconan might have hurt the Admiral enough that he might have brooded himself into the mood for payback," Christine continued with stark frankness. "That kind of thing happens. Damn it, he might even have been the one to blow the whistle on you. In certain circles, your affair with Harconan could very well be construed as 'dereliction of duty and conduct unbecoming to an officer'."

"Elliot is not that petty!" Amanda burst out before she could control the words.

"I didn't think so either, Boss Ma'am," Christine replied, openly grieving. "But it's the only thing that makes any sense."

Amanda knew that Christine had to be wrong in at least half of her assessment, the portion concerning the court-martial. But what about the other half? If Chris was right about Elliot?

She didn't need this now. She didn't need this at all! With both Indonesia and Phantom looming, there was no time to even consider the concept. Furiously, she stuffed the entire idea into a back compartment of her mind and firmly dogged the hatch down on it.

She took a deep breath. "Chris, this is just plain stupid," she said coolly. "And I will not hear any more about this."

"But ..."

"Drop it, Commander. That is an order!"

"As you wish, ma'am." Christine turned away to stare out across the bay once more. "I'm sorry for stepping out of bounds."

Amanda gritted her teeth. Reaching up, she rested her palms on the Intel's shoulders. "Chris, will you do a couple of things for me, please?"

The reply was almost inaudible. "What?"

"For one, believe in me and believe in the Admiral. No matter what happens. No matter what you hear. Believe in us and that everything is going to work out. All right?"

"All right." There wasn't much surety in the reply. "What's the other thing?"

"Take care of my damn palm tree for me."

Christine choked on her laugh. Spinning around, she locked Amanda up in a fierce hug that was returned in kind.

The brushed denim skirt and jacket Amanda had worn for the flight from Darwin to Sydney felt decidedly odd. It had been some time since she'd had a call to wear civilian clothing. Still, perhaps it was time to start getting used to it. If things went as planned, she'd have considerably more use for them.

According to her overt travel orders, she was scheduled for a twenty-hour holdover in Sydney before making the final transoceanic jump to Hawaii and to her hypothetical NAVSPECFORCE board of inquiry. But according to her covert instructions, she would be contacted by "someone" and diverted to "somewhere else".

If Naval Special Operations had been a challenging adaptation, this new level of cloak and daggerism was going to take even more getting used to. And this time, she had no one to blame but herself. When she had created the Phantom Force concept, she had not considered what actually living it would entail.

Amanda knew Sydney to be a beautiful and fascinating city to visit, but she didn't have any taste for sightseeing. Checking into her room in the Hilton, she grimly settled in to wait out the hours until contact. Without bothering to open her suitcase, she cast off her suit jacket and started to pace.

What else would be different in this new command? How would she have to change to fit into it? Phantom belonged to her, more than the *Cunningham*, more than the Sea Fighters. She had sketched out the parameters, the requirements, the methodology and doctrine for its use. But she didn't know the reality of it, the end result of the bare concept.

It was rather like being a virgin bride on her wedding night, she mused. Or possibly more like an expectant mother being wheeled into the delivery room.

Admiral MacIntyre had promised to scare up some of her old hands to work with her on this. She wondered who they might be and if she could rebuild the dynamic she'd once had with them.

And then there was the big one. Could she make it all work? She knew, if no one else did, just how fabulously lucky she had been with both the Duke, as USS *Cunningham* was known, and the Sea Fighters to have the quality and the compatibility of personnel she'd been given. Could she hope to be as fortunate a third time?

The obverse side was that, if Phantom did meet her expectations, and she could meet Phantom's, it would be the blade used for striking down Makara Harconan. And she must wield it to the death.

*Damn, damn, damn you, Makara! Why couldn't you have been satisfied with just being a multi-millionaire?*

And then there was that total insanity Chris had brought up. Where in the world had she gotten the notion that Admiral Elliot Edward MacIntyre could have any kind of interest in her beyond the professional? During her time with Naval Special Forces, they'd had occasions to talk outside of their duties, casual talk about things done and seen and about Elliot's family and her career and future in the navy. Certainly there had never been the slightest hint of … impropriety.

One of Amanda's eyebrows cocked. Not that the theoretical concept wasn't unpleasant. Elliot MacIntyre wasn't a bad man to think about at all. Only different. If Harconan had been a piercing torch flame stabbing at her points of vulnerability, then Elliot would be more like sun-warmed steel, something to lean against and draw strength from.

She mused for a moment, slammed the hatch shut on that particular space once more. She'd already made more than an adequate hash of her personal life. There was no sense in even contemplating such a titanic compounding of her problems.

Time inched past. She opened her travel book, Hayward's superb study of Nelson's battle tactics *For God and Glory*, and then slapped it shut again. The television was switched on for five minutes and then switched off. The room service menu was examined without any true interest and tossed aside. Only her relentless pacing and the darkening sky of the evening soothed her.

\*

A rented Range Rover drew into in the hotel parking lot, its driver looking up at the golden wall of glowing hotel windows. He already knew his objective. Room seven twenty-one.

He could also visualize the room's occupant, no doubt thinking furiously and wearing a path in the carpet.

He smiled to himself. He knew her well. He knew her mind, her spirit and her body, in pleasure and in pain. But that had been in the past. Now it would be different. It must be different.

He sat behind the Range Rover's wheel for a few moments more, thinking about other, possibly better times, then stepped out of the vehicle. Pulling a battered briefcase out of the Rover's back seat, he crossed the parking lot to the lobby entrance.

*

Amanda was standing on the small sundeck balcony, watching the landing lights of the airliners inbound to the airport when someone knocked softly at her door. She hesitated for a moment before going back into the room. It might just be a hotel maid coming to turn down the bed.

She crossed to the small entry hall – but, before reaching for the lock and chain or removing the wedge she'd molded from moistened bathroom tissue from under the door, she checked the security peep-lens.

Outside stood a slender dark-haired young man of average height clad in well-worn Levi's and a blue polo shirt. His features were Mediterranean handsome, but his eyes were an exceptionally piercing and memorable ice blue.

She had to brace herself against the door for a moment in sheerest shock. What was *he* doing here? Then she had to smile. When she considered it for a moment, where else would he be?

Toeing the wedge out from under the door, she fumbled the latches open. "What in the world ..." she started to say, opening the door wide.

Smiling, Commander Vincent Arkady lifted a hand and touched her lips with his fingertips, hushing her into silence. Moving swiftly, he brushed past her into the room, indicating that she close and secure the door behind them.

Amanda obeyed and looked on bemused as her former shipmate, lover and senior helicopter pilot from her days aboard the *Cunningham* crossed to the bed. Setting his flight bag on the spread, he popped the latches open and removed a small electronic device roughly the size of a pack of cigarettes. Thumbing the activation, switch he intently studied the minute display screen before speaking a deliberate test count. "Able, Baker, Charley, Delta, Echo ..."

The "bug sniffer" scanned the room's electromagnetic spectrum and approved.

"We're good," he reported, tossing the glowing bit of electronics on the bed. "All secure, Captain."

He held back the affectionate "babe" of their private times together, and made no move to draw closer or to touch her. Amanda was grateful for his wise assessment of the situation. Her own first instinct had been to burrow into the once-familiar comfort of his arms.

Once, she and this bold younger officer had run the risk of professional suicide by bonding in a potent and passionate love affair. Neither of them had regretted taking the chance at the time. It had been a needed and a good thing, to the point that a marriage had been a possibility.

It hadn't happened and the necessities of the service had drawn them apart. Now, this sudden turn of events was going to have to be examined very carefully before a new ambience could be established.

Even so, she was glad he was here; the probability of making Phantom work had just taken a sudden upward jump.

"My new CAG?" she inquired.

"And doubling in brass as your strike squadron leader."

She shook her head. "Eddie Mac promised me some of my old gang but I never expected this! The last time we talked, you were in Japan with the Joint Strike Fighter demonstration group."

Arkady shrugged. "I was. But you know how it is when something else interesting comes along. And this looks like it's going to be pretty interesting."

"To say the least." She bit her lip for a moment but couldn't restrain the words. "This might be violating security but I have to ask. Where is she?"

"She's tied up in Port Jackson right now."

Amanda lifted an eyebrow. "And do the Australians know about her?"

"They haven't got a clue. Call it a final phase security test. But first things first, skipper. Before I make the introduction, you've got the inevitable paperwork to do."

Arkady sat on the edge of the bed and removed a stack of manila envelopes from his flight bag. "These are all for you. Direct from Admiral MacIntyre at NAVSPECFORCE HQ."

Amanda sank down beside the aviator and accepted the first of the envelopes. Opening it, she found herself reading a formal request to the United States Navy Bureau of Personnel for an early retirement. Her own.

Even though this had been her own proposal, her throat tightened.

"That gets mailed to the Military Attaché at the United States Embassy here in Sydney," Arkady commented. "The post mark will reinforce the story should anyone be interested. The resignation has already been accepted."

Amanda managed to swallow. "I see."

He passed her the second envelope, then rose to his feet. With dead seriousness, he lifted his fingertips to his brow in a letter perfect salute. "I know I'm not in uniform, Admiral, but please allow me to be the first to salute your flag."

Amanda started to answer the salute out of reflex, then his words sank in. "What?"

She whipped the envelope open and stared at the documentation." Arkady, what is this?"

He laughed and sank back to the edge of the bed. "Just another example of Eddie Mac's masterful management of the military bureaucracy. You know the old navy tradition. When a senior Captain retires from the navy, it's customary that they receive a symbolic one grade bump up the ladder to flag rank. Well, you're retiring and you may consider yourself symbolically bumped."

"But my retirement isn't real ... or at least it's not supposed to be."

"Details! Details!" He indicated the second envelope. "This brings us to your new commission in the United States Naval Reserve. It won't be on public record but it will be held by the Joint Chiefs of Staff and the Navy. There's also a special rider attached to this particular reserve commission directing that, at the completion of this tour of special detached duty, your commission in the regulars will be restored with all back pay, privileges, seniority and, most especially, rank." Arkady paused. "Eddie Mac just fiddled the fine print a little so that you'll get recalled at your bumped retirement rank of rear admiral lower grade and not as a four-striper. "

Amanda had to laugh. "It's not intended to work that way."

"So? This has got to be one of the sweetest pieces of book-cooking I've ever heard of. You're putting your career on the line for the Phantom Project so the Boss is making double-be-damned sure you get it back again and then some when this thing is over. You know the Admiral. He always backs his people to the hilt."

"That he does," Amanda had to agree. "But doesn't Congress have anything to say about the creation of new flag officers?"

"You might want to have a look at the authorization signatures on that rider."

Amanda did so, then looked up again, trying to control the tremor in her voice. "The President and the Secretary of Defense?"

"How about that? It seems President Childress remembers what you've accomplished on his watch as well." Arkady reached for the next envelope in the briefcase. "And now that you're a retiree, you're going to need a job so you won't become a burden on the taxpayers."

Amanda read through the new sheaf of documentation. It was an employment contract from the Galaxy Maritime Consortium, hiring one Amanda Lee Garrett as a merchant marine shipmaster at a very pleasant salary and benefit package.

"You're also supposed to mail that contract in from here in Sydney. It's also a technicality. You're already on the payroll."

Amanda frowned. "Galaxy Maritime Consortium. I don't recognize the line."

"Sure you do," Arkady replied promptly. "Their personnel manager is an old navy buddy of your dad's. He's been trying to talk you into coming to work for their shipping firm for years. Given the current state of affairs, you've accepted. Got it?"

"Understood. Is anybody going to notice that I don't have merchant mariner's papers, much less a master's ticket?"

"Nope." Arkady handed her the last fat envelope. It contained all of the professional documentation she'd need for her new life. "You've been studying for your master's ticket on the side for some time now. If you don't remember doing it, somebody else will remember for you."

Amanda took a rather unsteady breath. She knew that she'd already made the critical commitment, but having the paperwork in her hands took it all to another level. "Phantom" was rapidly gaining reality.

She crossed her legs, gathering the hardcopy onto her lifted knee. She took another wavering breath, but her voice was steady when she spoke. "Arkady, can I borrow a pen?"

The aviator looked on silently as she signed and dated the paperwork, resealing the appropriate ones in their respective envelopes ready for mailing, the others going into her own briefcase.

"You'll need to take your luggage when we leave, Captain," he commented. "You won't be coming back here."

"Good enough," she replied, looking up. "But before we set out to save humanity again, would we have time to go out to dinner? Suddenly I'm starving."

A brief tropic rainsquall had swept over the harbor a short time before. The truck-battered tarmac of the long jetty glistened wetly in the glare of the overhead arc lights. The night air was moist and rich with the ocean scents of salt and marine organics, the smell of a port. A smell that Amanda Garrett relished.

The Range Rover bounced over the last cluster of potholes and Arkady brought it to a halt. "Here she is."

She didn't say anything in reply. All of her attention was anchored on the great living shape moored to the pier, outlined in the night by its own deck lights. Arkady smiled to himself, tasting the bittersweet. Once upon a time before, he'd lost this unique woman to a ship.

When he had learned that he was going to serve with The Lady again, he had wondered if ... Well, he had wondered.

Now, seeing the intentness in her eyes, her total focus, he understood. It hadn't been just that one time. Now, only hours after their reunion, there was yet another ship. There would always be another ship. If it was any consolation, he sensed that no other mere man would ever really possess any more of Amanda Garrett than he had. He was going to have to be content with that.

He let her get out first and alone, giving her a few silent minutes to introduce herself to her new love.

\*

Amanda let her eyes trail down the length of the great ship, pushing out her senses and instincts to take in every visible detail, every nuance of design.

She was a merchantman, an OB bulk carrier, riding low in the water under full burden. With her deckhouse set right aft and the row of seven big MacGregor hatches spaced out down the long, open sweep of her deck, the class signature was unmistakable.

This was right. This was as it should be.

Unlike the tanker or the container ship, the bulk carrier had an inherent freedom of operation. Designed for the cheap and efficient transport of "unimproved cargos" such as grain, coal and ore, the bulkers were the twenty-first century's incarnation of the old tramp steamer. Ranging the world's sea-lanes on no fixed route or schedule, they hunted for the most profitable payloads on the global commodities markets.

Amanda started to walk slowly, her heels clicking on the pavement, pacing the ship's length. She was a big vessel for her kind, although not one of the largest. Amanda judged her to be a Panamax, sized to fit through the Panama Canal. Still, it would be a tight squeeze through the Gatun Locks. She must be a good nine hundred feet in length, if Amanda was any kind of a judge, and she must displace at least sixty thousand tons, making her larger than any World War II vintage battleship or aircraft carrier.

She was also a handsome brute for one of her massive breed. Possibly out of a Japanese yard. They liked a pretty ship. She also had exceptionally fine lines for a bulk carrier, with an unusually long bow and forecastle and a sharply raked cutwater. Amanda would wager there was a streamlining bulb under that cutwater as well, a Yamato hull. Engined properly, she'd have speed.

That was also how it must be.

The ship was well maintained, her black hull and white superstructure freshly painted and free of rust staining. Given the antenna arrays on the main mast and on the auxiliary jackstaff at the break of the forecastle, she'd been well outfitted.

A pair of angular, side-by-side funnels were fared into the aft end of the large six-leveled deckhouse, clusters of sooty diesel exhaust stacks protruding from the funnel tops.

There were rents in the cloud cover over the harbor and Amanda squinted at the stars above the funnels. They shimmered slightly. Her mains were turning over, idling, ready to answer bells. She could feel the rapid pulse beat of the massive engines radiating up through the concrete of the jetty.

Multiple high RPM plants, diesel-electric propulsion. Quick to respond to Lee Helm commands and quick to crash start, should you need to get underway in a hurry. She would be multi-screw as well, for better maneuverability in tight waters.

Just as Amanda had wanted.

She could sense the critical, almost subliminal whir of ventilator fans, the sigh of air flowing through ductwork, the exciting whisper of a ship alive. A broad blue band circled each angular funnel, a spotlight playing up across it. Centered in each stack band was a white spiral galaxy symbol. Another set of spotlights illuminated the name board on the bridge wing.

GALAXY *SHENANDOAH*.

Was this the vessel she had imagined when she had first conceptualized the Phantom Force Project? Suddenly, she could imagine no other in the role.

Amanda heard a car door slam behind her and Arkady came to her side, carrying her luggage. "What do you think?"

"She's a beauty, Arkady."

He nodded in agreement. "She's a sweet platform," he agreed. "Having the deckhouse right aft takes a little getting used to, but nobody's having adaptation problems. Not even the Army guys."

"Excellent." Amanda glanced at him, her hands braced on her hips. "And how about you? You know the drill. Stark honesty, please."

He tilted his head and shrugged. "Semper Gumby, captain. I've learned a few things. You got yourself a good CAG."

"I expected nothing less," she smiled back. "Let's go find a war."

There had been only a single crewman on watch as they had drawn up. Now, two other men had emerged from the deckhouse to stand at the head of the steep aluminum gangway that extended down to the dock.

As Amanda climbed to the bulker's weather deck, she was hit with the second and third jolts of the night and she half-ran the last couple of steps.

"Welcome aboard, captain."

"Dix!" She didn't try to disguise the delight in her voice.

Lieutenant Commander Dixon Lovejoy Beltrain stood before her in a tropic white merchant mariner's uniform. Blond and ruddy, he still looked every inch the Southern conference quarterback he had been.

Beltrain had been another of her protégés, serving as her Tactical Officer aboard the *Cunningham*. She didn't ask why he was here; the first mate's shoulder boards on his uniform were self-explanatory.

"They seemed to think you'd need a good stealth man for your exec, ma'am," Beltrain said, "and I learned the trade from the best."

"Ha!" Amanda started to shake his hand but it occurred to her that, technically speaking, she was no longer a member of the United States Navy. Strict fleet protocols didn't apply to her behavior any more so she could damn well administer as many overjoyed hugs as she desired and she did so.

Another man – a tall, raw boned, hound-featured man in an engineer's coveralls – stood to as well. "You don't want to hug me, Captain, I'll get oil all over you."

Possibly so, but she still tightly gripped one of his callused tool-scarred hands in both of her own. "To hell with that, Chief. But damn it, you're retired! For real."

"Oh, I still am, sort of," Chief Carl Thomson, the *Cunningham*'s former senior engineering officer, replied. "I'm double dipping, same as you. I'm a civilian working under contract to Galaxy Maritime."

"But you had a consultant's slot with Lockheed Shipbuilding!"

He lifted his shoulders. "You know how it is, Captain. I got fed up sitting on the beach and I liked those old Glencannon stories I used to borrow off you. I figured this was as close as you could get these days to bossing the engine room on a tramp steamer."

Arkady, Beltrain, Thomson. Amanda looked from face to face, each so well remembered from her first command and from triumphs and disasters shared in Drakes' Passage and the China Coast. She tried to control the moist burning in her eyes, urgently wanting to not make a fool of herself.

She recalled her idle thought of the previous day. A warrior did have many homes. And she was returning to one of them now.

As Amanda unsnapped the latches on her suitcase, she sensed the deck beneath her feet pitch almost imperceptibly. The *Shenandoah* was taking the lift of the first open ocean swell. Pausing, she gauged the roll of the wave down the length of the mammoth bulk carrier, listening for any creaking play in the frames.

Nothing save for the steady rumble of the engines and screws. She was a tight "rigid" hull and Amanda smiled, pleased yet again.

The Captain's cabin was spacious – and, from a naval officer's point of view, positively luxurious, coming with indirect lighting, a large, built-in desk and full-length settee. There was even a bed, a genuine bed, instead of a bunk. All of the furnishings and fittings had been done in the dark blue and white company colors. Obviously, the Galaxy Maritime Consortium did not believe in parish-rigging its ships.

And there were windows. Not merely portholes but curtained windows. Beyond them, the beach lights of Sydney Harbor National Park were drifting past in the darkness.

Amanda swiftly unpacked the few things she had with her, staking her claim. Unzipping her boots, she slipped them off, wiggling her nyloned toes appreciatively on the thick fitted carpet. Taking her hairbrush with her, she crossed to the desk. Sitting down, she opened the laptop computer. A number of these "laptops" could be found spotted around the stern section of the *Shenandoah*, serving a multitude of interesting purposes.

Keying the computer to life, Amanda consulted the small cheat sheet she had been given. It would be a few days before she had the secure accesses down pat.

"Communications, this is the Captain," she said experimentally.

"Radio shack, aye," a voice promptly replied from the laptop's speakers. "Welcome aboard, ma'am."

"Thank you. I understand there is a logged message from NAVSPECFORCE headquarters for me."

"Yes, ma'am. You are instructed to personally notify Admiral MacIntyre of your arrival aboard and your assumption of Phantom command via direct link."

"Direct link?"

"Yes, ma'am. The Phantom Force commander has a direct secure access to the Commander and Chief NAVSPECFORCE at all times. Admiral MacIntyre's standing orders."

Amanda lifted an eyebrow. "Very well. Make it so." It would be after four o'clock in the morning in Hawaii but orders were orders.

From amid the cluster of exhaust stacks atop one of the *Shenandoah*'s funnels, a steel shaft like a submarine's periscope extended into the night. At its head, a finely polished mirror swiveled, aiming an invisible laser beam through a hole in the clouds to a Milstar communications satellite hovering in the southern sky.

Amanda had given her hair only half a dozen of her nightly hundred strokes when the call went through.

"MacIntyre here." The voice at the other end of the link was thickened by sleep. Direct link must mean through to MacIntyre's quarters as well. Amanda had a momentary image of the man coming up on one elbow, a sheet across his chest and his hair rumpled.

Possibly it was just her exultant mood but she found the image ... interesting. Someday, under more controlled circumstances, she might speak further with Christine on the subject of Elliot MacIntyre.

"Sorry to wake you, sir. This is Amanda Garrett. I'm aboard the *Shenandoah* and I have assumed command."

"*Shenandoah?*" MacIntyre's voice cleared instantly. "What's your status?"

"Operational, sir. I've had my first walkthrough of the ship and we are underway at this time."

"Excellent. Well, what do you think of her?" MacIntyre sounded amused but maybe slightly tense as well, as if hoping for her approval.

She drew her brush through her hair a seventh time and came to a decision. "I'm eminently satisfied, Elliot," she said, concluding that a Captain-under-God of the Merchant Marine could decently address an Admiral by his first name. "With the ship and the crew both."

The lounge bartender at the Darwin wondered if he was going to have a feminine drunk on his hands before the night was over. The blonde sitting alone in the mock Tudor shadows of the back booth hadn't quite made it yet, but she was working on it. She'd been brooding between her high voltage rum and Cokes long enough to not quite tip over the edge, but it was only a matter of time.

It was probably down to problems with some bloke, the bartender decided, shooting another glance at the grim little figure in the pink Capris. She was cute enough for it and there was a mix of anger and despair to her drinking. Maybe it would be best to drive the cork in on her now before he had a row to deal with.

The bartender's consideration was diverted by a new arrival passing through the door from the gentlemen's bar: a tall, broad-shouldered man clad in a sports shirt and Levi's, a Yank from the look of him. Likely one of the mob from the ships out in the harbor. Any number of them had been through of late. Good customers if you could cope with the peculiar accent.

The newcomer looked around the dimness of the lounge. Noticing the blonde in the back corner, he started over to her. If this fellow was looking for a Sheila, he was out of luck tonight. A couple of the local lads had made the try earlier on in the evening and the bartender had heard the snarled rejection clear across the room. Clearly the lady was not in the mood.

And yet, when the big man made his approach, she nodded, and the newcomer slipped into the booth across from her.

"A Foster's, please, ma'am," Stone Quillain said to the passing barmaid. Then he returned his attention to the small, sullen figure seated in the shadows. "I been hunting all over town for you, ma'am."

"I'm found," Christine Rendino replied.

Stone quashed a flare of annoyance. He could already sense he was dealing with what his father would call "a notional female."

"It would have been a sight easier if you'd left your damn phone on."

"Maybe I didn't want to make it easy," she murmured, taking a sip of her half-emptied drink.

"Damn it, Commander! We're on ready-to-move notification. We could get our sortie orders at any time now. You're bustin' shore leave protocols all to hell!"

A blonde eyebrow lifted. "And maybe I don't give a damn."

Stone Quillain was a gentleman of the old Southern school, the one that mandated you treat females with respect at all times. He even restrained his verbal explosion until after the waitress had delivered his drink.

"All right," he said, after taking a savage pull of the beer, "just what the hell is going on here?"

"Nothing."

"Bullshit!" he growled back. "For the past few days, you've been about as much use to the Task Force as a bucket of oily rags and you've been takin' your whole damn section down with you. Now maybe you figure you've got good reason to come down with the vapors just before we launch a combat op – but I'd like to know what it is. If my boys and me are going to get our asses blown away on account of bad Intel, we'd kind of like to have a reason."

"You are way out of line, Captain!" the Intel blazed back.

"The hell I am! All of the tactical units are sweating about the sorry feedback we're getting out of Intelligence. You're falling down on the job and I'm not risking a hit on my outfit over it! I'm takin' this to the TACBOSS!"

Christine killed the last of her drink in a fast gulp and looked up at him. "You do whatever you want! A court-martial may be the fastest way out of this shit outfit."

Stone Quillain took a deep, controlling breath. The Marine could recognize a notional female when he saw one – but, possibly to the surprise of some who knew him, he could recognize a hurt and heartsick one as well. "Commander ... ma'am. Something's wrong here. Something's real wrong. Will you please talk some about this? Maybe I can do something."

Christine studied the empty glass in her hand for a moment. Then she grimaced and shoved it away across the mock-wood Formica of the tabletop. "I'm sorry, Stone. You didn't deserve that. It's just that ... I don't belong here any more. I've never really belonged here."

He frowned. "What do you mean?"

"I mean I'm not supposed to be a damn naval officer! I've never wanted to be one. When I was in high school back in Ventura, I'd have laughed in your face if you'd even suggested it."

Stone took another sip of his beer. "Then why'd you ever join up?"

The Intel shrugged. "It was convenient. I wanted to go to college and my folks didn't have the money for it. Naval ROTC was a means to my end. I'd get my degree, go in for my hitch, play with the neat toys for four years – and then I'd be out and on my way to Silicon Valley. But it didn't work that way."

"What happened?"

"I ran into Captain Amanda Garrett," she replied. "She wasn't a Captain then, just a Lieutenant Commander, and we were both attached to the Operations Staff aboard the old Enterprise. We were assigned as cabin mates, we worked together, we became friends, and somehow I got sucked up into her slipstream."

Stone chuckled. "I know the feelin'."

Christine went on softly, her eyes fixed on the tabletop. "All of a sudden, the job and the uniform were important. I wasn't marking time any more, just waiting to get out. When my time came to re-up, I did. And when Amanda got the *Cunningham*, she asked for me. I've been working with her ever since."

"Yeah," Quillain agreed. "She's about the best skipper I've ever worked for, bar none. She is something special."

"She was." Bitterness crept into Christine's voice and she looked toward the barkeep, considering a survey on her drink. "She was the best they had and they cut her throat. The best fighting Captain in the fleet and the brass hats just *fucking* cut her throat!"

"It wouldn't be the first time a looter and shooter got crosswise with the metal officers an' the desk jockeys."

"Sure, but after all she'd done for him, Admiral Elliot Goddamn MacIntyre let it happen. Maybe he even made it happen." Quillain could hear the betrayal creeping in over the pain in Christine Rendino's voice, the disillusionment. "That all was bad enough. But she let them get away with it! She didn't fight it, Stone. When the pressure came on, she didn't stand up to them, she quit! She just damn resigned!"

"Maybe," Stone replied, his voice neutral.

Christine's unfocused gaze lifted to the Marine's face. "What do you mean?"

"I mean, I know the skipper," he replied. "She don't have quit in her. She'd fight. Even if she couldn't win, she'd be fightin' and figurin' right to the end. I know the Admiral too. I got to know him pretty good when we were goin' in on Harconan's big base on New Guinea. He didn't strike me as the kind of C.O. who'd crap out on a good subordinate."

"But he did, Stone! And she did!"

"Like I said, maybe."

Christine blinked the haze out of her eyes. "What are you talking about?'

He set his beer glass down with a decisive click. "Damn it, ma'am. You're the Intelligence officer! Work it out like a field problem! We got a formation under observation that is suddenly diverting widely from its standard operating procedures for no apparent reason. What must be assumed, given that situation?"

Christine frowned, making her mind work and reaching for the textbook answer. "That there is a factor or factors not apparent having an influence on that formation."

Stone nodded. "There you go. I'm not giving up on either the Skipper or the Admiral yet. There's something here we're not seein'."

"But what?"

It was the Marine's turn to frown thoughtfully. "I dunno. Could be we're not supposed to know. That sometimes happens when you're workin' Special Ops. Ever' once in a while, somebody will just step around a corner and disappear. No warning. No explanation. He's just gone and, if you ask about him, he's TDY or on extended leave or some other damn kind of a thing. Then, a year or two down the line, the guy will step back around that corner and pick up again as if nothing ever happened. And if you ask about where he was for all that time, he just sort of shrugs."

"Do they always come back like that?" Christine asked in a small voice.

He shook his head. "Naw. Sometimes, you hear they been killed in a 'training accident' somewhere – or sometimes they just stay gone and you never hear anything at all."

"Before she left the Task Force, Amanda told me to believe in her," Christine murmured more to herself. "And to believe in the Admiral."

"I'd listen." Quillain knocked back the last of the Fosters and stood up. "I'll see you back on the ship, ma'am."

"Fa'sure, Stone. Oh, and you don't have to see the TACBOSS. Intelligence section will get squared away, I promise."

Quillain grinned in the low light. "Hell, I don't have time to talk to that fella anyway."

Ten hours later, Christine Rendino popped her eyes open and the dawn light stabbing through the partially open drapes exploded in the back of her brain. She squinted at her surroundings, the touristy pastel room with the handful of discarded clothing scattered around it, and then at the radio clock on the end table. Then she huddled back under the thin sheet and swore at herself for being several different species of idiot.

She had checked into the Darwin the previous night after her drinking bout in the Lounge. She'd taken a twenty-four hour shore leave and there had been no sense in returning to the *Carlson*. She had a long and painful hangover to survive first. She also had some long and painful re-evaluation to do. Mostly concerning herself.

"No matter what happens. No matter what you hear. Believe in us and that everything is going to work out." Those had almost been Amanda's last words to her. Had they been a message that she, Christine, had missed?

"I'm not giving up on either the Skipper or the Admiral yet." Stone Quillain's flat statement shamed her, for she had done just that.

Where did that damn Marine get off, trusting in Amanda when she, Christine Rendino, didn't? The best friend and nearest thing to a sister she had ever been granted and, in her anger, idolization and disillusionment, Christine had had been quite willing to abandon that bond and go into a sulk like spoiled brat.

And the same with the Admiral MacIntyre. Eddie Mac inevitably backed his people to the hilt and beyond, even at the sacrifice of his own wellbeing. Hadn't he insisted in personally leading the assault to drag Amanda out of Harconan's base at Crab's Claw, even after he'd surmised Amanda's affair with Harconan? And wasn't the thought of the Admiral acting like a sulky pimpled juvenile maneuvered out of a Saturday night date just a little bit ridiculous?

Stone was right. Something else had to be going on.

Beyond that, just what in the hell did Amanda Lee Garrett or Elliot Edward MacIntyre have to do with Lieutenant Commander Christine Rendino and her duties and responsibilities? Maybe she had signed on for her first tour to buy her college degree and maybe Amanda had inspired her into reupping for her second. But what was her reason for her sticking around for a third?

How about because she had become good at a job she was proud to be doing?

Ignoring the throb in her temples, Christine reached down beside the bed and found her shoulder bag. Taking out her cell phone, she reactivated it.

As the phone's little screen illuminated, Christine winced to find half a dozen voicemails waiting for her on the Sea Fighter exchange. Marvelous.

God, but Amanda would have been furious with her over this pathetic performance.

Maybe she should start being a little furious with herself too. Damn it, she was a fricken' naval officer and the best Intel in the fleet. It was time to get back on the job. It was also time to find out just what Amanda was really up to. If someone thought mere JSOC security could keep her locked out they were sadly mistaken.

She threw off the sheet and in a few moments she was under a cold needle shower, blasting the lingering fuzz from her mind.

She was just toweling herself dry when her cellular chirped "Anchors Aweigh", the alarm she'd set for official Sea Fighter traffic.

Still drying her hair, she stepped out to where she'd left the phone and keyed the call accept. "Commander Rendino here," she said crisply.

"My standing orders were that all officers were to keep their phones on at all times when shore side, Chris." Sounding mildly annoyed, a familiar purring alto issued from the speaker. "I've been trying to reach you since last night."

Her damp towel slithered to the floor. Christine Rendino didn't think she could be going into the DT's. "Boss Ma'am? Captain ... Amanda?"

"Yes, Chris," the voice chuckled. "It's me. Now settle down and tell me where you are." The call had the slightly hollow sound to it that hinted at a long-range satphone link.

"I've got a room at the Darwin Hotel," the Intel replied.

"Are you alone and is your phone on secure encryption?"

The Intel hastily checked the settings. "Yes to both."

"Good. Now listen to me. You'll have to move fast. You're being detached from the Sea Fighters and are being placed back under my command."

"Your command?" Christine wondered.

"Don't ask questions now. We'll have plenty of time to go through it all later. A tactical field detachment from NAVSPECFORCE Intelligence will be arriving in Darwin within the next twenty-four hours. You will be exchanging places with the detachment's commander. He'll be taking your slot with the Sea Fighters, you'll be taking the detachment up to our embassy in Jakarta. Further orders will be awaiting you there. "

"Understood."

"Good. I think I've got some interesting work for us, Chris. As our old friend Arkady would say, *mucho divertimento*. Oh, and we'll be working with him again as well. Along with some of our other people from the old Duke."

"Amanda, I am just so glad to hear from you."

"I missed you too, Chris," the voice chuckled. "I'm sorry about any false impressions that might have been generated. There has been a reason for it all. You'll understand presently."

Christine sighed, no longer hungover but suddenly very content, as her universe snapped back into its proper configuration. "Not a problem, Boss Ma'am."

The other sleeping occupants of the sixth floor of the Darwin Hotel were jarred awake by a gleeful scream of "YES!"

Jubilantly, Christine scrambled back into her clothes. Humming under her breath, she sat down in front of the dressing table to do a quick hair and face do, planning a lavish breakfast. With the Admiral and Amanda back in their proper places, the world was beautiful again.

The Admiral and Amanda.

Suddenly, Christine's hummed melody trailed off as last dialog she'd had with Amanda back aboard the *Carlson* came crashing back to her.

The little blonde glared at the image in the mirror. "Christine Maude Rendino, you have a big frickin' mouth!"

The Seawolf Super Huey settled onto the ridgeline in a flurry of dust and sand. Scowling like a thunderhead, Captain Stone Quillain peered out of the open side hatch of the helicopter at the absolute desolation surrounding the grounded aircraft. Unbuckling his seat harness, he leaned over the pilot's shoulder. "Okay, dammit, what's supposed to be out here?" he yelled over the fading howl of the turbines.

Commander Richard "Cobra" Jackson, the C.O. of Light Attack Helicopter Squadron Three turned his helmeted head and looked back at the Marine. "What's here is this set of GPS co-ordinates." He held up a palm-sized "Slugger" Global Positioning Unit. "This is where you change buses. I bring you here. Somebody else picks you up. That's what I know."

"This has got to be the damnedest thing I have ever heard of!"

"Stone, don't ask me! I haul you all, that's all." The Aviator racked the Slugger onto its charging clip on the control panel and reached down between the pilot's seats. Coming up with a full canteen, he passed it back to Quillain. "Just in case they keep you waiting a while."

Quillain made a sour face. "Well, thank you kindly, sir."

"You're most welcome," the helo jockey replied. "See you later – I hope!"

"Ha! Ha! Ha! Why don't you go wax the steps at the Old Folks Home, Cobra? They could use a good laugh too."

Quillain caught up his sea bag and dropped from the open side door to the stony ground, hunkering low to keep below the helicopter's rotor arc. As he got clear, he heard the Super Huey powering up for lift off. He flinched away from the stinging sand whipped up by the rotor wash. When he looked up again, the Seawolf was airborne and paying off toward the northeast.

The sound of the helicopter rotors dissipated, leaving only the whine of the wind. From his position atop the low ridgeline, Quillain could see the glitter of the ocean several miles to the west. Inland, beyond an expanse of brush dotted outback, a mountain range thrust skyward, all bare, jagged, rust-colored rock. Overhead was empty sky, the color of faded denim and clumped with cumulous clouds. The full heat of the desert day hadn't settled in yet, but it was coming.

Beyond that, there was nothing.

Absolutely nothing.

Quillain tore off his utility cap and slapped his thigh with it, simmering.

This insanity had started aboard the *Carlson* the previous evening when he had been called in by his new TACBOSS. According to Captain Carberry, the Red Cross had contacted the Task Force. One of Stone's family had been taken ill, and he was being granted emergency compassionate leave, commencing immediately. Stone was to turn command of the Sea Dragons over to his Company exec and make all preparations to fly out to the States the following morning.

Naturally enough, Quillain made an immediate sat phone call back to his parent's farm outside of Valdosta, Georgia. He found that his mother, who had been pleased but somewhat puzzled to hear from him, was making fruitcakes for the Christmas bazaar at the First Baptist Church. His father was out in the equipment shed tinkering with his new John Deere and his kid sister was playing basketball down at Clyattville. Every other member of his family, up to and including his peculiar cousin Ray John up at the state prison, was in robust health and good spirits.

When he returned to the TACBOSS to request a clarification, he was told in no uncertain terms to shut up and make ready to move out. Until further notice, one of his family members was deathly ill and his presence was required. The Navy would inform him when that individual was well again.

His hand-over of the Sea Dragons had not been the crisis it might have been. Part of the "Garrett Doctrine" was that no one indispensable within the Sea Fighters. Every unit leader was mandated to have his own replacement ready for a seamless handoff of command.

All that was required was a sleepless night to check and sign-off the paperwork and hand over the reins.

Quillain had presented himself, grumbling, on the *Carlson*'s flight deck the next morning for the flight out to Darwin.

Only Seawolf One had not gone to Darwin.

Fifty yards down slope, a cautiously curious kangaroo peered from behind a knot of sun-blasted scrub.

"Will you kindly tell me just what in the hell is going on around here?" Quillain roared at the marsupial.

The 'roo fled in terror.

The Marine aimed a furious kick at a baseball-sized rock, the steel capped toe of his boondocker sending it bouncing for the length of a tennis court.

Half an hour later, Stone sat on his upended seabag, studying the canteen in his hand and telling himself that he really wasn't thirsty yet.

Then he heard the noise approaching, something like the familiar vibrant growl of a rigid-rotor helicopter but with an odd, trilling undertone. Stone got to his feet and squinted at the horizon as it grew rapidly in intensity.

Suddenly, to south, something bobbed over the ridgeline. Banking in sharply toward Stone, it came in so low that it trailed a slipstream-whipped wake of dust. Instinctively, the Marine ducked and yelled as the aircraft blazed past overhead. Straightening, he stared after the bizarre flying machine as it popped up in a steep zoom climb and reversed toward him once more.

Stone was no aviator, but he did know the weapons systems of the world backwards and forwards. This thing simply wasn't in the books.

All he could say was that it was a helicopter ... of some nature. It had a family resemblance to the Bell-Textron AH-1 Super Cobra series used by the Marine Corps, but there were differences, major critical differences.

There was no rotor mast, and the streamlined blade hub sat low atop the twin-turbine power pack, the mark of an advanced rigid rotor transmission system such as could be found on an Army AH-64

Apache. The familiar Cobra landing skids were missing, as well as the chin-mounted gun and sensor turret. The tri-barreled 20mm cannon peered from a fixed centerline mount below a sleeker extended nose faring.

Set at the mid-point of the fuselage were a pair of wings – not the usual stubby aerodynamic weapons sponsons, but honest to God, swept-back wings, a set of streamlined drop tanks mounted on hard points beneath them.

But the true strangeness began at the rear of the aircraft. Instead of the conventional tail rotor, the helicopter's tail boom flared into a set of cruciform fins and a circular shroud. Encased within that shroud was a pusher-style propeller and what appeared to be a set of elevator and rudder airfoils.

The overall impression the machine gave was more of a small jet fighter with rotors than of a conventional helicopter.

It had been painted a dull, grayish black and it was only as the aircraft slowed and circled back toward him that Quillain could start to make out "PHANTOM" lettering and insignia on its sides.

Whatever it was, it belonged to the United States Navy.

The machine slowed, flared and touched down a few yards off from Stone, daintily settling on the wheeled landing gear that had extended from its belly.

Beneath the pilot's cockpit, Stone could dimly make out a zero-zero designation number, the traditional Navy "double nuts" of a squadron or air wing commander. There was also a single, small patch of color, a cartoon decal of a curvaceous blonde girl clad in scanty harem garb riding a flying carpet, "Jeannie II" scripted with a flourish beneath the image.

The rotor growl faded back to an idling purr and the man in the pilot's seat lifted a hand to open the sun visor of his flame-decorated helmet. Regarding Stone steadily, he turned the action into a flippant two-finger salute.

Another peculiarity: the pilot's controls were in the forward cockpit, not in the rear as in a standard Cobra.

As the Marine hunched in under the machine's whickering blades, the aircraft's pilot swung back the side-opening canopy. Reaching down into the cockpit, he touched a control that popped open an access panel in the fuselage and Stone stuffed his sea bag into the empty magazine compartment of the internal cannon.

Swinging up onto a hard step on the fuselage, he leaned close to the aviator. "Okay," he yelled over the rotors, "before I get in this thing, how about telling me what's goin' on?"

The aviator with CMDR ARKADY worked into the flames on his helmet's visor shield looked at him through a penetrating set of blue eyes. "Captain Garrett sends her regards. How's that suit?"

Quillain slapped the cockpit rail. Now it was all clear. "Ha! I'd say that suits just fine!"

The rear cockpit and the flight helmet waiting in the seat for him were both a tight squeeze, but Stone was willing to accept them.

Within minutes, they had lifted off from the ridgeline and were over the Timor Sea, streaking due west at a meager hundred-foot altitude and hugging the water in a radar-avoidance flight plan.

Quillain had flown aboard any number of aircraft in his life, both fixed and rotor-winged, but never in anything like this one.

For one, it was decidedly faster than any conventional helicopter he had ever seen. For another, it simply didn't feel right. When they had first lifted off there had been the deep throbbing, all-inclusive vibration of a helicopter – but gradually, as their speed had increased, the vibration had faded. Now they were flying through the sky with the effortless smoothness of a commercial airliner.

"I gotta ask, Commander," Quillain said into his lip mike finally, "just what the hell is this contraption?"

Arkady chuckled. "It's a Bell/Piasecki AH/C-1A SPEED Cobra, a compound helicopter." He twisted in the pilot's seat and extended a hand back over his shoulder. "By the way, my name's Vince Arkady."

Stone reached forward and shook the offered hand. "Stone Quillain. I've heard Captain Garrett talk about you plenty."

"The Lady's been war dancing about you for the past few days as well.

She seems to think western civilization is doomed to certain extinction if we don't bring a certain leatherneck into the package."

Stone digested the statement. He was pleased that Amanda Garrett considered him indispensable, but for what? He decided to tackle things one question at a time.

"Okay, commander. What's a compound helicopter?"

The aviator laughed again. "It's the Holy Grail Piasecki Aircraft has been chasing ever since the 1960s. Another name for the compound helicopter is a convertaplane. It's a crossbreed of helicopter and airplane that can flip back and forth between the two flight systems."

"How d'you mean, sir?"

"As a Marine, you understand the concept of vertical envelopment and you must know all about the advantages and limitations of helicopters. Right?"

"I know they're damn handy because they can take off and land vertically," Stone replied. "But they got issues with speed, survivability and range."

"Exactly, mostly because of that speed limitation," Arkady said. "You can't shove a conventional helicopter through the air faster than about two hundred miles per hour because of rotor stall."

"I've heard helo drivers talk about that rotor stall business," Quillain confessed, "but I didn't know exactly what they were talking about."

"It's pretty simple, really," Arkady replied. "A helicopter's rotors are essentially its wings, only they generate lift independently of the aircraft's airspeed by rotating around the transmission hub. Thus, a helo can hover, land and take off vertically and fly sideways and backwards.

"But the rotor blades also interact with the airflow around the helicopter. As the helicopter accelerates in forward flight, each rotor blade loses a degree of lift. As it swings aft toward the tail, the rotational velocity and the airflow of the slipstream cancel each other out. But, as the blade swings forward again, the rotor velocity and the slipstream enhance each other, generating more lift. At a certain point, this imbalance becomes critical and the aircraft pitches out of controlled flight. Generally, you hit the wall at around two hundred miles per hour."

Stone glanced out at the wavetops flickering below the SPEED Cobra. "We're doing way better 'n that now, aren't we?"

"Yeah, our airspeed is currently about two hundred and sixty and we have another sixty in the can if we need it."

"All right, I'll bite, Commander. How are we doin' it? What about that rotor stall thing?"

"We are doing it because ..." The horizon tumbled as the gunship rotated through an effortless slow roll. "... at the moment, we're an airplane."

Quillain grunted and locked a death grip on his seat arms.

"Rotor stall doesn't apply to us," Arkady continued cheerfully. "Our rotors are completely unloaded."

Stone loosened his death grip. "Unloaded?"

"Yeah. They aren't producing appreciable lift. The cyclic and pitch of the rotors have been zeroed and locked, and the blades are only rotating to maintain rigidity."

The horizon pitched over a hundred and eighty degrees as the SPEED Cobra rolled upside down and remained there. "See? Our wings are loaded now, generating the lift keeping us airborne. We're controlling with our elevators, ailerons and rudder, and the drive propeller is pushing us through the air." The inverted sea and sky swayed as Arkady dipped the wings. "I say again, we're an airplane."

Hanging from his shoulder harness, Stone was certain his fingerprints were permanently stamped into the seat arms. "I'll take your word for it, sir," he said through gritted teeth.

The horizon snapped over again as they resumed a conventional flight attitude. "Where it gets fun is when we come down out of good cruise," Arkady went on enthusiastically. "I'll come back off on our throttle, or rather our 'Velocity Controller.'"

The Cobra nosed up into a shallow climb. As the airspeed fell away, Stone didn't detect any change in the sound of the power plant – but he did notice the growing return of a familiar vibration.

"As we fade back past the rotor stall limit, the fly-by-wire flight management system automatically diverts power from the drive propeller to the rotors and starts dialing in blade pitch. The rotors accept load and start to generate a growing percentage of our lift.

"As our speed continues to decrease, the control surfaces go to zero setting and the rotor cyclic unlocks." The compound helicopter began to weave sinuously through the air, this time in response to the tilting of its rotor disk. "And finally a thrust deflector swings out in the propeller duct. It diverts the blast of the airscrew laterally so it counters the main rotor torque like a tail rotor. So now, *bloop* ..." The aircraft came to a full hover and whipped around in a fast three-hundred-and-sixty degree flat spin. "We're a helicopter again."

Stone swallowed mightily and straightened in his seat. "Beggin' your pardon, Commander, but do you happen to know a lunatic helo pilot called Cobra?"

Arkady looked around his seat back. "Captain Quillain, I personally taught Cobra Richardson everything he knows about insanity."

"Kinda thought so."

"What's more," Arkady continued, his enthusiasm growing, "I can manually override the flight management system and make this beast do things you just won't believe ..."

"No! Uh, no, that's okay, sir. Maybe we just ought to be gettin' on to wherever it is we're supposed to be goin'?"

"I guess you're right." Arkady urged the SPEED Cobra forward, resuming his course and accelerating back through its flight modes. "The bottom line is an aircraft with a performance envelope about the equivalent of a World War II fighter-bomber, something like an F4U Corsair or an F6F Hellcat – only you're stealthy, you're night and all-weather capable, and you're a VTOL that can operate off a small surface platform."

Beyond being nauseated, Stone was also impressed. "Boy, the Corps has got to get some of these!"

"Probably they will," Arkady agreed. "Piasecki can make a compound conversion kit for just about any kind helicopter. The Air Commando boys in my air wing fly a SPEED conversion MH-60 Nighthawk. But for a while I suspect this tech is going to remain the personal property of the Lady and Phantom Force."

"What's Phantom Force?"

"Us." The aviator rummaged in a map pocket for a moment and then tossed a manila envelope over his shoulder into the rear cockpit. "Here's your piece of the action. You might want to start studying up. The skipper'll expect you to hit the ground running."

Frowning, Quillain broke the seal of the envelope and examined the heading on the thick hardcopy file it contained:

## Composite Operations Development Group Alpha

"Granted you sign aboard that is," Arkady added. "Phantom is all volunteer. "

Quillain didn't reply; he was already deep in the table of organization. He'd thought these compound helicopters were weird – but this was even more interesting. With the sea and sky beyond the canopy forgotten, Stone took a pen from the cargo pocket of his utilities and started jotting notes on the page margins.

Some time later, Arkady said, "Coming up on Point Item."

Stone looked up. Point Item was the naval term for a point of interception between a ship and aircraft.

On the horizon, the dark line of a ship's hull spearheaded a white streak of wake. As the range closed, Stone could make out that it was a merchantman, a big one with a stern-mounted deckhouse, steaming north at a fair turn of knots.

As the SPEED Cobra began its transition into helo mode, Stone noticed that the merchantman was starting a turn across the wind, the familiar maneuver of a vessel recovering a helicopter.

"We settin' down on that ship, Commander?"

"Something like."

As they came around the merchantman's stern, Stone made out a name and registry port.

Then he noted a slender, white-clad figure on the port bridge wing, watching them on approach, and he caught the flash of familiar ruddy hair. The Lady was indeed in residence and in command.

The landing gear thumped down and, suddenly, the centermost of the freighter's seven big cargo hatches opened, not buckling upward slowly in the conventional manner of a MacGregor hatch but slicing apart flatly. A helipad was revealed, strobe lights blinking sequentially in each corner.

The helo sidled in over the pad, flaring out and touching down with each maneuver flowing smoothly into the next. The instant the undercarriage made contact, Arkady throttled back and hit the kill switches and rotor brakes.

Quillain's stomach lurched as the deck sank away beneath them. The helipad was also a fast elevator. The Marine caught a momentary glimpse of stenciled printing along the deck lip.

THRU THESE HATCHES PASS THE BEST ... PERIOD!

Then the MacGregor was slammed shut overhead, cutting out the hot daylight and Stone Quillain murmured, "I will be forever damned!"

Arkady only chuckled, "Alice, welcome to Wonderland."

The United States Embassy
Jakarta, Indonesia
1010 Hours; Zone Time, October 19, 2008

Ambassador Randolph Goodyard looked out across the compound from the armored glass windows of his office and empathized with the Captain of the Titanic.

Watching one's "ship" sink with nothing to be done to save it is an agonizing experience.

Given the realities of the post 9-11 world, America's overseas embassies had been systematically rebuilt with enhanced security in mind, evolving into art deco fortresses designed to survive both terrorist attack and mob violence. This "Fort Apache" air had been enhanced at the Jakarta facility in recent days by the arrival of a FAST (Fleet Anti-Terror Security Team) platoon to reinforce the embassy's usual Marine security detachment.

From his vantage point, the Ambassador could see a Stinger Surface-to-Air Missile crew deployed on the roof of the parking garage. Armor-clad Marine sentries also paced the aluminum frame firing step that ran along inside of the blast wall circling the compound. They were a comforting presence, given what was happening beyond that white concrete barrier.

Smoke lay low over the city – not the usual pollution of deforestation and slash and burn agriculture that is the environmental bane of Indonesia, but a harsher, metallic contamination of blazing buildings and vehicles tainted with burning flesh, the stench of a city besieged and dying.

Through the partially open ventilation louvers of the window, the cry of sirens and the occasional crack of gunfire could be heard, sounds with an ominous, growing familiarity. The rioters were winning. The Indonesian government was slowly but steadily losing control of its own capital, as well as of the nation itself.

"It's not your fault, Randy."

The Ambassador turned to face his wife. Sharon Goodyard stood by his desk clad in a tropic weight pantsuit, a small suitcase at her feet. A slender middle-aged blonde of medium height, she still carried much of the fresh attractiveness she'd had as a freshman economics major back at St Paul University. Over the duration of their marriage. she had shared Goodyard's life and his political and economic career. Now, though, had come a time for separation.

"I wish you'd let me stay," she whispered.

Goodyard shook his head. "No, Sharon. Things are bad now and they're only going to get worse. I want you and the other dependents out of here, now, before things go completely to hell."

"And what about you?"

The Ambassador's features hardened. Always a spare man, the strain of the last few weeks had driven him into gauntness. "I'll stay until I'm forced out or until they recall me. I may have made a hash of things out here but, by God, I won't run from my responsibilities."

Tears glinted in his wife's eyes. She knew this man. She knew he was a politician and, by necessity, he had played all of the politician's games in his struggle to climb the ladder of government. But she also knew that, in all essentials, he was a good man with a heartlander's love of his nation.

She caught at his arm. "Darling, please! This isn't your fault!" she repeated with urgency.

Goodyard smiled and drew her close. "I know. This was coming long before I ever got the Ambassadorship. I suppose I can also take comfort in the fact that Harconan made fools out of far better men than me. I just wish I could have done ... something."

There was a light knock at the door of the office.

"Come in."

The young Marine officer commanding the standing Embassy detachment appeared in the doorway. It was still odd to see him bulked out in camouflaged combat utilities and an interceptor vest, instead of his usual, crisp high collared blues.

"Begging your pardon, Mr. Ambassador, but the extraction flight is inbound and on final approach. Sir, we'd like to make as fast a turnaround as possible, so if Mrs. Goodyard ..."

"We understand, lieutenant. My wife will be down presently. Thank you."

They waited until the door had closed before slipping into a fierce farewell embrace. "No sense in you coming down, darling," she murmured. "I'll say goodbye here. But please, if things start to get really bad, don't wait too long. To hell with duty."

He ran his hand down her back in a comforting caress. "I'll be fine, Sharon. They'll take be taking good care of us. You just relax and have a nice vacation in Australia."

His wife snorted derisively and kissed him once more. Then, slipping out of his arms, she took up her shoulder bag and suitcase, forcing herself to move quickly to the door.

When she was gone, Goodyard turned back to his office window, his face tight. Beyond the glass, the droning roar of the inbound evacuation flight could be heard.

The camouflaged MV-22B Osprey appeared beyond the compound wall, diving in fast in a combat approach and landing. The engine pods on the tips of its stubby wings swiveled upwards, its two huge propellers transmuting into helicopter-style lift rotors, and the big Marine tilt-rotor flared out like a hunting hawk. Swiveling about a hundred and eighty degrees, it aimed itself outward for a fast departure before settling onto the embassy helipad. Then, bouncing lightly on its undercarriage trucks, the VTOL's engines faded back to idling power, its airscrews feathering to kill the prop wash.

The Osprey's tail ramp dropped and a dozen or so men and women disembarked, clad in a mixed bag of dungarees, khaki, and camouflage. Sea bags, personal weapons and a number of hard-sided aluminum equipment cases were offloaded from the aircraft as well, making room for the outbound evacuees.

Goodyard recognized the incoming military personnel as yet another aspect of the building crisis. They were an Intelligence unit of some nature that would be using the embassy as a listening post.

Abstractly, Goodyard noted a small blonde woman in a summer weight naval officer's uniform among the newcomers. There was something oddly familiar about her, but before the Ambassador could place it, the departing embassy dependents were herded across the helipad to the aircraft.

His wife was among the little group of luggage-burdened civilians and Goodyard had attention to spare only for her. She waved from the tail ramp before disappearing into the Osprey's shadowed interior. The ramp closed and the turboprops spooled up to flight power, filling the embassy courtyard with a tornado-like flurry of dust wind and kerosene haze.

Lifting off, the VTOL swept over the compound wall, climbing away through the smoke of the burning city. Precautionary anti-infrared clusters rained flarelike from its countermeasures pods as it gained speed, converting from helicopter to fixed wing mode. Then it was gone, racing north for the comparative safety of the sea and the long, looping flight around Java to Australia.

Goodyard and his wife had been forced to say farewell on a number of occasions over the years. For the first time, the Ambassador wondered if this was for the last time.

Moving aimlessly, he drifted back to his desk. Sinking down into his chair, he cradled his head in his hands

*Harconan.*

Goodyard had once considered himself a fairly canny individual, well versed in the murky infighting politics and nobody's fool. But Makara Harconan had made him one.

When Goodyard had received the Indonesian ambassadorship, Harconan had been standing there, practically at the door of the aircraft, with his hand outstretched in greeting. Sophisticated, vastly wealthy, and well versed in the complexities of Indonesian politics and culture, the half Dutch, half Bugi merchant trader was one of the men of power within the archipelago. He had seemed a worthy asset to cultivate, to befriend, even to defend.

Then the bomb had exploded in Goodyard's face.

Makara Harconan, his confidant and comrade over the dinner table, was not the trade and industrial magnate that he had appeared to be.

Like the Makara, the mythical Indonesian sea beast the taipan had been named after, the amiability of the dolphin had concealed the soul and teeth of the shark.

Harconan had proven to be the organizer and leader of a international piracy cartel responsible for hundreds of millions of dollars in shipping losses and hundreds of deaths throughout the waters of South East Asia.

He was also the driving force behind a plan to not merely overthrow the government of Indonesia but to destroy its very national structure.

The piracy cartel had been broken by the intervention of the United States Navy. But the second phase of Harconan's master plan, the destruction of the Indonesian State, was now in full play and apparently close to success.

Being America's last ambassador to Indonesia was a distinction Goodyard didn't particularly desire. But it seemed the dubious honor was about to be forced upon him.

His brooding thoughts were disrupted by the attention tone of his intercom. He tapped the key for the speaker.

"Commander Rendino from the tactical Intelligence group is here, sir." The rough, youthful voice of the Marine sentry standing guard outside his office was a considerable change from that of his secretary.

"Very good. I'll see the Commander."

A moment later, the office doors opened and Goodyard felt the jolt of surprised recognition. He had already made the acquaintance of this particular military officer.

Only, on that occasion, she had been wearing a most revealing gold sequined mini dress.

Setting down a hard-sided aluminum computer case, the attractive little blonde came to an easy parade rest before the Ambassador's desk.

"Lieutenant Commander Christine Rendino, at your service, Mr. Ambassador."

"I believe we've already met, Commander."

Commander Rendino had been a member of the Sea Fighter Task, the Naval Special Forces unit that had broken the Harconan piracy cartel and revealed his anarchistic intents to the world.

At the time of their entry into Indonesian waters, Goodyard had considered them, loudly, to be a "needless provocation." He had named their capable but controversial commander, Amada Garrett, a "cowgirl" and a "Rambo."

"Yes, sir. At the Harconan reception on Bali."

The memory of that event and of things said there were yet another lash across Goodyard's memory. Once again, there was no one to blame but himself.

Abruptly, he stood and extended his hand across his desk. "Welcome to Jakarta, Commander Rendino. I wish I had talked a little less and listened a little more at the occasion of our last meeting."

Rendino smiled and accepted the handshake. "Mr. Ambassador, my Sea Daddy – who happens to be a woman – has taught me that making mistakes is part of the human condition. What you do about it afterwards is what counts."

In spite of the circumstances, Goodyard felt the corner of his mouth quirk up. "Captain Garrett?"

"Yes, sir."

"A remarkable woman, I understand. I wish I'd availed myself of the opportunity to get to know her better. I ... regret hearing about her recent difficulties. Please have a seat, Commander."

"The fortunes of war, sir. Thank you." The Intel sank gracefully into one of the brocade chairs facing the desk. There was something odd in the demeanor of the Intelligence officer. This woman had been a friend of the legendary Captain Garrett, yet there had been no tension generated with the mention of her recent forced retirement. Instead, there was almost an amused glint in her blue-gray eyes.

Goodyard settled back into his own chair. "I've been in communication with the Secretary of State. He advised me that I would be receiving a liaison officer from the military command being assembled to deal with the developing crises here in Indonesia. I gather that will be you, Commander."

"Yes, sir," Rendino nodded. "My unit is one of the Intelligence gathering assets for the Regional Intervention Force. Part of my job will be to keep you in the loop with the developing situation."

"You say you are one of the assets being deployed. I may assume then that there are others?"

"Yes sir," the young woman replied carefully. "You may assume that Intelligence gathering operations are underway on a number of levels within the archipelago."

"And these Intelligence gathering operations are being performed in preparation for a military intervention in the Indonesian crisis?"

Again, the slightest hint of a smile brushed across Commander Rendino's face. "The command authority of the Regional Intervention Force is preparing a series of contingency plans for a wide range of possible scenarios at this time, sir."

"And will I be advised on these 'contingency plans,' Commander?"

"Mr. Ambassador, I assure you that you will be fully informed of the Intervention Forces intents as the situation develops and the appropriate courses of action become clear."

Goodyard understood. This moment of diplomatic fencing had cleared the air and told him his place in the upcoming scheme of things without the necessity of having it spelled out. There was a third presence in his office at that moment. Some invisible personage stood at Commander Rendino's shoulder, silently stating in no uncertain terms, "Mr. Ambassador, we have a battle to fight here and it will be fought our way and not yours."

For a moment, Goodyard tried to assess the identity of this personage. MacIntyre of NAVSPECFORCE? He had been present at that much regretted reception as well. Or could it conceivably it be someone else who might have taken a step backward into convenient invisibility?

Whoever might be responsible, Goodyard could accept this unspoken ultimatum in only two ways: anger or humility. And anger, at this late date, would assuage nothing, not even his own ego.

"Very good, Commander. You may rest assured that I am ready to render any assistance I can to your operations."

The Intel, who really had a most charming smile, relaxed in her chair. "We never conceived of anything less, Mr. Ambassador. Would you care for the latest sitrep at this time?"

"Sitrep?"

"Milspeak for situation report, sir. Sorry."

"No need to apologize, Commander. I need to start learning the tongue of this new land I'm venturing into."

# Part Three

# **First Contact**

It was a frequent sight at many Third World ports, merchant ships loitering at anchor offshore, waiting. Waiting for pier or warehouse space to open up. Waiting for a dockworker's strike to end. Waiting for a cargo to be delivered or for shipping documents to clear.

Or waiting to see if their intended port of call was still going to be there come morning.

On the lee side of the Pulau Seribu, a small mixed bag of container ships, roll-on-roll-offs and break-bulks flying the flags of half a dozen nations, huddled together like a herd of wary elephants. Nervous anchor watches scanned the cloud-streaked horizons and nervous skippers watched CNN, mentally flipping nickels, pence or yen about cutting the owner's losses and getting the hell out of Dodge.

As the vivid green of the islands beyond the anchorage faded in the tropic heat haze, a newcomer joined the herd, a big, handsome bulk carrier coming in from the Sunda Strait. The Talk-Between-Ship channels crackled.

"Dottier av Dalarna, Dottier av Dalarna, this is Galaxy *Shenandoah*, do you read, over?"

"Galaxy *Shenandoah*, this is Captain Bolstad of the Dalarna. We read you, over."

"Good afternoon, Captain Bolstad. This is Captain Garrett of the *Shenandoah*. I'll be coming in to anchor about half a kilometer astern of you if you have no objections. Over."

"I have no problem with that, captain. That will be plenty of swing room. We have good holding ground here. Over."

"Thank you, Captain. What about the other local conditions? Any piracy reported?"

"No pirates, but everything else is going to shit. Over."

"What do you mean, Captain? Over."

"Look to the south. That smoke on the horizon is Jakarta burning. Will you take advice, Captain Garrett? Over."

"I'll take all I can get. Over."

"Then keep the power to your anchor capstan and your engine room ready to answer bells. We may all want to get out of here in one hell of a hurry."

*

The only boat available for port and customs duty had been an open forty-foot launch of dubious reliability. The two-hour run from quayside Jakarta to the outlying merchant anchorage at Pulau Seribu had been quite adequate to make Lieutenant Simando sun-scalded, salt-sticky and very unhappy.

With the declaration of martial law in the Indonesian capital, the navy had assumed control of the Port Master's office and Simando had been assigned to the duty of chief boarding and inspection officer. To his fellow officers, he had made much of the responsibility of the assignment. In reality, however, he knew that he had been given the job only because of his modestly good grasp of English, and because there was no one else available.

In truth, Simando loathed the duty. He was a landside staff administrator with no real grasp of the nuances of customs and inspection law. The foreign merchant officers and their frequent damn-your-eyes attitudes intimidated him, and, at the worst, he was not the best sailor in the world. Nausea was a constant companion aboard the launch and he had lost vast face heaving over the gunwale on more than one occasion.

He was also afraid. With anarchy engulfing the archipelago, being a government official ranging about in a small unreliable open boat was not a comfortable position to be in. Neither the pistol at his belt nor the two lackadaisical Indonesian Marines who accompanied him made Simando feel any better. Bluster was his sole defense.

"Bring us alongside! Smartly now!"

144

Unspeaking, the insolent Bugi helmsman swung the launch around the counter of the big bulk carrier. Simando didn't bother to look up at the name painted across the broad stern. He recognized the Panamanian flag of convenience and he could deal with the details when he got aboard.

Besides, his grasp of written English was considerably weaker than with the spoken word.

At least the crew of this ship had been civilized enough to put a gangway and a landing stage over the side. Scaling the towering black flank of the bulker's mammoth hull on a flimsy rope ladder would not have been a pleasant experience.

A reception committee awaited the inspection party at the top of the gangway, a slim dark haired Caucasian with a third mate's bars on his spotless tropic whites and a stocky Filipino in seaman's dungarees.

"Welcome aboard the Galaxy *Shenandoah*," the mate said crisply. "I'm Third Officer Carstairs and this is our Bosun, Mr. Devego. How may we help you?"

"I am Lieutenant Simando of the Indonesian navy. I am here to conduct customs and inspections of port security!"

The Caucasian frowned. "We were expecting the Jakarta harbormaster."

"The Indonesian navy now has control of these matters," Simando barked. "We have all authority here."

The Third Mate nodded respectfully, "Of course, Lieutenant. We will assist you in every way possible."

"Very good." Simando smoothed his artificially ruffled feathers, assured that he would receive the appropriate respect. "My men will conduct inspections. I will speak with your captain."

"Yes sir." The third officer looked to the Bosun's Mate. "Chief, you will assist the inspection team. Make sure they see everything they need. Lieutenant, if you will accompany me to the main salon, the captain is waiting for you with the ship's documentation."

"Very good," Simando replied in a lordly fashion. "I will see your captain now."

Simando's insecurity began to creep back as they entered the deckhouse and climbed the four levels to the salon. This vast vessel likely displaced more than the entire Indonesian navy and its captain was apparently something of a driver. The stark white passageways were all freshly painted and the cool blue linoleum that floored them was spotless – definitely a step above the usual merchant ship standards. Any captain who kept a ship of this size in this superb a condition with a small civilian crew must be a formidable personality.

Despite the air conditioning, Simando began to sweat again.

They stepped through a curtained door off the passageway and the flooring went from blue linoleum to blue carpeting. They were in the main salon, what would be the wardroom aboard a naval vessel.

"Captain, this is Lieutenant Simando of the Indonesian Navy. Lieutenant, this is Captain Garrett of the Galaxy *Shenandoah*."

Simando's jaw dropped. The captain was a woman!

Seawomen and female officers, even captains, were an increasingly common phenomenon within the world's merchant fleets – but to find one commanding this huge, glistening monster was a shock, especially since this one was decidedly attractive, at least by western standards.

Large golden lioness's eyes beneath a fringe of amber hair regarded Simando with a disconcerting directness. "Thank you, Mr. Carstairs. Carry on. I'll take it from here."

The woman had been seated behind the large dark maple mess table that dominated the center of the salon and she rose now, extending her hand across it. "Welcome aboard my ship, Lieutenant. May I have my stewardess bring you a cup of coffee or a cold drink?"

The Indonesian would have killed for an iced orange soda but he felt his mastery of the situation degrading rapidly. In a single, effortless and totally polite manner, this red-haired demoness had firmly established that he, Simando, was standing on *her* decks and that she was in charge here.

Simando ignored the extended hand and dropped his eyes. "No, I wish nothing, thank you."

The Garrett woman – Garrett, that odd name sounded familiar –

smiled and used the ignored hand to gesture toward the neat stacks of paperwork on the table.

"I believe you'll want to see these, Lieutenant. Here are my ship's papers, my crew documentation and the bills of lading for my cargo. You should find everything in order."

Still standing, Simando scowled down at the paperwork, making a show of riffling through the offered files and giving them a close scrutiny. For the sake of face, he wished he could find some flaw in the cool and rather intimidating efficiency he had been confronted with aboard this vessel. Something to challenge the capability of this western female captain. Her sense of calm-eyed surety was growing increasingly aggravating. Unfortunately, Simando didn't even know what he should be looking for.

"Your arrival in Indonesian waters was not scheduled, Captain. Why do you come here?"

She nodded toward her cargo manifests. "We're out of Central America with a load of pulpwood chips for a paper mill in Amsterdam. The brokerage our owners are dealing with could only scrape together three-quarters of a cargo out of Nicaragua, but they have a lead on another five thousand tons of pulp out of the mills on Kalimantan. We were diverted to Indonesian waters on the chance we can top off our holds. My owners have instructed me to remain at anchor here until cargo negotiations have been completed."

"We know nothing of this," Simando said stiffly. "You must realize that there are many problems here. Great difficulties. We have martial law. The military of Indonesia cannot be responsible for your business dealings."

The woman shook her head. "I never expected the Indonesian military would be so responsible. And they aren't my business dealings, Lieutenant. Those are matters for the owners to deal with. I just follow orders. However, I do hold the Indonesian military responsible for the safety of my ship and crew while we are in your national waters. Your country's internal problems are yours and not mine."

Simando's jaws clinched on the retort that the Indonesian navy was too concerned with trying to defend their own shipping to be bothered with a pack of damn *kasar* freighters. But such an admission would be an even more catastrophic loss of face. "I will inspect your cargo," he said, tossing the unintelligible documentation back onto the table, abruptly changing the subject as an escape.

For the first time, Captain Garrett looked slightly perturbed. "My cargo? Why? I've told you that all we're carrying is bulk pulpwood chips. You have the bills of lading right in front of you."

"I will see your cargo!" Simando insisted, pleased to be able to at last disconcert this woman. He would not be the only person to be inconvenienced this day.

The woman rolled her eyes toward the overhead, an expression universal among merchant masters around the world. "As you wish, Lieutenant. Come with me."

Leaving the salon, they descended to the bulker's weather decks once more. Captain Garrett moved briskly and Simando puffed a little to keep pace with the woman. He also strove mightily to ignore the fluid sway of her hips as she clattered down the ladderways ahead. Damn these western females who refused to acknowledge their place.

Going forward from the deckhouse, they reached a point adjacent to the first of the freighter's huge raised cargo hatches.

Here, a smaller personnel hatch had been set into the steel decking. Its dogging levers had not only been hammered tightly shut – a massive padlock had been added. Heavy industrial grade duct tape, marked with the international chemical hazard symbol, sealed the hatch and a criss-cross of adhesive chemical test paper had been tacked across it. Obviously, whatever lay under that hatch was more than a little furious.

"I thought you said you carried only the wood?' Simando exclaimed, goggling at the ominous portal. Looking about, he noted more sealing tape and chemical warfare test paper stripped around the seams of the cargo hatch.

"We are," Garrett replied calmly. "Raw pulpwood chips from a tropic environment. Before we can unload in Europe, the whole cargo has to be thoroughly fumigated for ecologically hazardous pests. We'd started the procedure before we were diverted here. To interrupt the process now, I'd have to stand offshore for a couple of days to purge my holds and unseal my deck hatches and I'm not going to do that until I'm assured I have a cargo to load. Methyl bromide costs money."

"M ... meth ...?" Simando couldn't recognize the word. He wasn't sure he wanted to.

Captain Garrett nodded casually and took a step back from the hatchway. "I can have my crew set up a containment tent over the personnel hatches and I can provide seawater hoses for decontamination afterwards, but you'll have to provide your own chemical suits and gas masks. I can't accept the liability of letting you use our emergency gear. I'll also need a signed release of responsibility for anyone going down into the cargo spaces. And if you get into trouble down there," she added grimly, "don't expect me to order any of my people to go in after you. They're not being paid that much."

Simando took his sodden handkerchief from his pocket and blotted at his cheeks." I have seen the manifests," he muttered.

Amanda watched from the rail as the chubby Indonesian officer descended the gangway, moving with a sweaty eagerness to be free of her ship. His two-man inspection team, who had spent the bulk of their time "inspecting" the galley while being feted by a friendly cook, followed him down to the battered launch.

Amanda took a deliberate breath. This had been, and likely would continue to be, a tricky bit, commanding a freighter that never actually carried any freight.

When the *Shenandoah* had been built, her designers had considered installing at least one functional cargo hold, but the space couldn't be spared. There was simply too much to shoehorn into the hull. *Shenandoah*'s cargos would exist only as a set of masterfully cooked books back at Galaxy Maritime and a stream of synthesized manifests from the documents section.

Should the Indonesian port authorities endeavor to verify her contracts, bills of lading and ports of call – an unlikely probability given the current chaotic state of affairs – the telephone calls and faxes would

149

somehow go astray. They would be answered by someone else, somewhere else, who would pass the Galaxy *Shenandoah* with flying colors.

Amanda wasn't exactly sure how that was supposed to work, but she suspected the fine hand of either the Christians In Action or No Such Agency and possibly both.

Amanda leaned on the cable railing, deliberately letting herself be seen from the launch as it pulled away from the stage. Did the coxswain look up and let his gaze linger on her for an unusually long moment? Possibly. And could it mean more than a man studying a rather exotic looking foreign female? Possibly again.

That was why Amanda had brought her ship into Indonesian waters under its true name and colors rather than under any one of half a dozen alternative identities. That was why she had also made herself prominent as her captain.

Even the most minor events within the maritime world of Indonesia would eventually leak back to the *Raja Samudra*. Harconan would soon learn that she had returned to the archipelago, theoretically in disgrace and as a free agent.

She lifted her gaze from the departing launch to the heat-hazy horizon. Would he smell a trap? That was entirely possible. She knew Makara to be as cunning and suspicious as a barracuda.

Still, might he also be bold enough to make a run at this particular bait? Either for revenge or possibly for other reasons? Amanda shook her head in bemusement. She simply couldn't imagine herself as a fair Helen capable of launching a thousand ships, or even one Bugi *pinisi*.

That was out of her hands. She could only stand poised to reel in the hook if the opportunity presented itself.

She turned and stepped to the deck phone mounted beside the superstructure door. Lifting the receiver from its watertight box, she double-clicked the talk button to access the all-ship system.

"This is Captain Garrett," she said deliberately, keying the voice identification circuit. "The Executive Officer, please."

"This is the Exec," Dix Beltrain's voice responded promptly.

"Our guests have departed, Dix. You may secure from hush mode and below deck isolation. Weather deck security protocols will remain in effect."

"Very good, ma'am. Will do. Be advised that, while our Indonesian friends were here, the *Remora* reported in. She's sitting on the bottom underneath us at this time. Request permission to flood the moon pool and bring her aboard."

"Proceed with the recovery at your pleasure, Dix. How did the SEALs make out?"

"Chief Gillespie reports four-oh, ma'am. No problems, no hostile contacts and the cable taps are in place and operational."

"Very good. I'll be joining you in the Combat Information Center presently."

Amanda hung up the phone and returned to the deckhouse. Descending one level below the main deck, she moved forward through a narrow side alley to the heavy transverse bulkhead that separated the stern section from the cargo spaces.

Here, a small oval watertight door was set into that bulkhead. According to the ship's blueprints, it was a service access for one of the wing ballast tanks in the upper corner of Number 7 hold, such ballast tanks being a standard aspect of a bulk hauler's design. Accordingly, the hatch was locked and prominently marked with the injunction that it must remain sealed at all times while the ship was at sea.

Before Amanda could activate the concealed voice authorization lock, the service hatch, heavy frame and all, swung outward with a sigh of hydraulics and a trio of navy seamen in dungarees and baseball caps swung through, heading to their duty stations in the stern.

"By your leave, Captain," the senior man said politely.

"Carry on, Mr ..." Her eyes flicked to the name tape on the seaman's shirt, "Shmitsky."

She could never be as close with this crew as she had with that of the *Cunningham* or with her old hovercraft squadron. There were simply too many personnel aboard, over two thousand in all. But she must make the effort. She must let this polyglot band of strangers know that their Captain did, in fact, give a damn about every one them.

There was no ballast tank beyond the hatch, just a short stretch of gray corridor with flush mounted access doors for systems bays and offices on either side, the paintwork and stainless steel fittings gleaming under bright florescent lighting. It was a corridor such as might be found on any naval vessel in the fleet.

The air was warm and stuffy. When hush mode was in effect, the ventilation and air conditioning in the hold spaces had to be throttled back to survival minimums. That state of affairs wouldn't last for long. Already Amanda could feel the vibration radiating up through the decks as the auxiliary power rooms over the keel brought their generator sets online and cooling drafts sighed from the duct grills.

She undogged and pushed through another thick fire and soundproof door into the hangar deck. Down the double-football field length of the huge workspace, the hurly-burly of aircraft maintenance and servicing was ramping back to its usual brisk levels.

The elements of the helicopter wing sat parked in long, angled rows down either side of the bay: the sleek Navy SPEED Cobras of the attack squadron, the husky Air Force MH-60 SPEED Hawks of the assault and lift group and the spidery AH-6 "Little Birds" of the Army Scout/recon section.

Painted stark white and Day-Glo orange, the two sleek Agusta Bell A-109s of the Coast Guard utility flight stood out amid the double phalanx of gray-black fuselages. One already bore the logos of a prominent Indonesian aero-tourism company, while the other was receiving the decal sets of a Red Crescent air ambulance service.

Squeezed in between the helos, or slung from the overhead beams with their wings and rotors folded, were the smaller aerodynamic shapes of the ship's drone complement. Beyond the twenty-six manned aircraft of the air group, *Shenandoah* carried an equal number of Unmanned Air Combat Vehicles configured for a variety of missions.

The faded denim blue of the Navy and Coast Guard dungarees intermingled with the camo patterns of Marine Utilities, Army BDUs, and Air Force tigerstripes.

On one of the great transverse beams above the hangar deck a placard had been mounted:

THINK PURPLE!

Purple was the color created when all of the United States service colors were blended together. It was an appropriate tint for the *Shenandoah*. She was a commissioned vessel of the United States Navy, but she sailed under the aegis of the Joint Special Operations Command. She was a multi-service platform, with elements of all the services serving on her deck. As the need for "jointness" relentlessly battered down the walls and rivalries between the military branches, this commando carrier pointed the way toward the unified defense forces of the future.

Amanda knew she must build on this concept, stitching these diverse elements into a unified whole. "Us vs. Them" must apply only to the enemy.

She continued forward, adding a personalizing word or two to her morning's greetings whenever possible. "Good morning, Sergeant. Mr. Devin, good morning. Carry on, ladies ..."

Aircraft had been pre-spotted on each of the three hangar deck elevators. A SPEED Cobra armed for air-to air with Sidewinders sat on number three aft. An MH-60 with Penguin antiship missiles under its wings had been positioned on number two amidships and an Eagle Eye tilt-rotor drone mounting reconnaissance pods was poised on number one forward. All were ready to be lifted topside through the deck hatches at a moment's notice.

Air operations would not be routinely undertaken during daylight hours, nor with another ship or aircraft above the horizon – but Arkady was still holding a strike set to launch, configured to cover any eventuality.

Amanda was pleased. Arkady had always referred to himself as just another rotorhead, but her former lover and current CAG was showing every sign of maturing into a very capable senior officer. As for how that maturity would apply to their personal lives, they'd still have to see. To date, neither of them had been given the time to worry about such matters and likely just as well.

Amidships, Amanda descended deeper within the massive hull. Barring the big nuclear fleet carriers, the *Shenandoah* was the largest combatant in the United States Navy – but she was still cramped. Her air wing, her landing force, her weapons systems, and ninety-nine per cent of her crew compliment, had to be concealed inside her hold spaces, the bow and stern having to remain configured as those of a standard merchant vessel.

Most of the time, the vast majority of her personnel couldn't indulge in shore leave or even be allowed a breath of fresh air on deck. Amanda recognized the potential for morale problems would be enormous. She must hit this problem hard right from the start. Maybe she could begin a rotating "ship leave" to the passenger cabins in the stern house whenever they were underway.

Two levels down, she dropped through a hatchway into a humid steam bath. She was on the berthing and training deck for the landing and assault force. Down here, the environmental control system could be reset separately from the rest of the vessel, allowing the euphemistically titled "Composite Development Group" to acclimatize to whatever environment they would be projected into. Stone Quillain was obviously preparing her Sea Devils for the tropic dankness of Indonesia.

From down a side passage, a roaring chorus of harsh shouts echoed from the ship's gymnasium, intermingled with a crash of heavy boot soles on steel decking.

"WHEN WAS THE LAST EASY DAY?"

"YESTERDAY, SIR!"

"WHEN'S THE FIRST HARD DAY?"

"TOMORROW, SIR!"

"GIMME FIFTY!"

"HOOYAH, SIR!"

The Sea Devils were yet another great experiment, an amorphous company-strength organization of Green Beret A Teams, Army Ranger Squads and SEAL and Marine Force Recon platoons, the very best of the best, with a permanent shipboard command-and-control cadre caged over them. The Composite Development Group was designed to be intensely flexible, fluidly altering its makeup to adapt to the ship's current mission and relying heavily upon the inherent professionalism and discipline of the Special Forces operatives involved.

Could it be made to work? Stone Quillain would let her know. If the experiment failed, it wouldn't be for lack of trying.

Amanda felt the first prickle of perspiration forming on her skin and she moved on to deeper and cooler realms. Another level down, she entered the Command-and-Control Block.

"Captain in the CIC!"

"As you were," Amanda replied to the traditional call as she pushed through the light curtain into the blue-lit dimness of the *Shenandoah*'s primary Combat Information Center.

It was a large workspace, commensurate with the size of the ship and of the decisions that would be made here. The overhead was low and cluttered with cable ducts and control clusters, while three of the four bulkheads were lined with rows of imaging and data display flatscreens.

Workstations ran down the port and starboard sides of the compartment, manned currently by the quietly efficient duty watch. The forward bulkhead was dominated by the glowing, four by two-meter topaz expanse of the Alpha tactical display.

Amanda scanned the displays, bringing herself up to date on the status of her ship and the world within a two-hundred-mile radius.

At the submersible operations console, a live video feed was running of the recovery of the *Remora*, the carrier's Advanced SEAL Delivery Vehicle. The stumpy conning tower of the minisub was just breaking the surface of the ship's moon pool while wetsuited divers plunged into the water around it, rigging the cable slings that would lift *Remora* into its servicing hangar.

At drone control, a slowly rotating overhead image of the US Embassy compound in Jakarta played across the display. They were keeping a stealthed Mariner RPV in a permanent sentry orbit above the Embassy, watching for untoward developments.

Forward, on the Alpha display, an antlike swirl of position hacks crawled around a map of Java. A real-time track of every sea and air vehicle on the move around and over the island was being maintained – not by direct radar imaging, as with an Aegis cruiser's SPY-1 arrays, but via passive sensor scans from remote sources. Air Force Global Hawk recon drones circling above the archipelago, and NSA and Naval surveillance satellites arcing high in their polar orbits, fed a continuous data stream to the carrier's battle management systems.

This cascade of information could be both exhilarating and a little overwhelming.

Amid all of the cold, cutting edge technology, there was a human link to a heroic tradition. A plastic display box had been mounted on the bulkhead just above the Alpha screen. The model of a sleek nineteenth century war steamer was silhouetted in the screen glow; the Confederate States Ship *Shenandoah*, the USS *Shenandoah*'s namesake and the greatest, most successful surface raider in the history of naval warfare.

Masquerading as a merchant vessel and sailing under the flags of half a dozen nations, the C.S.S. *Shenandoah* had been the relentless scourge of the Union merchant marine during the Civil War. The boldness, dedication and sheer audacity of her captain and crew made her admired even by the men sworn to destroy her.

In her Phantom paper, Amanda had sought to harness this same kind of audacity, applying it to a world where any nation or terrorist organization had instant access to the global infonets and to one-meter real-time imaging of the planet's entire surface.

The Commando Carrier *Shenandoah* was a sea wolf in sheep's clothing, armed as a multi-mission warship but maintaining the outward appearances of a merchant vessel. She was heir apparent not only to the Civil War's *Shenandoah* but also to the German surface raiders and the British Q-Ships of the World Wars, vessels that relied on camouflage and guile for survival as well as firepower.

Amanda had viewed the merchant raider as another form of "stealth" technology, one that could be used to secretly insert an appreciable military force and all of its supporting elements – air power, ground transport, logistics and C3I – into the heart of an enemy stronghold where it could be unleashed with devastating effect.

The First World's version of the car bomb.

The inevitable coffee and hot water urns had been set up beside the entry hatch. Amanda paused and rummaged among the selection of foil-wrapped tea bags in the small white crockery dish. Lipton wasn't Earl Grey but it would do. She built herself a cup.

The elevated Captain's chair was located in the center of the compartment, just behind the combat helm and tactical officer's station. As it had always been aboard the old Duke, it was facing aft ready to receive her. She settled in and gave the shove with one foot that swiveled it to face the Alpha display. The pivot was still a bit stiff, but it would loosen up with time.

Amanda closed her eyes, just for a second. She was a ship's captain again, not a mere senior tactical officer – and it felt very good.

Her exec came up to her side, passing her a loaded work pad. "Good morning, ma'am. Here are the division officer's reviews on yesterday's drill sequences. Looks promising."

"We're getting there, Dix, but we can always do better." She crossed her legs and tilted the chair back, taking her first sip out of the steaming mug. "Good morning, ladies and gentlemen. It's a beautiful day topside. Let's see what we can do to improve on it."

Slowly, Makara Harconan worked his way through the pile of color printer downloads. Taken from several angles and distances, they were photographs of a large black-hulled merchant ship resting at anchor. One of them displayed the name and homeport across the stern.

"The Galaxy *Shenandoah*," he mused. "What do we have on her, Lo?"

"An OB class bulk carrier rated for general cargos," his factotum replied from across the table. "According to *Jane's All the World's Merchant Vessels*, she was launched in 1992 for the Nordkapp Shipping Combine. She's out of a Finnish yard and, as originally built, she was a fifty-five thousand-ton Panamax with MAN maritime diesel propulsion and an ice-strengthened hull for Arctic work. Up until three years ago, she sailed under the Norwegian flag as the Nordkapp Sif."

"And then?"

"She suffered a major engine room fire while in port in Goa, India, and was put up for sale. Approximately two years ago, the hulk was purchased by the Galaxy Maritime Consortium and totally refurbished in the Sanyo yards in Japan. She was rebuilt with twin screws and Caterpillar/GE diesel electric propulsion, her hull was lengthened and her displacement increased to some sixty-six thousand tons. Currently, she's on her initial voyage under the colors of the Galaxy line."

"And what do we have on Galaxy Maritime?" Harconan lifted his chilled glass of Dutch lager and took a thoughtful sip. The afternoon shadows were striking across the lanai and, while the day's heat still lay over the island, the promise of evening had drawn the bite from it.

"A small American firm," Lo replied, "organized approximately ten years ago by a group of retired US naval officers. It uses a Panamanian flag of convenience, but the company headquarters is located in Boston, Massachusetts. The firm owns three other vessels, two handimax tankers on the African and Persian Gulf oil routes and a single handimax containership working a schedule of the lesser ports on the

Pacific Rim. The Galaxy *Shenandoah* is the largest and newest addition to their fleet. As for the Galaxy Maritime Consortium, it appears to be a conservative, well-run firm, apparently profitable. Its stock is not being traded on the open market at this time."

"I see." Harconan took up the last photograph in the file. It had been taken with a powerful telephoto lens and was slightly blurred, as if the camera mount had been unsteady.

Even so, Amanda Garrett's amber-red hair and intent, elegant features were unmistakable. She wore a merchant mariner's uniform and the Captain's bars on her shoulder straps were also unmistakable.

She stood on the bridge wing of her new ship, one hand resting on the rail, looking directly into the camera lens, her eyes narrowed slightly as though she might be studying the distant Bugi *prahu* that carried the cameraman.

A vessel like the Galaxy *Shenandoah* would be easy meat for his finely-honed pirate crews, especially when loitering at anchor as this one was. He merely had to reach out his hand to possess her again.

So very easy.

Or so it would seem.

"What have we learned about Captain Garrett's forced retirement, Lo?"

"A fragmentary story has reached the American media concerning Captain Garrett's capture and imprisonment by our forces, the inclination of the story being that her capture was due to certain errors in judgment on her part. Her resulting rescue placed US military personnel unnecessarily at risk and the blame for the casualties incurred has been placed at her feet. It is believed that, given her past services to her nation, she was offered an early retirement as an alternative to facing the ignominy of a court-martial for her actions. This is a procedure not unknown within the American military."

"And nothing further?" Harconan queried.

"It's reported that Captain Garrett has formally accepted all responsibility for the debacle and her professional and political enemies appear assuaged by her retirement. The story caused something of a flurry at the time of its release, but the American media and public tend to rapidly lose interest in the intricacies of military affairs."

Harconan continued his study of the photograph. It was only a single, simple picture – and yet he sensed an incongruity. The taipan was a master at targeting the weaknesses and vulnerabilities of an opponent and this was not a picture of either an embittered or a defeated person. In Amanda's posture, her expression, her aura, it simply wasn't there.

This was an individual not easily beaten. Once, by sheer luck, he had taken her prisoner for a time – but only after she had pierced his organization and shaken it to its very foundations. Even after the capture, after she had been spirited away, rendered theoretically helpless and stripped of every conceivable asset, she had still called hellfire down on him, destroying his most impregnable base.

She could have fought any court martial in the world to a standstill with what she had accomplished against him.

Could it be what she had done *with* him then? Did she fear that it might be learned that they had become lovers for a time?

Harconan found himself shaking his head and grinning wryly. Amanda Garrett had as little to be ashamed of in bed as she had on the battlefield. If challenged on the point, she wouldn't flinch from that confrontation either.

"What do you think, bapak? What is your opinion of Captain Garrett's return to our waters?"

The creases in Lo's weathered face deepened in concentration. "There is no evidence of a concrete nature that Captain Garrett, her ship, or the company that owns it and employs her is anything but as represented," he said finally. "The chain of events that returned her here is also plausible. There is no overt reason that all things could not be as it appears. However, I must state that I find it excessively ... convenient."

Harconan nodded. "I agree. It's very convenient indeed."

*Far too fast and far too convenient. Things are definitely not as they seem. You have a plan, my queen. You're trying to beguile me once more.*

Damn this woman and damn himself for a fool for ever seeking to possess her.

He could feel those large golden eyes peering at him, amused and calculating and he could recognize the extrapolations of her planning. She knew that he would sense the trap in her "convenient" presence. She would know that the sane thing for him to do would be to stay as far away from her as humanly possible. But she would also know that her flagrant presence would represent a nearly irresistible challenge, the equivalent of a slap across the face to a regency dandy.

*I am here on your doorstep, Corsair. Come dare the dance with me one more time.*

A voice of sanity countered these thoughts, telling him not to be a fool, that he had greater prizes in sight.

Perhaps so, but Amanda Garrett had learned the nature of his personal beast too well. She knew that Makara Harconan would always want it all.

The Indonesian Frigate Karel Satsuitubun
45 Miles North-Northeast of Damar Island, the Banda Sea.
2257 Hours; Zone Time, October 23, 2008

The Karel Satsuitubun was an old, tired ship. A modified copy of the British Leander class frigate, she had been originally built for the Netherlands Navy in the 1960s. The irony of her being purchased by a former Dutch colony had long since faded.

The Karel had been rebuilt and modernized several times, but there was only so much that new harness could do for an old horse. Her worn engines had lost power, her hull skin had wrinkled from wave stress, and rust was gnawing at her plates and frames. She deserved the peaceful oblivion of the scrapper's yard – yet she soldiered on, for the nation she served was in dire peril. She was all there was in a time when she might not be enough.

The Karel's failings had driven her captain on deck along with the majority of her personnel not on watch. In addition to a number of other secondary systems, the onboard air conditioning had failed, rendering the frigate's berthing spaces a humid, sleepless hell.

From his station on the starboard bridge wing, the Captain could see his crewmen sprawled on the weather decks, striving for a degree of rest and relief in the smothering airless heat of the tropic night.

Scattered among the sailors were the darker, camouflage-clad outlines of the company of KOPASSUS commandos they were carrying, a burden the Karel decidedly did not need but which must be borne. The remainder of the Army Special Forces Group with their vehicles and heavy weapons had been crowded aboard the Teluk Berau. If conditions were bad aboard the Karel, they must be agony aboard the elderly ex-East German LSM holding tenuous station off the frigate's port bow.

The Teluk had problems of her own. A steering gear failure had delayed their departure from Surabaya by half a day, and the leakage from a bad propeller shaft gland was barely being kept in check by her wheezing pumps.

Even the third and newest ship of the little task group, the Dagger class missile boat Rencong had started to report engine room casualties. The smaller vessel kept falling astern, laboring to keep pace.

Such problems were endemic within the Indonesian Fleet. Its ships, mostly aging cast-offs from the First World navies, were worn down from long years of hard service with too few rupiahs and trained man hours available for servicing and maintenance. In recent months, the situation had grown worse as government military units had raced from one hot spot within the archipelago to the next, fire brigading against open rebellion, slipping farther and farther behind the curve with each outburst.

Now the savages on Irian Jaya had gone berserk. The warriors of the Morning Star Independence Movement were attacking government outposts and facilities with a ferocity and strength no one had ever before seen. The native Papuans were now threatening to push the Indonesian authorities off the island all together.

Several key mining colonies had already been overwhelmed and Morning Star marauders were boldly striking at the outskirts of the island capital Jayapura itself. Casualties were reported as heavy and the fighting brutal. Pray to Allah that this last handful of reinforcements to the colonial garrison would be enough to stabilize the situation.

The Karel's captain looked aft and to starboard and scowled into the thick night. The Rencong should be keeping station on the frigate's quarter, a kilometer astern, but the missile boat's running lights were no longer in sight.

"Officer of the watch, why has the damned Rencong fallen back again?"

"I can't say, sir. We haven't heard anything from her," a voice replied from the interior of the bridge.

"Do you have her on the radar?"

"I'm sorry, sir." The voice was hesitantly apologetic. "The surface search radar is down. The system has overheated. The air conditioning ..."

The Captain muttered a curse under his breath and groped for a pair of night binoculars from the bridge wing storage rack. "If the cursed

Talk-Between-Ships still works, get on with her and find out what silly buggers they're playing at."

Lifting the binoculars to his eyes, the Captain swept the stern arc, searching for the errant missile boat. Nothing but darkness. Nothing ...

Wait!

Well off the starboard quarter there was a flickering flash like ruddy heat lightning. A second followed a few moments later, a sequence of them. Was that the Rencong? Was she on fire? His grip on the binoculars tightened and he peered down the bearing more intently.

Another flicker, growing brighter rapidly. No, growing closer rapidly ...

The Karel's captain was frozen in place by surprise and total, stark disbelief. When he managed to break the lock on his muscles, there was no time left for anything but a single scream of denial.

The first Exocet anti-ship missile slammed into the base of the bridge, homing on the largest radar cross-section of the ship. Detonating, the one hundred-and-sixty-five kilogram warhead ripped away the entire forward end of the frigate's superstructure, hurling it over the side and shredding the tightly packed bodies laying on the foredeck with a storm of shrapnel.

The maimed were still arcing through the air from the concussion of the first explosion when the second Exocet gutted the helicopter hangar aft.

Neither of the ship-killers had traveled a great distance; the bulk of their propellant was unexpended. Flaming chunks of solid rocket fuel joined in conflagration with kerosene from the tanks of the Karel's demolished Sea Lynx helicopter, setting her ablaze from bow to stern.

The handful of duty crewmen in the Karel's engineering spaces were trapped screaming under a roof of flame.

And from below came the water. Aged hull plates yielded under the whiplash shock of the warheads. Welds fractured; seams gaped open. In a hundred places, the sea poured in, unchecked by the watertight doors and hatches that had been left open to promote a wisp of air circulation within the hull. The damage control men who should have been closing them lay dead amid the jagged, sizzling steel topside.

Slowly, groaning in her final agony, the Karel Satsuitubun capsized, far from the chill North Atlantic waters that had given her birth.

The meager handful of crew who yet lived were likely unaware that the Teluk Barau, the transport they had been escorting, was also dying in the night.

Initially at least, the Teluk had been more fortunate. One of the pair of Exocets fired at her had "gone stupid" and missed. Only a single missile found the LSM, striking her well aft. On fire and with her engines dead, she was finished as a ship. But there were many survivors, a few officers coherent enough to give orders and a little time to don life jackets and get the life rafts over the side.

Only there were too few life jackets and too few life rafts. The LSM had been catastrophically overloaded. The Titanic disaster would be repeated in the midst of the Banda Sea.

But here, in these tepid tropic waters, hypothermia would not be a concern. Here, death would take another form. Tuned into blood and turbulence in their realm, the sharks were already converging – not in hate or anger, for those were human concepts, but merely in hunger.

Suddenly, a searchlight slashed across the oil-smeared surface of the sea. A ragged cheer arose from the men lingering on the Teluk's slanting deck or clustered around the floating rafts as illumination flares arced into the sky and burst alight, raining down their piercing metallic glare.

The chunky outline of the Rencong could be seen rapidly closing the range. Their comrades of the fleet coming to their rescue. Again, a hoarse cheer of gratitude and deliverance rang out.

The missile boat's engines throttled back and she settled out of plane, swinging broadside to the sinking ship, clearing her firing arcs. In the flare light, maybe only one or two of the survivors noted that the gaping mouths of her Exocet tubes were charred and smoking.

Then the Rencong opened fire. The big 57mm Bofors forward, the 20mm Reinmetals amidships, the twin 40mm aft. For maybe three minutes, the autocannon raged and probed and slew until the screams had all died away and the riddled hulk of the Teluk Berau had slipped beneath the waters.

The engines of the Rencong, good reliable engines suffering from no mechanical difficulties, rumbled to life and the big missile boat accelerated smoothly away from the massacre site, bound to the northwest under new orders.

The first sickle-shaped fin cut the water, trailing a thin line of luminescence. Unconcerned with the treachery of men, the lords of the Banda Sea began reaping their harvest.

Point Man Base
The United States Embassy, Jakarta, Indonesia
0702 Hours; Zone Time, October 24, 2008

Christine Rendino twisted and stretched, wondering muzzily for a moment just where she was.

The bedroom was dark, with daylight leaking around the perimeter of the heavy, drawn curtains. The furnishings were expensively French provincial and its soundproofing was excellent. The only noise existent beyond the purr of the air conditioning was the impatient warble issuing from one of the row of laptop computers deployed on the dressing table.

Then Christine's mind snapped clear and she stretched once more. Switching on the bedside lamp, she slipped from under the sheet and padded barefoot across the thick velvety carpeting to her ad hoc workstation. Tapping the monitors out of screen saver mode, she checked the address of the incoming message on the PC she had dedicated as a communications unit. Satisfied, she accepted the call and keyed the webcam for audiovisual.

"Good morning, Boss Ma'am," she caroled, sinking onto the dainty chenille-covered chair.

Amanda Garret's image filled the screen against the backdrop of her sea cabin. "Good, morning, Chris, it took you ... What in the world are you wearing?"

The Intel smugly fingered the neckline of the filmy green peignoir. "Oh, this little thing, just something the Assistant Secretary of cultural affairs left behind when she evacuated to Australia. The ambassador assigned me her quarters for the duration and I thought I might as well take advantage of all the amenities."

Amanda just shook her head.

"Just because some people don't have a clue on how to fight a war in a civilized manner," Christine continued loftily, crossing her legs and drawing the lacy silk around her.

"Whatever, Chris. I'm just glad I'm not making this call from the

Combat Information Center. I want a sitrep on whatever's going on in the Banda Sea."

Christine did a fast call up on a second laptop, verifying that nothing new had been added to the file since she had retired three hours before. "The only answer I can give is that nobody seems to know, including the Indonesians. Our taps into the Indonesian Defense Ministry and the Presidential Palace are smoking, but all we're getting is hysteria. All anybody can say for sure is that a three-ship Indonesian naval task force carrying reinforcements to New Guinea has vanished."

"It hasn't disappeared, Chris," Amanda replied grimly. "It's been destroyed, totally wiped out. We've shifted a Global Hawk over the Banda Sea area and we've spotted a debris field. There's nothing left but wreckage, an oil slick and a school of bloated sharks."

The Intel's lips pursed into a soft whistle. "I think the Morning Stars may just have won their Papuan Republic. The Indonesian garrisons on New Guinea are barely hanging on by their fingernails and that reinforcement group was their Old Guard, their last major reserve formation. They don't have anything left."

Amanda's brows dipped. "This is it, then? The nation killer?"

Christine shrugged. "Very close, Boss Ma'am. One more good shot and I suspect President Kediri's government goes into Chain-Stokes respiration."

"Damn, damn, damn! He is going to beat us!" Amanda looked off-screen for a moment, concealing emotions. After a moment, she looked back. "How did he do it, Chris? How did Harconan take out an entire blue water task force in the open sea? His Boghammer packs and raider schooners are good inshore and against merchant shipping and small craft – but not for something like this! Where did he acquire this kind of fire power?"

"I simply do not have a clue," Christine replied frankly. "It must be like his underground base at Crab's Claw peninsula. Harconan has developed assets we never expected or imagined."

"Could he have gotten hold of a sub somehow?"

"It's conceivable," the Intel replied. "Maybe he's cut a deal with an admiral in some other South East Asian nation and he's renting one with a mercenary crew. Or he's picked up a flight of fighter-bombers-with–a-fast-side-of-fries and he's staging them out of an old World War II airbase somewhere. We'll have to start looking. All I can say for sure is that, no matter what precautions we've taken with Harconan, we've always underestimated him ..."

She paused, an odd expression crossing her features.

Amanda caught the break. "What's the matter, Chris?"

"Unless, just possibly, we might be over-estimating him," the Intel replied, drawing out her words.

"What do you mean?"

"Something just occurred to me, Boss Ma'am. What if we might be getting tunnel vision? What if Makara Harconan isn't the source of all evil? "

"I say again, Chris, what do you mean?"

"I mean that Army outfit that was taken out was literally the Indonesian Old Guard," Christine replied. "They were Kommando Pasukan Khusis, the Indonesian Army Special Forces. KOPASSUS is an elite outfit with an officer and NCO cadre dedicated to Kediri and his government. Among their other missions, they're the dedicated presidential guard unit. That's why the Ministry of Defense and the ABRI high command was hesitant to release them. They are, or they were, the regime's pet coup busters."

"That could be significant," Amanda agreed, warming to Christine's suspicion. "Do you think the elimination of this specific formation could be more than the mere fortunes of war?"

"I don't know," the Intel frowned. "This might take some contemplation. In the meantime, is anything going down at the anchorage?"

"Yes. I think Harconan may be nibbling the bait. We're being sharked."

Christine sat up straighter. "Are you sure?"

"I'm positive. The question is by whom." Amanda looked down at her keyboard and the screen image shifted to a picture of a slim-hulled, outriggered prahu, the smallest of the standard Bugi sea craft.

Perhaps thirty-five feet long, the prahu had a tent-like canvas shelter in the bow and a powerful outboard motor at the stern. Two men were aboard, one manning the motor, the other half concealed in the shadow of the bow shelter. The image of the man in the bow windowed up and filled the screen. He was peering through a powerful pair of binoculars. The tube of what might have been a telephoto camera was also propped against the gunwale beside him.

"They've been dancing around us for at least the last two days," Amanda's voice continued to issue from the laptop speakers. "They're pretending to be one of the fishing boats from the Pulau Seribu, but we've drone tracked them when they've withdrawn at night and they're not returning to any of the local villages. They're laying up in an isolated cove on the island closest to our anchorage. They could conceivably be setting up a conventional pirate boarding, but they seem to be ignoring the other ships holding out here and focusing on us."

Christine nodded in slow agreement. "A bulk hauler wouldn't be a pirate's first pick. Fa'sure those are Harconan's personal emissaries. I'd love to have a word or two with these guys."

"So would I." The image of the prahu and its crew blinked off screen and Amanda reappeared. "I've been considering that option – but, if his scouts disappear on him, Harconan will likely assume that we've got him spotted and that the *Shenandoah*'s a set-up. He could spook on us."

"Yes and no, maybe and maybe not," Christine replied, looking thoughtful. "Could I get airlifted out to the ship tonight? There's something kind of crazy I'd like to try."

Amanda went wary. "Define 'crazy', Chris."

"Crazy even for me."

Drawing on the butt of his clove cigarette, Malang Sengosari lay back and watched the cloud tails swirl across the stars overhead. The strapping young Bugi seaman felt the little prahu fishing boat bobble and tug at its stone anchor as his shipmate Mahmud rolled over in the bow, grunting and mumbling to himself.

They had completed their fourth day of spying and the duty was beginning to wear. They were living on the fish they caught, eaten raw for the most part, and they drank the water from the passing rain squalls caught and rung out of their ragged shirts. What was worse, this miserable remnant had been their last cigarette.

Still, he and Mahmud were Bugi and they obeyed the commands of their ship's captain as he obeyed their clan chief and as the clan chief, in turn, obeyed the Raja Samudra. They had been ordered to watch the big merchant ship and to watch for the red-haired foreign woman aboard it. They would continue to do so.

Regretfully, he flipped the butt over the wooden gunwale of the prahu, hearing it hiss out over the lap of the wavelets against the hull. Their mothership would return soon to collect what they had learned and they would have more cigarettes. Sengosari allowed his eyes to close.

*Thump!*

They snapped open again. Something had struck the hull of the boat. Lifting his head from the wadded blanket he'd been using for a pillow, the Bugi swiftly looked about.

They still lay forty yards off the mangroves, beyond the reach of mosquitoes. The waters of the inlet were glassy smooth, and to westward, beyond the mouth of the inlet, the anchor lights of the moored merchant ships twinkled.

It must have been nothing. Sengosari let his head sink back to his pillow.

*Thump!*

A harder blow.

The corsair came up onto his knees. Ripples were spreading out from around the prahu. Under the water there was a faint, moving luminescence. Sengosari groped for the pistol under the wadded blanket.

From up in the bow, he heard Mahmud scream.

Startled, Sengosari looked up. Powerful arms suddenly burst out of the water around the prahu's low set stern, clawing at him, gripping him, dragging him over the side. Sengosari tried to scream as well, but the dark waters closed over him, gagging his cry as the black demons drew him down into their wet hell.

The captain of the Karel Satsuitubun thought he had been miraculously lucky to survive the sinking of his ship. Now he wasn't so certain.

Blown over the side in the first moment of the attack that had destroyed both his vessel and the LST they had been escorting, he had witnessed and escaped the systematic massacre of the survivors by the rogue missile boat.

For black, endless hours, he had clung to a piece of floating wreckage, listening to the screams of the other survivors as the sharks had closed in. When they had come for him, he had beseeched Allah and beaten them off with his fists, his flesh tearing on their thorny skin.

The captain had been on the verge of yielding to his death when the rising sun had revealed the graceful silhouette of a Bugi *pinisi* bearing down upon him.

He had survived the blood-sodden night, only to find himself a prisoner. Roughly bound and blindfolded, he had been carried aboard the schooner to somewhere. There, he had been loaded aboard a small amphibian aircraft and carried to somewhere else, to this small windowless cinderblock room that smelled of copra and the sea.

Here, his bonds and his blindfold had been removed. His wounds had been treated and he had been given food and drink. But two silent, heavily armed Chinese guarded the door and his final fate seemed very much in question.

Then came his interrogator, the tall, handsome near-European with the pencil line moustache and the crisp safari suit. Outlined in the glare of a hissing gasoline lantern, he sat across the room's rickety table from the captain, asking questions. The Indonesian naval officer answered them. He had no reason not to.

"Why?" the stranger asked finally.

The captain shook his head. "I do not know. I swear by the sacred names of Allah, I do not know. Our own ship, our own men, murdered us. There was no warning. No reason. If you know the explanation, I beg you to tell me why my crew and all of the others were so betrayed."

The big man was silent for what seemed a long time. "I honestly don't know either," he said finally.

He rose and started for the door. Then he hesitated and looked back for a moment. "You will not be harmed, Captain. You will be my prisoner for a time but you will be well treated and you will see your home and family again. You have my word."

For the first time since the sinking, the Captain of the Karel Satsuitubun dared to believe this might be true.

Makara Harconan walked slowly back to the lanai of the plantation house, his security team hanging back in the shadows, vigilant but unobtrusive. Harconan made no note of them, nor of the piercing stars overhead, nor of the susurrus of the trade wind in the palm groves. He was lost far too deeply in thought.

Lo waited on the lanai, a spare black-suited shape standing at parade rest in the flickering light of the candle lanterns. Harconan gestured his factotum into one of the rattan chairs drawn around the table before taking one himself. "The missile boat that conducted the attack, do we have any sighting reports on it?"

Lo shook his head. "No sir. The archipelago is extensive, even for our people. It has apparently withdrawn to some island base unknown even to the Bugi."

Harconan smiled without humor and waved away the servant who had appeared at the plantation house door. "I believe this is what is called being hoist on one's own petard. This is a strange turn of events, bapak, very strange."

"I must agree, Mr. Harconan, but possibly it is also compatible with recent events in Bali."

"What's the latest from our people down there?"

"More strangeness, sir. Indeed, as per your orders, our operatives have been seeking to avoid discord there. The potential for an ethnic and religious holocaust is too great. However, someone is most definitely seeking just that. Intelligence Group Bali has identified a number of covert action cells that are apparently attempting to promote such a conflict."

"Who are they, Lo?" Harconan demanded. "Who do they belong to?"

"Unknown at this time, sir. The operation appears to be well-organized and its personnel skilled in covert activity. As yet, our Intelligence sections have been unable to penetrate their organization. Beyond knowing they're there, and that they are inspiring confrontation between Muslim and Hindu, we know little about them. Clearly, however, there is a third agenda in play."

Harconan interlocked his fingers and leaned into his joined fists, tapping his chin lightly. "Suppositions then, Lo. Who might they be?'

"I have no concrete hypothesis. However, their level of expertise and the recent events in the Banda Sea suggest some cabal within the Indonesian military or government, although obviously one not supporting President Kediri."

"Have these cells cropped up anywhere else?"

The Chinese nodded. "There are hints that they may be in place on some of the Christian islands of the archipelago such as Timor and the Ambion group, although they do not yet appear to be active. This hints at a possible theory about this third faction's motivation."

"Which is?"

"We must assume that some individual or group of individuals is attempting to co-opt your concept of revolutionary change within the archipelago. But for reasons of their own, they're seeking to take events one step farther. They are not merely endeavoring to foment the collapse of the standing Indonesian governmental structure, but they are seeking to promote a large-scale conflict among the peoples of Indonesia, pitting race against race and religion against religion."

"But for what reason, Lo?"

"No doubt they pursue some goal they perceive as beneficial to their interests. Possibly they believe that an Indonesia occupied by only a single religious or cultural group would be easier to control than an Indonesia occupied by many. I believe the current popular geopolitical term for this is 'ethnic cleansing'."

It made sense. Lan Lo did not speak unless his words made sense.

"Damn them!" Harconan's fist exploded onto the tabletop, cracking the wood. "Whoever they are, damn them!"

"Sometimes," Lo said quietly, "when one plows a field for planting, the intruding weeds grow faster than the intended crops."

"All secure! Take her up!"

Hoist motors howled and the brick-shaped hull of the *Remora* lifted out of the moon pool, water cascading off her camouflaged casing. The cradle arms swung down and engulfed the Advanced SEAL Delivery Vehicle, locking it into hard dock. Grillwork decking sections swung down from the sides of the big sea lock, fitting around the secured minisub.

"Recovery completed, Captain," the CPO bossing the hangar crew yelled up to the gangway that ran overhead. "All secure."

"Very good, Chief. Carry on," Amanda called back. At her side, Christine Rendino almost danced in impatience. Earlier that evening, a utility flight helicopter had lifted her out from Point Man Base to the *Shenandoah*. The Intel had insisted that she conduct this particular field interrogation personally.

The dogging wheel atop the minisub's stumpy conning tower spun open. A wetsuited man, with the solidly muscular, almost chunky build of a Navy SEAL, swung the hatch open and jackknifed out onto the deck. Looking up to the gangway, he lifted a fist with the thumb extended. "We got 'em, Captain."

Christine couldn't wait. "Did you get them clean?"

"Clean and sweet, ma'am. We put 'em in a sleeper hold the second we got 'em underwater. They never knew what hit 'em."

"Are they alive?"

The SEAL team leader looked slightly offended. "You wanted 'em alive. You got 'em alive. We got 'em into the sub and breathing again inside of three minutes. Doc's put 'em on your soup as per the ops plan."

Even as he spoke, a team of pharmacists mates were working around the *Remora*'s hatch, maneuvering an intravenous bag and the limp body attached to it up onto the deck where a basket stretcher awaited it.

"Yes, yes, yes!" Christine yipped with glee and slapped the gangway rail. "I love it when a plan comes together."

Amanda gave her friend a dubious glance. "I'm still not exactly sure just what this plan all constitutes."

"I suppose you could call it an experimental interrogation technique. If we can make it work right, nobody's going to know these guys have ever had their brains drained. Not even them."

*

Idly, Malang Sengosari wondered if he was dead. Not that it mattered greatly, for he found death quite tolerable: a relaxed float in a warm, pulsing darkness to a backdrop of distant celestial music. And, as the Prophet had promised his warriors, the seventy virgins awaited him in this paradise.

So far, there had only been the one – but she was a most pleasant virgin, beautiful, naked and pliant, with fingertips like warm living silk. It boded well for his future as a dead man.

Or perhaps he wasn't dead. For pleasurable though she was, his comely companion was not quite what he had expected as a celestial virgin. He hadn't visualized them as being pale blue with silvery hair.

Possibly she was a sea jinni. Didn't he recall something about being drawn down into the water? And this place he was in seemed to waver as if with the sweep of the waves. He must be a captive of the sea jinni as it was told in the sagas of the Bugi storytellers. For a lusty fellow such as himself, such captivity didn't promise to be too onerous.

That was it. His comely companion must be a jinni. That would explain not only the odd color but the odd inflection and accent. Who could expect one of the jinn to speak Bahasa Indonesia perfectly? It would be amusing to teach her; she seemed most eager to learn.

Indulgently, he murmured answers to her childlike questions ...

*

Christine Rendino, clad in a beach jacket, bright blue body makeup and a thin hazing of silver glitter pushed through the outer door of the interrogation space's light and sound lock.

"How did it go?" she asked.

The two civilian interrogation specialists manning the biomedical console didn't at all look like CIA agents. The man far more resembled a skinny, balding insurance salesman, while the woman had the look of a motherly, graying RN.

"Very good, Commander," the male half of the team replied. "Even under stimulation, we were able to maintain the psychopompic dream state. He remained disengaged but reactive throughout the interrogation sequence."

He activated the printer unit of the lie detector and let it rasp out a long strip of hardcopy. Christine tore it loose and ran an expert's eyes down the jagged response lines, matching Sangosari's biological responses to the carefully phrased sequence of questions she had asked.

"He wasn't stressing," she said finally. "There are no fear-anger peaks and he sure didn't seem to be fighting me in there. I'm seeing an over-all truth reaction. I'd say he was giving me the straight stuff."

"I'd agree," the interrogator nodded.

"Then let's call it a good run." Christine folded the print-out and set it on the console. "What's the current status on both subjects?"

"When you gave us the prompt word for the first subject, we edged him back down into true sleep," the female specialist replied. "Subject two is holding in the sleep state and we can surface him whenever you'd like."

Christine glanced at the military clock on the bulkhead. "Okay, we're still good on time. Hit number one with the 'scop, take him deep and package him for transport. Then bring the second subject up to interrogation level. I want to try for some cross references."

"It shouldn't be a problem, Commander." Keeping her eye on the EKG and heart monitors of the subjects, the female tech typed a series of commands into her control display, making minute alterations in the complex drug cocktail feeding in through the intravenous needles.

At the rear of the workspace, Amanda Garrett, an unspeaking and somewhat bewildered observer until now, got out of a metal-frame folding chair. "What have you got?" she demanded.

"We have indeed been graced by the personal emissaries of the Raja Samudra," the Intel replied, parking a lightly clad hip against the edge of the console. "The name of our friend in there is Malang Sengosari – or Sengosara – and his sidekick is Mahmud, no last name. They're Bugi pirates from the same village on Mataram.

"Their raider was diverted to Pulau Sebus within twenty-four hours of our anchoring here. They were ordered to keep the *Shenandoah* under observation and specifically 'to watch for a European woman with red hair'. They were to get photographs of her. They even received special instruction on how to operate a telephoto camera."

Amanda nodded. "We found the camera, along with a couple of pairs of high-powered binoculars, in their boat. What we didn't find was any kind of radio or communications equipment."

"That makes total sense. Harconan is clearly interested, but he's also suspicious. He's figuring that any radio transmissions in the vicinity of the *Shenandoah* might be monitored. According to Malang, their mothership circles back every two or three days to collect their Intelligence and issue new orders. They're due through tomorrow."

"We can designate the ship and establish RPV surveillance when they do," Amanda replied, crossing her arms. "So far so good, but how much closer will this get us to Harconan?"

Christine shrugged. "It'll be a start. We've pierced the first cell of Harconan's network and we've found the second. We'll just have to see how it goes."

"We have a time factor, Chris!"

"I know we do," the Intel replied calmly. "But, as you have often said, Boss Ma'am, 'Softly softly, catchee monkee.' Working up the chain of a tight cell-type security system can only be done one step at a time. There aren't any short cuts."

Amanda caught her breath. "I understand that, Chris, but damn it, we still don't have anything!"

"Sure we do. We know that Harconan is interested and that he's sniffing the bait. We're also inside his network and, with a little luck, he won't know about it."

"I'm still not sure just how that's supposed to come about. Just as I'm still not sure about what you think you're doing." Amanda gestured at the Intel's decidedly distinctive appearance.

"Oh, this," Christine, glanced down of herself. "It's a little exercise in reality disassociation."

"Reality disassociation?"

"Well, say you're walking down the street one day and suddenly you're grabbed by a number of large, decidedly unsympathetic men who drag you off to a grimy back room somewhere and ask you a bunch of very pointed questions. You would assume you were being interrogated, correct?"

"Correct," Amanda nodded.

"But what if you're walking down that street and you suddenly just sort of drift off to sleep. When you wake up again, you find yourself in bed with ... oh, say, Errol Flynn, Johnny Depp and Sean Connery, who entertain you with casual conversation between bouts of passionate dalliance."

"I'd say that I was either drunk, stoned or had totally lost my marbles," Amanda replied flatly.

"Quite so, Grasshopper. You would have undergone a surrealistic experience that could not be coordinated with conventional reality. These dudes are currently undergoing the same kind of dis-coordinated experience. We grabbed them off their boat this evening. Tomorrow morning, they're going to wake up back aboard that boat with no solid, overt indication that anything has gone on. They'll only have some hazy, disjointed memory that, in the interim, something very strange happened."

Amanda cocked an eyebrow. "Like receiving a deep body massage from an azure masseuse."

"You've got it. Here's how the package works. At the moment, our subjects are being fed a continuous stream of short-term tranquilizers and hypnotics that suppress the will and rational thought. They're also floating on a couple of blood temperature waterbeds in a darkened, soundproofed space."

"Sensory depravation?" Amanda asked with some concern.

Christine shook her head. "Oh no, just sensory control. We're being careful to feed them a scootch of local, easy-listening music to keep them from slipping into depravation shock. We're also being careful to hold them in a pleasure state that doesn't trigger any of the animalistic, instinctive fear-flight reflexes. Trust me on this, Boss Ma'am, these guys are enjoying themselves.

"This environment we've established is also irrational. It doesn't connect or relate to any kind of normal, rational experience, so it doesn't invite normal, rational reactions like a resistance to questioning."

Amanda decided she'd pretend to understand. "I thought you always said that interrogations under truth serum couldn't be trusted."

"We're dealing in generalities here, not rocket fuel formulas," Christine replied. "The advantage to this interrogation technique is that we don't have to disappear these guys. We can reinsert them back into their environment without their being able to recognize what's happened to them."

"Are you sure about that?"

"Pretty sure." Christine gestured toward the biocontrol console and the interrogation team working it. "Right now, we're hitting the first subject with a massive dose of scopolamine, the same stuff they sometimes give to women during childbirth so they can't clearly remember the pain of the experience. It can't erase the memory totally but it will further blur an already blurry event to the point they shouldn't have any kind of coherent recall.

"Most Indonesians – be they Muslim, Hindu or whatever – still have a very strong connection to a native mythology that's just crawling with gods and spirits and demons and all sorts of other unearthly entities. If they don't consider this just one exceptionally wild dream, they may very well pass it off as some kind of supernatural event or visitation. With a little luck, the last thing they'll think of is that they were guests of the bad guys."

Long ago, Amanda had learned the wisdom of leaving esoteric specialties to the specialists. "I'll take your word for it, Chris. Stand on."

Amanda started for the passageway door, then paused and looked back. "What you've been doing here, this whole procedure, sounds a great deal like some of those alien abduction stories I've read about. You know, the ones involving the little gray space men from the flying saucers. I don't suppose ..."

Christine Rendino looked acutely uncomfortable.

Amanda held up her hands. "I know, I know. You could tell me but then you'd have to kill me."

"Uh, not exactly, Boss Ma'am." She indicated the CIA team. "I could tell you but then they'd have to kill us both."

The insurance salesman and the motherly RN looked up and smiled pleasantly.

*

Malang Sengosari jerked awake and sat up. The high riding sun reflected off the waves of the inlet and stabbed deep in his eyes.

They had slept far too late. His head was exploding and his mouth was foul as a week dead fish. Mahmud was sitting up in the bow, looking haggard and somewhat green under his seaman's tan.

Something had happened. Something had come out of the sea – and there was the girl ... the blue-skinned girl who had smiled and whispered ...

Allah and all his Prophets, what had happened?

Malang took up a gourd of rainwater and drank off half its contents. Mahmud moved aft and took the gourd from his hands, draining off the other half. For a full minute they crouched in the bottom of the prahu, looking at each other. Finally, Mahmud said. "I'll get the anchor up. It's late."

Malang nodded. "I'll get the engine running. Let's have another look at the anchorage before the *pinisi* comes."

Eventually, when he was a gray-bearded clan captain yarning with his respectful crew, Malang would tell the tale of a night spent in the arms of a beautiful sea jinni. But not today and not for many long years to come.

The Temple of Pura Luhur Batukaru
Northern Tabanan Regency, Bali
1200 Hours; Zone Time, October 25, 2008

Located deep in the cool, mist-streaked rainforests at the foot of the sacred mountain Gunung Batukaru, Pura Luhur Batukaru is the ancestral temple of the Tabanan princes.

As it is dedicated to the deities of mountains and lakes, every other temple in Western Bali, in turn, has a shrine dedicated to it. Legend says Pura Luhur Batukaru was founded in the eleventh century by the Hindu sage Kuturan, but ancient stone monoliths have been unearthed that indicate the temple site has been a place of mysticism and veneration since prehistoric ages.

Flanking the main shrine complex, steps guarded by demon statues lead down to a small square pool with a tiny island in its center, a symbolic microcosm of the Hindu Mount Miru. Placed on the tiny island are two platforms, one dedicated to Gunung Batukaru, the other to the deities of the Three Lakes – Tamblingan, Buyan, and Bratan. Nearby, sacred hot springs bubble and steam on the moss-sheathed riverbanks.

It is a place of great spirituality to the followers of the Science of the Holy Waters, and a place of great power.

That was what had brought the four Muslim teenagers to the temple.

Likely they meant no true harm. They were city youths, the sons of Javanese government officials and businessmen from the regency capital at Tabanan. Heir families were well-to-do for the island and, as is frequently the case with privileged adolescents all around the world, the boys were cursed with an excess of energy, time and hubris.

As youth elsewhere might have fallen into the trap of drugs or alcohol, they had fallen into the pit of excessive religion.

Islam in Indonesia was, for the most part, a far different thing than the militant Wahhabism of Saudi Arabia or Afghanistan. The beer-sipping or bikini-wearing Indonesian Muslim generally had a far mellower and more tolerant world view.

Therefore, to this small band of restless, callow young people, Islamic radicalism was a road to individuality. It was a way to feel "special," to stand out from the crowd, and it provided a moral high ground from which attacks on parental authority could be launched. The responding parental outrage only made the forbidden fruit sweeter.

These youths were far from the suicide bombing stage, however. Today's long planned expedition to the temple of Pura Luhur Batakaru was more an act of public defiance, a personal pledge of dedication to Allah and a slap in the face of public propriety.

They did not intend to die.

The aged Imam in their school of religion who had encouraged them in this act did not mean for them to die either. He was an embittered, intolerant man who did not know the Balinese Hindus and who did not want to know them. He did not understand that he was blindly flicking ignited matches at a spilled pool of gasoline.

In due course, he would die for his ignorance and bigotry as well.

The four Muslim youths left their battered Toyota in the small parking area below the temple. Carrying their prayer rugs, they swaggered up the lichen-covered steps to the broad terrace in front of the gates, pretending not to notice the cold stares aimed at them from the scattering of other temple visitors, but secretly relishing them.

With exaggerated meticulousness, they oriented their rugs toward Mecca and knelt. Loudly, they began their noon prayers, brandishing their sacrilege of one of Agama Tirta's holiest shrines under the nose of propriety. They were young, they were immortal, they were the favorites of God. Besides, the Hindus were a race of pacifists.

Were they not?

Deep in their devotions, they didn't notice the crowd gathering on the steps of the terrace, a silent, staring throng that filtered down the paths to cluster around the interlopers. The Muslims had no way of knowing that they were not the first to intrude at Pura Luhar Batakaru.

During the previous night, one of the subsidiary shrines in the forest around the temple had been viciously vandalized. The shrine's *pemangu* had been beaten and left for dead, and these villagers had spent their morning washing animal filth off the representation of the gods and picking up shattered bits of sacred tablets and artwork.

The four Muslim youths had played no part in the vandalism – more calculating minds than theirs had planned the desecration – but none of the outraged present particularly cared. The crowd pressed closer. There was no sound save for the words of prayer and then they trailed off into silence.

The Muslims looked up to find themselves walled in by a solid mass of stone-featured Balinese: grim, silent, impassive, totally unlike the islanders they had known. Now they sensed the building wave of wordless implacable rage. Again, the Muslim teenagers prayed – this time wordlessly, not out of bravado but in terror.

A child, an eight-year-old girl struck the first blow, hurling a stick at the quailing youths. Then the crowd swept forward.

One of the Muslims momentarily broke free of the mob. With his shirt and most of his skin clawed from his torso, he fled to the temple parking lot, a hundred silent people on his heels. His hand closed on the door handle of the Toyota just as a multitude of hands closed on him.

And through it all, there were no outcries of fury, no curses, no yelling. The only sounds were his screams – and the other noises produced when a human being is torn literally limb from limb.

"What have you got?" Christine Rendino demanded, trotting into the Op Center from her interrupted dinner in the Embassy dining room.

"Some kind of trouble on Bali, Commander," the watch officer replied, looking up from his workstation. "We're getting heavy traffic on the Ministry of Defense taps from police command in Denpasar, indicating an outbreak of large-scale violence in Tabanan regency."

"Define 'large-scale' and 'violence'," Christine said, donning her command headset and clipping the palm-sized receiver box to her belt.

"Denpasar isn't too sure itself, ma'am. The trouble appears to be centered around the regency capital but it's spreading. And it's not conventional civil disobedience or rioting, but systematic bloodshed in the streets, apparently directed against the Muslim minority."

"Oh my god!" Christine breathed, a chill rippling through her. "When did it start? How widespread is it? Are the local authorities getting it under control?"

The watch officer shook his head. "No answers to any of the above, ma'am. Communications are apparently breaking down in the Tabanan area."

"This is not good. This is extremely not good. Do we have any drone coverage over Tabanan?"

"No, ma'am. Not at the moment."

"Then contact Global Hawk command at Curtin Air Force Base and get me some! Then get me a sat link to the *Shenandoah*. I need to talk with Captain Garrett immediately."

"Right away, Commander." The duty officer felt his own unease grow. Their easygoing, slightly oddball, detachment C.O. was suddenly as serious as a new coffin. "What do you think is going on over there, ma'am?"

"Judgment day. Now get me on line with the Lady!"

"Put it on the Alpha Display," Amanda commanded.

The low murmur of operations-speak scaled back within the darkened interior of the Combat Information Center. The watch officers and duty SOs cut quick looks over their shoulders at the imaging on the big forward bulkhead screen.

They saw a high, side-angled view of a small city, the regency capital of Tabanan, surrounded by green un-ripened rice fields. Multiple smoke columns were rising from its eastern end. The view rotated slowly as the Global Hawk drone circled the objective at sixty thousand feet.

Amanda leaned forward in the Captain's chair, eyes narrowed, jaw set. "Magnify."

The drone control officer murmured into his headset, passing the word to the *Shenandoah*'s RPV control node.

Half a thousand miles away, the lens system in the drone's camera turret responded to the command, zooming in on target. Tabanan was, or had been, a neat community, ordered and growing rapidly into modernity. Now, flames could be made out dancing at the base of the smoke clouds.

"That was the mosque," the control officer said, blipping a target box around the largest fire. "That's the police station. Those other buildings along the main street – those residences near the mosque. They probably belong to the local Muslim population."

"Probably. Take us in closer."

"Aye, aye. Going to max mag."

Once more, the cameras pulled the ravaged city closer until people could be seen, the living crowds massing in the Hindu temples and the smaller number of the dead. The still forms of men, women and children lay in lines along the roads and in the town marketplace. They were not sprawled or scattered. There was a grotesque orderliness to the way they lay, the mark not of passionate violence but of deliberate execution.

"Pull back. Zero the magnification."

The scan widened and the world fell away, pulling back above the stripes of wispy cloud until the ground was a dozen miles below.

"Rotate the scan, three sixty."

The camera view panned slowly across the verdant terrain of Bali, the patchwork pattern of the rice fields, the paler patches of the scattered villages, the great craggy bulk of Mount Karangasem to the northeast and the azure of the sea to the southwest.

Smoke plumes writhed into the sky in at least four other locations.

"Is this being seconded to the Embassy?" Amanda inquired.

"Yes, Ma'am. And to NAVEX 7.2 Flag and NAVSPECFORCE Headquarters."

"Very good." Amanda tapped the transmit key on her own lip mike. "Signal Intelligence, this is the Captain."

"Signal Intelligence, this is Captain Montgomery," a crisp feminine voice replied.

"Captain, are we getting any signal intercepts out of the Bali Global Hawk? Anything that can tell us what's happening on the ground?"

"Nothing definitive, Ma'am, just continued generalized indications of large-scale anti-Muslim terrorism and a general collapse of civil authority. Tabanan regency appears to be the flashpoint of the disturbance and we have heard references to an event or incident at one of the local Hindu religious shrines."

That seemed ominously similar to the execution style death patterns they were seeing. The worst-case scenario would be for the angered *pedanda* of the Science of the Holy Waters to call for an exorcism of the Muslim "demons" living on Bali as they had done with the communists in the 1960s. If such were the case, if a call for the mass cleansing of the island in the name of the Trisakti were indeed flashing from temple to temple, then this was only a hideous beginning.

"The civil telephone net's gone down throughout the central regencies – as have the security force radio nets," the signals officer continued. "All we're getting is random traffic from a scattering of isolated tactical units. The police headquarters are apparently being targeted by the mobs."

"That's to be expected. Most of the senior police cadre on Bali are Javanese Muslim. What are you getting out of Denpasar?"

"Not much. Civil radio and television are starting to make references to civil disobedience and rioting in some northern towns and villages, but the deaths and the extent of the outbreak are being downplayed. The authorities are 'reacting' to the situation. We're also seeing repeated calls for national unity and the 'we are many but all are one' ideal. I'd say it was a classic 'whistling in the graveyard' package from a very scared administration."

"What are the authorities doing?"

"Police headquarters in Denpasar was sending out repeated demands to the regency stations for more intelligence on the situation, along with orders to suppress the outbreak at all costs. Lethal force authorized. Then, about twenty minutes ago, Denpasar dropped off the net completely. We're receiving fragmentary traffic on the civil emergency services channels, indicating a massive explosion at the police brigade command post, possibly a car bomb."

"Damn!" Amanda murmured. "This couldn't get worse."

"Yes, ma'am, it could," Montgomery said, remorselessly. "Very much so. We've started to pick up something else over here that I think you urgently need to listen to."

Amanda had not known Captain Janet Montgomery of US Army Intelligence for very long, but Amanda sensed that she was usually a very understated individual.

"I'm on my way."

*

The Signal Intelligence bay was a division of the larger Joint Intelligence Center aft and to starboard of the CIC. Its soundproofed confines were jammed with radio receivers capable of monitoring the entirety of the communications spectrum. An avalanche of words poured continuously through Sig-Int, but the workspace itself was exceptionally quiet.

The babble of voices was contained within the headphones of the hand-picked team of Bahasa-speaking Intelligence and communications specialists. The only loose noises were the purr of air conditioning and the occasional sporadic clatter of computer keys.

Captain Montgomery was a very intent young woman in army camo with dark eyes and dark hair drawn tightly back from her face. As Amanda entered her realm, Montgomery spoke without preamble. "Ma'am, we've encountered another very disturbing turn of events. It involves the situation on Bali but it's taking place on Java and Sumatra."

The Army woman reached over and punched an access key on a workstation. A voice issued from an overhead speaker. Amanda couldn't understand the words but she could recognize the anger, the hysteria, the hatred. "Who is he? Amanda asked. "And what's he saying?"

"This is Ishmael Muarasi," Montgomery replied. "A very prominent Indonesian radical mullah. If you trim away the frills, he's issuing a fatwa call for jihad against the Balinese Hindus, demanding their extermination by the faithful. This is only one of several such broadcasts."

Montgomery pushed a series of buttons on the console. With each channel switch, the voice changed, but the hate didn't.

Amanda frowned. "Given the circumstances on Bali, that almost had to come next."

Montgomery shook her head. "You don't understand, ma'am. About an hour ago, four powerful civil radio stations, two on Java and two on Sumatra, ceased conventional programming, all at essentially the same time. Then these same four stations all started to broadcast this barrage of fatwa calls, along with a steady stream of hyped atrocity stories from Bali. The key point is that all four stations are broadcasting the same exact thing. Not just the same kind of programming, but the same, exact, pre-recorded broadcasts. This is no spontaneous event. This has got to be part of a pre-planned propaganda campaign."

Amanda's stomach gave a lurch. "It's a set-up?"

The Army officer nodded. "It must be. There are no specifics of time and place being mentioned in any of the fatwa broadcasts, and no coordination between the atrocity stories and any of the real-time events actually taking place on Bali. These are generic broadcasts prepared ahead of time in the expectation that the Balinese explosion was going to take place."

"By the same people who provoked that explosion."

"Exactly, ma'am. None of the other Indonesian national stations has even mentioned the Balinese outbreak yet. Jakarta is apparently trying to suppress the story. The stations broadcasting the fatwa traffic must be under the control of someone else with the intent of escalating the crisis in the archipelago and collapsing the Kediri government."

Amanda Garrett's face was immobile, but the universe twisted wildly around her, established projections and patterns exploding and reforming. There was no time for disbelief, denial or recrimination, or even to acknowledge that faint, indefinite nagging in the back of her mind that something about this scenario had been wrong from the very beginning.

Like a fencer instinctively countering an unexpected thrust by an opponent, there was only time for reaction. "Miss Montgomery, have you apprised NAVSPECFORCE Intelligence of this situation?"

"Yes, ma'am," the army woman replied promptly. "We're downloading to them continuously."

"Very well. Develop a strike template for a signal suppression mission against the radio stations conducting these propaganda broadcasts. The air group commander will be on with you about this presently. Keep me informed of any further developments."

Amanda left the Intelligence Center, heading for the stern section. As she strode down the passageway leading aft, she hammered orders into her command headset.

"Captain to Bridge!"

"Bridge, 'by."

"Mister Beltrain, lay to your sea and anchor details. Make all preparations to get underway."

"Aye aye, ma'am!"

"Captain to CAG."

"This is Arkady in Air One."

"Mission to fly, Commander. Fangs out! This is not an exercise. Get on with Montgomery in Signal Intelligence. She'll give you the dope. Get a signal suppression strike package developed and ready to launch! Night ops! Multiple targets! Covert profile! Optimize your weapons load out for minimum collateral damage! All speed, Arkady! All speed!"

"You've got it, Captain," Arkady replied crisply.

"Captain to Communications!"

"Communications, aye."

"Set up a conference call in my quarters. I need to speak with Commander Rendino at Point Man Base immediately. Then get through to Admiral MacIntyre's Chief of Staff and tell him that it's imperative I speak with the Admiral as soon as possible."

\*

Both of the laptops on her cabin desk were active and networked into the ship's systems. The NAVSPECFORCE test pattern filled the screen of one, while a harried Christine Rendino peered from the other. In the background of the webcam image, Amanda could see the Intelligence team working their ad hoc operations room. Sidearms were being worn and body armor, helmets and carbines were stacked ready at hand on the desktops.

"Chris, what's the situation in Jakarta?" Amanda inquired.

"Quiet so far, but nobody knows how long it will last," the Intel replied. "The city is on full lockdown. A twilight curfew has been declared and there's a heavy police and army presence in the streets. The word's spreading about the Bali massacres and the locals are getting pissed. They're not exactly sure who they're going to be pissed at yet, but they are considering their options. "

"What's the embassy status?"

"We're on full lockdown with FAST Marines on the walls," the Intel replied. "Other than the Australians, we're the last foreign embassy left in the capital and the Aussie ambassador and his skeleton staff are forted up with us. We're acting as the collection point for the remaining international community in Jakarta and our Marines have been escorting evacuee convoys out to the airport all afternoon. We're also seeing another disturbing trend developing. Members of the Balinese Hindu community here in Jakarta are starting to show up, asking for protection from mob violence. They don't trust the Muslim authorities."

"What's Ambassador Goodyard doing?"

"He's granting it, along with generally kicking ass and taking names. He's made it clear that he intends to stick 'till the last cat in the alley's dead. Foggy Bottom can be proud."

Amanda half smiled, "It sounds like he's matured a bit since our last run in with him."

"He's learning the ropes, Boss Ma'am," Christine agreed.

"What are you getting from the Kediri government?"

"Heavy commo traffic between Jakarta, Canberra and Washington. Currently, President Kediri is in conference with our Secretary of State and the Australian Foreign Minister."

"What are they talking about, Chris?"

The Intel looked uncomfortable. "Uh, those communications are on secure State Department links, Boss Ma'am. I'm not authorized to access ..."

"Chris, what are they saying?"

She sighed. "Kediri's asking – no, cancel that, he's begging – for help. He says that he doesn't have the forces available to deal with the Bali uprising and that his government is on the verge of collapse."

"And?"

"And the Regional Intervention Force is being committed to evacuate the foreign nationals in the archipelago and to keep the Straits of Malacca open. And that's all."

"So they're cutting him loose," Amanda murmured. "They're judging Indonesia as a lost cause."

Christine shrugged. "What can I say, Boss Ma'am? Harconan's got us beat."

The heel of Amanda's hand slammed down on the desktop. "Not Harconan, Chris. That's just the problem. It's not Harconan!"

"What?"

"It's not just Harconan. There's somebody else!"

She was interrupted by a voice issuing from the speakers of the second laptop. "Captain, this is communications. Admiral MacIntyre is on channel from NAVSPECFORCE."

"Bring him into this call, please."

The screen of the second laptop filled with the image of Elliot MacIntyre in the Naval Special Forces briefing room. He appeared to be alone and the tension in him was obvious. "Amanda, we've got major developments in the situation down there."

"Commander Rendino and I are already working the problem," Amanda replied. "We understand that the Indonesian government is in imminent danger of collapse over the Bali situation. We also know President Kediri has asked for assistance and that the Intervention force is being sortied."

MacIntyre gave a wry half-smile. "I should have guessed." He glanced toward what must have been a second conference screen. "Good evening, Miss Rendino. I'm pleased you're on top of things. It will simplify matters and God knows we need all the simplification we can get."

"The primary overt mission of the Intervention Force," Amanda demanded, "has it been altered?"

"Not appreciably. Evacuate all foreign nationals trapped in country and maintain freedom of the seas. That's still the program."

"And no mission expansion?"

"Nothing is on the boards so far. Our Joint Naval Expeditionary Group and the composite ANZAC squadron are to move north from Darwin to Bali. They'll establish a beach head on the southern peninsula, secure Negura Rai International Airport and the harbor facilities at Benoa for use as a central evacuee collection point and operations base."

Amanda frowned. "Seizing a port facility isn't exactly SOP for an evacuation mission, Elliot."

"Let's say that somebody's thinking long-term. If we're seeing the Balkanization of the Indonesian Archipelago, we might be needing a permanent base in the region."

"What about our people? The Sea Fighters."

"They've been detached from the main body of the Expeditionary Group and are acting as an independent rapid response unit. They're proceeding to Labuan Bajo on Flores to clear the tourist resorts there. After that, they're off for the southern coast of Sumatra."

Amanda nodded. "And what are Phantom's orders, sir?"

"You are being redeployed to an operating location off the northern coast of Bali. You will continue to operate as a regional Intelligence gathering platform and you will stand by to assist the Bali Occupation Force as required."

"So we're abandoning both the nation-saving mission and the Kediri government."

MacIntyre grimaced and studied his desk. He was not a man who suffered defeat easily. "No one is saying so in so many words, but the back-room consensus is that we're trying to revive a dead horse. Kediri and Indonesia are finished, Amanda. Our friend Harconan's won."

"That's just the problem, Elliot. We're not fighting Harconan. At least not now and not in Bali!"

MacIntyre looked up sharply. "What?"

"The scenario has altered. There's a third faction intervening in the archipelago. Someone with a different agenda than that of Harconan."

Speaking rapidly and concisely, Amanda related what she had learned from the *Shenandoah*'s Signal Intelligence section concerning the fatwa broadcasts.

"It sounds to me like just another example of Harconan's chaos theory revolution in action," MacIntyre said when she finally paused.

Amanda shook her head. "No, this is a decisively different game plan. Yes, Makara Harconan wanted to inflame the various rebellious factions within Indonesia. And yes, his intentions were to turn them

196

against the government to bring about a division of the archipelago into a number of independent republics and kingdoms. But he did not want to set the peoples of Indonesia irreversibly at each other's throats!" Amanda shoved her chair back and started to pace. "Fomenting a jihad between the Indonesian Muslims and Hindus would do exactly that. The scenario that is being set up on Bali is not part of his plan. There's somebody else involved. Somebody far more ruthless."

"We've seen no evidence of any such third faction operating in the archipelago, Amanda," MacIntyre replied.

"Because their operations were masked by Harconan's! I suspect we've got a group of opportunists out there co-opting Harconan's plan for their own ends – and, given their willingness to foment an open war between the two largest religious factions in the island, those ends can't be good ones."

MacIntyre impatiently shook his head. "I'm still not seeing any essential deviation from the set strategy we've seen Harconan use before."

On the first screen, Christine Rendino was suddenly looking thoughtful. "It's not a matter of deviation sir, but of proportion. The Bali event is escalating the chaos factor doctrine to a new and unnecessary level. Harconan was already achieving all of his goals. There's no need to foment this kind of potential holocaust. Captain Garrett's right. The Bali event would actually be counter-productive to Harconan's stated desires and goals."

MacIntyre scowled. "And how do we know just what those desires and goals truly are, Commander?"

"I know!" Amanda snapped back. "I've heard his intentions and his goals from his own lips and I know that this action is simply not right for the man."

MacIntyre stared out of his screen at her. "And are you sure you know the man that well?"

She met his glare head on. Suddenly, and for one flaring moment, it wasn't about Indonesia or military strategy and tactics. "Damn it, Elliot,

I slept with the man! If anybody in the world has the right to say they know Harconan's mind, it would be me."

"That's right, Amanda." MacIntyre's voice was dead cold. "You did sleep with him."

"On several occasions." Amanda braced her hands on the edge of the desk and held MacIntyre's eyes. "And you knew that, Elliot, and you still gave me Phantom and sent me in here to kill him. Now is one hell of a time to start questioning my judgment in this matter!"

The three-way circuit was silent for what seemed a long time. Then Christine Rendino spoke. "Admiral, a while ago I was reminded of an Intelligence truism. When there is a deviation from an established norm for no apparent reason, then there must be a reason that isn't apparent." She took a breath. "Amanda's theory of a third faction could account for a number of inexplicable events we've seen recently, like the sinking of that Indonesian task force in the Banda Sea. If you were to ask me to make a professional assessment of this third faction theory, I would have to say that it could very well be valid."

"Very well." MacIntyre had yielded his position. "Let's grant the possibility. But we're still operating with just opinion – damn it, Amanda, even if it is yours and Christine's. We don't have anything solid to go on."

Amanda could only shrug. "You're absolutely right," she replied quietly. "But opinion is all we have right now. If we wait until we have something more concrete, we're going to lose. It's death or glory time. We can cover our collective asses or we can try and win this damn war. We have to decide now."

MacIntyre sat back and ran a hand through his iron-streaked hair. "So, let's assume that we have a third faction in play. What do we do about it? Amanda, the keystone of this theory is essentially your personal assessment of Harconan. Are you sure enough on this assessment to be willing operate on it?"

"If I wasn't, I wouldn't have approached you with it," she replied somberly.

MacIntyre studied her for a moment more. Then he sighed and a wry, self-derisive smile crept across his face. "All right, Amanda. I suppose I've come too far to change horses at this late date. But, even if I might buy this package, I can promise you that it won't sell in Washington. We're going to need to show proof of the existence of this third faction to the State Department and the National Command Authority. And that doesn't even begin to address the question of what we might be able to do about it, if they're even willing to try."

"I suggest we eat the apple one bite at a time," Amanda replied, sinking back into her desk chair. "Over the short term, we have to buy ourselves and the Kediri government some breathing room until the situation clarifies and we can develop the necessary evidence to prove the existence of this third faction. Do we still have our covert orders to prevent the breakup of the Indonesian government?"

MacIntyre lifted an eyebrow. "Those have not yet been altered to the best of my knowledge."

"Then that gives us our sanction to act."

"What do you propose?"

"That we take a little detour on the road to Bali."

Somewhere Within the Moluku Island Group.
2150 Hours; Zone Time, October 25, 2008

Makara Harconan glanced out of his bedroom window, the one that looked out across the inlet. The big twin-engined Canadair amphibian was just touching down on the glassy waters, its wake a white streak in the starlight.

They would have to refuel the plane before departure. He still had a few minutes.

Zipping up the single waterproof diver's carryall he would take with him, he slid the big Browning Hi-power under the waistband of his jeans, distributing the stack of fifteen round magazines among the pockets of his safari jacket. Then, taking up the bag, he strode into the main room of the plantation house.

Lo and half a dozen of his silent Nung bodyguards stood there, the Nungs clad in camouflage with assault rifles and sub-machineguns slung over their shoulders.

"The plane has arrived, sir," Lo said quietly. "We're in contact with the Sangeang raider group and they'll be standing by at the rendezvous point. As per your orders, all uncommitted clan vessels in the Java and Flores Seas and in the lesser Sundas are converging on Bali."

"What's the situation on the island itself?"

"Continuing to deteriorate. Our colonies are evacuating to Flores and Sulawesi using their own sea craft. Our armed cells have gone active and are covering the withdrawal, engaging Hindu extremist groups where necessary."

"What about the government security forces on the island?"

"Overwhelmed, sir, and crippled by sabotage. For all intents and purposes, they no longer exist."

"I never thought to hear myself saying this about the police, but that's unfortunate. Lo, make sure our captains know they're to lift out anyone who wishes to leave Bali; Muslim, Christian, Hindu, anyone who wishes to go. This is a command of the Raja Samudra."

"It shall be done, Mr. Harconan." The Chinese hesitated, subtleties of expression hinting at some massive internal struggle. "Mr. Harconan, I must protest this action on your part as ... imprudent."

Such a thing was unheard of and Harconan smiled. "Why so, bapak?"

"By moving out of concealment, by resuming active command of the clans in this manner, you are placing yourself at risk, sir. Grievously so."

"Possibly, but I suspect that both the government and the other regional powers have other concerns at the moment."

"But what of this third faction, Mr. Harconan? We have yet to determine their identities, their capabilities or their intentions toward you."

"None of the answers will be good, I suspect, but we shall see. At any rate, it's irrelevant at the moment. I can't deal with this situation hiding out here like an old orangutan in his tree. I've got to be with my captains. I've got to regain control of this situation. And that reminds me – have we discontinued all arms deliveries to everyone except the Morning Stars and our own clanspeople?'

"As per your orders, Mr. Harconan," Lan Lo replied. "But I submit to you that the situation on Bali has passed beyond any man's control, including your own."

"Very possibly, but a man must try." Harconan hesitated. "What is the latest from Intelligence Group Amanda?"

"The Galaxy *Shenandoah* has just taken its departure from the anchorage at Pulau Seribu and is apparently leaving Indonesian Waters."

"And there was no indication of ... abnormalities?"

"No sir, all collected Intelligence indicates that Captain Garrett is merely a merchant marine officer and her ship a common freighter."

Harconan grimaced and shook off a random hope. "It is a true thing, Lo. You must be careful about what you wish for – for the Gods may be cruel and grant you your wish." He hesitated. "Mind things here, Lo. I must be going."

MacIntyre tucked his shaving kit into an exterior pocket of the single B-4 bag he carried into the field. Zipping the pocket shut, he swung the battered bag down from the coverlet of his bed, setting it on the floor beside his brief and computer cases.

Taking the phone from the lamp table beside the bed, he dialed through to NAVSPECFORCE headquarters. "Duty Officer, please. This is Admiral MacIntyre. What's the status on my command aircraft? Very good. Send a staff car to my quarters and notify Hickam security that my daughter will be accompanying me to the flightline. Thank you, Commander."

He hung up the phone and took a last look around the small beige bedroom with its pale gray curtains and matching spread, checking for anything forgotten.

He liked this room. His daughter had decorated their quarters with both taste and economy, making them a calming place to live. It was a pity he'd been able to spend so little time in them. He smiled and gave a nod to the photograph of his late wife on the lamp table. Then, catching up his uniform cap, the old sea-worn one with the sun-scarred visor, he went down the hall to the living room.

His daughter Judy sat curled on the couch in slacks and a sleeveless top, her feet tucked under her. When she was intent on something she looked so very much like her mother – and, at the moment, that intentness was focused on the television.

On the screen, a column of gray ships stood outlined against a gray horizon. Caught by a low-light television camera, their running lights scintillated while a news anchor spoke off-screen.

"The Regional Intervention Force, composed of elements of the American, Australian and New Zealand navies, sailed this evening from Darwin, heading north into the growing chaos that is Indonesia. This handful of ships and the elite troops they carry may be the last hope for the thousands of foreign nationals trapped in the archipelago by the discontinuation of civil air service. Likewise, they may be the last hope for the embattled government of President Ahsan Kediri.

"Diplomatic exchanges continue around the clock between Washington, Canberra and Jakarta, seeking a way to stabilize the deteriorating situation, but CNN's international affairs experts are not hopeful. The bloody religious outburst in Bali appears to be the deathblow for the world's fourth largest nation ..."

Judy killed the image with a stab of the remote button. "You're going back there, aren't you?"

"Yes," he replied, sinking down on the couch beside his youngest child. "We've got something of a situation developing down there and I want to have a look at the operations. Did you call Captain Grayson's wife?"

"Yes, Dad," the teenager replied patiently. "She'll be checking with me every day and keeping an eye on the house and I'll check with her before I go out anywhere. Are you going to be in the fighting like last time?"

MacIntyre gave a brusque shake of his head. "Last time there were extraordinary circumstances. This is just routine."

Judy smiled, dismissing the sophistry. "Dad, you've shown me the war room down at headquarters. If you wanted to 'look at operations' you could do it just fine from there."

"There are certain things you have to see up close and personal, kitten. Now, the bills are covered for this month and you've got a thousand dollars and the emergency Visa in my desk safe. Remember that credit card is only for emergencies."

His voice trailed off as his daughter nestled against him, resting her head on his shoulder. "Dad, what's really wrong? You never used to feel guilty."

Damnation, Judy had inherited so much more than her mother's beauty; the deep perception was there as well. "I suppose it's because they keep getting younger as I get older," he replied, slipping his arm around her. "And it keeps getting harder for me to order them out. I can't simply sit in front of an Alpha display, drinking coffee and watching the casualty counts climb. I know that's how it's supposed to be done these days – and there are excellent reasons for it – but I'm just not strong enough any more. I'm sorry, Judy, it's not fair to you, but if there's going to be a fight, and it looks like there is, I've got to be down there with my people."

"Is it because I'm putting my application in for Colorado Springs?" she asked.

He sighed, "To be absolutely honest, yes and no and possibly and not really. Your brothers were both a lot easier to cope with. They're sane and want careers in the private sector."

Judy sniffed. "Brian and Steve are both puss-wusses. Somebody has to uphold the family honor."

MacIntyre laughed and hugged his daughter once more. "Seriously though, before you put in your application, there's someone I'd like for you to talk with first. Even today, career women in the services have a lot of challenges to face and this lady will be able to fill you in on the realities a lot better than I or any orientation officer could."

"Captain Garrett," Judy said, lifting her head.

"Well, yes. Amanda Garrett."

A sly smile crept across his daughter's face. "You're going to be working with her again, aren't you?"

"Ms. Garrett isn't under my command or in the navy any longer, Judy."

Her answer was a derisive feminine snort. "Yeah, right. Tell me another one, Dad."

MacIntyre scowled. "What do you mean by that?"

"Because Captain Garrett is no more out of the Navy than you are – or, if she is, she's working for the CIA or somebody as part of some big secret thing."

MacIntyre straightened and stared at his daughter. "Judy, what makes you say that?"

His daughter looked insufferably smug. "I have my reasons, Daddy."

Judy never called him daddy except when she wanted to be infuriating. "Name them, young lady! Now!"

"Oh Dad, you've told me so yourself. It sticks out all over you. For one, you'd never send me to someone for career advice if they'd actually been thrown out of the Navy in disgrace. For another, you'd never have let them throw Captain Garrett out in the first place. For a third, I saw the expression your face when those political hacks on the television were badmouthing her ..."

MacIntyre cocked an eyebrow. "What about my expression?"

"It was just like that time in Naples when that drunk said that awful thing about Mom and you decked him."

"Oh Christ!"

"And finally," Judy concluded, coming up to kneel on the couch, "you wouldn't be having this hemorrhage if you weren't worried about a security breach involving something horrendously top secret."

MacIntyre gripped his daughter firmly by the shoulders. "Judy, Amanda Garret is out of the navy and has absolutely nothing to do with NAVSPECFORCE any longer. Everything is just as it has been represented. Do you understand?"

"Of course I do, Dad. Just like you know that nothing that is talked about in this house ever gets mentioned anywhere else."

MacIntyre unwound and ruffled his daughter's hair. "Why couldn't your mother have given me another son?"

Judy chuckled, "You really like her, don't you?"

"Who, your mother?"

"Amanda Garrett. You really like her."

"Now what in the devil makes you say that?" MacIntyre demanded.

"Like the other thing, if somebody really knows you, it sticks out all over. It's like ..." Judy bit her lip, pausing to organize her thoughts. "When Mom died, something about you died too. You were still Dad and you were still the Admiral – but something else ... left. I could feel it. You just weren't all of you any more.

"But whenever I've seen you around Amanda Garrett, like when you brought her out here for dinner when the Sea Fighters were working up – or sometimes, just when you're talking about her – that part of you comes back. And that's all right. God knows, Mom would want it to be like that."

This transcended naval security. This was about lying to his daughter about himself and he'd had one hellishly tough standard to hold himself to. Anne had always told her children the truth, even when it was the worst truth conceivable.

"Judy, it's conceivable there's something to what you say." MacIntyre slouched back on the couch. "But what your damn fool of a father may feel about Amanda Garrett is not all right. Not in the slightest."

"I know all about chains of command and no fraternization and all that kind of thing, Dad," his daughter said with some impatience. "But none of that matters now."

"Why not, child?"

"Gee, Daddy. There's no harm in dating a freighter captain if you want to. After all, Amanda Garrett has absolutely no connection with the Navy or NAVSPECFORCE any more."

MacIntyre groaned and swiped his giggling daughter's hair over her eyes. "A third son. Would that have been too much ask for?"

With all topside lights extinguished, the *Shenandoah* thundered through the night, her bow slicing cleanly through the waves, working up to speeds that no common bulk carrier had any right to reach.

In main engine control, Chief Thomson paced slowly behind the power management stations, watching the engine output bars creep steadily to the top of the CRT displays.

"Engines answering all ahead full, at standard civil power," the senior watch motor mac reported. "Motor loads and shaft RPM's holding steady. Transformer temperatures holding in the gates."

"Good enough, Shimski. Stand by. Johnson, call the status on the Auxiliary Power Rooms?"

"All APRs report up and ready to integrate, Chief."

"Right. Recalibrate all systems to War Power. Integrate APR power flow."

The rank of multimode flatscreens blinked out and snapped on again, displaying an entirely new set of engine performance readouts. The main engine output bars dropped to half-speed ahead.

"Let's put her to the wall." Thomson lifted his voice. "All engines ahead full, war power!"

The trembling of the deck plates increased and the howl of the main motors climbed to an even more piercing intensity. The integrated electric drive system was now effortlessly absorbing the combined current flow from both the main generator sets and from the Auxiliary Power Rooms in the hold section. Like so much else aboard the commando carrier, the horsepower ratings and load capacities marked on her motor casings were a flagrant falsehood.

\*

Topside, on the weather decks, powerful hydraulics sighed and hissed as a sequence of remarkable transformations took place. The short jackstaff mast forward disappeared, retracting smoothly into a tunnel inset in the hull. Cargo hatches two, four and six split and slid open horizontally. The panels of number two hatch locked into the false tops of holds one and three. In turn, the panels of number four locked into three and five and number six into five and seven, a reshuffling of steel that created a flight deck.

The elevators howled up from below, filling in the last of the gaps, each lift carrying a load of aircraft and personnel. Muscles creaked and men swore under their breath as multi-ton flying machines were rolled to their launching spots by raw manpower. Moving in the fuzzy green world of their night vision visors, the plane crews of the strike squadron SPEED Cobras swarmed over their charges like ants over a grounded dragonfly. Wings were lowered, rotors unfolded, and slim, deadly shapes slid onto launching rails.

Methodically, Marine First Lieutenant Keith Pinkerton – call sign, Pink – plugged himself into his aircraft: seat harness, oxygen mask connector, microphone and helmet headset leads, power and datalink for his helmet mounted display and night vision visor.

"Pink" was not the running name Pinkerton would have chosen for himself. He would have infinitely preferred something like "Thunderbolt" or "Fireball" – but, by longstanding military tradition, one's call sign was chosen by a peer group who almost inevitably chose something as humiliating as possible.

Unless, of course, you were someone like Pink's squadron commander Vincent Arkady, who was "Vince" to the entire known universe. A respectful running name meant something in this profession.

Someone slapped Pinkerton on the top of his helmet, and he looked up to find Arkady peering over the cockpit rail.

"You set to do this thing, Pink?"

"I hope so," Pinkerton replied with all honesty. "I mean, when is the last time anyone actually performed a combat launch like this?"

"You mean going over the bow without using a catapult?"

"Among other things, yeah."

Arkady considered. "Maybe fifty years or so, I guess."

"Do you ever stop to consider that maybe there could be a reason for that? Like maybe us getting run over by a big ship if something goes wrong?"

"Look at the bright side there, fellow. If you do screw things up, there won't be anyone left around who can criticize you."

"I hope you realize that statement could be taken in a number of different contexts."

"Pink, it's totally cool. We're gonna have fun!" Arkady dropped from the cockpit step to the anti-skid and jogged to the spotted double zero aircraft.

Pinkerton could only shake his head. "Where have I heard that before?"

*

"Stand clear of exhausts, intakes and propellers!" the deck boss chanted over the topside loudspeakers. "Stand by to start engines!"

Turbines whined to life and rotors began to spin, their blade tips barely clearing amid the tightly packed helicopters. A microlight was inset into each blade tip, invisible to the naked eye but readily apparent in the NiteBrite visors worn by the aviators and deck crew. Each helicopter became crowned by a shimmering halo of luminescence that marked the deadly arc of the blade sweep.

The major drawback to the compound helicopter conversion was weight. The wings and additional onboard systems, while greatly increasing the aircraft's over-all payload capacity, cut into the weight the helicopter could lift in a "hover-up" vertical liftoff. Tonight, each SPEED Cobra would be carrying a maxed payload of fuel drop tanks, missiles and cannon ammunition.

So burdened, each machine must conduct a rolling launch, like a conventional aircraft, using the combined lift of both rotors and wings to reach the sky.

What had been old was new again. To utilize this latest addition to the naval aviation arsenal, they must hark back to the early days of dive bombers and leather flying helmets.

Pink had done rolling launches before – on the training LPDs, in the simulator, and even a couple of times off the *Shenandoah*'s narrow patchwork flight deck. Still, he swallowed and wished he had a canteen within reach.

"This is Delta Strike Lead to the Lady." There was a choppy, digital edge to Arkady's voice. They were using a frequency-jittering difficult-to-intercept radio, with an unusual formality to his words. "All strikes standing by to launch."

"This is the Lady," a cool purring alto answered from out in the night. "You may launch the strikes."

Talk about running names, the commando carrier's captain was another of those rare individuals who had the personality to win a respectful one. She had a reputation that bordered on the legendary and his squadron leader insisted that every word of it was true and justified. Pink knew Arkady had put in a couple of cruises aboard Captain Garrett's guided missile destroyer; there was even a certain degree of intriguing scuttlebutt that she and Arkady had once violated a few naval regulations together. Pink couldn't say. Arkady was his friend and wing mate – but there were some questions you just didn't ask, no matter how well you might know a guy.

Forward and to port, Arkady must have thrown his ready salute to the launch boss standing at the edge of the deck. Pink could feel the buffeting of rotor and propwash as his flight leader throttled up to flight power.

The launch boss, the "deck monkey", went through his traditional exaggerated disco step launch gesture, ending on one knee with his fist thrust forward.

Pink's aircraft shuddered under the air blast as Vince pulled pitch. Arkady's Cobra started its forward roll down the limited length of the flight deck, gaining speed with an unnerving slowness. First, its landing gear broke contact; then, it cleared the end of the flight deck and the forecastle. Moments later, as it lost ground effect going over the bow, the Cobra dropped like a rock.

Pink almost strangled on his own heart. Then, the flickering halo of Delta Lead's rotor lights bobbed back into view, climbing free into the black sky.

Pink would have a few, a very few, extra feet to launch with. He swallowed his own heart back into place and ramped up to flight power, throwing his own salute to the waiting deck monkey.

*

Four SPEED Cobra attack teams went airborne, each helicopter carrying a pair of AGM-88 Advanced Anti-Radiation Guided Missiles on its wingtip mounts. The "radiation" referred to in the missile's nomenclature was not of the atomic variety, but the electronic. The AGM-88 was a radar killer, designed to blind air-search and anti-aircraft radars by honing in on and destroying their transmitter antenna. But the AGM-88 was not only a lethal but a versatile predator. It could be programmed to sniff out and kill other energy emitters, such as the broadcasting tower of a radio station.

Two Cobra flights doubled back toward Java, targeting the radicalist propaganda transmitters in the cities of Bandung and Semarang. The third cut down through the Sunda Strait to hit the stations on Sumatra's underbelly at Padang.

Flying northwest, paralleling the northern Sumatran coast, the fourth flight flew through the darkness toward the most distant objective, the transmitter at Pakanbaru.

The SPEED Cobra's communications system recognized and acquired a long range satlink carrier wave and a voice sounded in Arkady's helmet phones.

"Star Child to Delta Strike Lead. Be advised Alpha Strike has engaged initial target. Target is down. Alpha is clear and returning to base. Star Child out."

Arkady squirted an acknowledgement back over the satellite link with a blip of the coder button on the HOTAS grip. "That's one, Pink," Arkady murmured into the talk-between-pilots channel.

"Hey Vince, you mind if I ask a question about this run?" Despite the close proximity of the two aircraft, Pinkerton's voice was faint. "Difficult-to-intercept" radio didn't mean "impossible" so they had their transmitter power backed down to minimums.

"Course not, Pink." Arkady's eyes flicked continuously from the navigation display to the sea's surface a meager fifty feet below his Cobra's belly. "Shoot?"

"There's something about the mission profile that I don't get," his wingman replied. "How come we're engaging the targets sequentially? If we'd staggered our launches, we could have hit these guys as a time-on-target attack, putting all of our aircraft and missiles in at the same time."

"Now why would we want to do that?" Arkady inquired mildly, breaking off his established eye movement pattern to twist and flex his neck. The weight of a night vision visor always gave him aching vertebrae.

"Uh, how about survivability? If we hit all of the targets simultaneously, we'll have surprise on our side and we could didibop the hell out of here before anyone could do anything about us. As is, we're the last in line to launch. If the bad guys figure out that somebody's picking off their radio stations one after another, they might react to it. And if they do, they're going to react all over us."

"Can't argue with that logic," Arkady agreed.

"I don't want you to argue with it," Pink replied plaintively. "I just want to know how come?"

"It's like this, buddy. Strike Alpha is 'Wha' hoppen?' Strike Bravo will be, 'I think somebody's shooting at us!' Strike Charley will be, 'Hey, somebody is shooting at us!' And Strike Delta, that's us keen guys, will be ..."

"Let's kill the bastards!" Pinkerton finished, sounding unpleased with the concept.

"Essentially, Pink. Even as we speak, there's a perilously cute little blonde on the ground in Jakarta doing all sorts of spy stuff to spot who's getting mad at us. It could answer a lot of questions about what's going on out here."

"I'm so happy. Tell me something, Vince. Are we going to be doing a lot of this kind of shit flying off of that hermaphrodite freighter?"

Arkady chuckled. "Pink, you're working for the Lady now. You're going to be doing things you won't even believe you're doing, even while you're doing them."

The tea in Amanda's mug was bitter, the mark of one nervous cup too many, and her eyes burned from too many hours of staring at Large Screen displays.

She stood in a corner of Air One, the smallest and yet one of the most critical of the operations centers within the _Shenandoah_'s command-and-control block. Here rested the brain of the air group and the heart of all flight operations. Half a dozen workstations were spaced around the bulkheads of the dim little compartment, while a computer chart table in its center took up the bulk of the remaining space.

This was Vince Arkady's corner of the ship and he was already imprinting on it. Color copier downloads of classic naval warplanes had been taped into odd corners of the bulkheads and a poster from the Tokyo Air Show graced the inside of the door. Amanda couldn't help but note the sentiment added with a marker pen to the lower corner.

"With fond thanks and memories, Akiko."

Even under the current load, Amanda couldn't help but be woman enough to wonder who Akiko was and what she was fondly thankful for.

Alpha Strike had already been successfully recovered and stricken below. The helicopters of Bravo could be seen on the topside monitors, descending on the deck lifts – and Charley Strike was clear and coming home through the Sunda. Only Delta was still outbound, its position hack just reaching the end of its projected flight plot, the circle that marked the firing arc of an AGM-88. At its center was Delta's target.

"Signal Intelligence, are the propaganda broadcasts still coming out of Pakanbaru?"

"Yes, ma'am." Captain Montgomery sounded as tired as Amanda felt. "We're also picking up traffic on the Indonesian military's tactical channels. There's a firefight going on somewhere in the Pakanbaru area between government forces and a band of Aceh separatists. The government troops have been trying to reach and retake the radio station without success."

"Maybe we can save them the trouble. Stay on it, Captain – and give your people a well done. You've all done premier work today. It will be noted."

"Thank you, ma'am." Montgomery sounded like she'd be willing to trade any medal in the world for an uninterrupted hour in a bed.

"This is Delta Strike lead to Star Child." Vince Arkady's voice on the other hand sounded as steady and strong as a man risen from a refreshing night's sleep. "Be advised that we are coming in on target. Cleaning up and climbing to attack altitude."

Amanda glanced up at the overhead speaker, visualizing in her mind's eye the discarded drop tanks splashing into the sea beneath the two distant SPEED Cobras, the slender dragonfly aircraft nosing up into a climb.

Now was the moment of greatest risk as the strike abandoned its sea skimming flight profile. Various technologies had been applied to the compound helicopters to render them more difficult to detect – retinal schiff-based radar absorbent paint, RAM body panels, radar transparent thermo-composite rotor and propeller blades – but such "cheap stealth" applications could only reduce the helicopter's radar cross section, not eliminate it. The SPEED Cobras were stealthy, not full stealth. They were vulnerable to the brush of a sweeping air defense radar.

"Climbing to two thousand, Pink."

"Angels two it is. Right with you, Lead."

Air One was directly accessing the Talk-Between-Pilots channel now as the easiest mode of monitoring the strike, the voices of the two aviators issuing from the overhead speakers.

"Let's heat 'em up, Pink."

"Roger, Vince. Arming missiles. Got good arming lights."

"Okay Pink, come left to 210 degrees true. Set your signal gates and start hunting."

"Rog."

"You'd think if they wanted to protect their transmitter, they'd just shut the damn thing off," the fighter direction officer murmured from the main console.

"That would be an option if they had permanent possession," Amanda replied absently. "But whoever our friends in the Third Faction are, they probably realize they're only going to have a limited number of broadcast hours out of those facilities. It's only a matter of time before the Indonesian government recaptures those transmitters or cuts their power. Until then, they'll nurse as much propaganda mileage out of those stations as they can."

The overhead speaker sputtered and emitted a whisper of hysteric Bahasa, a backdrop for the voice of Vince Arkady's wingman. "Delta Lead, I've acquired the target."

"Rog on that, Pink. I'm still not acquiring. Let's take it in a little more."

The position hacks of Strike Delta crawled closer to the Sumatran coast. A third blue bat-shaped aircraft symbol paralleled them, holding farther offshore, the Air Force Global Hawk that was providing radar imaging and electronic Intelligence for the mission.

Suddenly two more aircraft hacks appeared on the display from the northwest. Only these pulsed a warning red.

Instantly, the fighter director pounced on his transmit key. "Strike Delta, be advised you have two hostiles factoring from the northwest, climbing out from Medan Air Force Base. We are indicating active airborne radars. Targets are vectoring for intercept!"

"Roger that, Star Child." Arkady's voice was bland, a workman going about a well-practiced trade. "We got 'em on the threat boards. We are being painted. We still have room and we are continuing to close with the target."

Amanda leaned in over the fighter director. "What have we got?"

"An Indonesian interceptor flight, ma'am. They're only BAC Hawk strike-trainers, but they'll be carrying ASRAAM air-to-air missiles and cannon and a rudimentary air intercept radar."

The SPEED Cobra flight was just going feet dry, crossing the coastline

– but, as they continued to close on their objective, the swifter Indonesian fighters continued to close on them. On the large screen display, the interceptors trailed a golden glowing flight track behind them. Amanda could see them edging around, incrementally aligning on the helicopters as the Indonesian pilots obeyed their own ground controller's intercept vectors.

The overhead speakers hissed and muttered, picking up an underbreath mumble. "Come on, you bitchkitties! You can hear him out there. Why won't you lock up?"

Amanda figuratively gripped herself by the throat, throttling down the screamed command to break off and get the hell out of there. Vince Arkady knew his business.

"Hey, Lead, I got threat warnings. We're being painted air-to-air. We got Hawks in a pursuit curve. Thirty seconds to ASRAAM range." Pinkerton's voice was as laconic as Arkady's.

"I'm on it, Pink. I have to reset a circuit breaker here ... Got it! I have acquisition lights! Take your shots! Let's kill him!"

"Affirmative! Shooting in three, two, one ..."

Whispered rasps issued from the speakers as a sound-actuated mike responded to the missiles roaring off their wingtip rails.

"Missiles away! Good birds!"

"Roger D! Brake left, Pink! Break hard left! CHAFF! CHAFF! CHAFF!"

An extensive glowing blob blossomed on the large screen display as the countermeasures systems of the SPEED Cobra's kicked out blocks of radar jamming metal foil. The tracks of the compound helicopters and those of the Indonesian jets merged within the chaff cloud.

There was a fearful moment of indistinction; then the two tracks reappeared, separating. The frustrated jets punched out of the cloud heading west, the American aircraft to the southeast, diving and reversing out from under the guns and missiles of their pursuers.

"Star Child, this is Delta Lead. We have serviced the target. Endeavoring to disengage."

In Air One, Amanda snapped her fingers and pointed to a second systems operator. Without needing a verbal instruction, the young woman called up the signal intercept channel. Over the airwaves, the booming angry voice of an imam was just reaching a crescendo of religious revilement when, abruptly, it was cut off as if by an angered and profaned Allah.

On the hillcrest above the town of Pikanbaru, four streaks of light dove meteor-like toward a tall gridwork tower. Bitten through by multiple warhead hits, the radio antenna swayed, buckled and crashed to the Earth.

The job was done. Now to get the workmen home.

The SPEED Cobras ran to the southeast, paralleling the Sumatran coastline but staying feet dry. Amanda recognized Arkady's logic. In a race, Hawk against Cobra, the Cobras had no chance. Likewise, venturing back over the sea would present a downward-looking airborne radar with a pair of clean returns against a flat uncluttered background. But by staying low over the land, Arkady could exercise the snakish virtues of twisting, turning and hiding amid broken terrain.

"Keep it in tight, Pink." The voices over the tactical channel continued to tell the story.

"Right behind you, Lead. I got tail warnings on infra-red."

"I got 'em too. Descending ... Range closing ... They're coming back around on us. Let 'em set up and then we'll pogo to the right over to the other side of the ridge. I'll call the break. Stand by on your flares in case they pop a missile."

The words were still casual but accelerated breathing rasped in the mikes. Lungs fought for oxygen in Air One as well, but no one spoke; there was nothing constructive to say as the Indonesian interceptors once more aligned on the fleeing helicopters, gingerly probing down through the night, trying to acquire their flitting targets.

The Indonesian pilots were being cautious. They weren't exactly sure what was lurking down in the hill shadows.

"Here they come." Arkady would be stealing glances at this same Global Hawk download on his own master display. "Let's let 'em come in just bit more. Come on down and play in the dirt, boys! Okay, Pink! Break right and climb! Break and climb!"

"Breaking now! Still with you ..."

"Roger! Poppin' the ridge. Takin' it down. Takin' it down!" There was a sudden pause. "SHIT! CABLE! CABLE! CABLE!"

"GOING HIGH! GOING HIGH! VINCE, WATCH IT!"

Both of the blue position hacks vanished from the screen. Amanda's heart stalled in her chest.

"Vince, you okay?" a tentative voice queried from the speaker.

"Yeah. I'm okay, Pink. Heck of a place to put a high line logging rig, huh?"

Amanda and a couple of others suppressed their sighs of relief. Delta Strike's jink over the distant ridgeline had only broken their contact with the Global Hawk radar.

"Man, you went *under* that sumbitch, Vince!'

"Yeah, well, you were going over it. Where are you, Pink?"

"Coming up on your four. Where are the bad guys?"

"Climbing out at ten o'clock. Gimme a threat board check, Pink."

"I'm showing clean, Lead."

"Okay, I'm getting bored with this. Flare back and go helo. We got some clear ground ahead. Let's squat and wait these guys out."

"Squat?" Amanda queried.

"Yes, ma'am," the fighter director replied. "They're going to try hovering down below tree level. It'll kill the Doppler contrast and merge their radar returns into the ground."

"Will it work?"

"It depends, ma'am, on if the radar on those Indonesian Hawks can pick up a rotor flicker or if they have infra-red detection capacity."

"When will we know?"

"In pretty short order, ma'am."

There was only dead air over the radio channels. On the Global Hawk's radar scan, the Indonesian fighters could be seen flying a cloverleaf search pattern centered over their last fix on the compound helos, the jets snuffling through the sky like a pair of frustrated bloodhounds quartering for a lost scent.

The hunt went on for perhaps five minutes or five centuries for the occupants of Air One. Then the laws of aviation science ruled in favor of Delta Strike. Maneuvering at low altitude, the Indonesian jets guzzled fuel. They made one final pass and then broke away for home, climbing into the northwest. No fresh flight came to replace them.

The fighter direction officer let the Hawks draw well clear, then spoke into his headset. "Delta Strike, you are clear. The interceptors are no longer a factor."

A long pause, then, "Roger that, Star Child. Mission accomplished. Taking departure. Returning to base."

The pair of blue aircraft symbols blipped back into existence on the screen and resumed their long run for home.

Amanda couldn't resist jumping on the channel. "Situation report, Delta Lead."

"We're fine, captain." A hint of amusement had crept into Arkady's voice. "Although I can't say the same for at least one Sumatran small holder."

"Say again, Delta lead?"

"We had to hover down in this poor guy's farmyard. We blew over his chicken coop and outhouse and stripped all the thatch off his roof. Given the war dance he was doing, I don't think he was too pleased with us."

"Hopefully he won't be the only one. We'll see you when you recover, Delta Lead."

It suddenly struck Arkady that this was the first time he'd been aft since he had been aboard. The transition from the tightly-packed militarism of the camouflaged hold section to the airy civilian elbow room of the stern house was striking.

He'd been totally involved in getting the air group fully operational to range far from Air One and the hangar deck, but he hadn't been invited aft. There could be a lot of reasons for that; both he and Amanda had been given a lot to think about lately.

As he climbed the 'tween deck ladders, he could feel the stern lifting and trembling under the thrust of the propellers. The commando carrier had come about immediately after recovering Delta Strike and was now steaming hard to the east, obviously going somewhere in a hurry.

He knocked on the door of the Captain's cabin, hearing multiple voices beyond it.

"Enter." Amanda Garrett was as he had seen her so often aboard the *Cunningham*, on her feet and pacing, running on willpower and nervous energy, her eyes shadowed and yet bright from sleeplessness. She glanced toward him and fired of a brief, welcoming smile. "Come in, Arkady. Join the family circle."

She was alone, physically at least. The other voices had issued from the brace of laptop computers parked on the cabin's broad, cluttered desktop. Arkady had no difficulty in recognizing the faces that filled the two screens.

"Good morning, Admiral. How you doing, Chris?"

Christine Rendino was seated in a rather elegant bedroom suite while MacIntyre hunched in the cramped communications bay of an Orion C and C aircraft, the faint background moan of turboprops testifying that he was airborne.

"Good morning, Commander," MacIntyre's filtered voice replied. "Congratulations on a successful mission."

"Thank you, sir."

"The same from me, Arkady," Christine interjected, "plus a big kiss on the cheek – or wherever! You were fabulous, as usual."

"I know it, sis, but taking down a few radio stations wasn't that big of a deal."

"You've done considerably more than that," Amanda said, crossing her arms. "You've provided us with solid evidence of an impending military coup against the Kediri government."

Arkady set his flight helmet on the edge of the desk. "The provocation angle worked then?"

"It did. Chris, bring Arkady up to speed with what you've been telling us."

"My pleasure," the Intel replied. "Here's the deal, flyboy. It hasn't been what we've been seeing over the past few hours; it's what we haven't been seeing. According to the commo traffic we've been monitoring in and out of the Ministry of Defense and the Palace complex, President Kediri and his people are appalled by the Balinese situation. They can recognize a government-killer scenario just as well as we can and they can also recognize the potential for a bloodbath that could set the Muslim and Hindu communities of the archipelago at each other's throats for the next century.

"Unfortunately, there isn't a whole hell of a lot they can do about it. Their military and security elements are so widely dispersed and heavily committed that it will be days before they can mass an effective reaction force."

"And it's beginning to look like somebody planned it just that way," MacIntyre added from his screen.

"Exactly, Admiral sir," Christine nodded. "We saw the mechanism in effect tonight. When those radio stations went rogue and started blasting hate propaganda over the main islands, the Presidential Palace ordered those broadcasts stopped at all costs. But again, the security forces were either out of position or they reacted sluggishly. That's how we ended up having to do the job for them."

"How are the Indies reacting to our intervention?" Arkady inquired.

"Nobody seems to know exactly who or what you were or where you came from, but the Indonesians can recognize a HARM when they see one. Shortly after the Alpha and Bravo Strike went in, the Ministry of Defense passed an event assessment to the Palace that indicated a US intervention was underway."

"What did the Palace answer back?" Arkady asked.

"To go with it! The Indonesian Defense Forces were not, repeat emphatically not, to interfere with the HARM missions taking out those radio stations."

"Wait a minute," Arkady said slowly. "If that order was issued after Bravo Strike went in ..."

"Exactly," Amanda interjected. "The interceptor launch against you out of Medan was not authorized by Jakarta. The Ministry of Defense hasn't even been informed of the attempt."

"Shit!" Arkady braced his hands on his flight-suited hips and considered the permutations. "The only way that could work is if the whole damn base was in somebody's pocket!"

"If not the entirety of the Sumatran military command," MacIntyre added. "Commander, over the past twelve hours, these ladies have managed to convince me of a couple of things. One is that a faction within the Indonesian military is taking over the Harconan revolution for their own purposes. And two, that they are an exceptionally bloody-minded crew."

"And three," Christine interjected, "that this outfit is probably ready to make its move to seize power, possibly within a matter of hours."

"Ah, hell!" Arkady exploded. "In other words – a stinking situation has just gone totally impossible."

"Not necessarily." Arkady was the only member of the conference to hear that whisper. "Not necessarily."

He looked around to see Amanda standing at her cabin window, looking out into the night. Her reflection in the glass was intent, as if she were studying something out in the blackness that no one else could see.

Lake Toba, North Sumatra Province
The Island of Sumatra
0634 Hours. Zone Time, October 26, 2008

"So far, the death toll is believed to be over two thousand, Admiral."

"Believed to be, Captain?" There was mild reproof in Admiral Ketalaman's voice. He disliked inexactitude. Perhaps that was one of the reasons he found such comfort in this command center sunk into the lava cave behind his villa; the gray-black basalt solidity of the low cavern ceiling, the cold, blue illumination from the workstation screens, the low disciplined murmur of the systems operators at their designated tasks, the very coolness flowing up from the bowels of the mountains. The order of it was soothing.

"Exact casualty counts are difficult to obtain, sir," his Chief of Staff replied carefully. "Conditions on Bali, especially in the northern provinces, are increasingly chaotic. This, in itself, is a clear indicator of the success of the operation. Also, the assassination of Colonel Penyu, the *Polici* brigade commandant for Bali, has been accomplished with a car bombing of police headquarters in Denpasar. Our agent, Major Malioburo, is now in command and he is initiating his designated strategy of provocation and withdrawal."

Ketalaman nodded. "That is satisfactory. And the overall picture?"

"All indications are that the Hindus have indeed initiated a total religious purge of the Balinese Muslim population. Even if the Jakarta government could find reinforcements to send, the situation is already quite beyond their control."

The Admiral noted the flicker of concern or possibly conscience in the eyes of his CoS and he smiled. "Don't worry commander, the Hindus will pay in due course. The story of this atrocity will serve us well when we retake the island, a justification for stern measures. Now what of the Australians and Americans?"

"The main body of Regional Intervention Force has sortied from Darwin and is steaming northward. They should arrive off Bali within the next twenty-four hours. The Singaporean and Japanese navies have also commenced patrol operations in the Straits of Malacca."

"Has there been any indication of a commitment of additional forces or of any change in their mission?"

"No sir, the RIF mission statement remains the same: to ensure freedom of the seas and to evacuate all foreign nationals from the archipelago."

"Excellent! We'll allow them to get the foreigners out. It will simplify things greatly. One less justification for any future intrusion into our affairs."

The Chief of Staff managed a faint smile of his own. "The foreign media representatives are already referring to the 'Indonesian quagmire', sir."

"Another good omen. And what of the situation in Jakarta?"

"Our forces are moving into position, sir. The seventeenth brigade has assumed the capital garrison duties and the majority of the assassination and sabotage teams are positioned and ready to launch on your command. We can go at any time now, but Brigadier Tagang would like another twenty-four hours to move some last pro-government elements out of the Jakarta district."

"I think we can give him his time, Captain. We'll want to give the hysteria over the Bali massacres a chance to grow among the civilian populace a bit more. It will improve the justification for our actions."

The CoS started to speak again, than hesitated. Ketalaman frowned. "What is it, Captain?"

"In relation to that factor, sir. There has been an irregularity in that area."

"What do you mean, an irregularity?"

"Last night, we launched the anti-Balinese propaganda campaign as per the Psyops plan. The radicalist commando teams successfully seized the designated radio stations and began the fatwa broadcasts. However, the seized stations were silenced after only a matter of hours."

"We expected that Kediri would eventually be able to stop our transmissions."

"That's the problem, sir. Government forces weren't involved. The station transmitters were destroyed by anti-radiation missiles. We believe they were American-made AGM 88s."

"Where were they fired from?" Ketalaman demanded.

"We don't know, sir. All anyone can say is that the missiles came in from the sea."

"Such weapons require a launch platform, Commander!"

"I know, sir. There were no known government ships or aircraft in the launch areas at the time of the events. Nor were there any identified Regional Intervention Force elements. There were some fragmentary airborne radar contacts off the Sumatran coast, but nothing that could be positively established. The strongest possibility is that ..."

"They were launched from a stealth platform of some nature. The Americans." Ketalaman pursed his lips. This was an unwelcome disruption of order. He had assessed the potentials of an American involvement and, as long as it evolved along conventional channels, he was not excessively concerned. But this proactive intervention by some unidentified and apparently invisible agency was disconcerting. It was like having a vengeful *hantu* ghost standing at one's back. It hinted that the giant might be taking a greater interest than had been expected.

"Step up our reconnaissance of the Regional Intervention Force and increase our monitoring of the US Embassy in Jakarta. If there is any further indication of excessive meddling by the United States, I wish to be informed of it immediately. Also inform Brigadier Tagang that we may not be able to give him his twenty-four hours."

"Yes, sir. At once." His Chief of Staff flipped to the next page of the morning's briefing file. "There is another event to report. In relation to the Harconan question, there has been a fortunate turn of events."

"How so, Captain?"

"A police launch on a patrol of the north coast of Sumbawa island encountered a plane crash in an isolated inlet north of Mount Tambora. A Canadar amphibian was found run up on a reef close inshore. A number of islanders were observed on the beach who fled into the hills at the approach of the launch. An investigative party was landed and a number of concealed drums of aviation fuel were uncovered. Apparently, the amphibian was making a refueling stop when it ran aground."

A Canadar amphibian? "Has the owner of the aircraft been identified?" Ketalaman asked.

"The aircraft had been repainted and its identification numbers falsified, but the airframe and engine serial numbers match with that of Makara Harconan's personal aircraft."

"Ah," Ketalaman said softly. "Was any Intelligence recovered?"

"A hasty attempt had been made to burn the aircraft, but several charts and an intact Global Positioning Unit was recovered. The aircraft was apparently returning from an open ocean rendezvous off Lompoc Island."

Ketalaman concealed his eagerness. "What was its point of origin?"

"A small plantation island in the Moluku group, sir."

"Has this information been relayed to the Ministry of Defense?"

"The launch's commander is one of our men, sir."

Ketalaman allowed himself to nod in satisfaction. "Very good, Captain. This is a favorable event. Most favorable."

Nancy Aimsley sat on the bed in the humid, airless darkness of the cheap hotel room and held her children close, thinking about Vermont and Christmas and whether they would live for another day.

She'd made the few feeble gestures she could, locking the sliding glass doors that opened onto the beach and drawing the drapes tightly closed. She had even wedged the room's few pieces of flimsy furniture against the inner door.

Soon though, she would have to go outside and into the madness again. There was no electricity. There was no water. They had already eaten the scant bagful of snacks and soft drinks she had snatched out of her apartment kitchen. There was nowhere else to go and no one to turn to.

The only other occupants in the beachfront motel were an expatriate Australian couple in their seventies, who were slipping steadily deeper into a detached state of shock, and a pair of vacationing college girls from Denmark who had lost their English in their terror and who cowered in their room, weeping and seeking solace in a baggie of marijuana.

The establishment's owners were simply gone. Just where, Nancy did not like to contemplate. They had been Balinese Muslims.

Nancy lifted her cellphone once more. Even though the screen still glowed with the "No Service" prompt, she pushed the redial button for the US Consul in Denpasar. Like the last fifty times she had tried, there was no response – and now the low battery warning blinked as well.

She felt the moisture gathering in her burning eyes, the fresh tears joining the drying streaks on her face. She wished someone, anyone, would answer. She wished that she and her children were anywhere other than Bali. She wished that time could be made to run backwards so that the last forty-eight hours could be made to disappear, or even the past six months.

The offer of a posting in Bali for Suncrest Fashions had been a dream assignment. Combining good money with a beautiful and exotic locale, it had been a perfect escape from her exploded marriage. Nancy found a lovely apartment on the fashionably upscale Benoa Peninsula near her office, a good private school for foreign students for her sons – and even a Balinese housemaid to deal with the cooking and cleaning.

There had been talk about the troubles in Indonesia, but she had been assured that didn't apply to Bali. "The Balinese are the kindest, gentlest people in the world!" And so they had seemed.

It was paradise, or as close to it as a sophisticated, independent businesswoman could obtain. Perhaps that was why she had resisted being driven from it.

The first warning from the American Embassy in Jakarta advised that instability within the Indonesian archipelago was growing and that all American Nationals should make preparations to evacuate at short notice.

But that couldn't possibly mean from Bali.

When the second warning arrived, advising that all American nationals should depart Indonesia immediately, the American Benoa community elected to take action. They gathered at the home of a University of California political science professor on sabbatical and discussed the situation over coffee.

The professor explained in detail how the evacuation notice was merely a political ploy by the current reactionary administration, seeking to drum up support for a needlessly interventionist foreign policy. He went on to insist that there was no real risk to anyone willing to deal with the Balinese in a fair, nonjudgmental manner.

Comforted, Nancy stayed on. Others – the Johnsons, the Vales, the Smiths – had not been so comforted. They had left.

Then came the third and final notice, the one that stated in the strongest of terms that the United States Embassy could no longer be responsible for the lives and safety of any American national who remained in the archipelago.

At last, Nancy Aimsley had grown concerned. Perhaps it would be wise to return to the States for a time. She could visit her parents, and Walter had been complaining about his parental visitation rights. She wouldn't really be running away.

Nancy called her travel agency, only to find its Denpasar office closed. Then she called the airport directly. After a long wait, and several disconnects, she was told that there would be no seats available off island for at least a week.

The following day, the rumors of the rioting and the atrocities began.

The television and radio stations in Denpasar reported that the local authorities were "reacting decisively to the situation." Then the radio and television stations went off the air.

The following morning, the maid did not come to work and the electricity was off. Nancy took her sons with her to the Suncrest offices, not to work but to look for friendly faces. The stores and shops were closed and the streets were eerily empty.

The other American members of the Suncrest staff had also rallied at the office, but the only constructive course of action anyone could suggest was to contact company headquarters. The problem was, the phones, both cellular and landline, were dead.

Now the true fear started to grow. Nancy and her compatriots had been born into a world of the Internet and instantaneous telecommunications. There was always someone to call. Someone to listen to their concerns. Someone paid to give a damn.

Mr. Juita, the Javanese district manager, arrived shortly thereafter. But he provided neither information, comfort, nor leadership. He spoke only to say that, should anyone ask, he was not in, nor had he been there. His words were curt but his eyes were fearful. Then he went into his inner office and locked the door.

The heat and humidity crept into the silent office suite, untempered by air conditioning. Her colleagues Terrie and Frankie's nervous string of jokes had given out and the futile rehashing of the situation was abandoned. A rare car swept past in the street beyond the building. Once, a police siren honked tentatively in the distance. The sensation grew of a storm building to break.

They came shortly after the noon hour. Some of the men were strangers. Some were Balinese who had worked in the same building with the Suncrest people. Some were local Suncrest employees.

Smiling politely, they begged the pardon of the office staff and asked for Mr. Juita. Hesitantly, Nancy and the other Americans replied as they had been instructed, denying the presence of the Javanese Muslim. The Balinese continued to smile. Then they knocked on Mr. Juita's door and requested that he come out.

When Mr. Juita refused, the Balinese apologized once more and broke down the door. They carried the manager screaming out of his office and down into the courtyard, and there they cut his throat from ear to ear.

Fear blossomed into panic then, the frenzied consensus being to try and reach the US Consul at Denpasar. The staff started out in an automobile convoy for the island capital, but the closer to the city, the greater the savagery.

Houses and cars burned on the roadsides. Blood smeared the pavement and bodies sprawled. The mosques, small and few in number on Bali, were either in flames or were being wrenched apart barehanded by the mobs.

The line of refugee vehicles had snaked down one side-street after another, seeking for a route not closed by rioting or roadblocks. They were slowed by intermittent stops to argue about maps and directions. Cars started to separate off as frightened, angry people sought their own way to safety or perdition. For the first time Nancy could remember, Tommy and Aaron, her boys, were quiet in the car, their eyes wide and terrified.

The remnants of the convoy were finally stalled by a solid mass of people packed into the street. The Balinese flowed in around the Americans' cars, peering intently through the windows, studying faces, deciding if anyone within needed to die.

Nancy Aimsley would have lost her sanity there and then, were it not for the presence of her children. Only the need to be strong for them kept her from hysteria on the floorboards of her car.

And then a police armored car had suddenly appeared around a corner, machine gun fire spewing from its gun ports. People screamed and ran and the windows of the Settermans' Volvo just ahead of Nancy's car had dissolved in a spray of glass, blood and brain matter.

Nancy convulsively floored the accelerator of her Nissan and wrenched the wheel toward an alley. There was a thud and a gagging squeal as someone went down under her tires – and suddenly Nancy and her children found themselves away and alone.

Abandoning the futile quest for the consul, she turned west, fleeing into the quieter green refuge of the countryside where the death was not so overt. She had tried to reach Ngurah Rai airport, but as she neared the facility, she could see there were no planes climbing into the sky, just a dense plume of black smoke boiling up from the burning terminal buildings.

After that, the drive became aimless. She was stopped twice in the smaller villages but each time, when it was seen that she and her children were not Muslim, she had been allowed to pass. Corpses stacked in the ditches had told of what would have happened if she had been a follower of Muhammad.

That was how she had come to this beachside motel in the Kuta district on the western coast. Kuta was not the refuge Nancy would have chosen for herself and her children. It was the haven of cheap tourism, the wilder, younger, surfing crowd from Australia and the States. But this was where she had run out of gasoline and options.

Once more, by rote, she pressed the redial button on the cell phone. No connection, and this time the battery failed completely.

Tommy and Aaron were being so good, so brave for a six and an eight-year-old, somehow sensing that this was a time to be obedient and quiet. But the questions had started. "Mommy, when are we going home? Mommy, why are you crying? Mommy, what's the matter with that man?"

And finally, "Mommy, are we going to die?"

The questions would begin again when they awoke and she would have no answers for them.

Nancy looked toward the window. The sun would be rising soon. She would have to find some way to deal with another day.

The airless room was suffocating her. Carefully, she worked her way free of her sleeping boys and crossed to the glass doors. Then she undid the latch and slid the door open. Running her fingers through her short, sweat-wet hair, she inhaled deeply of the sea scented air. Out in the dying night, the shadows still lay heavy on the ocean, the pale break of the waves on the beach marking its edge.

The rumble was so low and deep-toned that its moment of inception didn't register. When it did, Nancy first thought it was a roll of thunder, but it lasted for too long. Then the building began to vibrate. An earthquake?

The sound grew in intensity, dividing into several separate thunders, sweeping closer and setting the glass doors vibrating in their frames. A wave of dark shapes roared overhead, momentarily occluding the last stars.

Tommy and Aaron awoke screaming.

Nancy slammed the door and snapped the latch. She comforted the boys for a hasty moment, then hurried back to the windows, peering through a slit in the blinds.

The sky was empty now, but not the sea. Things were coming out of the sea! A line of great, angular monsters boiled and bellowed out of the surf.

Sand and spray spewed from track wells and dimly silhouetted gun turrets traversed hungrily. The shapes lurched to a halt momentarily, each giving birth to a horde of smaller shadow shapes, two-legged, hunchbacked, the lesser following the greater as they resumed their lurching charge up the beach.

Slender-trunked trees and bamboo fencing splintered as the raging machines circled around the building. The dark men came rushing inside. Doors crashed open. Hoarse voices shouted. In her terror, Nancy couldn't comprehend the words.

"Is anyone in here? Are there any Americans here?"

She threw herself back on the bed and clutched her children. Down

233

the hall, doors splintered under boot kicks. The brittle, wooden door of their room exploded inward and the furnishings stacked against it were bulldozed aside.

A terminator strode into the room, armored, helmeted, camouflaged, a lethal-looking multi-barreled weapon shouldered and leveled, the piercing red beam of a laser sight lashing ahead of him. An eyeless, visored face turned, peering into the corners.

Nancy Aimsley screamed her final scream.

The visor turned toward her. "Are you an American?" the monster inquired, lowering its weapon.

"Yes," Nancy managed to squeak.

The monster flipped up its helmet visor. In the dimness, she saw the glint of eyes and an amazingly warm and compassionate smile. "We've come for you, ma'am. We're setting up a security perimeter and we'll get you and your kids and everybody else moved out to the ships as fast as we can. You take it easy now. You're going to be okay."

The kindly monster flipped his visor back down and strode back into the hall.

Nancy Ames hugged her children so tightly the boys whimpered in protest. They were indeed going to be "okay". As she sobbed in silent, hysterical relief, she understood and treasured an ancient, hackneyed cliché.

"The Marines have landed and the situation is well in hand."

Pesanggaran Highway interchange, North of Benoa Port, Bali
1334 Hours; Zone Time, October 28, 2008

For the hundredth time, 2<sup>nd</sup> Lieutenant Jordan Spokes of Marine Expeditionary Unit 7.2 ran his orders through his mind. "Hold the highway interchange. Permit no passage south into the Regional Intervention Force zone of operations. Aid and assist all foreign nationals seeking evacuation. If possible, avoid confrontation with the indigenous population."

They were simple enough to remember, but as the young Marine officer was rapidly discovering, nothing was ever simple in war.

His LAV 25 armored scout vehicle with its embarked recon team had been assigned to reinforce the unit manning the Pesanggaran checkpoint on the main ground approach to Bali's deep-water harbor.

It was a critical station on the security line the RIF had thrown across the Bukit Badung peninsula, and Spokes had been rather pleased to be going where the action seemed to be. But upon arrival, he found Koala Charley Five manned by only a single Australian Army squad and that he, Spokes, was now senior officer on site and the checkpoint commander.

The Australian NCO, a lean, sun-leathered man called Gregson, lithely scaled the side of the big eight-wheeled armored car, using only a single hand in the climb. The other was occupied with a half-eaten John Wayne bar from an American MRE pack.

"How's she lookin' from up here, lieutenant?" he asked, coming to stand beside the LAV's turret.

"Dead quiet so far," Spokes replied, finding himself pleased with his own answer.

The LAV and the Australian's long wheelbase military Land Rover were drawn across the paved two-lane to create a sketchy roadblock. The infantrymen had deployed in the fields on either side of the highway, trying without much success to dig firing positions in the mucky soil.

There was nothing in the way natural cover. The checkpoint had been placed deliberately where there was none. Fire superiority and a clear field of vision were considered a better defense. Still, it made one feel very naked.

About a quarter of a mile north along the highway, a low shaggy clump of trees brooded in the heat haze. Within it lay the temples and clustered buildings of a small farming village. So far, its inhabitants had remained unseen and the road empty.

"I dunno." The Aussie shifted the sling of his AUG Steyr assault rifle and took another bite of the chocolate bar. "Doubt she'll stay that way. It looks to be a pretty rum go."

"Yeah." On his drive across from the landing beaches, Spokes had seen the beheaded bodies of men, women and children.

Suddenly, a voice echoed up from the LAV's interior. "Hey, LT, we got action in the village area!"

Spokes' sensor operator crouched in the crew compartment, a laptop controller pad across her knees. To augment their local security, they'd launched a Mini-Dragon RPV on their arrival at the checkpoint and now the model-airplane-sized drone was circling above the grove, its tiny television camera peering downward.

"What do you have, Scotty?"

"I can't exactly say, sir. But we have a big bunch of people moving fast in our direction."

The sun-heated rubber of Spoke's binoculars burned the skin around his eyes as he lifted and aimed them up the road. A figure appeared from beneath the tree shadows, running down the road toward the check point. Through the heat shimmer, Spokes could make out it was a man bearing some kind of burden in his arms. And behind him were other shapes, more men running. Steel gleamed hotly in their hands."

"Stand ready!" Spokes yelled. "Prepare to engage!"

Gregson finished his candy in a single bite and sprang down from the LAV's deck, unslinging his rifle as he dropped. "Look alive, you blokes! We've got trade!"

The Aussie manning the pintle-mounted GPMG in the rear of the

Land Rover drew his bolt back and the LAV's turret indexed a few degrees as the Marine gunner acquired the targets in the sights of his 25mm autocannon. Spokes swung the OCSW 20mm grenade launcher around on its scarf ring.

"Grenadiers and shotgunners, load non-lethal! Scotty, hit the loud hailer! Warn these guys off."

"Lieutenant, watch it!" Gregson yelled, whipping his rifle to his shoulder. "That first bugger's carrying something!"

Spoke's gut lurched. Suicide bomber!

He pressed his eye to the sighting module of the OCSW, his thumb resting on the magazine selector, balancing the switch between the teargas loads and the anti-personnel flechettes.

The crosshairs of the module zoomed on the chest of a boy of maybe fourteen, his face distorted in a rictus of exertion and fear, his bare feet hammering on the blistering asphalt.

The bundle he carried had long black hair.

"Hold your fire! He's just a kid! They're both just kids!"

Spokes lifted the gun sights. A good dozen men were chasing the boy. Their faces were intent, focused in their pursuit, yet also calm, almost at peace, belying the knives and machetes swinging from their hands.

Spokes' hand came up to the transmit button on his lip mike. "Dingo Alpha! Dingo Alpha! This is Koala Charley Five! We have an incident! We have an incident! Over!"

His helmet earphones were clogged with channel chatter, none of it a reply directed at him.

"Dingo Alpha! Dingo Alpha! This is Koala Charley Five! We have an incident! I say again, we have an incident! Respond! Over! Scotty, hit the loudspeakers! Warn these guys off!"

The LAV's hull amplifiers thundered a pre-recorded warning message, one that ordered a crowd of Bahasa Indonesia speakers to stay back.

At the electronically shouted command, the pursuers broke stride, slowing to a hesitant stop, perhaps fifty yards off. The pursued, however, ignored both the order and the leveled gun barrels. He raced up to the side of the LAV and collapsed in its shade, his chest heaving with each shuddering breath. Looking down from the turret, Spokes could see that the child the boy carried was a big-eyed little girl, her arms locked in a death grip around her brother's neck. Sucking gasps of air, the boy tried to speak.

"Scotty, kill the recording. Sergeant, can you talk to this kid? I need to know what's going on here!" Once more, Spokes tried his radio, "Dingo Alpha! Dingo Alpha, this is Koala Charley Five! Respond please! We have an event in progress! Over!"

The Australian NCO sank down on one knee beside the Indonesian youth, speaking a couple of hesitant phrases in Bahasa.

The reply was a wheezing rush of words.

"What's he saying?" Spokes tried to split his attention between the mob on the road and the prostrate figures sprawled beside the LAV.

"Trying to sort it out, lieutenant. Something about him an' his sister needin' help ... Something about his mum and dad ... Right. He and his family are Balinese Muslims – they were trying to get off the island when they got jumped by the Hindus up in that next village."

The Australian looked up, his pragmatism cracking. "The bastards killed the parents! They want to kill the kids too! He's asking us for help! For sanctuary! Christ, Lieutenant! The girl's only four!"

Spokes looked up. The clump of villagers on the road had grown to a group of around thirty. Their faces were impassive, but an air of anger hovered over them now, becoming almost palpable. Some were stepping closer to the roadblock.

"Scotty, hit the loudspeakers again. Order those people to back off!" Spokes crushed down the transmit key. "Dingo Alpha, do you copy? Damn it! This is Koala Charley Five! Roll the Mike Force! We need some help out here!"

Hold the interchange. Permit no passage south into the Regional Intervention Force zone of operations. Aid and assist all foreign nationals seeking evacuation. If possible, avoid confrontation with the indigenous population.

Like every set of operational orders ever written, it seemed so complete, so absolute, so all-encompassing, right up until they had to actually be applied in the field.

Permit no passage south ... by anyone? Aid and assist all foreign nationals – but did a Muslim amid an island of angry Hindus count as a "foreign national?" If possible, avoid all confrontation with the indigenous population. Was it possible to avoid this one without condemning a young boy and a little girl to death?

The recorded voice was barking over the loudhailer but it wasn't holding the mob. They were bunching closer, building their energy for a rush to reclaim their prey. Gregson lifted his rifle once more, coming up in the classic kneeling firing position, picking the target for his first burst.

But the leveled guns weren't holding the mob either.

The Muslim boy, too weary and wind broken to run farther, clutched all that was left of his family closer. Looking up, he addressed Spokes directly. The Marine couldn't understand his words but he could recognize the plea in them.

Spokes reached for the transmit key again but stopped. He understood now that there was no aid, no advice that could reach him in time. There would be no superior to pass the buck off to. He also understood why the officers got the salutes now, the extra pay, the extra privilege or two. It was a pathetic remuneration for moments like this.

"Sergeant, get those refugees to the rear!"

"Right, Lieutenant!" Spokes barely caught the "Good on ya, yank" that was spoken under-breath – but he clearly heard the shouts of anger from the Hindus as the Muslims were hustled out of sight and to safety.

He heard his call sign finally being repeated in his helmet phones but the commander of Koala Charley Five couldn't be bothered with that now.

"Jellybag and teargas rounds on target! Everything else over their heads! Stand ready! Here they come! Commence firing!"

The mission profile of the Regional Intervention Force had just undergone a radical expansion.

Bali, the Northern Regencies
Late October, 2008

What do you when the world goes insane? What do you do when order disintegrates and law vanishes, when a creeping madness infects neighbors and friends turning them into coldly murderous enemies? What do you do when the cities burn and blood of your people flows freely in the streets?

You run. You gather all who are dear to you and you flee, seeking for refuge, seeking for some lingering pool of sanity where you can hide. Your priorities change. Property and possessions lose their value. Nothing remains but precious, irreplaceable life.

By car and truck, by motor scooter and bicycle, on foot, the Muslims of Bali fled. But they fled with no destination. The government they had relied on no longer existed; their officials ran in terror with them. They had no God, for the Mosques were the first to burn and the Mullahs the first to die. They had no safe road to follow for any path might lead to a grim-eyed, throat-slitting mob.

For the Muslims of southern Bali, there was the check line and the guns and sanity of the Regional Intervention Force.

For those left in the north there was only one whisper of hope. *Get to the sea!*

The word spread among the survivors, passing from cluster to cluster of the dispossessed and frantic. No one knew who passed the word but the message was always the same. *If you wish to live, get to the sea!*

The desperate exodus began to the beaches and the ports. The Balinese Muslims did not know what might await them there. Perhaps a miracle and a way out; perhaps only an empty promise and death.

It didn't matter; it was all they had.

<u>The MV Galaxy *Shenandoah*</u>
<u>Off the Northeastern Coast of Madura Island</u>
<u>1210 Hours; Zone Time, October 29, 2008</u>

Amid the growing chaos in the islands, the big bulk carrier made its way eastward to Bali, its passage ignored as violence unfolded around it. In typical Third World conflicts, neutral merchantmen frequently possessed an odd form of immunity. Like a mail or paper deliverer passing through a neighborhood, they were frequently a faceless, ignored factor. At least until someone came up with a reason they should be shot at.

So far no one had come up with a reason to shoot at the Galaxy *Shenandoah*.

In the captain's cabin, Amanda Garrett was involved in an unauthorized but necessary bit of backdoor Intelligence collection. Captain Ken Hiro, the current commanding officer of the USS *Cunningham*, was not on the highly compartmentalized JSOC listing of personnel authorized to know about Phantom Force and of Amanda's current status. However, Amanda had placed her old exec on her own personal need-to-know list and she was making use of it now.

"What's your situation, Ken?"

"We're still holding off Benglulu harbor on the southern coast of Sumatra and we're still pinned down," Hiro replied, his voice faint but clear. They were speaking via a cobbled secure communications link between their two ships, laser com from the *Shenandoah* to one of the commando carrier's Mariner reconnaissance drones and from the drone on to the *Cunningham* via encrypted commercial satphone.

"This was supposed to be a fast-in-and-out, evacuating a group of U.S. and Australian business people and a Japanese tour group – but it hasn't panned out that way. The Sea Dragons and a naval landing party are on the beach maintaining a defense perimeter. At the moment, they're the only thing standing between some two thousand Balinese Hindu expats and Indonesian Chinese and about ten thousand pissed off Muslims."

Amanda lifted an eyebrow. "Why are they mad at the Chinese?"

"You know how it goes with the Chinese merchant class in South East Asia, Captain. They're economically successful but outside of the cultural mainstream. When things go sour, they make a convenient scapegoat. Be that as it may, if we pull out we're going to see a massacre."

"We're becoming acquainted with the phenomenon. What about the government forces?"

"We've got a few police and Indonesian Army troops on the perimeter with us, but they'll last about ten minutes if we disengage."

"Are the Sea Fighters themselves under attack?"

"The ships are uninvolved so far, and we haven't been hit with anything ashore that we haven't been able to deal with non-lethally. The locals don't seem willing to take us on directly, but they're keeping up the pressure. I suspect it's only a matter of time before we start taking and delivering casualties."

Hiro sounded tired. "Beyond that, we've got major logistical problems. The refugees need food, shelter and medical care, way more than we can provide. It's one royal mess, Captain."

"We're seeing the same scenario everywhere, Ken," Amanda replied, wishing she had something more encouraging to say. "Only with differing casts of characters. There's way too many of them and not nearly enough of us. What are Captain Carberry's intentions?"

"He's started an evacuation of the Indonesian refugees up the coast to the big government garrison at Padang, using the PGACs and our one LCAC. It'll take time though – and what they'll do with them at Padang, I don't know."

"Acknowledged. We're bound for the north coast of Bali to see if we can accomplish anything there. Tie a knot and hang on, Ken."

"Will do, Captain. I'm glad you're still out here with us."

"No I'm not, Ken. Remember that. I'm just the lowly skipper of a tramp steamer now. I'll talk with you later."

She returned the phone to its cradle and stared at it for a long minute. Damn, damn, damn! She had failed in her first attempt to stave off this disaster and now she was failing in her second. It would be a comfort to say that this had all started long before she had ever come to the archipelago, that it was destined to happen and that no one could have stopped it. But such rationalization was not acceptable to her nature.

She ran her hands through her hair, fingers tightening until her scalp ached. Tie a knot, Amanda. Tie a knot and hang on!

Subliminally, her mariner's senses registered a slight change in the way the *Shenandoah* reacted to the sea. Looking up, she saw the light and shadow patterns drifting across the cabin floor. Standing up from her desk chair, she crossed to the cabin windows. They were starting their turn to the south.

Her windows looked to port and she could see the cloud-capped green peaks of Kangean Island rising out of the shimmering sea, looking like a stage setting for South Pacific. Without having to look, she knew that Rass Island would be on the horizon to starboard and that they were running the passage from the Java to the Bali Sea.

She had come to love the exotic, musical names common in these waters: Laute Kecil, Savu, Karimunjawa. If one had a good sailing craft, like one of the Bugi schooners, one could spend an entire lifetime just sailing from one mystic name to the next.

And she'd had the chance to do just that. The classic South Pacific fantasy: an existence free from responsibility or any physical or monetary want, a life spent in lovemaking and peaceful adventure in an oceanic wonderland. Just the sun on her back by day and a strong passionate man to rest beside at night and a white-sailed ship to aim at the next horizon. All of the paradises of her adolescent imagination.

The purchasing price would have been the mere sale of her soul and the ignoring of a holocaust.

"Damn you, Makara!"

The interphone on her desk rang with the alternate trill that indicated a call from the hold spaces. She was across the cabin in an instant.

"Captain here."

"Ma'am, this is the duty officer in CIC. We have a situation developing you need to have a look at."

She was beginning to hate those words.

"I'm on my way."

The captain of the little inter-island passenger ferry was a brave man. If he hadn't been, he wouldn't have risked this last run into Singaraga. But he was a capable seaman and, as such, a profound realist.

His ship was growing overburdened; he could feel it even tied alongside the dock. And yet the refugees continued to press their way aboard and the line of frightened, fleeing people still ran the full length of the pier and beyond.

He hesitated for a last moment, but then could hesitate no longer. May Allah forgive him – but this must be the end. His ship was far beyond its maximum capacity and he could squeeze no more aboard and hope to survive the passage to Java.

The ferry captain reached up and yanked on the cord of the air horn, sounding the signal he had prearranged with the tense crewmen waiting at the mooring lines. Then he threw the idling diesels into reverse and spun the helm hard over, springing his vessel away from the pier.

It was time to cut and run.

As the water boiled under the ferry's stern, a great wailing cry arose from the pier. In an instant, the line of refugees on the pier collapsed into a frantic mob. This was the reaction the ferry captain had feared. Singaraja harbor had emptied of small craft and shipping. His was the last boat out. The last escape from the burgeoning madness.

Hands reached beseeching at the ferry's railings. Members of sundered families screamed to those left behind. People tumbled off the edge of the pier into the widening gap of water, victims of the roiling crush of humanity. Some never surfaced again and went unmissed.

Sluggish under its living burden, the little ferry came about and lumbered toward the harbor mouth and the distant safety of Java. It would not be back again.

"It's like this, Skipper," Stone Quillain said. "We got us a real mess comin' together in Singaraja."

"Why should they be any different than anywhere on Bali?" Dix Beltrain inquired from the chair next to Amanda's.

"Volume, Dix. Sheer volume," Vince Arkady interjected. The aviator was the last member of the abbreviated Operations Group. They were clustered around the chart table in the Command Block briefing room, its bulkhead displays dominated by the real time imaging steaming in from one of the *Shenandoah*'s reconnaissance drone outriders.

"What do we have, Arkady?" Amanda asked quietly.

"Singaraja has been a primary escape route for the Muslim population of Northern Bali. It's the largest north coast port. It's had the strongest government and police presence and it's been a fairly cosmopolitan environment where the wave of religious fanaticism hasn't hit as hard as in the highlands. That situation is changing."

He stood and moved to the master flat screen, running his hand across the imaging of the Singaraja port facilities. Abandoned automobiles and trucks jammed the adjacent city streets and the piers and pier aprons swarmed with a milling mass of people. "We've got a backlog of several thousand refugees piled up in the waterfront district, looking for evacuation craft. The problem is, there aren't any. The last government ferry has sailed and all of the private shipping has hauled out."

Amanda nodded in the screen glow. Oddly enough for an island people, the Balinese were not great mariners. Most of the coasters serving Bali were Muslim owned and manned, and Bali would be a most unattractive port of call at the moment. If there were still any Balinese seamen or ship owners to be found, it was unlikely they would challenge the judgment of their Gods to show the Muslim "demons" any consideration.

"What about the Indonesian navy?" she asked.

"We've been trying to inform them of the situation through Regional Intervention Force Command. I don't know how much good it's going to do because the nearest Indonesian naval unit is over a day's hard steaming away."

Amanda felt her mouth tug down in a frown. "The Indonesian Navy hasn't established a presence in Balinese waters?"

Beltrain shook his head. "Nothing appreciable, Ma'am. Their eastern fleet units are mostly operating off New Guinea, while their western fleet seems to be massing around the Malacca Straits. We haven't seen any major retasking since the start of the Balinese crisis."

Amanda's frown deepened. That seemed to track with the scenario of applied stupidity they'd been seeing develop. She'd have to point this out to Chris just as soon as she could salvage a spare second. "I gather there's a more immediate crisis related with events in Singaraja?"

"It looks like it, Captain."

The image on the screen was changing as the Mariner drone slowly circled above the port city. Another massive clot of people came into view, considerably larger than that along the waterfront, filling the streets around an open building complex.

"We're seeing mobs assembling around the town's Hindu temples – especially around this southern one, the one dedicated to Shiva. The cultural Intelligence database indicates that this is bad, really bad. The Gods are being consulted on matters of life and death. This behavior pattern has been seen just before mass executions start."

Arkady looked away from the screen toward Amanda. "Once these mobs start to move on the waterfront, we're going to be seeing blood, guts and feathers raining down all over the landscape."

"What about the local security forces?"

"From what we can gather from radio intercepts, they've collapsed. The Balinese Hindu rank and file have deserted and are with the mobs – and the Muslim upper echelons have either bugged out or have forted up in the town police headquarters. They are no longer a factor."

"What about a conventional military intervention? Ours or the Indonesians?"

Quillain shrugged. "Too many commitments, Skipper. Not enough assets. The RIF is fully involved down south. The Indies say they've got nothing available and they couldn't get it here if they did."

Amanda gritted her teeth and wished she could set aside her captain's imperturbability long enough to ask for a Tylenol. "What options do we have?"

Down the table, Quillain, Beltrain and Arkady exchanged glances. Quillain took the lead in the reply. "We could deal with it," the Marine said. "It would mean landin' the full Sea Demon force, backed by an armed naval security detail to establish and secure a defensive perimeter around the dock areas. After that, we start lifting the refugees out with the SPEED Hawks."

"The Peleliu can give us some help with their Ospreys and Sea Stallions," Arkady said, taking over the thread of the dialog. "Even so, we'll still have several thousand people to move with a small number of small aircraft. It doesn't matter if we lift them out to a reception site on Java or behind the RIF check line on the southern end of the island, we're going to have long flights and low cyclic times. We're going to be pinned down for a couple of days doing this, and it's going to take a huge bite out of our fuel stores and available flight hours per airframe."

Dix Beltrain kept his head down, minutely examining a pencil. "I think the big point will be the time and overt operations factor, Ma'am. This isn't a raid or hit and run scenario. For the *Shenandoah* to intervene effectively in this situation, we will be required to function as a conventional amphibious warfare force. We'll have to hold close offshore. We'll have to launch large numbers of aircraft around the clock and we'll have to put boats and amphitracks over the side. Generally, we will have to advertise that the United States has a large block of combatants somewhere that we shouldn't have any. We'll blow our cover, Ma'am, sky high."

All three men went quiet. It was obvious that they had reached their own consensus before summoning her into the loop for the blood call.

Amanda looked down at the cool gray tabletop and lightly rubbed her forehead with her fingertips. Elliot MacIntyre would be in Darwin by now, en route to join them. It would be easy enough to kick this upstairs to him or to fuss around with busywork considerations until the intervention window closed and the whole question became irrelevant. But she'd never worked that way and she wasn't going to start now.

"Gentlemen," she said, "to put it bluntly, shit happens. Today, it's going to happen in Singarajah. Given the current parameters of the situation, we cannot effectively intervene without destroying the present and future utility of Phantom Force. Monitor and report, that's all we can do."

Her people agreed with their continued silence. There wasn't much to be said when you had just condemned several thousand men, women and children to death.

Amanda was about to dismiss the O Group when the overhead speaker clicked. "Briefing Room, this is drone control. Be advised we are observing an anomalous situation developing in the Singaraja approaches."

Amanda lifted her head and keyed the mike of her command headset. "Drone Control, this is the Captain. Define the situation."

"It looks like a large cluster of native coastal shipping, Ma'am. But it almost looks like a convoy. They seem to be running in formation."

"A formation?" Amanda's brows knit. "Let's see the imaging."

"Aye aye. Putting it up."

The main wall screen flicked between views to an overhead of a glistening azure-green ocean. A ragged formation of Indonesian Pinisi, nine vessels in all in three triple columns, appeared. Some were classic, schooner-rigged craft. Others were mastless, motorized coaster conversions with blocky deckhouses. All of them were churning toward the mouth of Singarajah harbor with a definite air of businesslike determination.

"What the hell is that all about?" Beltrain murmured.

"I'm not certain," Amanda replied, her eyes narrowing. "Drone control, this is the captain. Can you zoom in on the first schooner in the center column?"

In reply, the screen image centered on the designated ship, boxing and expanding until it filled the plasma screen.

It was one of the schooners, a big craft for a Pinisi. Slim-hulled, low set and rakish, its gaff sails were furled and it was running on a powerful auxiliary diesel. There was also a blue glint of polished steel at its bow and stern. A battery of heavy machineguns had been mounted and manned on its forecastle and raised quarterdeck. Men, armed men, were also clustered in the waist of the ship, assault rifles and grenade launchers apparent.

"That's a Bugi raider," Amanda murmured.

"Lord God Almighty," Quillain said. "This is the limit! Don't those folks in town have enough on their plate as it is? Now they got the damn pirates movin' in on them."

Amanda shook her head. "No, only those three column leaders look to be armed vessels. Those other *pinisi* are just standard motor coasters. It's like an escorted convoy ..."

Amanda pushed her chair back and got to her feet. "Drone control," she said, stepping closer to the wall screen. "Maximum magnification on the quarterdeck of that lead schooner!"

Again the camera imaging scaled up and refocused, centering on the helm station of the raider and the cluster of men gathered around it. One man strikingly stood out, standing literally head and shoulders above the other Bugi. Clad in jeans and a faded safari shirt, he carried a pistol belted around his waist and he was gesticulating vigorously as if giving orders.

"Harconan," Amanda breathed.

"What?" Beltrain looked from the screen to Amanda and back again. "You mean that's the guy we were sent after?"

"Yep," Stone Quillain nodded. "Sure enough. That is the gentleman in question."

Arkady keyed his headset. "Air One, this is the CAG! Do we have a clear horizon to launch? Roger that! Arm and spot an anti-shipping strike on the lifts. Expedite!"

Amanda whipped around. "No! Wait! Belay that order!"

250

The aviator looked up, a scowl on his face. "Captain, we have a clear shot at our primary target! This is the guy we were sent here to take out!"

She lifted her hand. "I know what our orders read, Arkady, and I know this man is our target! But right now he might be something else!"

"What are you talkin' about, Skipper?" Stone interjected, his voice low and cautious.

The three men could see Amanda's mind racing as she studied the plasma screen. She reached up and tapped Harconan's image with a fingernail. "This man is indeed our designated objective. But he's also the solution to the mess in Singaraja and we are not going to do a damn thing to interfere with him." She turned back to face her officers. "Don't you see? That's an evacuation fleet. Harconan has come here to pull those refugees out!"

"How do you know that, Captain?" Beltrain asked.

"It's the only thing that makes any sense at all, Dix. It's the only reason he'd surface like this! I've been working this question with Chris and Admiral MacIntyre. The growing body of evidence is that we have another faction attempting to achieve dominance in this conflict. A bloodbath on Bali is not part of the Harconan game plan. Here's the proof! He's actively fighting it."

Stone mused, "Yeah, I can see it. That big son of a bitch might be a son of a bitch but I never figured him to be that big of a son of a bitch."

"That's one way to put it, Stone. And just now Harconan has the sea lift and the boots to put on the ground to do what we can't."

"Well, that might resolve the Singaraja situation anyway," Beltrain said. "At least if he can get them off before those Hindu mobs start moving in on the port. If those pirates and the Balinese mix it up, we could still get the blood, guts and feathers."

"Now that's something we can do something about." Amanda turned to her CAG. "Arkady, we will need that strike flight of yours – but armed for riot suppression. We can take Harconan down later. For now, we're going to give him air support!"

The raider eased alongside the ferry pier, its engine backing with a grumble of reversing propellers. There were willing hands waiting to catch the schooner's mooring lines, but the majority of the crowd drew back from the grim phalanx of armed men that stormed down the gangway.

"Captain Arimbi, have your men cover the streets leading in from the city – but have them stay close!" Harconan bellowed down from the quarterdeck. "Try and hold any mobs back by shooting over their heads. No killing unless you're forced into it. And I will personally cut the throat of any man who loots!"

"Yes, raja." The raider's captain's reply was prompt enough, but still somewhat bemused by the decidedly unusual role being thrust upon him and his crew. "It will be done."

Harconan had to agree. Those weren't the orders a Captain Kidd or a Blackbeard would have given, but times and circumstances change.

He rested a hand on the sun-heated breech of the schooner's .50 caliber stern mount and watched his other vessels nose into the harbor piers.

His own place in the scheme of things was changing as well, but Harconan wasn't sure what his new position would eventually be. He had a new enemy, but he didn't know the identity of this new foe or of his intentions and resources. He knew only that his goals were not Harconan's own and that they must be resisted. He also knew that the fight must begin here and now.

This evacuation of the Muslim refugees from Bali was a gesture, a temporary damming of the flood of blood that his new opponent desired. But after that, what?

For the first time in his life, Makara Harconan wasn't sure – and uncertainty was a frightening thing.

His planned implosion of the Indonesian government and state had been a comparatively simple matter. The creation of chaos is always easy when compared with the restoration of order. And now he,

Harconan, must restore some semblance of order to a situation spinning wildly beyond all control.

He needed to take counsel with someone expert in the art of order. He needed to find new, uncontaminated allies. But, just as he didn't know who his enemies were, he didn't know who his new friends might be.

*You tried to warn me, didn't you, Amanda. You knew what I was letting out of its cage in my hubris and pride.*

Abruptly, he was diverted by a call from the lookout at the schooner's masthead. "Aircraft warning! Warplanes! Coming from the north!"

His brooding thoughts erased, Harconan stepped back from the heavy machine gun, letting the crew clear their weapon for action. Whipping his pair of binoculars up from around his neck, he scanned the northern sky.

There they were. Half a dozen of them, flying in a dispersed "loose deuce" formation. Helicopters, moving fast, exceptionally fast. Gunships, American-made AH-1 Cobras. But Indonesia hadn't purchased the AH-1. The only force in these waters flying the Cobra would be the United States Marines ...

But the American Marines didn't fly any Cobra that looked like that!

The leader of the weird flight pulled out slightly ahead of its formation and dipped. The damn thing was dipping wings that it shouldn't have! The strange machine's pilot was making the universal aviator's signal for a friendly aircraft.

Harconan tore his walkie-talkie out of its belt holster. "Hold your fire!" he roared to other captains of his squadron. "This is Harconan! Hold your fire! I command it! Hold your fire!"

Refugee and Bugi seamen alike goggled up as the black flight shrieked overhead, not even sounding like conventional helicopters. The aircraft ignored the evacuation fleet, obviously intent on other business in Singaraja.

And then Harconan knew. He knew without the faintest shadow of a doubt.

"Amanda."

\*

The waterfront of Singaraja flowed under the nose of the Jeannie II as the suppression flight crossed the coast.

"Little Stinker Lead to Stinker Flights. Like we briefed it, people. Pom Pom, your flight has the center temple. BoJoe, you guys have the north. Pink, you're with me. We'll take the big one."

"Affirmative, lead."

"Rog that, Commander."

"Right with you, Vince."

"Good enough, guys. Bestow the choke and puke and beat it out of there. Watch for ground fire. They're not going to be happy with us here presently. Little Stinker Flights ... Ready? Break, break and break!"

Wingtips snapped up as the two-aircraft elements peeled off, the white cylindrical bomblet dispensers prominent on their hard points.

Arkady thumbed the coolie hat switch on the velocity controller, calling up his weapons displays and arming his own dispenser pods. Flicking a glance down at the ground, he picked up Gajah Mada Road, the main highway south from the port area. Then, swaying the SPEED Cobra in line with the highway, he followed it toward his own objective.

In the spare seconds he had before acquiring the target, he mused that he had undertaken any number of peculiar missions for king and country, especially under the command of Amanda Garrett – but he had never been ordered to bomb a church before.

"This is Little Stinker lead. Watch your dispersal interval, Pink," he murmured into his oxygen mask. "Descending to drop altitude."

"Still with you, lead."

Arkady pushed the SPEED Cobra into a shallow dive. Ahead, beyond the city cemetery, lay the pura dalem of Singaraja, the temple of Shiva the Destroyer.

The temple grounds, the terraces surrounding them and Gajah Mada Road, were jammed with people, a mob-to-be working itself up into a religious frenzy for the final march on the massed Muslim refugees in the port.

This mob was the target to be destroyed.

Destroyed, but not killed.

Arkady caught the flow of motion across the surface of the crowd as thousands of faces turned up towards the black monsters that came intruding out of the sky, the howl and growl of rotors and turbines crashing through their chimes, drums and chanting. Around the perimeter of the massed populace, he saw a few scattered flaming sparks and he heard the 'tack' of a rifle bullet glancing off ceramic fuselage armor.

Third World mobs did so dearly love to shoot at helicopters.

Then they were cutting across drop zone at the keyed altitude. "Little Stinker lead is in and hot!" he chanted into his hot mike, triggering his sub-munitions dispensers. "Drop! Drop! Drop!"

A soft patter of detonations rippled from beneath the wings of the SPEED Cobras and hundreds upon hundreds of baseball sized bomblets sprayed out in their wakes, raining down upon the people massed around the temple.

As each bomblet was hurled from its launcher tube, a tiny chemical cell activated within it. A supercharged relation to simple kitchen baking soda, the cell fizzed into life as the bomblet fell, pressurizing the thin plastic shell from within. While still twenty to thirty feet in the air, the shells popped like a multitude of soap bubbles, each bomblet spraying out a cupful of a clear oily fluid.

The released fluid pattered down upon the assembled multitude, the fall catching the majority of the people clustered around the temple. For a few moments, nothing happened beyond a puzzled exchange of looks. Then the biochemical witch's brew began to react with the oxygen in the atmosphere.

It was a peculiarity of twenty-first century warfare that, in an age when mass annihilation was available in an unprecedented number of formats, one of the primary concerns of the modern First World military was the development and employment of new and improved ways of not killing people.

In a world of asymmetrical warfare, peacekeeping had become as critical a military evolution as warfighting. Terrorists and tyrants alike cowered behind the innocent and helpless; "holding babies over their heads" had become a favorite defensive tactic. As a counter, non-lethal weaponry had become the new cutting edge. Weaponry such as the CCD-N (Chemical Crowd Dispersant Non-lethal) 6 "Pigeye" cluster munition.

Chemical crowd dispersants such as tear gas and red pepper spray had been an anti-riot mainstay for police agencies around the world – but Pigeye took simple teargas a broad step further.

Within seconds of exposure, skin began to tingle and then to itch and burn, first aggravating, then maddeningly and finally agonizingly, the ultimate combination of sunburn and Alaskan mosquito bite. Eyes began to water, then itch, and then swell shut, tears gushing.

Noses gushed with a massive flood of mucus. Genetically engineered neural trigger agents carried by tissue permeation compounds crawled through skin and entered the bloodstream. As they reached the brain, the triggers targeted their selected ganglia centers. Intense, writhing, nausea struck with accompanying explosive vomiting. Bowels and sphincters released beyond the control of their owners.

And, over everyone touched, rose literally the most appalling stench conceivable, a fiendishly blended perfumer's nightmare of the scents instinctively repellant to the human animal, distilled into their most concentrated form. Skunk squared.

There was no protection from the riot agent barring a full MOPP biochemical warfare suit – and, barring the massive application of detergent and hot water, there was no escape from the effect until the volatiles of the compounds had completely evaporated in somewhere between one and two hours.

And Pigeye was not simply an area weapon. The rioters were not merely affected by the ghastly miasma; they carried it with them, inescapably bonded to their own living flesh.

The two-fold intent of Pigeye was simple: to break up the dangerous massed humanity of a riot by making the presence of the rioters intolerable even to each other, and to destroy the focus of those rioters by making them so totally miserable that any conceivable political or emotional motivation was irrelevant.

The Little Stinker flights climbed away from the city, circling to observe the effect of the dispersal attacks. Below them, the mobs seemed to explode outward as the individuals involved frantically attempted to get as far away from each other as possible. A faint ghost of the stench at ground level penetrated the strike group's cockpits, triggering a hasty tightening of oxygen mask straps.

"I think I'd rather be hit with napalm, thank you," Pink Pinkerton commented over the radio link.

*

The same scene played out across the screens in the Joint Operations Command Center. Amanda couldn't suppress her chuckle.

"I think we've bought our friend Harconan all the time he'll need for an unmolested evacuation." She keyed her headset. "This is Star Child to Little Stinker Flight. Mission accomplished. Very well done. We are still clear horizon. Return to base."

"Roger that, Star Child," Arkady's distant jubilant voice replied over the squawk box. "Smelly but victorious, we are inbound."

"Before we stand down from flight stations, I'd like to get somethin' else done," Stone interjected as the channel shut down.

"What's that, Stone?"

"I'd like to put another Mariner drone up to park on this ol' boys quarterdeck." Stone pointed toward the Bugi flagship centered on the main screen. "A dedicated mission. Now that we got Harconan dead in our sights, I want to make extra special sure we can't lose him until we're ready to take him."

Amanda caught the shadow of sadness before it could reach her face. "That's next on the agenda," she replied. "From the look of things, Harconan is embarking some of the refugees aboard his flagship, so we can't simply blow him out of the water. But, given the best speed of those *pinisi*, there are no off-Bali evacuation points they can reach before nightfall. We'll move in and take him after dark. I'd like to do it non-lethally if possible."

Quillain nodded. "I don't think it's goin' to be much of a deal at all

257

Skipper. I've been sittin' here working it out. It should be a pretty simple rush and board."

He consulted the yellow legal pad in front of him, already covered with a collection of notes in his loose, looping handwriting. "We'll have the helos hose him down good with flashbang grenades and Pigeyes, drivin' everybody below decks. Then we'll run an AAAV in under his stern and bust off his rudder so he can't maneuver. Then we'll bring the RIBS alongside with the SEAL and Force Recon teams. That load of passengers will hamper the fighting capacity of his crew just about as bad or worse than it will us. Unless he wants to be a totally suicidal asshole about things, not too many folks should get hurt."

"He's not suicidal, Stone," she replied quietly. "At least not when it comes to other people's lives."

"How about the other ships in his flotilla?" Dix Beltrain inquired.

Stone shrugged. "We herd 'em off with more flashbangs and Pigeyes and put rockets and cannon fire across their bows if they don't get the message. After that, if they want to push the fight beyond all common sense, it'll be on their heads."

"True enough," Amanda cut him off, her words abrupt. "Dix, recover Little Stinker Flight and launch the dedicated Mariner as Stone requested. Maintain continuous covert observation of Harconan's ship from high altitude. After the Bugi squadron sails, commence shadowing, keeping us below their horizon at all times."

"Aye aye, Ma'am."

"Stone, work up your ops plan for the boarding. Co-coordinate it with Mr. Beltrain and with Mr. Arkady to select your optimum engagement point." She glanced at her wristwatch. "We'll have another O Group at 1900 Hours to finalize the strike package." Suddenly, the overhead loudspeaker interrupted, "Captain, this is the Watch Officer. We have an emergency, ma'am." The voice was urgent in its inflection.

Amanda responded instantly, "This is the Captain! What's going on?"

"We've been ordered to return to Jakarta will all possible speed, ma'am. A military coup has been launched against the Kediri government and the US Embassy is under attack."

# Part Four

# Primary Conflict Initiated

President Ahsan Kediri was a weary, middle-aged man. At one time, not long before, he had been vigorous and solidly set with hair that had still been black. The gauntness, the graying, the slump to his shoulders had come with his presidency. The tension, the long hours, the perpetual string of compromises with others and with his own conscience, had worn him down.

He had been a rarity in Indonesian governmental circles: a national leader who had not risen from the highly political Army officers' cadre. By profession, he had been a banker who had entered civil service out of a genuine desire to change his nation for the better. But instead, the nation had changed him, distorting the idealism he had brought with him to the office. "Making do" had become the watchword of his administration –and, as his nation had slid ever deeper into its apparently terminal crisis, Kediri wished with a growing frequency that he had never heard of politics or of the Presidency.

Now the American Ambassador stood before his desk telling him that, at long last, it might be coming to its end. In a way, he should have been relieved – but there was still a flicker of the old idealism left, a stubbornness to not submit to the final indignity of defeat.

"The threat of a military coup is a sword held over the head of every Indonesian administration," Kediri replied. "I cannot abandon my duties in the face of a mere prospect."

His private office was a testament to this threat. Windowless and buried in the heart of the main building of the presidential palace compound, its tastefully expensive blend of European and Asian interior decor only partially concealed the fact that it was as much bunker as office.

At the moment, Kediri was alone with the two American diplomatic representatives, at their request.

"Nor does my government desire that you do so, Mr. President,"

Ambassador Goodyard replied. "We have supported your administration from the beginning of this crisis and we continue to do so now. That's why Commander Rendino and I are here, to present you with the evidence we have uncovered indicating that a military coup against your government may be imminent and to urge you to take due precautions."

"What do you propose I do?" Kediri replied. "Abandon my post, my nation, in this time of disaster? I cannot! It would be the equivalent of surrender to these selfsame revolutionary factions."

"If I may interject, Mr. President." It was Commander Rendino, Goodyard's military advisor – who, surprisingly to Kediri, was a young golden-haired woman. "We do not propose any kind of abandonment. We only suggest that you shift your point of authority out of the capital to one of your garrisons on one of the outlying islands where it will be easier to maintain both governmental control and your personal security. Our Intelligence indicates that the major threat against your administration may be located here on Java and on Sumatra, the primary islands."

Kediri shook his head. "That would also be out of the question! Java is Indonesia and Jakarta is Java! Fleeing Java would fully be the equivalent of fleeing the country!"

The young woman murmured something under her breath, something like, "So much for *Bhinneka Tunggal ika.*"

"Mister President," Ambassador Goodyard resumed, "is it so inconceivable that this threat is not real?"

Kediri shook his head. "No, Mr. Ambassador, not in the least. I readily fear that such an event may, indeed, be possible and imminent – my own Intelligence resources are not so as inept as you may perceive – but, as a very wise man once said, I must not take the counsel of my fears. I must trust in those in my service that I am certain are faithful to Indonesia and to myself."

"Mr. President," the young woman said slowly, "are you certain you know just who those faithful are?"

Kediri opened his mouth to reply but hesitated, groping for a response that even he could believe. "I have personally ... aided in the selection of the current senior officer corps of my military, men chosen for their dedication to the people and the government."

"But which government, sir?" the young woman asked pointedly. "Theirs or yours?"

Kediri escaped into confusion. "I do not understand you, miss."

"Commander Rendino," she replied. "We have evidence that major military operations have been conducted involving units of the Indonesian military that are not being ordered by or reported to your Ministry of Defense. We can point out a series of recent redeployments of Indonesian military units that make no strategic sense, except to weaken your government's hold on Java and Sumatra. We have assessments that indicate certain phases of this current round of civil unrest are not being instituted by the Harconan group. There are even indications certain units of the Indonesian military known to be faithful to your government have been fired on and destroyed by other units that most certainly are not! Mr. President, putting it bluntly, the fix is in – unless you act now, you're screwed!"

"How do you know these things?" Kediri's voice rose.

The young woman gave a dainty, impatient snort. "Because we've been spying on you, of course."

No one, including Ahsan Kediri, would ever know how he would have responded to that statement.

A sudden shrill electronic tone sounded in the room. The American woman stiffened in her parade rest, then whipped a small device like a cellular phone out of a belt holster. Flipping the device open, she studied its small screen.

"We've just had a security breach in here," she announced. "A burst bug just went off in this office."

"A burst bug? What do you mean, Commander?" Ambassador Goodyard demanded.

"It's a sophisticated spying device, sir," the woman replied. "It digitally records conversations or data and then transmits them to a remote station in a high-speed microburst. They don't register on a conventional bug sniffer." Apparently, the young woman's equipment was unconventional, for she was intently studying the north wall of the presidential office. "They conduct data dumps either at a preset timer or on a remote command. One of them downloaded within twenty feet of us just a few seconds ago. Either this was sheer coincidence or somebody is extremely interested in what has just been said in this room."

"That is impossible, Commander," Kediri said, using anger to mask his sudden upsurge of fear. "This room has been thoroughly inspected by my own security staff."

"I'd give those words very careful consideration, Mr. President." She clapped the faceplate of the sensor shut and returned it to her belt. "Ambassador Goodyard, we are at risk and we are out of here. I am invoking security protocols and we are returning to the Embassy immediately."

"Do you think we may have a problem?" Goodyard asked, frowning.

"We'll know in the very near future, sir, likely after somebody unfolds and listens to that download." She looked across the desk at the President of Indonesia. "President Kediri, I'm only a junior naval officer and a guest in your country. I have no official standing whatsoever outside of my service and it is not my place to advise the elected leader of a sovereign nation. But if you would be willing to accept a friendly suggestion from a concerned onlooker, run like hell!"

"Asses and elbows, guys!" Christine snapped as she strode into her ad hoc operations center. "I want all stations manned! We may have problems! Drone monitors, pick up your real-time scanning of all Jakarta garrison sites. I want to know about any troop movements."

"Would you mind having an interested observer, Commander?" Ambassador Goodyard asked grimly, following her into the Embassy's converted reception room. "If anything's going to happen, I suspect you will know about it first."

"You're more than welcome to stay as long as you like, Mr. Ambassador. We'd set you up with a workstation but I suspect it's going to get a little busy in here."

"I can look over shoulders, Commander. Just tell me what I need to know and, if I get in the way, just shove me to one side."

"As you wish, sir," Christine smiled back briefly. This gentleman was learning the ropes.

Christine crossed to one of the field desks that had been set up in the big room and spoke with the systems operator behind it. "What are we getting out of the presidential complex? Gate specifics for unusual or priority traffic out of the presidential office or on the reserved presidential links during the last ... oh, twenty minutes."

"Yes, ma'am," the SO replied, her fingers dancing across the keys of her mil-spec laptop. "Yes, we have a usage spike – on the lines from the public relations office but using the presidential use codes. Calls to the Foreign Minister ... and the Chairman of the Golkar Political Party. President Kediri made the calls personally."

"Access transcripts of the calls."

Slim fingers danced again. Lines of computer translation flowed across the screen. "The Chairman and the Foreign Minister have been ordered to report to the Presidential Palace immediately."

"You've penetrated the Indonesian government's security to that extent?" Goodyard said, slightly awed and a little disturbed.

"Um hum," the Intel replied absently. "We can even tell you how many times the presidential throne gets flushed in a day."

"Hm," the Ambassador grunted, thinking of his own office. "Whatever happened to 'Gentlemen don't read each other's mail'?"

"If we can do all of this, Mr. Ambassador, just think of what someone who actually has access to the palace can do."

"If that *was* a bug over in Kediri's office, do you think our visit may have triggered something?"

She shook her head. "I don't know. Let's assume the potential coup masters have Kediri zeroed and wired and are waiting to take him out at the appropriate moment. If they think that Kediri might be about to do a fast fade on them ... We'll have to see."

"Commander Rendino, we have more Presidential traffic out of the Palace," the systems operator interjected. "It's to the Presidential flight at Halim Air Force Base. Translating ... It's a request for the President's aircraft to be prepared for take-off. No destination given. Now we have a request for an immediate helicopter lift out from the Palace complex ... Halam acknowledges ... A helicopter is being scrambled."

"He believes us. He's running," Goodyard commented.

"Sometimes the better part of valor, sir." Christine removed her glasses from her blouse pocket. Settling them on her nose. she removed a Krackle bar from a dish filled with Hershey's miniatures that had been set on the edge of the field desk. Unwrapping it, she munched thoughtfully.

*

It might have been an old time Western movie before the big showdown. The largest public square in a city of ten million people was empty, occupied only by its heroic statuary. The golden tip of "Sukarno's last erection" glinted dully. The mullahs called no one to prayer at Istiqial Mosque. The tourists were long gone from the Hotel Borobudur International. The only movement to be seen was the pacing of the nervous sentries at the perimeter roadblocks.

"Situational change at the Sunter bivouac site!" a voice called from across the reception room.

"What do you have?" Christine snapped.

"Troop movement," the systems operator replied, his field terminal linked to the sensor download of a circling Mariner drone. "A ground column. 4X4s and light armored fighting vehicles – a heavily reinforced company, maybe a rump battalion. They're making their turn in toward the central city, advancing down Jalan Agung Boulevard."

"Do you have any unit IDs?"

"From that garrison site, they'd be elements of the 137th *Polici* Special Security Battalion and the 17th motorized brigade. These guys are moving fast."

"Do you know these people?" Goodyard inquired.

"They aren't part of the regular city garrison force," Christine murmured, almost to herself. "They're outfits brought in as reinforcements during the civil unrest. It would be a natural move to reinforce palace security at a time like this. Drone control, keep that column covered. Communications, have we had any traffic between the Palace complex security office and the Suntir garrison site?"

"No, Ma'am. Nothing showing on the logs – but we do have pertinent traffic on the Jakarta police net. One of their tactical commanders is asking his headquarters who the hell these guys are?"

Christine frowned. "I'd call that a big uh-oh. Communications, ring up the Palace Complex security commander. Discreetly ask if he knows anything about an inbound armored column."

The Bahasa-speaking Green Beret manning the communications desk lifted a phone to his ear and hit a predial button, then a second, then a third.

"Commander, the Palace complex phone lines have gone dead." The Beret took another moment to consult his tactical display. "All telecommunications in the capital district have just crashed, land line and cellular."

"A milspec cascade jammer has just come on-line somewhere close by," the signal Intelligence guard announced excitedly. "A big one. Standard radio is down! "

"Let's escalate that to an ah shit! This is it. They're isolating the Palace and the Ministries." Christine turned to Ambassador Goodyard. "Sir, I suggest you get through to Washington on the satellite link and advise them that the government of President Kediri is falling. Fa'sure we got us a coup!"

*

The military coup was an art form in Indonesia. Unlike the United States Military, where it is hammered into the heads of the officer cadre that they *must* remain answerable to the civilian government and that they *must* not dirty their hands with politics, the Indonesian military considered it an aspect of their duty to set the civil government to rights if needs be.

Unfortunately, the exact definition of "to rights" is somewhat open-ended.

When their radios were jammed, the Jakarta police detachments sensed what was happening – and weary, sweating men mentally flipped a five-rupiah piece, deciding which side of the line they would come down on.

*

The weight of Christine's Interceptor vest dug into her shoulders and perspiration prickled down her spine. "Get that parabolic mike set up," she commanded, "and the long-range video rig. I want to see and hear what's going on over there."

The Intelligence detail wasn't alone on the compound wall. The Embassy had gone to full alert, with all perimeter gates closed and both the FAST platoon and its own security detail at their battle stations, their helmeted and MOLLE harnessed forms spaced along the security gangway, their weapons resting on the concrete parapet.

Christine considered donning her own K-pot helmet and decided she wasn't quite that scared yet. "Okay Owens," she called into her lip mike, "what's the latest?"

"The armored column is about a mile out, ma'am, coming on fast."

"What about Kediri's evacuation helo? Is it inbound?"

"It hasn't launched, ma'am. There's no activity around the presidential hangars at all."

The Intel grimaced. "Great! The fix is in there too. Have you advised the *Shenandoah*?"

"Affirmative. We're giving them a real time feed on all events. Captain Garrett advises that she's moving to support us with all possible speed."

"Have you been able to get through to the palace or to the Ministry of Defense?"

"No ma'am. All local commo is still down. We could send a courier across the square?"

Christine rejected the idea. "Negative. We're way out of time for that."

"What's the latest, Commander?"

Christine looked up to find Ambassador Goodyard standing on the security walkway beside her. He'd shed his suit coat in favor of a flak vest and his tie had been yanked down impatiently.

"Ambassador, you shouldn't be up here just now."

"Damn it! Don't start that with me, Commander. This is my embassy and I intend to see what's happening to it."

Christine was in no position to argue. "It's your call, sir."

He ran a hand through his thinning hair. "Thank you, commander. Now what's the situation?'

"Things could start to get noisy in a few minutes, sir. If they do, duck!"

"Activity at the Jalan Perwire street check point!" a sentry at the corner outpost yelled.

Christine and the Ambassador swung their field glasses onto the north-eastern corner of the square. The lead vehicles of the mobile column, a Cadillac Gage Ranger armored command car and a scorpion light tank, had arrived at the police roadblock. An argument could be seen going on between the checkpoint commander and the occupants of the Ranger.

The confrontation didn't last long. The men manning the barricade didn't have a tank backing them up. Soon, troops from the column could be seen disarming the police.

The barricade was drawn back and the column rolled through into the square. The duty officer's voice spoke in Christine's headset. "The armored column is dispersing. Elements are maneuvering on the side streets to surround the palace complex."

"Very well, maintain your surveillance."

A dozen vehicles had drawn up across the front wall of the palace grounds, blocking the main gates. Ground troops dismounted and fanned out. The sound of a voice distorted by a loudspeaker could be heard echoing across the square.

The man on the parabolic mike winced and lifted his headset away from his ears. "They're calling on the criminal Kediri to surrender himself to the Will of Allah and justice of the Indonesian people."

Christine sighed. "Once, just once, I'd like to hear one of these outfits just come out and say, 'Yo, dude, you're out of here!' But no, they've always got to do the deathless prose for the ages."

Goodyard lowered his binoculars for a moment. "Excuse me, Commander, but this is my first military coup. Are they always this ... polite?"

"It depends, sir. And I don't hear any fat ladies singing yet."

The amplified voice repeated its demand three times, then fell silent, a silence that protracted painfully. Then the main palace gates began to draw open.

"Show's over," someone announced, prematurely as it turned out.

Suddenly, from half a dozen firing slits on the palace walls, automatic weapons opened up, raking the coup column. Infantrymen crumpled under the fire storm and vehicle commanders died in their turrets.

"Get down!" Christine shoved the ambassador to one side and below the balustrade as bullets snapped and whickered overhead. Back on her knees, she got her binoculars out just in time to see a big Mercedes

270

limousine roar out of the Palace gate to plow into the two Land Rovers blocking the exit.

Given the way the two military vehicles spun out of the way, the Mercedes must have been a heavily armored security vehicle. The point was proven as teargas sprayed from concealed vents under its frame and submachine gun muzzles flamed from gun ports under the windows.

Two more limousines tore out through the gap created by the first, likewise streaming gunfire and tear gas. In an instant, the entire square became a war zone. The vehicles in the rebel column returned fire, turrets and ring mounts traversing after the fleeing cars. The gun positions in the palace continued to engage, and now some of the other police outposts around the perimeter of the square were opening up, tracer streams intertwining across the open spaces and ricocheting off the statuary.

The low-velocity 90mm cannon of one of the Scorpion tanks chuffed angrily and one of the limousines was lifted off of its wheels, thrown into a flaming death roll. The other two cars continued their headlong race across the square. Swerving wildly to evade gunfire and ignoring curbs and roadways, it was apparent they were heading for the US Embassy.

*Where the hell else did they have to go?* Christine thought wildly.

She hunkered beside Ambassador Goodyard, who still lay sprawled on the gangway. "Mr. Ambassador!" she yelled over the gunfire. "We need a command decision right now. What's left of the Kediri government is headed right for the Embassy. I suspect they're going to ask for sanctuary. What are your orders, sir?"

It was the moment Randolph Goodyard would be remembered for. "Open the gates!" he bellowed, drawing himself up. "Open the damn gates!"

The heavy steel bar grillwork of the embassy entrance retracted into the blast walls and the anti-vehicle barriers sank flush with the ground. Barely slowing down, the two bullet scarred sedans tore into the refuge of the Embassy compound, the gates and barriers closing behind them.

A line of enraged armored fighting vehicles were now advancing across Freedom Square toward the Embassy, and the slugs that dug chips from the compound walls were no longer accidental. One of the light tanks coughed out another shell, its detonation cratering but not piercing the thick concrete.

"Return fire!" the FAST platoon leader yelled. A Predator anti-tank rocket streaked away from an embrasure and the Scorpion dissolved into a black and orange fireball.

The siege of the Jakarta Embassy had begun.

There was no conferencing among the freighter captains. No group decision developed. It was just time to cut and run. Civil sideband and satcom channels crackled with radio messages to owners and brokers.

*Local situation untenable! Damn the contracts! We're pulling out!*

Coasters, schooners and small craft streamed out of Jakarta port. Burdened with refugees fleeing from the convulsing capital, they fled past the anchorage, seeking the refuge of the outlying islands and the open waters of the Java Sea.

*All hands turn to! Stand by to heave round! Engine room, stand by to answer bells!*

A pair of Indonesian Air Force jets screamed low over the sea. Reversing, they circled the anchorage, the rocket pods under their wings glinting in the fading sunlight. They orbited twice, as if thoughtfully eyeing the nervous merchant vessels, then banked off toward the mainland.

Anchor lights flicked off. Running lights came on. The fleeing freighters moved in silhouette against a flaming twilight sky.

"Where away, captain?"

"The fastest course out of this hell hole! Engines ahead full!"

The merchantmen scattered, heading northwest for the Karimata Strait, southwest for the Selat Sunda, northeast for Makassar Passage. A handful of refugee boats too small or ill-equipped to make the run to safety trailed in their broadening wakes, desperate passengers waving handfuls of rupiahs, begging for a passage out to anywhere.

The urge for flight was becoming infectious, instinctive, like wildlife fleeing before a coming hurricane. A nation was in its death throws.

Only one lone ship raced up the Javanese coast, inbound to Jakarta.

Goodyard had donned his conservatively cut blue pinstripe – not the new tropical weight he'd purchased before being assigned to Jakarta but the old reliable that had served him well back in Lincoln, Nebraska, a crisply unworn Brooks Brothers white shirt and, for luck, the indigo tie that had been a birthday gift from Caroline.

The role he was about to play was more daunting than any he had ever imagined for himself. For the next few minutes, he must be the living embodiment of the United States of America. He must speak for the most powerful nation on Earth and possibly set its policy in this developing crisis. It was the legacy of Ambassadorship that extended back to Benjamin Franklin and all of the cutting-edge telecommunications in the world couldn't ease the burden or the responsibility. Goodyard really hadn't considered that factor when he'd accepted his appointment, but he was more than aware of it now.

He was seated at his desk, a silver pen in his hand, when the knock came at his office door. "Come in."

He didn't look up from his writing as Commander Rendino and the Embassy Marine Detachment leader entered, ushering in a third figure, an Indonesian Army Officer. The two American military personnel were in camouflage. The Indonesian was in semi-dress uniform, decoration ribbons bright on his chest and an empty pistol holster at his belt. His posture was nervously belligerent.

Goodyard continued to write, keeping the man waiting for a good minute. Then he deliberately set his pen aside and looked up.

"This embassy has been fired upon and has been surrounded by hostile troops," he said coldly and without preamble. "This situation is totally unacceptable and I demand to know who is responsible for this outrage."

The Indonesian who had been intent on making his own demands was jolted by this preemptive strike. "I am Major Tetari of the

274

Indonesian Army of National Reunification. We have no desire for any conflict with the United States, but this embassy is harboring a criminal wanted for crimes against the people of Indonesia." His English was accented but precise.

"I know of no such criminal currently within this embassy," Goodyard replied. "Our embassies are not havens for such individuals."

Major Tetari swallowed. "We request, in the name of the people of Indonesia, that you turn over the former President Ahsan Kediri for arrest and trial on the charges of corruption, terrorism and malfeasance in office."

"I know of no such charges currently held against the current President Kediri by either the People's Consultative Assembly of Indonesia or by any other recognized judicial tribunal anywhere," Goodyard replied. "Nor does the United States recognize the existence of any organization called the Indonesian Army of National Reunification. As we hold that Indonesia is, in fact, one nation united under a valid, elected government, an Army of Reunification is both redundant and unnecessary. Now, we request – no, correction, we demand – that the hostile forces arrayed against this embassy be withdrawn immediately!"

"This will be done when the criminal Kediri has been ..."

"We have already disposed of the question of President Kediri's criminality, Major," Goodyard cut the rebel officer off sharply. "The United States continues to recognize President Kediri and his administration as the lawful government of Indonesia. As a friend and ally of the United States, he is welcome to remain as a guest within this embassy for as long as he chooses to stay."

Tetari swallowed and moistened his lips. "Then will you give us assurances that your guest will not be allowed to perform actions hostile to the interests of the people of Indonesia and the Army of National Reunification."

"As I stated previously, Major, the United States does not recognize the existence of the latter organization. Furthermore, as a friend and ally of the United States, President Kediri is welcome to utilize the facilities of this embassy in whatever fashion he so sees fit to further the interests of the legitimate Indonesian government."

"That is unacceptable," the Indonesian blurted out. "We insist that ..."

"You may insist on nothing, Major!' Goodyard roared. "Not here and not today!"

"Our forces can take this embassy at our pleasure, Mr. Ambassador!"

"I am well aware, Major, that the damn fools of this world frequently perform acts of incredible stupidity. If your Army of National Reunification desires to prove this point, you may launch your attack at any time."

Goodyard took up his pen and returned his attention to the paper before him on the desk. "Lieutenant, I'm finished with this gentleman. You may show him out."

"Aye aye, sir," the Embassy Marine replied crisply. "Major, if you will follow me, please."

The seething Indonesian had no choice but to allow himself to be ushered from the office.

Christine Rendino lingered behind for a moment, just long enough to deliver an irreverent wink and thumbs up.

Goodyard grinned back and replied in kind.

Glancing down, he considered his fifth rewriting of "Mary had a Little Lamb."

Lake Toba, North Sumatra Provence
Sumatra
0012 Hours; Zone Time, October 30, 2008

Admiral Ketalaman stared past the faces of the other men seated around the conference table at the wall of the cavern bunker, noting the crystalline flecks glittering in the dark basalt, and the work-broken facets of the raw stone.

*Draw strength from the mountains. Be as the stone: strong, hard, impassive in the face of all adversity.*

Renewed, he let the hesitant words of the reporting officer flow over him.

"The American Ambassador refuses all negotiation over the matter of President Kediri and apparently he has the support of his government in the matter. It is also apparent that their embassy is under orders to offer armed resistance to any effort to take Kediri by force."

"They have only a handful of troops," the Islamic militia liaison interjected impatiently. "A platoon or so. Easily overwhelmed."

"Barring the fact that we would be declaring war on the United States of America," a third, more militarily realistic voice interjected dryly.

"The sword of Allah is mightier than any nation!"

"The sword of Allah be damned! We'd be biting a tiger in the ass!"

"Enough!" Ketalaman did not lift his voice but he did inject iron into it. Discipline was at its most critical in times of reversal. "This has been an unfortunate event. Kediri's continued freedom and the American intransigence are complicating factors but not insurmountable ones. They will be dealt with in due course. But first we must deal with the weakness that allowed this to happen. General Mytari, you are our Javanese Operations officer. Why was this allowed to happen? Why was Kediri allowed to reach the American Embassy?"

Ketalaman could see the general swallow in the low lighting. "It was unexpected. When our Intelligence monitors learned that the Americans were advising President Kediri of our plans and activities,

277

we were forced to launch an ad hoc operation. We were not fully prepared to seize the palace grounds at that time."

"You should have been," Ketalaman said softly. For ten heartbeats, Ketalaman held the thunderbolt over the cringing officer. "I desire that you conduct an immediate investigation into this matter and that you procure a list of the officers directly responsible for this failing. We will consider this matter further when you have done so."

"Yes sir, at once." The man whose life had just been returned to him tried to discreetly backhand the sweat from his face.

In actuality, the general's fears were groundless. Ketalaman had never had any real plans to order his death – he was a reasonably capable and dedicated officer whose death would have caused needless turbulence within his command structure – but the admiral had no intention of letting his subordinates know that.

In all probability, there was no true fault to be found in this incident. Military coups were an inexact science at best. In due course, the general would present his list of names and, in due course, Ketalaman would order their execution. Discipline would be served and the general would be an even more conscientious officer in the future.

"Now," the Admiral continued, "concerning the Kediri matter. This is a problem that may rectify itself. Even with the support of the United States, the Kediri government might still fall on its own. The administration has been critically disrupted and the majority of its senior members are either dead or in our hands. All will depend upon the response of the commanders of the outlying garrisons and island administrations. If they swear allegiance to us, or fragment into individual satraps, then the day is ours and Kediri and his allies, no matter how potent, are irrelevant. If Kediri maintains control, however, further actions must be considered."

*The Leader must always have a plan. Or at least he must give the impression he has one.*

"We will continue operations to secure the Capital area and we will continue our propaganda programs and our monitoring of the outlying islands. We must also expedite negotiations with the uncommitted commanders of the government military. We must make them see they are futilely supporting a lost cause.

"We must also tighten our perimeter around the United States Embassy in Jakarta. No one is to be allowed in or out. Kediri must not be allowed to escape again, no matter the cost or outcome. Is that understood?"

An acknowledgment rippled around the table.

"Very well," Ketalaman continued. "In twenty-four hours, we will reassess the situation. In the meantime, commence the planning and preparations for the seizure of the Jakarta embassy. If it is required, then it shall be done. We have come too far to turn back now."

This time, the acknowledging murmur was somewhat more hesitant and thoughtful.

*As the mountains, Ketalaman. Let not a hint of your own fears and reservations escape.*

"Now, to other matters. What of the Harconan strike?"

"The aircraft has launched and should be arriving over its target shortly," his aide reported, pleased to be able to report a positive event. "All is going according to plan."

"Excellent."

Tonight, Makara Harconan must become an ally, a prisoner or a dead enemy. It would be best if he could be made an ally, albeit an unwilling one. With the pirate chief's assets gathered into the fold, he, Ketalaman, would be in a far better position, even given the Kediri setback.

But, as with Kediri, there was no certainty. They had Harconan's headquarters targeted, but there was no guarantee that he would be present. There had to be a backup plan in place to cover that eventuality.

"Captain Menjual."

"Yes, Admiral?"

"I have orders for the 1st Surface Battle Squadron. Have them take immediate departure from their forward holding station and proceed with all speed to the waters off Southern Sulawesi. I will have further orders for them later."

"Here's the situation as it currently stands, sir," Van Linden said. "President Kediri, his Foreign Minister, Assistant Defense Minister and several senior members of the Peoples Conservative Assembly have reached our embassy in Jakarta and have been granted sanctuary by Ambassador Goodyard. Fighting between pro and anti-government factions of the Indonesian military is continuing within the city and is spreading rapidly throughout Java and Sumatra. Several Indonesian radio and television are announcing the overthrow of the Kediri government and the formation of a new 'Government of National Unification' under an Admiral Ketalaman of the Indonesian navy."

"What's the status of the embassy itself?" President Childress inquired. Clad in slacks, sports shirt and cardigan sweater, he looked rumpled from a hasty dressing. He sat with his elbows braced on his desk blotter, his fingers interlaced.

"They are not under fire at the moment – but the embassy compound is surrounded by Ketalaman's troops. They want Kediri and his people, but they don't quite want a shooting confrontation with the United States over it. At least not yet."

Van Linden was in a suit and tie, but his clothing showed the signs of more than a day of continuous wear. He sat deep in his chair, his shoulders slumped with exhaustion. A White House butler appeared, bearing a sliver tray with a coffee service and a small plate of pastry. Childress silently indicated the corner of the desk closest to his Secretary of State.

Van Linden allowed a cup to be poured for him and he accepted it, black. "Thank you, sir." Then he said, "We suspect we may have inadvertently triggered Ketalaman's coup prematurely. He wasn't quite ready to make his move yet. This might just give us some options."

"Just who is Ketalaman and what does his move entail?"

Van Linden frowned and took another sip of steaming coffee. "That's

280

a problem. Nobody seems to know a great deal about who Ketalaman really is. We're dealing with something of a Martin Bormann here, a secretive individual, very astute at collecting power without drawing attention to himself. We do know that he's a senior naval officer – but he's from outside the usual maritime communities of the Indonesian archipelago. He's a Sumatran from Aceh province, traditionally the seat of conservative Islam in Indonesia."

"So he's a Muslim extremist then?" the President asked.

"No, sir, we don't think so. He even comes from a Christian family. We do believe, however, that we are dealing with a consummate opportunist. We suspect Ketalaman can talk a good game of radical Islam but that he considers the radicalists simply as a useful addition to his power base. He's using them as a way to achieve his own ends, just as he's also using his military position and the Harconan revolt. "

"And those ends are?"

"We believe to seize the two primary Indonesian islands of Java and Sumatra. At least that's what his current mission intent seems to be. He's smart enough to recognize that he can't secure all of the islands in one gulp, but with a Javanese-Sumatran power base under his control, he will eventually be in a position to move outward to absorb the rest of the archipelago."

"In other words, yet another tin pot military dictator involved in a power grab."

Van Linden drained his cup and wondered briefly how much coffee he'd consumed that day. "Essentially – but an intelligent, patient, tin pot dictator. Ketalaman must have been quietly putting the infrastructure for this coup in place over a period of many years, never instigating but always preparing, waiting for some large-scale crisis that would give him his chance. Harconan's assault on the Indonesian central government played directly into his hands."

President Childress nodded and steepled his fingers. "Your Martin Bormann comparison is very apt: the quiet, patient powerful man who obtains power by swaying with circumstance."

The Secretary of State set the cup back on the tray. "When I saw the

Harconan scenario developing, I was afraid there might be someone like Ketalaman waiting in the background."

"Sometimes it's hell to be proven right," Childress grunted. "What are our options?"

"We've had a couple of lucky breaks so far. Ketalaman's move on President Kediri was advantageously timed for us, and Kediri and his people did make it to our embassy before they could be taken into custody. Thus there's still a valid Indonesian government and there are still pro-government forces in the field engaging the rebels. Ketalaman has not yet secured his power base.

"But the pro-government elements need leadership and the Indonesian government itself needs to prove that it still exists and that it is valid, both to its own people and to the world community.

"Here's our point of decision, Mr. President. Do we grant President Kediri and his people not merely refuge, but access to the communications they need to co-ordinate action against Ketalaman's forces? In effect, do we allow the Indonesian government to operate from our embassy compound?"

"The related question is how Ketalaman will react to our allowing Kediri to operate from our embassy," the President countered.

"A very good question indeed, sir. Ketalaman has already issued a demand that Kediri and his people be turned over to him – and there were certain thinly veiled threats involved. I suspect, if we allow Kediri and his people to operate, Ketalaman will order an attack on the embassy to take them out. The man has pitched his penny and has absolutely nothing to lose."

As he and as so many occupants of this office had done before, Childress brooded over his thoughts, balancing the words he must speak next.

"We've known from the beginning that the standing Indonesian government had its decided flaws, but it also had the promise of growing into something better. I can't see that promise in an expansionist military dictatorship willing to cuddle up with radical Islam. We'll stand with Kediri."

Van Linden nodded. "We're going to have to get Kediri and our people out then. Their current position is untenable. That's going to mean an escalation of involvement, Mr. President. We must assume that Ketalaman will not allow Kediri to simply waltz out of Jakarta. It will be an extraction under fire. Nor do I think we can wait very long before taking action, because Ketalaman won't wait. He will want to finish Kediri off, even if it means invading our embassy compound."

"I don't think we have worry about excessive Congressional debate in this matter," Childress replied. "No one is eager to see a new version of the Iranian hostage crisis. Will the Regional Intervention Force be able to handle the extraction mission?"

"No, sir. The RIF is fully committed at this time. Beyond that, should an overt military force move toward Jakarta, it could trigger Ketalaman's attack. However, Joint Special Operations Command has covert elements in the area that are deploying at this time ..."

The drag of the diver's bag bobbing behind him on the tether slowed Harconan's swimming slightly, but not enough to matter. His powerful crawl carried him across the course line of the Pinisi flotilla and through the interlocking wakes that streamed behind them.

Pausing to let himself float upright, he looked around to orient himself in the night, seeking for his objective. After a moment, he spotted the tall, scimitar curved bow looming against the stars, its passage foretold by the rumble of its engines, and underlined by its luminescent bow wave.

Once more, Harconan struck out, a few powerful strokes placing him directly into the path of the oncoming coaster. He lifted his head, intently gauging his distance as the cutwater hissed down on him. The bow wave burst across his face and the curve of the hull rushed past, the little converted schooner suddenly growing huge.

Harconan's fingertips brushed down the ship's wooden flank and found the knot-studded rope that trailed from the deck. Lunging, he grasped out and found himself being hauled through the sea and battered against the coaster's side.

The Nantucket sleigh ride lasted for only a few moments. Silhouetted heads peered down from the railing and waiting, willing hands draw him up and out of the water.

The decks and cabin of the vessel were crowded with refugees, but a space along the railing had been cleared for Harconan. A cluster of Bugi seamen, the majority of the *pinisi*'s crew, drew respectfully around him on the deck as he caught his breath. "I ask leave to come aboard your ship, captain," Harconan said to their leader.

"Your presence honors my ship, my chief."

Harconan clapped the shipmaster on the shoulder. "The honor is mine. You and your men did well this day. Many will live who would have perished. Now, there is no time to lose. I need a radio."

The shipmaster passed him a Chinese-made Citizens Band walkie talkie. Harconan lifted it to his face and spoke a few words into it. It was a brief, totally innocuous phrase, but every other captain in the evacuation flotilla was guarding this channel, waiting for it.

With the passage of the word, helms were swung hard over. Wakes curved as the evacuation flotilla suddenly scattered in a bomb burst maneuver, each of the nine craft swinging onto a new and widely divergent heading.

Harconan grinned to himself. Amanda had kindly come to his aid in Singaraja this afternoon, but now he must thwart her. He had no doubt as to what her real mission and intents were. It would be only a matter of time before she struck at his flagship.

He could imagine her red-haired fury at finding that he had slipped away. Her boarding parties would find nothing but an innocent Bugi schooner carrying a cargo of hapless Balinese Muslim refugees. The schooner's armament had followed him over the side. He was not certain of the capabilities of her exotic new command yet, but he could make a few educated guesses. He doubted that she would have the assets to board all of the scattering ships of the flotilla simultaneously.

And if, by chance, she did, he'd worry about it then. Either way, contesting with her again was stimulating. Freighter captain indeed!

"You may have my cabin, sir, if you would wish to rest," the coaster's shipmaster murmured.

Harconan shook his head. "That isn't necessary, Captain. Until we reach the next rendezvous, all I need is a patch of deck like any other sailor."

"If you please, my chief. It is a matter of my ship's honor and my own."

"As you wish then, Captain. You command here."

The captain's cabin was a mere dog's box behind the wheelhouse, but it came with privacy and a moderately clean towel. Harconan dried himself and exchanged his sodden swim trunks for the dry clothing from the diver's bag. Then he stretched out on the narrow bunk and once more considered his options.

Today was a start, an act of defiance against the individual or individuals who were corrupting his plan. But he must begin to think beyond mere gestures. He must find his new enemy, close with him and get his hands around his throat.

It was going to be a matter of adaptation motivated by necessity, like balancing a stock portfolio to react to radically changing economic conditions, or changing a ship's course in the face of inclement weather. Harconan was a man who recognized that clinging to obsolescent goals was act of abject foolishness. He must open a whole new page in the ledger.

Amanda, the Regional Intervention Force, even the Jakarta government – he must begin anew with them as well. He must begin to look upon them as potential assets to be turned against a greater enemy.

Especially Amanda.

She must be here with some American special operations battle force, and that bulk carrier she commanded must be more than it appeared to be. Given the decisive and timely way she had intervened this afternoon, she also must be operating with a very large degree of independence. She must also be recognizing that Bali was not of his doing and that a greater threat existed.

If he could only talk with her for ten minutes, just ten, as equals and allies and not as prey and predator ...

It was something to consider. But first he had to establish the identity of their mutual foe. That would give him a coin to bargain with.

As a step in that direction, he knew he had to reestablish communications with Lo and update himself with the latest developments. Possibly his Intelligence groups had already procured him his answer.

He rose from the bunk and again reached for the diver's bag, removing the lunchbox sized waterproof case of the sat phone. After deploying the saucer-sized dish antenna on the cabin's crude table, he switched the system on, allowing the phone to seek for an active and in range communications satellite. It acquired one almost instantly and the oncoming call light snapped on. Lo was trying to reach him.

Then Harconan's spine abruptly stiffened. The digital readout on the phone display glowed with the crisis call number.

The C-130 Hercules was one of the few long-range transports available in the Indonesian Air Force inventory, just as the platoon of KOSSUS commandos it carried were the Army's last uncommitted special operations force. That was why Admiral Ketalaman had held both carefully in reserve for a moment such as this.

The C-130 stayed at twelve thousand feet as it made its approach. It would never transit closer to the island, or even come within five miles of its shoreline, but it didn't need to pass overhead to deliver its payload.

To any observer on its island objective, it would remain a distant twinkle of navigational strobes and a faint moan of aero engines, a harmless traveler passing in the night, en route to some other destination.

The jump light flashed green within its cargo bay and black-clad men tumbled out of the open tailgate into the darkness. Camouflage-patterned nylon streamed and batlike rectangular parafoil parachutes cracked open. The commandos swirled for a few moments like a flock of night hunting swallows, then lined out in a long silent glide for the island, each squad rallying and guiding on the dim, colored glowtube taped to the back of its squad leader's helmet.

The platoon hissed in over the reefs, flaring out expertly against the trade wind to whump down on the narrow strip of beach or to splash into a landing in the hip-deep shallows. Parafoil chutes collapsed and were hastily wadded up, while code words were whispered into microphones.

The heavily-armed body of men broke into two groups and double timed down the beach in opposite directions. Their objective was located on the far side of the little island and they intended to engulf it from both sides, ensuring that there would be no escape.

*

Lan Lo awoke instantly to a long burst of automatic weapons fire. He recognized the light, angry crackle of a Steyr assault rifle, the preferred arm of the Nung security detail. He lay still for a moment, waiting. Then the burst was answered by an angry volley from a heavier caliber weapon. An FN FAL, Indonesian Army standard issue.

So it had come.

Lo arose and switched on the small bedside lamp. The main generator had been shut down for the night, but the auxiliary batteries were adequate for several hours. He dressed with swiftness and precision, completely down to his necktie, listening and assessing as he did so.

The volume of fire had grown rapidly and now issued from multiple points around the perimeter. Occasionally, a random bullet would strike the plantation house with an angry thwack, splintering wood or shattering glass. They were close. The discharges of the heavier Indonesian rifles also decisively outnumbered those of the defenders. They were many.

There were tasks that must be completed and there would be little time for them.

There was a quiet knock at his bedroom door. Lo slipped a tiny Seecamp's .32 caliber automatic, a weapon that had served him well in times before, into the pocket of his suit coat and answered it.

The commander of the base security detail stood in the doorway. "We are under large-scale assault, sir," he reported. "The compound is surrounded. We cannot hold."

"Prospects for an evacuation?" Lo kept his own words pared down to a minimum.

"Not possible. The attackers have already seized the pier and boathouse. We are cut off."

"I see. I will require a few minutes."

"You will have them." The Chinese mercenary drew his sidearm and strode down the hall to the front of the house. There would be no surrender. He was Nung as his men were Nung. They fought for money, but they died for personal honor.

Lo closed the bedroom door and twisted the key in the lock. Then he turned to the bank of laptop computers, radio receivers and satellite phones that ran the length of one wall. This was all that remained of the once formidable Harconan business empire and Lan Lo had insisted on overseeing it personally.

The transmitters and satellite phones had been used only sparingly for security's sake, but that was irrelevant now. Lo selected the crisis phone, the one only to be used in situations such as this. No matter what might be said over this phone, its activation alone would tell Harconan that all had been lost here.

Lo punched through the call code and lifted the satphone handset. He frowned as the call was not picked up. He knew that this was off the regular contact schedule and that Mr. Harconan might be unavailable. That was a pity; it would have been best to inform him of the situation personally.

Leaving the sat phone active, Lo began his final duties.

A large open-ended steel drum sat incongruously in one corner of the bedroom, its bottom filled with a thick layer of crumpled celluloid film.

The single rack of CD storage media and the single small stack of unshredded and unburned hardcopy that Lo had allowed to accumulate went into the drum. One unit after another, the laptops, the small printer with its integral memory and the radio transceivers with their digital frequency modules, followed them.

The equipment had been carefully organized to make the task quickly and easily done. In less than a minute, it had been accomplished.

The gunfire outside had grown to a crescendo and a rifle slug drilled through one thin wall. Lo took up a last object from the equipment desk, a small metallic cylinder with a pull ring at its top.

There was a roar and a concussion from the front of the plantation house that shattered the last of the glass and shook the structure to its foundations. Shrapnel whined hungrily out in the hall and the defending guns went silent. Hand grenades in all probability. Lo drew the pin from his own, smaller grenade and dropped it into the incineration drum. Harsh blue-white light glared from the mouth of the barrel, a geyser of smoke and flame following. Around him, the air filled with the choking bite of burning plastic.

*Satisfactory.*

All sources of information useful to Mr. Harconan's enemies had been eliminated, save for one. Lo slipped a hand into his pocket, then noted the answer light glowing on the crisis phone. Lo caught up the handset and keyed the reception button.

There were heavy footfalls and voices somewhere outside. Only seconds remained.

"Lo, this is Harconan! What's happening back there?"

"Mr. Harconan, your headquarters have been located and are lost to you. I believe it is the new enemy. I regret ..."

The bedroom door splintered under a boot kick and there was no time left for regrets, only for the very last duty. Lo pressed the muzzle of the Seecamps to his temple and pulled the trigger.

Benoa Port
The Island of Bali
0941 Hours; Zone Time, October 31, 2008

The elegance of the modern Naval Expeditionary Group was that it was far more than a mere accumulation of ships. It was an entire self-supporting miniature military that could be positioned anywhere on the Earth's surface where there was adequate water to float in.

Ground troops did not have to be lifted in. A Marine battalion reinforced with attached armor, artillery and reconnaissance assets was an integral part of the package. Airfields didn't have to be constructed or repaired. The flight decks of the amphibious ships served as the home base for dozens of helicopter gunships, VTOL transports and jet strike fighters.

Supplies didn't have to be accumulated, for the amphibs could carry enough beans and bullets to keep their landing force and air group operational for up to two weeks. Defenses didn't have to be established, for the escorting Aegis cruisers could deal with any manner of threat, ranging from submarines to theater ballistic missiles.

There was only one major drawback to the Naval Expeditionary Group: there were inevitably too few of them.

\*

The world was ordered around the USS *Pelelieu*. The massive queen bee of NAVEX 7.2 lay at anchor in the center of Benoa Harbor, surrounded by her swarm of bustling workers. Landing barges and LCAC hovercraft shuttled between her docking bays and the shore and a steady stream of Ospreys and helicopters lifted from and returned to her decks, servicing the ground force outposts on the Badung Penninsula.

The great artificial island that held the primary port facilities had been secured and was operational under the control of a mixed force of US Navy Seabees and Coast Guard. Royal Australian Navy stores ships and high-speed catamaran transports were docking and landing reinforcements and support assets.

All was well here – but Benoa Port and the Badung Peninsula were only a small part of the island of Bali, and Bali was but one island among thousands.

Aboard the *Pelelieu*, the tension in the Task Force Commander's office was palpable. Two men confronted each other across the TACBOSS's desk. They were alike in many ways: both were career military officers, dedicated to their service and their nation, both were combat veterans; both were skilled, capable and admirable in their own right.

But one man was a line officer and the other Special Operations. Despite all of the emphasis on "jointness" within the services, walls remained.

There was one other difference. One man wore a single star on the collar of his crisp tropic whites. The other had three on his travel-wilted khakis.

"We're happy to provide NAVSPECFORCE the aircraft you need," Admiral Sorenson said stiffly. "But there is some difficulty with this scheduling. Your mission isn't scheduled to fly until tonight, but half of my Osprey group has already been taken off-line. We have missions for those aircraft now."

"I understand, Admiral," Elliot MacIntyre replied. "We're taking a hellish bite out of your lift capacity and, if we'd had time to bring in one of our own Special Ops Osprey squadrons, we would have. But we couldn't and we have to borrow yours. It is absolutely imperative we have four Ospreys and a pair of spares on station at Jakarta skybase tonight. It's the same with your F-35s. Yours are the only full-stealth aircraft we can get within range in time."

"We'd have gotten them there," Sorenson insisted. "My people don't fall down on the job."

"I never thought that they would, Admiral." MacIntyre knew the real source of the edge in Sorenson's voice. No commander liked having their quarterdeck violated and NAVSPECFORCE had been directly tinkering with NAVEX 7.2's internal operations, a titanic bending of naval etiquette. But, at the moment, MacIntyre didn't give a damn about bruised egos. Those Ospreys *had* to be on station tonight with well-rested aircrews aboard and with clean maintenance cards, wounded feelings be damned.

"Another point, Admiral MacIntyre," Sorenson continued. "My aircraft and my aircrews will be playing a major role in the evacuation of the Embassy in Jakarta and, as yet, my tactical officers have received only a very abbreviated briefing package of the operation."

*What you mean, you hard-headed Swede, is that you have received a very abbreviated briefing package on the operation,* MacIntyre interjected silently.

"My people have no idea who we will be working with and who they will be relying on," Sorensen went on. "That's highly unsatisfactory, sir."

"But necessary, Admiral," MacIntyre replied, "absolutely necessary due to a variety of critical security concerns that I am not at liberty to discuss. You have my personal assurance that your aircrews will receive all the information they require for the successful conduct of this operation."

MacIntyre heard the breath hiss from behind Sorenson's clenched teeth. "Then a final point, Admiral. You have reserved one of my Ospreys for your *personal* use tonight. So far, my AIRBOSS has received no information at all as to your intended flight destination."

"That's correct, Admiral," MacIntyre replied, speaking succinctly. "Your aircrew will be provided with all of the navigational data they'll need after we are airborne. They will also be placed under specific orders from the highest authority to not reveal anything, about anything, to anyone about what they might observe on this flight."

"I see ... Admiral."

"I'm pleased that you do, Admiral."

## The North Coast of Lompoc Island
## 1200 Hours; Zone Time, October 31, 2008

Makara Harconan paced the sun-striped floor of the clan chief's hut, trying to will away his awareness of time. The isolated Bugi village had offered him the best they could. The best food, the best lodging, their best ship and crew ready to sail at a moment's notice. What they could not provide was an easing of his mind.

There are things a man can sacrifice in pursuit of a goal. His wealth, his position, his comfort, personal welfare and safety, his Dutch father's heritage, the very world he has built for himself. Harconan had done so willingly, staking it all on a roll of the dice.

But there are some things a man, a true man, cannot cast aside at his convenience. Harconan had never been afraid to stand alone if needs required it. But if standing alone meant that all of those you had ever cared for must perish …

He didn't know. That was the worst. The satphones and radios were down at his headquarters and Lo had missed three calls on the emergency contact schedule. If he missed this fourth call …

Abruptly the satellite phone, sitting active on the table in the center of the room, buzzed for attention. The channel register indicated an incoming call on the crisis link. Harconan pounced on the receiver.

"Lo?"

"Makara Harconan?" Even through the static, it was a voice Harconan recognized.

He only wished he didn't.

Harconan understood everything now. It all fell into place and he could see it all. That was Lan Lo's last precious gift to him: understanding.

"Good afternoon, Admiral Ketalaman."

"Good afternoon, Mr. Harconan. I'm pleased we have finally reached you. We have important matters to discuss."

"As I have been eager to speak with you as well, Admiral. Only I didn't know it."

It was Merpati Ketalaman of Sumatra, the Admiral who hated the sea. The controlled one. The man who always spoke softly. Harconan had purchased him years before as a useful asset to his piracy operations. Ketalaman had been a most pragmatic individual, one who could be totally trusted – at least for as long as his actions were in his own best interests.

"What's happened at my headquarters?" Harconan demanded. "What have you done with my people?"

"As I said, I have been eager to speak with you," Ketalaman continued. "We had a most successful relationship when you were conducting your piracy operations and it has been my desire to co-ordinate activities with you once more. But you have been rather difficult to locate recently."

"My *people,* Ketalaman." Harconan's voice was deadly.

"I regret to say there has been an unfortunate incident. When we approached your base, there was a conflict between my men and your security forces. It was most regrettable. If you had been present, I'm sure it could have been prevented."

"And my assistant, Lan Lo?"

"I also regret to say that he is dead, but I give you my word that it was not at the hands of my men."

Harconan felt his mouth twist. "I can believe that."

It wasn't a matter of believing Ketalaman. It was a matter of believing in Lo. To allow himself to become a threat to Harconan would have been unacceptable.

"You seem to have gone to a great deal of trouble to renew acquaintances."

"I have, Mr. Harconan. I believe that, as two realistic men, we can be of use to each other once more."

Harconan's instinct was to scream at this man to go to hell, but his voice remained calm as he replied. "How so, Admiral?"

"We are essentially working to the same goal. You desire the disruption of the Jakarta government. So do I. You desire the political disassociation of the islands of the Archipelago; I do as well. I desire control only of Java, Sumatra and certain small subsidiary territories. As our intentions parallel, I suggest that we meet and discuss combining our operations. I believe you would make a useful ally."

"I'm flattered, Admiral," Harconan replied, bitterness leaking into his voice. "But why should either of us bother?"

"Because your alliance would be helpful to me and wise for you. You have resources that I would find of use in stabilizing the situation on Java and Sumatra. Your Bugi sea clans would then be assured of my good will in the future."

"I see. And the maintenance of your good will is something the people of the sea should be concerned about?"

"It would be most wise to do so." The voice on the far end of the satellite circuit was almost gentle, as if Ketalaman felt himself talking with a child.

"What assets of mine would you desire, Admiral?" Harconan replied.

"We can discuss the exact details when we meet." Ketalaman sounded pleased. "Suffice to say that I will have sealift requirements for both personnel and supplies. There will be various Intelligence matters I'm sure you'll be able to assist me with, and my forces will require access to the arms stores you have positioned around the archipelago."

"Is that all you will require of me, Admiral?"

"For the immediate future, yes."

"Then you may kiss your own ass, Ketalaman. I didn't seek to deliver the peoples of Indonesia from a petty tyranny just to hand them over to a greater one."

Harconan heard the ghost of a sigh over the channel. "Very dramatic but vainglorious, Mr. Harconan. I will contact you at this time tomorrow. You will have changed your mind by then."

The circuit broke. Harconan slammed his own receiver back into its cradle and hit the off switch. He had found his new enemy. Now he must start his search for new allies.

"Captain, this is Air One. Admiral MacIntyre's aircraft is on approach. The ship is across the wind and we have clear horizons."

"Very good, Air One," she replied into her headset. "Bring him aboard."

She was alone in the topside darkness. She had no personnel to spare for an honors party. All hands labored below, racing to meet the "Trick or Treat" timeline. Nor did the tactical situation permit ceremonials. The *Shenandoah* was circling at her initial point, positioned to jump off into the attack.

Amanda stood at the foot of the short ladder that led to the top of number four MacGregor hatch. Instinctively, she took a grip on one of the rungs as a wisp of vertigo brushed her. The *Shenandoah* rode easily on the low swells and she had both her sea legs and her darkness-adapted vision, but night on a blacked-out deck could still be disorienting.

All of the commando carrier's topside illumination had been extinguished and the coastal lights of Java lay below the southern horizon. Even the sky glow of Jakarta was absent. The city was blacked out, but not by choice; its power grid had collapsed in the chaos.

There was only the horde of stars in the dome of the sky and the uncertain, transitory biolight kicked up by the turbulence of the *Shenandoah*'s passage.

"Captain, the Admiral's aircraft is turning final."

Now Amanda could hear the moan of turbines over the hiss of the bow wave and the rumble of the ship's engines. An MV-22 Osprey was coming in from leeward with its power pods already lifted into helicopter mode. Skimming the sea like a titanic bat, it was visible only as a mobile patch of occluded stars.

The tilt-rotor flared back and decelerated as it came in over the *Shenandoah*'s deck and Amanda was whipped by her own hair as the lift wash passed over her. She felt the thump of the Osprey's undercarriage slamming down on the helipad.

She scrambled up the ladder to the hatch top in time to see a single shadow spring down from the transport's open tailgate. Then she had to close her eyes and duck back below the hatch edge, clinging to the ladder rails as the renewed blast of the rotor-props battered her. When she could lift her head to look again, the Osprey had climbed clear. Swinging away from the ship, it headed for its distant home aboard the *Pelelieu.*

The figure it had left behind tugged open the zip on his wind cheater and removed an officer's cap. Pulling it on, he strode toward the corner of the helipad carrying a single B-4 bag with him.

Amanda finished the climb to the hatch top. Straightening, she snapped off her salute.

"Welcome aboard the *Shenandoah,* sir."

"It's a pleasure to be aboard, Captain." MacIntyre hesitated and she heard a hint of wryness creep into his voice. "Damn it, Amanda. You're setting the protocols out here. What am I supposed to do about honoring the colors? Damned if I'm going to salute the Panamanian flag."

"Carry on, sir. We're flying our battle flag tonight."

*

The green-tinted image on the flat screen wavered as the hand-held NiteBrite camera panned across Merdeka Square. "As you can see," Christine Rendino's voice narrated from the overhead speaker, "we don't have a lot of action in the square itself. The rebels seem to be keeping the entire government district isolated. I think that'll work to our favor. We're not going to have to worry about a lot of collateral casualties. They lost a couple of tanks to our Predator rockets. You can see the burned-out wrecks right there."

The plasma displays spaced around the bulkheads of the Command Block briefing room were filled with continuously updating tactical maps and status charts. Even this real-time data stream was proving inadequate and stacks of printer hardcopy were mounting up on the large central table, along with a steadily growing number of coffee mug rings.

"How many Predator rounds do your boys have left?" Stone Quillain looked up from the strip of printer paper he'd been consulting.

There was a murmur of mixed voices off mike on the Jakarta screen. "Lieutenant Trennan says we only have three left," Christine replied. "But the Indonesians are keeping their vehicles pulled back onto the side streets around the square. They don't want to give us any more freebies. They do have infantry and security troops deployed on the roofs and inside the buildings around the square though. I'll try and give you a zoom in."

The camera image rushed in on the roof of the Gambir train station on the eastern side of the square. Then it traversed unsteadily down the length of the flat roof line, showing helmeted heads peering over a sandbagged revetment.

Amanda leaned forward, her arms crossed on the table. "What about anti-aircraft, Chris?"

"It's like with the AFVs, Boss Ma'am. There's no heavy stuff within line of sight of the Embassy. There could be MANPAD SAMs on any of these roofs around here though. Fa'sure you've got light automatic weapons and grenade launchers – I think there might even be a heavy machine gun position on the roof of the Defense Ministry. I'm going to try to show you ..."

The image swung back to the west side of the square and elevated, the person aiming the camera standing erect to get the angle.

"Chris, stay down!" Amanda snapped into her headset. "That's an order!"

The video image blurred and bounced back below the concrete balustrade. The camera came out of telephoto mode and reversed onto the face of Christine Rendino, peering out from under a camo-covered K-Pot helmet. "Hey, it's okay. They're playing nice. We haven't taken any fire for hours."

"Those would make excellent famous last words, Commander," MacIntyre interjected severely from where he stood behind Amanda's chair. "Don't claim them for your own. You are ordered to stay alive until we can get you out of there. "

"Will comply, Admiral sir. That's about all the tactical I have. Everything else, the drones and sats can give you better than I can."

MacIntyre grunted, "I don't suppose the opposition is conveniently using the communications centers at the Ministry of Defense and the Palace compound?"

"No joy, Admiral. President Kediri's heroic defenders, the bastards, managed to sabotage their commo systems and our signal Intelligence taps before falling gloriously in battle. All we're getting is the operational stuff on the Indonesian tactical radio nets."

"What's the situation inside the Embassy?" Amanda inquired.

"The embassy staff are burning the hardcopy files now. All computer memories have been purged and blanked and the hardware has all been wired for destruct. We'll be ready to move whenever."

"Don't make any long-term plans, Chris. We'll get back to you."

The Intel cocked an eyebrow. "It's not as if I'm going out for a latté. This is Point Man Base, out."

Christine's video and audio links went down.

A few long moments of silence followed in the briefing room. "Believe in yourself. Amanda," MacIntyre said quietly. "You'll get her out."

"This one is just a little more difficult, Elliot."

She heard him give a soft rueful laugh. "Tell me about it. Every time I send one of you out it's always just a little more difficult."

For the first time in several days, Christine's revelation about Macintyre flared back into Amanda's mind. Unlikely though the concept might be, that touch felt rather comforting at the moment.

"It could be worse," Stone Quillain said, providing a welcome distraction. "Between signal Intelligence and the drone imagin', it looks like the rebels only have themselves a reinforced brigade and a few other odds and ends in and around Jakarta. That ain't a hell of a lot of manpower to hold a major city."

Amanda nodded. "There are still pockets of resistance holding out. *Polici* mostly, but they'll complicate the equation for the people running this coup."

"That is something." MacIntyre lifted his hand from her shoulder and paced over to a second large screen display. This one held a computer map of the Jakarta environs, a scattering of red position hacks widely spaced across it. "They're spread thin and they don't have the total support of either the military or the populace. Obviously they were, and are, counting on the total decapitation of the Kediri government as their road to power. As long as Kediri is out there alive and giving orders, they could still lose it all."

Amanda frowned. "That doesn't bode at all well for our Embassy. We've got to get Kediri and our people out of there now, before the rebels get that little bit more desperate."

MacIntyre glanced back at her. "I've got you your wish list from the Regional Intervention Force and the Australians, but it will be at least another forty-eight hours before we can get any additional surface platforms in here or kick loose any additional Special Ops ground units. My sense is we don't have that time."

"We don't," Amanda agreed. "We have to go tonight and we have to go with what we have aboard the *Shenandoah*. Those are the parameters my planning staff and I have been working with."

"What have you got?"

"Something a little bit unusual." She got up from her chair and joined MacIntyre at the map display. "We started with two extraction options, either over the beach or out by air, neither of which we were happy with. It's over four miles from the harbor to the Embassy through what they call the old Batavia district. My ground advisor here was exceptionally unhappy with the ground option."

"Oh yeah," Stone nodded. "You got your narrow old-timey streets and the old city canal system to deal with. You got choke points all over the place where a small armored column could get stalled up and piled on. Beyond that, we've got a hundred and twenty-eight souls to get out of that compound. We don't have near enough tracks to move that many people in and out in one cycle and I can guarantee you right now we ain't goin' to get two."

"We even considered taking our AAAVs and RIB raiders down either the Banjii or the Gunung-Sahari canals," Amanda added, running a fingertip along the glowing blue lines on the screen. "But again, there are just too many bridges and choke points where a handful of rebel troops could pin us down. If we're going to do this, we've got to do it by air."

"I'd agree, but with some massive reservations." MacIntyre reached over to the trackball controller and keypad beside the display. Using them, he blew up the core section of the map until it filled the screen. "You've got the helipad inside the compound and you've got plenty of open landing ground in the square," he said. "But the closer to the central government district you get, the worse the urban buildup, including high rises. That's not good helicopter or VTOL country. You could very well develop a Mogadishu scenario if you get some downed extraction aircraft."

"I know it," Amanda replied. "That's why we've come up with a twist on things that may help to give us an edge on this situation."

MacIntyre lifted a shaggy brow at her. "What kind of a twist this time?"

"We're going to turn the classic ground support equation around backwards."

"Backward?"

Amanda nodded. "Normally, you bring in air power to support your ground units. Tonight though ..." She reached up and tapped a point on the map, an empty area along the coastline of Jakarta Bay labeled 'Ancol (Dreamland) Park.' "Tonight, we're going to bring in the ground units to support our air power."

A million dollars worth of processor boards and chipsets crunched under crow bars and carbine butts.

"Everything but the radios and relays, people!" Christine Rendino called over the sound of the destruction. "Sergeant MacGuffin, you and Stacy stay on the Indonesian tactical monitors right up to the last second. Have the det cord in place and ready to blow as we go out the door."

"No problem, ma'am," the noncom replied. "There's not going to be shit left in here when we're done."

The once elegant Embassy reception room looked like the interior of a bombed-out electronics plant. There would be no time or lift available to evacuate the Point Man equipment, only the people. But none of the sophisticated Intelligence gathering systems would be left intact. The same kind of organized demolition was being repeated in the Embassy communications and encryption centers.

One of the civilian embassy staffers appeared at the doorway to the reception room. Clad for practicality in jeans, blouse and running shoes, she cringed a little at the sight of the organized devastation. "Commander Rendino, the Ambassador would like to speak with you if it's possible."

"Sure, Sally. On my way. MacGuffin, keep busting things until I get back." Trying to assume a proper air of military *savoir faire*, Christine scooped her helmet and P90 Personal Assault Weapon off a nearby desktop and followed the staffer.

Ambassador Goodyard and President Kediri were both waiting in Goodyard's office. Seated behind his desk, Goodyard was dressed in a golfing shirt and slacks, while Kediri paced the floor clad in the same rumpled safari suit he had worn on the day of the coup. A pair of Kevlar helmets and interceptor vests lay across the desktop and the office seemed warm, despite the laboring air conditioning.

Goodyard looked up as she entered. "Good evening, Commander. May I offer you a cold drink?"

"No, thank you, sir," Christine replied with matching politeness. She didn't need anything more to throw up.

"I know you're heavily involved at the moment – but I was wondering if you could give President Kediri and me an update on the extraction operation?"

"Preparations for the Embassy evac are essentially complete, Mr. Ambassador. We'll be ready to go when the time comes."

"And that will be ...?"

"All I can say is soon. A flexible timeline has been established for the operation, dependent on a number of variables. We'll give you a warning when we get the word."

Christine looked at the impassive Kediri. "Mr. President, in a related question, have your people been able to establish the status of that Indonesian frigate currently holding off Jakarta?"

Kediri shook his head. "The Surabaya Fleet Base has been attempting to raise the Wiratno all day. They do not reply."

"That's unfortunate, sir," Christine replied carefully.

Kediri grimaced. "This entire situation is unfortunate, Commander."

Christine could only agree. "When the time comes, you, Ambassador Goodyard and the other members of your government will be evacuated on the first aircraft. By our estimation that should be the safest flight out. You'll be moved from here in the main building to the rallying point in the compound gymnasium and from there to the Osprey. Just follow your escort's instructions and you should be fine."

"And where will we be evacuated to?" Kediri inquired with a degree of suspicion.

"To Bali, Mr. President."

"Bali?"

"Yes sir," Christine nodded. "To the ships of the Regional Intervention Force in Benoa Port. That way we can provide you with both the personal security and the command-and-control facilities you'll need to maintain your government while keeping you within

Indonesian territory. It wouldn't be politically sound to have you declared a government in exile."

"I feel Surabaya Fleet Base would be more appropriate," Kediri said stiffly.

"But more dangerous for you, sir. Not all of the rebel commanders within your military may have declared yet. Aboard our ships, we know we can keep you alive."

Kediri subsided.

"Our embassy will be moving there as well, Mr. President," Goodyard said, placating. "A temporary matter for both of our governments." The Ambassador looked back to Christine. "Will you be joining us, Commander?"

Christine shook her head. "No, sir. My people and the Marines will be going elsewhere."

"I see." He rose from behind his desk and extended his hand. "In case we don't have the opportunity again, I'd like to thank you for all you and your people have done. You've given me a considerable education on a number of subjects."

Christine accepted the strong handclasp. "You've been a good student, sir. It's been an honor serving with you."

"I take that as a great compliment, Commander."

MV Galaxy *Shenandoah*
The Jakarta Approaches
2305 Hours; Zone Time, October 31, 2008

The wheelhouse of the Galaxy *Shenandoah* resembled that of most other large modern merchantman. It ran the full width of the superstructure, watertight weather doors opening onto the bridge wings, a broad paned windscreen providing a superb overview of the main deck and beyond.

It would take an expert's eye to note that the windscreen was made of bulletproof armored glass and an electric drill to prove that the steel plating was underset with a thick layer of polymer armor.

In its standard operating mode, the bridge was sparsely outfitted in comparison with that of a warship. There was a combined helm and lee helm station, equipped with a set of remote engine and steering thruster controls, and a combined chart table and navigation systems console with a radar hood. A pair of raised swivel chairs stood ready for the Captain and the Watch Officer and the ship's interphones and the TBS radio flanked the hatchway leading aft to the chart and main communications rooms.

This night, with business at hand, the conventional bridge instrumentation had been augmented by half a dozen of the ubiquitous milspec laptops. Velcroed to the consoles and tabletops, and networked into the *Shenandoah*'s integrated combat system, they stood duty as battle management repeaters, uplinking the data stream from the CIC.

Beyond the bow, a thick band of a deeper darkness lay across the southern horizon, a thin scattering of dim sparks glowing across it: the island of Java and the few surviving lights of Jakarta.

With all standard running and deck lights switched back on, the *Shenandoah* nosed in toward the coast at an easy eight knots, tracking on the standard harbor approach channel like any other foolish but innocent merchant vessel.

Her electromagnetic signature was also innocent. Electronics and signal Intelligence systems would register only a single, standard Decca navigational radar. The powerful night-piercing optronic sensors and the frequency-hopping data links that bound her to the remote eyes of her vigilant drone net were also undetectable.

Amanda leaned forward and studied the tactical display on one of the laptop repeaters. The Combat Information Center was the usual battle station for the captain of the modern man of war. It was the informational nexus point where a commanding officer could best "see" the battle evolve through the medium of the ship's sensors.

But tonight, Amanda had chosen to start this fight from the traditionalist's post on the bridge. MacIntyre was managing things in the Command-and-Control block, and she wanted to be topside. She wanted see her new ship through her first battle with her own eyes.

There was only a single surface contact hack on the miniature Alpha screen, circling slowly beyond the shipping channel and glowing the yellow of an unverified target. Amanda called up the signal Intelligence sidebar, watching the register of a sweeping radar beam.

"We're being painted," the watch officer spoke from behind her shoulder. "He knows we're out here."

"It seems so, Mr. Carstairs. And likely he intends to do something about us."

"Begging the captain's pardon, ma'am, but do we know which side this guy is on yet?'

"Not exactly, but he's had all the opportunities he's going to have to come to Jesus."

She tapped in her command code, accessing the targeting designations. Using the laptop's touchpad, she boxed in the Indonesian warship, shifting its threat rating from yellow-unknown to red-hostile.

"Mr. Carstairs, notify the moon pool that they are cleared to flood and to open the belly doors. Arm all drop collars and configure for surface engagement. We'll use the Mark 48s."

"Very good, ma'am." She could hear the subdued tension in the young officer's voice. Probably this would be the first live fire order he had ever relayed. The first blood chit to cash. It was a rite of passage for all in the profession of arms. Amanda lay awake at night remembering hers.

A pair of shadowed figures, one towering with bulky equipment, the other slight in comparison, pushed through the bridge entry light curtain. Amanda shot a brief glance back over her shoulder. "Good evening, gentlemen. Status report please."

"The transverse bay has been flooded down, skipper," Stone Quillain reported, his voice a quiet rumble. "Tractor crews and beaching force are aboard and ready to disembark. Sky Island and Special Boat chalks standing by, ready to load."

"Is it still your intention to go in with Sky Island Able?"

Quillain's gear harness clicked lightly as he shrugged. "If you're gonna lead, you got to be out in front."

"I've employed that useful sophistry myself on more than one occasion so I can't ethically call you on it. Arkady, what's the last word on the air group?"

"We had one hundred per cent availability, all mission slots filled. We're set to commence launching as soon as we convert the deck."

"We will be doing so shortly," Amanda replied, not taking her eyes from the monitor display. "Arkady, what's the word from the Sky Base AWACS?"

"All sky base elements and all support flights are holding on station. They are standing by for mission commit."

"Very good. We have one final problem out here to deal with. Then we'll commence air and landing operations. After we take out the Indonesian guard ship, we'll ring down to full stop to put the tractor platoon and the raiders over the side. As we perform that evolution, we'll convert the deck and vertical launch the Eagle and Hell Eyes. Then we'll turn into the wind and start working back up to flank speed. Arkady, as soon as you get adequate wind across the deck, you may launch the manned aircraft." Amanda turned to face her two subordinates. "Fluid, flexible and fast, gentlemen, that's how we play it. Good luck to you both. May we be discussing a clean victory over breakfast tomorrow."

"I wonder if any of the mess men aboard this tub know how to make fried mush," Quillain mused. "Nothin' sits better after a night's huntin' than a good plate of sausage and fried mush."

"I'll make the appropriate inquiries, Stone. Commander Arkady, if you'll remain for a few moments, I need to speak with you."

"As you wish, ma'am," he replied formally.

Quillain took his departure and she led Arkady out to the portside bridge wing. There she sought for a pocket of isolation and dogged the wheelhouse door closed behind them.

Slipping her command headset down around her neck, she leaned against the bridge wing railing looking out across the bow, hoping Arkady would catch the invitation to informality in her posture. After a moment he joined her, shoulder to shoulder at the rail.

She and Arkady still had a lot of exploring to do in this new relationship of theirs. She was afraid that her orders tonight might not make things any easier.

"For some reason, this reminds me of that night off Shanghai," she began. "That first one when we accidentally ran down the Red torpedo boat."

She watched his silhouette nod. "I was just thinking the same thing. The feel is the same."

"Very much so. Different, but the same." That summed up their current personal situation quite well. "Arkady, may I ask you something?"

"Sure thing ... ma'am." She caught the hesitation in his voice, that floundering frustration in just who she was and what he was supposed to be.

"Did you really throw that engagement ring off the end of my father's boat dock back in Norfolk?"

She'd caught him by surprise as she had intended. Arkady tried to suppress an explosive snort of laughter. "How the hell did you find out about that?"

She smiled to herself. She'd found the right tension breaker. "Dad told me all about it. He wanted to make sure I knew just how badly I'd blown that particular opportunity."

"It wasn't your fault, b ..."

"Arkady, it's still me in here," Amanda said levelly. "Go ahead and say it."

"It wasn't your fault, babe." The old comfortable endearment of their affair rolled out of him in relief. "It wasn't anybody's fault. It just wasn't meant to happen."

Amanda shook her head. "No, we can't fall back on that fudge either. Let's face it, Arkady. What we had together was very, very good – and I have never regretted a moment of it. Something could have built on that. I suspect we could have probably made a marriage work if we'd wanted to. Lord knows, we'd both considered the point. But when the time came to make the decision, we made another choice. Or at least I did."

"Why?" he asked simply. They couldn't really see each other's eyes in the night shadows, but she could tell he was looking into her face. She took a deliberate breath. She owed him a long-deferred answer to that question, but she wasn't sure how acceptable a one she had.

"I don't know if this will make much sense, Arkady. It hasn't to me on the frequent occasions when I've thought about it. But, for all of my life, I've trusted and reacted to my instincts. So far, it's worked for me. I hope you can trust them on this point, too."

"To date I haven't had any complaints either. Try me."

Amanda took a deep breath. "As you wish. Back when I was with the Sea Fighters, we had this one little Motor Mac who was blessed, or cursed, with what they call 'The Touch'. She always seemed to know beforehand if a mission was going to go clean or ugly. Or if someone was going to die or not. Have you heard of the phenomenon?"

"You always hear the stories," Arkady replied uncertainly.

"And sometimes they turn out to be true," Amanda continued. "Well, on that day, I ran out on you for that job into West Africa, I had this ... sense that it just wasn't supposed to be. That there was some other kind of destiny, of fate, waiting for me somewhere. One that I didn't want to draw a very caring and loving and slightly wonderful young man into."

"Ah, Christ."

She felt his hand come up to touch her cheek. For one sweet, familiar moment, she tilted her head into the caress. Then she lifted her own hand and caught his in a tight grip, lightly kissing his stick-callused palm. "Damn it, Arkady. We're always going to hold a piece of each other – and, God knows, I need you now as much as I've ever needed you. I need you to stand at my shoulder and tell me when I'm right and when I'm wrong and to lend me a little extra strength when I need it."

The pause between her heartbeats seemed to last for a long time. The Sir Lancelot's role was a difficult one for even the best of errant knights to play. It took a big-hearted man and friend to take it on. Then she felt the strong responding grip of his hand.

"Hell, what do you think? You knock 'em down. I'll stomp on them. Same as always."

She bit her lip for a moment. That was the wonderful thing about a good grade of steel. It could be reforged.

"I'm very happy to hear that, Arkady. More so than you'll ever know. Because I have a special job for you tonight. Just one bitch of a job."

"Call it, babe. It'll get done," he said briskly.

"Okay, here it is. Tonight, when your strike group goes in over Jakarta, you stay out of it. You stay high and you stay totally defensive. You do not engage unless you receive a specific clearance from me. Those are specific orders, Commander, and they are not open for tactical interpretation."

She knew her sudden shift of topic had thrown Arkady off-balance. "Begging your pardon, Captain, but that'll be my squadron out there!"

She continued before he could further challenge her. Lifting her hand, she extended two fingers. "Two reasons, Arkady. For one, you are my air group commander. You're senior command personnel now. You need to be out there, doing the big job of coordinating air ops while letting your people do theirs. Get used to it. You're going to be doing a lot of it from now on."

Personal time was over. "Yes, ma'am."

"Now for reason number two. I have to know that you and your wingman are out there, over the primary engagement zone, in fully armed and undamaged aircraft, ready to act at a moment's notice. I know your capabilities and I am holding you in reserve. You are my thunderbolt, Arkady. If something should go radically wrong out there, and I have every reason to believe that it will, I will be counting on you to pull us out. Are there any problems here?"

She caught the glint of his grin. "None whatsoever, Captain." He held out his hand and they gripped palms tightly.

"Captain?" The voice sounded faintly from the headset looped around her neck. The handclasp broke as she one-eared the headphones and spoke into the lip mike, "Captain by."

"We're being hailed by the rebel frigate. They're maneuvering to cross our bow. Range fifteen thousand yards and closing slowly."

"Initiate deception program and prepare to engage. All elements, stand by to initiate primary mission timeline!"

Arkady already had the bridge hatch undogged and open. "Luck, Captain," he called back.

"Luck, Arkady and good hunting." She hoped he could hear the unspoken "And thank you, love," she added.

*

"Merchant vessel, merchant vessel! Identify yourself. " The warship, an ex-East German Parchim class frigate cut slowly across the shipping channel. "This is the Wiratno of the Indonesian Navy of National Reunification. You are violating our national waters. Identify yourself!"

"This is motor vessel Chiku Shan of Taipei," a thickly-accented voice replied over the Talk-Between-Ships circuit. "We are inbound to Jakarta."

"The port of Jakarta is closed to all shipping. Reverse course! Reverse course now!"

"This is Chiku Shan. We do not understand!" The voice on the TBS was plaintive. "We are scheduled for a Jakarta port call. We are scheduled!"

"Chiku Shan, reverse course and leave this area or we will fire on you."

Amanda lowered her nightbrite binoculars, and glanced down at the laptop screen. They were live-streaming video from the submersible launch bay.

The *Remora* had been jacked up to the highest level of its hangar, and the midnight blue depths of the open moon pool roiled with the turbulence of the ship's passage. The drop collar arms extended over the pool from the port and starboard bulkheads, each cradling the cold steel length of a Mark 48 ADCAP torpedo.

"CIC," she spoke deliberately into her lip mike, "do we have a range and firing solution on surface target, Master Zero One?"

"Bridge, range is now fifteen hundred yards and we have a valid firing solution."

"CIC, clear your safety interlocks. You are cleared to fire ... Fire one."

A Mark 48 fell away from its drop collar, the forward shackle releasing a split second before the aft so that the torpedo sliced into the moon pool in a clean, angled dive.

"Fire two."

The torpedo drives engaged as they pulled out of their dive below the *Shenandoah*'s keel. Accelerating smoothly, they raced toward their target, guidance wires unreeling from their spinnerets.

"Torpedoes away, Captain. Running hot, straight and normal."

Amanda lifted her binoculars once more and leveled them beyond the *Shenandoah*'s bow. She reacquired the slim, low-riding hull of the frigate, shimmering a soft blue-green in the night vision optics.

The accented voice barked from the overhead speaker once more: "Chiku Shan, this is your last warning! Reverse course now or we will fire on you!"

Through her glasses, Amanda could see the frigate's autocannon turrets indexing to bear on the *Shenandoah*. In a few moments more it would be irrelevant.

They would have no further warning. The trudge of the freighter's propellers on the same bearing as the torpedoes would mask the hot, venomous hiss of the propulsors. Guided by the commando carrier's sensors, the Mark 48s steered in under the target. As they reached the end of their run, they pulled up sharply and knifed into the belly of the frigate.

Amanda's night vision glasses momentarily overloaded with the blue-white glare beneath the sea. Then she caught an impression of the little warship, buckling upward amidships, her back broken over a boiling dome of water.

The *Shenandoah*'s deck and running lights blinked out as the Commando Carrier returned to blackout. Amanda let the glasses drop to her chest, rapid-firing a string of orders. An entire chain of events must take place instantly, before the rebel military command shore-side could react. She would sing the verse, her officers replying in chorus.

"Lee Helm! All engines back full! Bring the ship to full stop."

"All engines backing full, ma'am!'

"Air One! Be advised you are cleared to convert the deck! Launch the air group!"

"First flight on the elevators, Captain."

"Landing Force Operations Center, you may land the landing force!"

"Landing force going over the side."

"CIC, inform the Embassy and Sky Base! We are initiating the Operation Trick or Treat timelines. All phases – commence, commence, commence!"

That was all she could do. The *Shenandoah*'s moment as a shooter had passed. It was all in other hands now.

There was no physical structure to Sky Base. It existed merely as a set of navigational coordinates around which a large and varied formation of aircraft circled in a wide racetrack pattern.

The heavy iron consisted of a pair of militarized Boeing 767s, one a US Air Force AWACS II airborne command-and-control aircraft and the second a Compass Call Bravo electronic warfare plane. A burly KC-10 Extender air-refueling tanker also held in the formation, intermittently topping off the Sky Base's swarm of Little Friends.

The two four-plane flights of Royal Australian Air Force F/A-18 Hornets had staged out of East Timor and were armed for air to air. The flight of USMC F-35 Joint Strike Fighters had launched from the USS *Pelelieu* and were configured for surface strike.

Holding at a lower altitude and a tighter orbit another tanker, a Marine turboprop KC-130J circled, trailed by the *Pelelieu*'s gaggle of MV-22 Osprey tilt-rotors. With their passenger bays empty, they would serve as the primary extraction aircraft.

Over the short term, sky base could provide a strike package with all of the support assets of a ground basing facility, barring rearmament and the opportunity for an aircrew to stretch their legs.

At the initiation order, the Compass Call bird went on the electronic offensive, its array of powerful cascade jammers blasting a deafening scream of white noise across the standard Indonesian military radio channels and data links.

Simultaneously, the four F-35s retracted their radio antenna and refueling probes within their stealth envelopes. Invisible now to radar, the Marine fighter-bombers peeled off and accelerated to transonic velocity, streaking toward their targets in and around Jakarta.

*

Five miles off the coast, the *Shenandoah* shuddered to a full stop under the thrust of her backing propellers. Down either flank of the commando carrier, hull panels, their edges camouflaged by false welding seams, swung open. Power davits howled and four ten-meter-long RIB (Rigid Inflatable Boat) raider craft swung outboard from their concealed boat bays. Each raider carried its Special Boat crew with a four-man SEAL detachment to ride shotgun. Each raider also carried a massive load-out of armaments and ammunition.

There was a degree of swearing and fumbling as the boats hit water and davit shackles were cast off. There had been little time or opportunity for live-drilling this particular evolution, but SB personnel manned both the RIBs and the launch bays and there was little or nothing they did not know about the handling of small craft.

Amidships, to port and starboard, another set of hatches swung upward and half a dozen blocky tanklike shapes lurched out of the transverse amphitrack bay. Lurching and wallowing like water buffalo, the Marine Advanced Amphibious Assault Vehicles tilted out of their semi-flooded hangar, their diesel exhausts kicking up plumes of spray as they plunged into the sea. Bobbing back to the surface, the big machines furiously churned away from the flanks of the commando carrier, their spinning tracks doubling in brass as paddle wheels.

Clear of their mothership, a miraculous sequence of changes began, fully the equivalent of a warthog transforming into a gazelle.

The tread assemblies of the AAAVs – tracks, bogie wheels and all – retracted into their angular hulls. Streamlining doors closed over the track wells to create a smooth planing surface, and the armored forward hull plate hydraulically tilted outward at a steeper angle, becoming a hydro ski.

Inboard, safety interlocks disengaged in the amphitrack's engine compartments, unleashing the full twenty-six hundred horsepower of their massive MTU/Detroit Diesel power plants. Hydrojet drives blasted astern of each assault vehicle, horizontal geysers boiling the sea. There was an abrupt forward and upward surge and the AAAVs half-lifted their hulls out of the water to skim the wave tops with the grace and ease of a ski boat.

At thirty knots, the AAAV platoon lined out for Jakarta harbor, the four RIB raider boats pulling into an escort diamond around it.

*

As the beach assault force had gone out of the *Shenandoah*'s side hatches, her weather decks had been had reconfiguring to air operations mode.

Every element of her air group was being committed and every machine had to be put into the sky as rapidly as possible. First on the decks were the tactical scout and attack RPVs, the Boeing Textron Eagle Eyes with their reconnaissance pods and the Hell Eye variants with their brace of Hellfire surface-to-air missiles, the remote-controlled eyes and fangs of the ship.

A dozen of these miniature cousins of the tilt-rotor Osprey VTOL were spotted on deck in a double row. With their mini-turbines screeching and their twin long-bladed air screws swiveled into lift rotor mode, the little fish-shaped machines stood poised to explode into the sky like a covey of quail.

*

In the heart of Jakarta, the sound of the torpedo hits registered as a hint of distant thunder. The Indonesian patrollers and sentries deployed around Merdeka Square looked up, mildly puzzled. Then, abruptly, they had more urgent concerns.

A closely-spaced series of piercing cracks and rolling booms echoed within the square.

The NCO leading a patrol past the abandoned Greek embassy had his head explode without warning. The sentry manning the lookout on the observation deck of the MONAS memorial spire toppled from his post and plummeted four hundred feet to the pavement. Two soldiers manning the gates at the Ministry of Defense crumpled simultaneously. An officer peering out of a window of the Aryaduta Hyatt was hurled backwards with a massive crater blasted in his chest. At multiple points within the arc of fire and sight around the US Embassy, men started to die.

The Marine Corps appreciated the sniper. Every Fleet Anti-terror Strike Team platoon had a pair of two-man sniper elements attached to it, their weapon of choice being the big .300 Magnum variant of the Remington M-40C bolt action rifle. In addition, at least one man in every FAST squad had gone through the Marine tactical snipers course to learn how to get the maximum out of the extended barrel variant of the M-8 assault rifle. And finally, within the Embassy's security force, there was one Montana boy who had received no formal sniper's indoctrination – but who had been given his first deer rifle on his twelfth birthday.

All through the afternoon, these men had been spotting the surrounding Indonesian sentry posts and patrol routes, building their targeting priority lists, and checking their ranges and engagement patterns. Now, with great precision, they were making the vicinity of the US Embassy a very unhealthy place to be.

*

"How are we doing?" Amanda demanded, pushing through the light-curtain into the shadowy blue dimness of the Landing Force Operations Center.

"The timelines have initiated," MacIntyre replied, pacing the narrow aisle behind the double row of systems operators' stations. "The Embassy has started their area sterilization and the fire base force is approaching the Beach. The Sky Base strike group should be at their drop line within the next thirty seconds."

"We're on the track." Amanda shed her helmet and flak vest and looked around in the dimness for some place to stack them. With nothing apparent, she heaped them on the deck in a back corner of the space, impatiently kicking them as far out of the way as possible.

The Landing Force Op's Alpha Display had been locked onto a computer graphics situation map of the Jakarta area. Amanda came to stand beside MacIntyre, focusing totally on the wall screen. There was no sense in a questioning look at the combat watch hunching over their consoles; if this massive untested assembly of machinery and humanity were to fail, it would likely happen as this first massive load came onto it. There was no sense in wondering or worrying. Soon she would know.

The position hack of the fire base force crawled steadily toward its designated beach head at Jakarta's Ancol amusement park.

She sidled a half step closer to MacIntyre. At this particular moment, it was good not to be quite so alone. "What's the word from Air One?" she inquired softly.

"The RPV group is spotted and ready to launch," Macintyre replied, his own voice low. "Drone control reports they have good control on all units. The Strike and Sky Island elements are ready to go on the lifts as soon as the drones clear. All we need is clean sky."

Suddenly, four blue bat-shaped aircraft hacks flickered into existence on the Alpha display. For a few instants, they manifested themselves in a broad arc across the Jakarta engagement area from a point perhaps ten miles off the coast. Then, as rapidly as they had appeared, they vanished once more.

"And there's Marine Air checking in," MacIntyre murmured.

*

Inland, at the Jakarta Regional Air Defense Center at Halim Perdana Kusuma Air Force Base, the systems operators also caught a momentary flash of airborne targets offshore. But the contacts were so brief in duration that the Indonesian radarmen hesitated before reacting, puzzled over just what their phased arrays had detected. By the time they understood, it was too late.

The transitories had signaled the beginning of the end for the Indonesian air defenses. They had been caused by the cycling weapons bay doors of the approaching Marine F-35s, their opening causing a momentary gap in the fighter-bomber's stealth sheathing.

Pairs of AARGM-88 anti-radar missiles fell away from each aircraft. Igniting, they blazed toward the coast, the sonic booms of their passage resonating over the city.

Seconds later, the radar screens at the Regional Air Defense Center went blank as the HARMs obliterated the transmitter arrays, blinding the system. The Indonesian radar men never caught the second return from the Marine stealth birds as they launched the remainder of their load.

The strike fighters salvoed a variety of munition forms from their bomb bays, alike only in that each mounted a "Diamondback" Joint Direct Attack Munitions glide and guidance package. Razor-edged air foils snapped open and lift strakes caught the thin atmosphere at twenty-five thousand feet. Brought awake by its departure from its launch aircraft, each weapon locked onto the guidance signals of the Global Positioning Satellite network and began to steer toward the specific one-meter set of geographic co-ordinates that marked its final destiny.

The F-35s cranked hard over and reversed away from the coast, never once going "feet dry" over the city. Their packages delivered, their job was done. The bombs themselves would take it from here.

*

On the Alpha Display, they could see the Diamondback JDAMS radiating outward fanlike from their launch points.

"HARMs are in and the Indonesian radars are down, Captain," an SO reported. "We have clean sky!"

"Very good. Inform Air One that they may commence launching operations. Communications, advise the Embassy that they have incoming."

*

The initial detonations at Halim Perdana Kusuma airbase were unimpressive, a series of rapid flickering flashes above the runways and a faint crackling sound like a protracted string of firecrackers. A soft whickering whisper followed as a multitude of soup-can-sized metallic objects rained out of the sky.

Each soup can hit the ground, bounced, flipped upright on its coil spring landing gear and exploded, its shaped charge warhead drilling down through the thick concrete. Lightning danced across the ground and taxiways; runways and parking aprons unzipped, dissolving into impassible rubble. Nothing with wings would be taking off from Halim Perdana Kusuma for the foreseeable future.

As a double insurance, each patch of shattered runway had a silent circle of sentries. More Intelligent soup cans sat upright, ominous and unexploded. These were "area denial munitions", the politically correct Nelly phrase for land mines. Loaded into their bomblet bus with a more powerful ejection charge, they dropped around the edges of the havoc wreaked by the primary cratering charges. They would have to be dealt with, gingerly, before the runway repair crews could set to work.

*

East of the city, beyond the Sunter canal, the support elements of the 17th Motorized Brigade had established their base camp for the occupation of Jakarta. Here, within a fortified laager, were the critical "brains and guts" elements of the mobile force: the command and communications vehicles, the logistics trucks and fuel tankers, and the brigade's battery of 105mm field howitzers, the only heavy artillery currently in position to cover the city and its approaches.

The brigade was a good one. Its commanders were not fools. They had dispersed their equipment and they had dug in deeply against the possibility of air attack, their sweating, swearing soldiers throwing up earthen blast berms and filling and emplacing multitudes of sandbags.

They had also positioned a portion of the brigade's air defense troop of British-built Stryker combat tracks, armed with French-made Mistral surface-to-air missiles to cover the lager site. They thought they had made themselves ready for any eventuality.

Possibly that's why no one was immediately concerned when more strings of flickering flashes were seen in the sky beyond the laager perimeter, especially when no ground explosions or other mayhem seemed to follow.

It didn't occur to anyone that the flash strings were all taking place upwind. Nor could anyone see the armada of hundreds of small parachutes drifting in above the camp.

Dangling beneath each parachute was a flat, disc-shaped "skeet" loaded with a carefully shaped charge of high explosives and a tiny but discriminating package of electronics. Each skeet scanned the ground directly beneath it with microwave and infra-red microsensors, seeking for certain distinctive, recognizable geometric shapes: a truck, a tank, an artillery piece. When the "smart" sub-munition found such a shape, it exploded but in a most unique fashion.

The bottom of the skeet was made of an exotic copper alloy that was reshaped by the focused blast of the explosive charge into a semi-molten, armor-piercing dart that lanced straight down out of the sky like God's own vengeance.

A jet of vivid green fire struck and pierced the deck of a Stryker anti-air vehicle positioned on the edge of the camp, and the track burst in a bubble of flame. More flame streaks rained down as scores of the skeet swarmed over the laager site. Command and communications vans were gutted. Fuel tankers fire-balled. Ammunition trucks exploded. Cannon were sawed in half. The deeply dug complex of field fortifications were irrelevant. The strikes all came from the most vulnerable point, directly overhead.

The doom bolts targeted only vehicles and equipment. The hapless soldiers trapped in the fire squall merely got in the way.

*

The bombs that took out the Indonesian Ministry of Defense and its garrison were not in the least exotic. Simple one-ton chunks of high explosive, they drilled through from its roof to its sub-basement, gutting the structure and caving it in upon itself.

In the Point Man Operations center, half a mile away across the square, Christine Rendino's chair bounced a solid three inches into the air, the crash and tinkle of imploding windowpanes following the bludgeoning thunder of the explosions.

She shook the ringing out of her ears. "I think I hear our ride coming."

*

The friendly position hacks were multiplying on the Alpha Display as air traffic built rapidly over Jakarta.

At the highest altitude, some sixty thousand feet, circled the big US Air Force Global Hawk surveillance drones, beaming down real-time radar and video imaging of the developing battle.

Below, at thirty-thousand feet, the Australian Air Force F/A-18s were establishing a Combat Air Patrol over Jakarta, ready to pounce on any outside aerial interference. Lower yet, the *Shenandoah*'s wave of scout and attack RPVs were sweeping in over the city.

On the ocean's surface, the AAAV landing force was lining up on its objective beach while, the RIB raider boats peeled away from their escort slots, moving toward their own targets along the port waterfront.

More friendly hacks were blipping into existence on the display with every passing second. Muffled by the interceding decks, a continuous vibrant roar came from overhead. The topside monitors showed a stream of helicopters lifting off from the commando carrier: SPEED Cobras, SPEED Hawks and Little Birds, everything in the *Shenandoah*'s inventory. Yet more contacts were crawling down the screen from the north, the evacuation Ospreys moving up to their holding line.

Operation Trick or Treat was boiling down into one titanic air traffic control exercise.

"Captain, this is drone control," a voice sounded in the earphones of Amanda's headset. "All elements on station. Ready to start trolling."

323

Amanda replied into her headset mike, "Drone control, stay high and mark targets of opportunity. Do not engage until we get the fire base operational."

"Aye aye, ma'am." There was disappointment in the reply. It was obvious the RPV team wanted to start the hunt, but they couldn't be wasted. Not yet anyway.

The Landing Force Op center was growing warm with the heat of computers and bodies. Someone slipped in through the light curtain and wordlessly passed around cold sports drinks and cans of soda. Amanda automatically took a sip without tasting what she was drinking.

"Sea Demon Six to Star Child. We're holdin' at departure line. Sky Island flight ready to commit." Stone Quillain's voice was torn with wind roar and rotor blast. To provide the lift weight for the four-man Sky Island teams and their small mountain of equipment and ammunition, the Army AH-6s that carried them had been stripped of their integral armament and their fuselage door panels until they were little more than flying skeletons. Stone would be clipped into a monkey harness, sitting on the bare deck of the Little Bird, his legs dangling over a thousand feet of empty air.

"Strike Lead to Star Child," Vince Arkady's voice interjected. "Strike group is up and on station above Sky Island flight. We are ready to rock this town."

"Acknowledged Strike Lead. Acknowledged Sea Demon Six. Stand by all air elements. Hold and orbit at your check lines. The fire base force is crossing the beach at this time."

Ancol Park was the playground of the city of Jakarta. A complex of amusement rides, sports fields and public gardens, it stretched for over a mile along the shore of the Java Sea, east of the city's port facilities, its broad yellow beaches a favorite escape for the city's populace when the environment became too sweltering for even the tropic born to cope with.

In proper, sane times it was a crowded, happy place, meant for pleasure and relaxation.

Of late however, it had been a place of desolation and emptiness, occupied only by shadows, a handful of fearful squatters displaced by the fighting inside the city and an occasional rebel military patrol.

Now an ominous set of newcomers intruded. The *Shenandoah's* AAAV platoon snarled out of the surf. Their tracks redeployed, the big amphibious fighting machines bulldozing aside the occasional picnic table as they scrabbled up the sand to the firmer ground of the soccer fields beyond the beach area.

Once on the grass, their line abreast formation bowed outward into a defensive arc, the vehicles positioning so that their heaviest armor and armament would bear on any intruder approaching the beach head.

The point was proven within seconds as an Indonesian Army motor patrol tore onto the soccer field from inland, investigating the growl and chatter of engines and treads. The Indonesian Land Rover skidded to a halt as its headlights fell on a massive, sleekly angular camo-painted shape crouching on the grass. The corporal commanding the patrol reached for his radio microphone, but never completed the move as the AAAV's bushmaster turret whipped around and spat out a quick-draw burst of 25mm fire.

Tailgates dropped and a mixed team of US Army Rangers and Force Recon Marines poured down the ramps. The majority of the troops fanned out to establish a wider defense perimeter beyond the arc of the vehicle line. The remainder began to hastily offload and deploy the base plates, tripods, and tubes of a pair of 120mm heavy mortars. Cases of shells followed, and ordnance men carefully began to lay a series of ugly black sausage shapes on the ground, each finned projectile having a glassy, quarter-sized lens inset in its nose.

*

"The landing force reports perimeter secured and mortars up!" a Marine force SO reported. "Ready to commence firing."

"Very good," Amanda replied. "Mortars may commence firing as they get designation. Drone control, start trolling. You are cleared to fire and designate at will."

*

In the drone control center, twelve young men and women sat encased in a computer synthesized world. Each manipulated a pair of throttle and controller grips and each wore a blank-visored video helmet that turned and nodded as they scanned an environment ten miles distant.

They were of a generation that had teethed and grown up with videogames. Now, they were turning their skill with an amusement into a grim profession. They were the first generation of warbot warriors. Many others would follow.

Peering through the telepresence eyes of their robotic airborne alter-egos, they peeled off and dove recklessly into the streets canyons of Jakarta. As they descended, they flicked on the navigational strobe lights of their RPVs. They wanted to be seen. It was their mission to be shot at. It was their expectation to die, at least cybernetically.

Tracer streams shot up at them. Even with their brigade command-and-control networks knocked out, the individual rebel commanders at the company and battalion levels were convulsively reacting to the attack.

A Scorpion light tank sat parked on the bridge where the Samanhudi Boulevard crossed the Ganung Sahari canal. The vehicle commander elevated his anti-aircraft machine gun and blazed at one of the impudently blinking sets of lights in the sky.

The targeted RPV's operator, a nineteen-year-old "geek goddess" from Cleveland, Ohio, responded as she had in a thousand games of "Unreal Tournament" and "Doom III", bobbing, weaving, evading and countering with one of her drone's brace of radar-guided Hellfire missiles.

The hundred-and-ten-pound Hellfire had been designed to deal with armored fighting vehicles much larger than the Scorpion. Consequently, the little British-built scout tank was flattened like a tin can.

Satisfied, the Geek Goddess from Cleveland went back on the hunt.

*

Farther east, an Eagle Eye operator stalked a previously spotted target, a pair of Rhinemetal 20mm anti-aircraft twin mounts emplaced in one of the open display areas of the Jakarta Fair Grounds. His recon RPV carried no weapons of its own, only something just as deadly: a laser designator pod.

Gingerly, the Eagle Eye operator "hovered up" over the roof of the Airport International Hotel and "started the music," the invisible infra-red beam of his designator whipping out to paint the first of the anti-aircraft guns.

In the Landing Force Operations Center, a Marine fire control officer had been "piggybacking" the Eagle Eye operator, accessing the video feed from the RPV's low-light television cameras. As the targeting crosshairs settled on the anti-aircraft gun and the active designation box snapped into existence on his telescreen, he spoke a command into his hot mike.

Ashore, inside the beachhead in Alcol Park, an Army Ranger let a 120mm round slide down the throat of his mortar, ducking back to avoid the muzzle blast as the shell struck the firing pin at the bottom of the tube.

The mortar had been pre-registered on the general area of the Fair Grounds. As the shell, a creation of the superb Swedish munitions firm of Bofors, pitched over the high point of its trajectory, the laser sensor in its nose went active. It sought for, and found, that one particular speck of modulated coherent light reflecting off the designated target. Its guidance fins trimmed as it adjusted its course.

*Wham!*

One round fired. One target eliminated. The ultimate in military efficiency.

The designator beam traversed and pointed accusingly at the second gun.

*

To the west, another Eagle Eye, its propeller/rotors tilted up into helicopter mode, stalked down the Jalang Torman Raya, keeping below the roof lines of the high-rise buildings along the boulevard. Focused on his precision flying, its operator was taken totally by surprise when a pickup truck load of Indonesian infantry darted out of a side street.

A light machine gun and half a dozen automatic rifles hammered up at the slow, low flying drone. Bullet streams ripped through the Eagle Eye's structure and its systems operator swore as scarlet battle damage warnings flared around the perimeter of his vision field. As the fatally damaged drone began to plummet from the sky, its SO gave his controls one last savage wrench.

The cheer froze in the throats of the Indonesian infantrymen as the death plunge of the RPV they had downed changed into a flaming kamikaze dive straight into the bed of their truck.

Aboard the *Shenandoah*, the systems operator tore off his virtual reality helmet in disgust. Game over, for him and for others.

Back and forth over the city, the RPVs worked the target, provoking responses, building distraction, running risks manned aircraft couldn't dare. And the robots paid for it, absorbing casualties from the growing volume of ground fire as they sterilized a corridor for men to follow.

In what had been the headquarters of the Jakarta *Polici* Harbor Patrol detachment, an officer hunched over the shoulder of the enlisted operator of a field radio, making said operator even more nervous.

"Damn it private! Can't you get through that jamming? I need brigade now!"

"I'm sorry major, but this is something more than the jamming. I'm getting fragmentary traffic from the other tactical units, but brigade is completely off the air! There's nothing on either the primary or the backup channels."

It was not difficult to guess why. Beyond the walls of the harbor-side building, the continuing cackle of automatic weapons fire and the thud of explosions could clearly be heard.

An NCO pushed through the door from an adjoining office, illuminating his way with a flashlight beam. With the city power down, the detachment's Honda emergency generator was barely adequate to maintain the radios.

"Were you able to get through to the Defense Ministry on the landlines?" the officer demanded.

"No, Major, but I was able to reach Lieutenant Sirhi at Gambir Station. There's no Defense Ministry left. It's been destroyed."

"What?"

"Yes sir." The Sergeant mopped at his sweat-slick brow with his sleeve. "American precision-guided bombs. The building has been leveled and the Merdeka Square command post destroyed."

"Are they sure it's the Americans?"

"It must be. Damned if we have anything like this." The noncom waved out at the darkness. "They're hitting us with a complete Baghdad package. That means Brigade must have been taken out. The Americans must be coming for their people at their embassy and they have already made a landing somewhere in the area."

"Why do you say that?" the major demanded.

"Mortar fire, sir. You can hear it outside. They're using heavy mortars on targets in the city."

"The motor patrol in Dreamland Park is not reporting, sir," the radio operator interjected. "We might not be hearing their calls over the jamming – but it could be something else."

"In Muhammad's name," the Major groaned. "What next?"

He was answered with a spray of shattered glass as the picture windows looking out across Jakarta harbor imploded under multiple bullet impacts.

The officer, the sergeant and the private hit the floor as a fifty-caliber slug sent the field radio flying.

A pair of RIB Raiders lay a hundred yards off the harbor patrol headquarters, systematically riddling the building, its finger piers and the moored patrol boats, with machine gun and grenade launcher fire. The SEALs and Special Boat men were engaged in one of the first Naval Special Forces missions, "beach jumping," the spreading of chaos and confusion from the sea amid the ranks of a land-bound enemy.

The raiders maintained their barrage until the fires blazed ashore with an adequate brightness. Then their crews kicked a few smoke and flare floats over the side and roared off in search of more trouble to make. Jakarta had a long stretch of waterfront and the possibilities were numerous.

*

The Sky Island flight went feet dry over the city, buzzing in above the shadow-filled streets. Trusting in the nylon webbing of his monkey harness, Stone Quillain leaned out of the open side of the Army AH-6, scanning ahead through his night vision visor.

The only ground illumination came from the occasional set of racing headlights and a few distant burning structures. Sporadic shell bursts flamed greenly in the night and tracer snakes crawled through the darkness.

None crawled in the direction of the Little Birds, however. The multitude of diversions was working, permitting the small helicopters to slip through unengaged. But they would have to build on that even further before they could risk bringing the Osprey lift ships in to the embassy.

That was what the Sky Island mission was all about. The legendary Chinese General Sun Tsu had once written in the first textbook on military strategy and tactics that, "You must take the high ground or you shall most certainly perish in the valley."

That rule was as applicable in the heart of a great city as anywhere else. Ahead of the Little Birds, Jakarta's high ground loomed. Four huge hi-rise resort hotels rose above Merdeka Square, overlooking the embassy compound and its approaches: the Sriwijaya to the north, the Transaera to the east, the Aryaduta Hyatte to the southeast and the Metropolitan to the southwest. Blacked out and abandoned, the travelers and tourists they had served were gone, but this night they would serve a different kind of sightseer.

Stone reached up one-handed and called up the air command channel on his Leprechaun transceiver. "Sea Demon Six to Strike Lead!" he yelled over the rotor roar. "All Sky Island elements positioned to insert!"

"Roger that, Sea Demon," Vince Arkady's relaxed reply came back through Stone's headset. "Strike elements – Baker, Charley, Dog, Echo – stand by for sterilization passes on Sky Islands. Roll in ... now!"

Stone's helicopter bobbed for an instant as two larger, sleeker, chunks of darkness blasted past overhead. Looking up through the NiteBrite visor, Stone caught a belly view of a pair of SPEED Cobras, weapons pods studding their underwing hardpoints. Fangs out, they were diving on Stone's future command post, the roof of the Hotel Sriwijaya.

It had to be assumed that the Indonesians read Sun Tzu as well.

Again, Stone leaned outboard to watch events develop. This was going to be interesting.

Someone hostile was in residence on the hotel roof. Clearly visible through the photomultipliers, small arms fire sparkled from the balustrade, aimed at the approaching gunships.

The lead Cobra replied with what looked like a glowing green death ray that swept along the edge of the hotel roof, wiping away the flyspecks of rifle fire. Stone could recognize the tracer stream of a 20mm "Vulcan Lite" Gatling gun when he saw one. He could also appreciate good shooting.

He had a little more trouble with what he observed next. The sterilizing SPEED Cobra pitched up steeply, bled speed and flared into a side skid. At first, Quillain thought that the compound helo had been hit, but then he realized that the Navy gunship was still under precise, deliberate control.

As the wingman climbed and circled, the flight leader jinked around the top of the hotel, in an odd, sidling dance, edging closer, side slipping a few feet to one side or another, climbing slightly or dipping its nose.

Then it hit Quillain. He'd seen this kind of thing before, back home on his father's farm. Ol' Rebel, their venerable gray barn cat, would lay moves like this on a mouse he was chasing. The helo pilot had missed someone on his first firing pass, and now he was hunting the fugitive through the maze of ventilator stacks and elevator heads on the hotel roof, trying to line up a finishing shot.

Blooded veteran or not, Quillain felt a cold shiver ripple through him. He lifted a hand to the Leprechaun keypad clipped to his chest harness and tapped into the designated Talk-Between-Pilots channel.

"You need a hand down there, Lieutenant?" the Cobra wingman inquired

"Negative, negative, this guy is just being a pain," an annoyed feminine voice replied. "Where'd he go, dammit? Just a sec ... Okay, got him cornered. Going to grenade. Gotcha!"

The rotor-winged mouser pounced. A single shell belched from an underwing gunpod, a fireball blossoming on the roof. Then the SPEED Cobra was wheeling clear and climbing away. "Sea Demon Six, this is Strike Flight Bravo. The LZ is clean and we're out of here. Your sheets are turned down and the mint is on the pillow."

"This is Sea Demon Six. 'Preciate ya, Bravo. We are in."

With a droning whine, the AH-6 settled onto the roof of the hotel and its handful of passengers disembarked with an explosive rush.

The Sky Island force consisted of the three four-man diamonds of the Green Beret A-Team and the Sniper/Designator element of the Marine Force Recon Platoon. As a gesture of jointness, Stone had attached himself to one of the Army Special Forces sections – but, with the camouflage patterns of their uniforms washed out by his night vision system, it was impossible to tell the difference between Dogface and Leatherneck this night.

Once more, Stone slapped the key pad of his transceiver. "Star Child, Star Child, this is Sea Demon Six at Sky Island Alpha. We are down and operating."

"Acknowledged, Island Alpha."

Wordlessly, the four-man Special Forces unit broke down into two smaller segments, the sniper/observer team rushing for the cannon scarred balustrade that overlooked Merdeka Square, while the security team moved to secure the rooftop access doors.

Once again, the lethal mystique of the sniper came into play. A single, skilled marksman, dealing precision death from a distance could paralyze a far larger body of troops. Even a blooded combat veteran, inured to the possibility of random death on the battlefield, might freeze when confronted with the thought of having a single, specific bullet aimed at him with cold blooded determination.

The tactical snipers on the embassy walls had initiated this paralysis; now the Sky Island marksmen would set the final seal upon it. They were armed with the "Big Fifty", the Barrett M82A1 .50 caliber anti-materiel rifle

With an unhurried swiftness, the Green Beret Snipers deployed, extending the bipod of their massive primary weapon and finding a brace point and firing position. Uncapping the lenses of the thermographic rifle sight and observer's scope, they set out a row of massive reload clips and their range tables. In less than a minute, gunner and spotter were behind their scopes and hunting targets.

Quillain flipped up his visor and lifted his own NiteBrite binoculars, then panned them across the city. Intermittent flashbulb bursts of mortar and missile fire flared, answered by occasional sputtering tracer streams from anti-aircraft guns. The defensive gunfire was thinning out rapidly, however. The concentrated flak suppression program being put down by the RPVs, SPEED Cobra's and mortar crews was making the firing of an anti-aircraft gun a very dead-end proposition.

Off to the southwest of their position, across the broad open space of the square, the ruins of the Indonesian Defense Ministry sent up a dense plume of smoke. A steady popping of rifle fire came from the US Embassy compound in the southeastern corner, along with the occasional rip of a machine gun or thud of a grenade. Mostly it was outgoing from the compound walls; the FAST Marines were maintaining a furious fire, hosing down the local environment.

As yet, there was no sign of coordinated activity from the rebel forces surrounding the embassy. The shock paralysis of the attack was still in effect. They didn't know just who the enemy was or what his intents were, nor from where the next blow might fall. The individual company-level commanders were waiting for orders to come down or for the situation to clarify before taking action.

Stone could recognize the logical but insidious trap the Indonesians were sliding into. When you were under attack, it was always better to do something, anything, constructive immediately rather than to stand around figuring out what would have been best after it was too late.

He swung his glasses back across the square and caught movement at the base of the MONAS monument. A squad of Indonesian infantry crouched behind the base of the towering obelisk, taking shelter from the fire from the embassy. Through his powerful NiteBrite glasses, Stone could see one of the soldiers had something lifted in front of his face: a radio. Apparently, the squad leader was trying to establish contact with his superiors, intent on asking just what in the hell he was supposed to do now.

Stone wasn't the only one to spot the infantry squad.

*C-R-A-A-A-C-K!*

Even standing ten feet away from the weapon, the muzzle blast of the Barrett Big Fifty was a stinging physical slap.

The Barrett fired the Browning .50 caliber machine gun round, a venerable projectile designed shortly after the First World War that, by sheer accident, turned out to be the most accurate long-range cartridge ever created in the history of ballistics.

The Browning .50 hadn't been meant for use as a sniper's round. Originally, it had been intended to knock out tanks and shoot down airplanes. When used against the far more fragile human body, the effect could only be called spectacular.

The Indonesian squad leader exploded under the impact of the massive, hypervelocity slug. In Stone's thermographic binoculars, he dissolved into a spray of hazy green mist that engulfed the remainder of his squad.

"Boy howdy, that's doing the job," Stone commented mildly.

"Yeah," the lead Beret sniper replied, not lifting his eye from the sighting module. "I'm using one of the new Norwegian HE loads. It ramps things up."

*C-R-A-A-A-C-K!*

Half a mile away, another target at the base of the obelisk dissolved. Some of the Indonesians dropped their weapons and fled wildly, preferring the random death that might be encountered in a dash across the open ground of the square to the certainty of being crushed under the pointing finger of God. Others just crouched, frozen, incapable of action as the sniper methodically emptied his magazine. Either way, none of these soldiers would be a factor for the remainder of this fight.

Stone was satisfied. "Star Child, Star Child, this is Sea Demon Six at Island Able. It's as good as it's going to get. Let's get these folks out of here."

*

In the Landing Force Operations Center, Amanda Garrett decided that she was passionately in love with Remotely Piloted Vehicles. Almost half of the *Shenandoah*'s tilt-rotor drone group had been shot down performing the close recon and flak suppression mission, and yet it would only be a matter for the US taxpayer and Boeing Textron to deal with, not Graves Registration.

She studied the continuously updating symbology on the primary displays and was nominally pleased with what she saw. The Indonesian command-and-control nets were still down. Their ground units were still semi-paralyzed from assault shock and all identified anti-air positions had been nullified by precision guided mortar and missile fire. She decided Stone was right. It wasn't going to get any better.

"Air One, this is the Captain. Proceed with the primary evacuation phase. Put the blanket down over the primary LZ and commit the Ospreys."

"This is it! Let's go!" Christine yelled.

Swapping their headsets for K-Pot helmets, the Systems Operators abandoned the last functional workstations and headed for the door, snatching up their personal weapons as they came. Sergeant MacGuffin and Christine were the last out of the Point Man Base operations room, MacGuffin trailing a detonator wire behind him.

Detcord had already been looped around the tactical scanners and relay radios. As the Sergeant connected the firing leads to a hand clacker firing unit, Christine took a last wistful look into the cluttered reception hall. It had been an odd first independent command but it had been hers.

"Fire in the hole!" MacGuffin yelled and Christine ducked back behind the wall.

The clacker clacked and a linear explosion lashed around the interior of the room, shutting Point Man Base down permanently.

As they trotted out of the embassy building, the thud and roar of the night washed over them and they were engulfed in the stench of burning buildings and gun smoke.

"Sarge, rejoin the main party and make sure all chalks are ready to load. I'm taking a final look from the wall."

"Okay, ma'am. Watch your ... Well, you just watch it!"

"Always do."

Christine scrambled up the ladder to the parapet gangway stretching across the forward wall of the embassy.

The FAST Marines and the Embassy security force were strung out along the walls like the defenders of a medieval castle. A thickening layer of ejected gun brass glinted on the parapet decking. Around her was the continuous, deliberate, bap, bap, bap, of aimed, suppressive fire.

Peering through their night sights, they overwatched Merdeka

337

Square and the faces of the surrounding buildings, sending rounds in at any hunt of movement or even into places where movement might be. They were burning through ammunition at a terrific rate, but it was critical to keep hostile heads down for the next few minutes.

They still weren't taking much answering fire and Christine peered cautiously over the parapet lip. She was using only the mark one eyeball at the moment and the vista was positively Satanic: the blacked-out buildings of central Jakarta were a jagged mountain range around the valley of the square, with the burning defense ministry an erupting volcano, its flames glittering off acres of broken glass in the perimeter streets. In the square itself, the statuary seemed to writhe, dancing in agony in the smoky light.

It was a terrifying scene and Christine noted abstractly that a part of her was indeed terrified.

A loudhailer call suddenly rippled around the embassy compound. "Chemical Alert! Chemical Alert! GAS! GAS! GAS!"

The suppressive fire staggered as the marines snatched for the protective gear slung from their harnesses. Christine fumbled with her own gas mask, trying to remember the donning drill. If she didn't get it right, she was likely to be very unhappy for some time to come.

*

The next movement in the intricate aerial ballet began. The Air Commando MH-60 flight swept inshore, flying nose to tail down a narrow corridor designated by their GPU systems, a corridor that passed upwind of the Merdeka Square area.

The Air Force compound helicopters carried multiple sub-munitions scatterpacks under their wings. Smoke and teargas grenades rained from the launcher tubes as they transited beyond the square. Hundreds of ghostly white plumes rose from the streets and rooftops, merging into a wall of eye-burning artificial fog that began to roll over the square and the embassy.

Smoke screens were not as commonly used as they once were – but no weapon or tactic ever becomes entirely obsolete.

The SPEED Hawks jettisoned their empty scatter packs and swung back toward the sea and their holding line. They would have another role to play shortly.

*

From his position atop Sky Island One, Stone Quillain watched the rivers of chemical vapor flow into the open reservoir of the square and soak into the surrounding buildings. He was well above the maximum concentration level, but he felt the first tingle of the tear gas and hastily pulled his chemical warfare hood down over his face.

"All Sky Island sniper teams, this is Sea Demon Six. Go to thermographic sights and keep knocking 'em down! Keep 'em off the lift ships!"

The Marine and Beret gunners flipped their sighting system modules from low-light to infra-red targeting. Peering through the man-made smog bank, they continued their turkey shoot.

*

The first Osprey VTOL swept down out of the sky, smoke swirling tornado-like in the wash of its rotorprops. Its pilots had switched to their own haze-piercing thermographic vision systems. Passing over the compound wall, the Osprey pivoted, popped its landing gear and dropped onto the embassy helipad.

"First chalk load up!" the Marine pad boss bellowed over the turbine scream. "Move your ass! Go!" That he was yelling at a United States Ambassador and the leader of a major foreign power was irrelevant.

From her position on the wall, Christine Rendino watched as Ambassador Goodyard, President Kediri and their staff were hustled into the waiting belly of the impatient aircraft. In all probability Goodyard couldn't see her, but she lifted a hand in farewell.

By the clock, the first Osprey was on the ground a bare thirty-five seconds. Then it was lifting off, climbing through the smoke screen for the sky, the sea and safety. The primary mission was accomplished. That which Admiral Ketalaman desired was out of reach. Technically, logically, there was no reason for the battle of Jakarta to continue. But as with all wars it was easier to begin than to end.

*

The Rebel NCO crouched in the corner of the Gambir station waiting room, his eyes tear-blinded and his uniform splattered with the brains of his company commander. "Yes, the damned Americans are pulling their people out of the embassy!" he yelled over the jamming warble in his transceiver. "No there's nothing we can do! We're being cut to pieces here! If you want them stopped we'll need help! Everything we can get! Everything ... and hurry!"

Flashlights and headlights blazed. Shouted orders reverberated amid the dank concrete pillars. Engines roared to life, thickening the air of the underground parking garage with throat-tickling fumes. Vehicle crewmen squeezed into turret hatches beneath the low ceiling and mobile troopers piled into armored passenger compartments.

Shielded by multiple levels of concrete, they had been safe from both observation and from the fire and thunder haunting the night. Now, as one of the last uncommitted and intact elements of the Jakarta city garrison, it was their turn.

"Osprey Bravo is airborne." The word came in from Air One. "The Australian Ambassador and his staff are clear. Osprey Charley is going in."

"Those are all of the big-ticket items," MacIntyre murmured.

"It's still so far so good, Elliot," Amanda replied, her eyes roving constantly over the Alpha display. "We're in and we're getting them out. That's what counts."

"Very true." She glanced in his direction, making out his craggy silhouette in the screen glow as he studied the tactical situation with the same focused attention. "But we still have a long way to go, young lady."

Amanda could only agree. On screen, the red hostile unit hacks were beginning to move. Like white corpuscles attacking an infection, they were starting to converge on Merdeka Square and the landing site. As yet, the convergence was slow and erratic – but there was an increasing deliberation to it.

The Indonesians were still shocked but they were recovering command-and-control.

"Osprey Charley is airborne, Captain. That's the first of the civilian refugee chalks."

*Good. That's good!*

"Captain," another voice interjected. "The beach Firebase reports they're down to four rounds per tube and they're starting to get increasing ground fire on their perimeter."

*That was bad.*

"Tell Firebase to check fire! Save those rounds for getaway ammunition. Order all Special Boat elements to converge on the Firebase support stations. Prepare to cover the extraction."

The tide of the American raid was cresting. Soon it must begin to ebb.

The fourth of the Ospreys boomed past the top of the high rise. Climbing steeply, its engine pods swiveled to horizontal flight mode. Anti-IR flares rained down in its wake, underlighting the ground smog of tear gas and chemical smoke.

Sweat burned hot and slick under Stone Quillain's chemical warfare hood, and he urgently wished he could perform the simple act of swiping his arm across his face.

The Barrett Big Fifty had fallen silent, the sniper team manning it surrounded by a half-circle of smoking shell casings. "We've learned 'em, Captain," the spotter reported. "They're keeping their heads down."

"Keep 'em there. When they start pullin' the Embassy garrison out, we're goin' to lose the suppression fire from ground level."

There was a sudden shock against the soles of his combat boots and the hollow thud of a nearby contained explosion.

"We got activity!" The yell came from one of the cover team at the hotel's roof access. A couple of protracted bursts of M-8 carbine fire followed.

"Maintain the cover!" Quillain yelled over his shoulder to the snipers as he cut back across the roof to the top of the stairwell. A thin haze of explosives smoke leaked out of the stair house. The Beret guards were kneeling on either side of the open door, aiming down into the darkness.

"What's happenin'?" Quillain demanded, dropping down beside the team leader.

"Somebody just yanked open the fire door at the bottom of the well. We had it wired – whoever it was got a Claymore right in the face."

It had only been a matter of time before the Indonesians figured out what was going on over their heads.

Stone took a cautious look down the well. Through his night vision visor he could make out a blast-buckled fire door and what appeared to be a combat boot. The foot in it was no longer attached to a leg.

Over the whine of the idling Little Bird, Quillain caught the sound of orders being shouted on the floor below.

Stone unhooked an M-67 fragmentation grenade from his MOLLE harness and gestured the Beret to stand back. Expertly gauging the angle of the partially open door at the bottom of the stairwell, he pulled the pin. Allowing the safety lever to flick away, Stone hurled the grenade down the well with all of his considerable strength. The metal sphere whanged off the door, skittering and bouncing down an unseen corridor. There was another shock against his boot soles and Stone ducked back as shrapnel ricocheted up the well.

"We should be able to keep 'em off the roof, sir," the Beret commented.

"Yeah," his partner added. "As long as they don't lug explosives up here and blow the whole roof out from under us."

The last Osprey lifted off from the Embassy helipad carrying the final handful of civilian refugees. No one remained within the compound walls save for the security details and the Intelligence unit, fewer than seventy-five people in all.

The civilians were all outbound for the RIF fleet and, eventually, for Australia. The Embassy garrison was to be routed to a different, much closer destination.

Crouching down behind the firing parapet on the compound wall, Christine Rendino tried to keep her voice steady as she spoke into her lip mike. "Star Child, Star Child, this is Point Man! The last of the civvies are clear! We're ready for flight two."

"The first of flight two is inbound, Chris." Amanda's calm reply was as steadying as a drink of cool water. "We're on the downside now. We'll have you out of there on the next bird."

Christine forced a swallow down her dry throat. "Negative. I'm ... I'm on the last ship."

Amanda's voice lifted slightly. "Chris, the Intelligence detail is the next out."

"I know, Boss Ma'am. But I'm senior officer present. This is my watch. I go out with the last flight."

There was a hesitation at the far end of the circuit. "Acknowledged. Carry on, Commander."

"Thanks. Fa'sure I hope you know this is what you get for being such a damn good role model."

A rueful chuckle came back. "Thank you for the compliment. Take care, Chris."

With its side hatches open and landing gear extended, the first of the *Shenandoah*'s SPEED Hawks dipped down into Merdeka Square. Side-slipping past the MONAS spire, it swept over the Embassy wall, slewed in line with its escape route and settled onto the helipad. The posed members of the Intelligence detail scrambled aboard and the SPEED Hawk was on its way out.

"First and second squads, off the wall!" the FAST Platoon leader yelled over the tactical channel. "Chalk up to lift out!"

The volume of fire streaming from the embassy shrank and the first stars glittered through the thinning smoke screen.

Over half of the Eagle Eye and Hell Eye control stations had been powered down. The "dead" drone pilots, their virtual reality helmets tucked under their arms, loitered in the control bay, studying the repeater screens of their fellows still in the fight, critiquing them under their breath.

"Sandy's sure got the moves with that Eagle Eye of hers."

"Yeah, we gotta get her flyin' a Hell Eye. She'd kick ass."

"What we gotta get is a way to carry more goddamn ammo. This two rail limitation sucks!"

"You're too frickin' impatient, Tyrone. You got to learn to wait for the fat shots, man!"

These young enlisted SOs were the first generation of the warbot warrior. Although they had no realization of it, any more than the first aviators, tankers or submariners, they were building a database and a set of traditions for a whole new way of warfare.

Then, at one of the still active control stations, an operator stiffened, looking "down" over Jakarta. "I have hostiles! Major hostiles! Glodok sector!"

Every eye in the darkened service bay went to the repeater over his station.

"Jesus! Where did those guys come from?"

"They're coming out of an underground parking garage. They must have been lying doggo."

"Shit! Look at 'em all! Tyrone's right! We need to carry more ammo!"

"Situational change in the Glodok sector! Enemy armored column!"

"Let's see them," Amanda snapped.

The drone-generated imaging appeared in a corner of the big plasma screen, a view looking down into a blacked-out high-rise canyon. Land Rovers, Cadillac Gauge APCs and Scorpion light tanks – more than a score of vehicles – could only mean a full mixed-team mechanized company, intact, unengaged and moving under orders.

"Where the hell did they come from?" MacIntyre demanded.

"I don't know, sir," the center duty officer replied. "There wasn't any armored formation of that size showing anywhere on the boards in that sector. They must have been holed up in a warehouse or a garage. Some kind of a reserve force."

Amanda checked the compass rose in the corner of the screen. "They're heading south, straight for Merdeka Square."

"For all appearances, ma'am."

"How long until they're a factor?"

The duty officer made a fast judgment call. "Through that built up environment, maybe five minutes, six at the outside."

"Get the SPEED Cobras in there!" Amanda snapped. "Engage targets! Take those bastards out!

"Belay that order!" Admiral MacIntyre said heavily. "Do not engage!"

Amanda twisted to face him. "Elliot, that column is moving on the embassy. They'll be there in a matter of minutes!"

"Take a look at the strike environment, Amanda. That column is passing through a dense residential area. Those are apartment complexes on either side of that avenue, and it's outside of the central city district. The Indonesians haven't evacuated those buildings!"

He didn't have to elaborate. Given the cracker box construction common in Asia, putting fire into the enemy column in the close confines of the city streets would cause what was euphemistically referred to as "collateral damage" on a massive scale: civilian casualties, men, women and children.

Elliot was right and she slammed her palm down onto the console top. "Damn, damn, damn! Put me through to Strike Lead."

Arkady's voice came up in her headset in a matter of seconds, speaking over rotor thunder. "This is strike lead 'by. What's up, Captain?"

"New target! Non-lethal! Armor inbound from the Glodok sector toward Merdeka Square. Hit them with the Pigeye flight. Try and slow them down."

Amanda was fully aware that matching non-lethal weaponry against a real combat unit using blood armament was not sound doctrine. The rebels need have no concerns at all about putting their own people at risk while the United States would be crucified by the world media if they didn't make every effort to minimize civilian casualties, even to the point of placing American lives, the lives of her people, at risk.

But whoever said the Universe was fair?

"Acknowledged." Arkady sounded dubious. "Pigeye flight on the way!"

Amanda forced herself on to other concerns. "What's the status on the Embassy evacuation? How many more lift flights to go?"

It was MacIntyre answered. "SPEED Hawk Echo is on the ground now with Foxtrot holding to land. Foxtrot is the last evac bird."

"Then maybe we can beat them out." She turned to the Duty Officer. "The Firebase and the Special Boat Sections are to commence an immediate withdrawal. They can't do us any more good – so get them out of there. Have the Sky Island sniper sites stand by. AIRBOSS, this is the Captain. Move your crisis flight to the inshore check line and get on with SPEED Hawk Foxtrot. Tell them to expedite the extraction. We're running out of time!"

"We're pulling out! Fall back! Mount up!

The mortar crews horsed their weapons – base plates, tubes, bipods and all – up the tail ramps of the AAAVs, not bothering with conventional tie-down procedures. Around the firebase perimeter, the thin line of Marines and Rangers collapsed upon itself, the ground fighters backing toward their vehicles, blazing into the darkness in a concentrated mad minute of full autofire.

Standing close offshore, the RIB gunboats emptied their shot lockers, raking the probing Indonesian troops with a focused hail of grenades and machinegun fire.

At the tailgate of each track, squad leaders counted and double counted every man back aboard.

"We're in! We're all in! We're good! Go, go, go!"

Ramps lifted and slammed closed.

"Track Lead to all track elements! Commence extraction! Cover your sectors! Maintain firing!"

Turrets traversed, autocannon and co-axial machine guns snapping off bursts. The AAAVs backed slowly down the beach, the sea boiling up around their hulls. With pursuing bullets glancing off their armored hides and waterspouts lifting around them, the big war machines wallowed back into the safety of the night.

"Yeah," Stone replied into his lip mike. "I hear you, skipper. We'll be ready."

He crouched beside the shrapnel riddled stairwell house. He and the security team had been engaged in a very diverting game of hand grenade baseball with the growing number of Indonesian soldiers on the floor below. Thanks to their holding the high ground, Stone and the Sea Demons were still decisively ahead on points.

Stone switched back to his tactical channel, speaking to his snipers and his escape helo pilot. "Heads up, boys. We're goin' to be getting out of here pretty quick."

He shifted position again returning to the roof edge. There was only one evac flight left to go – but the last bird out was always the bitch of the litter.

Through the thermographic sighting system, the line of rebel armored fighting vehicles glowed like a string of internally illuminated beads being drawn through the city's streets. From his station orbiting at ten thousand feet, Arkady could note and bitterly appreciate the erratic path the task force was following towards the Embassy.

Whoever was commanding the column was deliberately keeping to the narrower residential streets, keeping his force shielded by apartment houses and private homes, daring the circling attack aircraft to fire on them at the price of innocent and uninvolved civilian lives.

Holding babies over their heads.

"If I could get you bastards alone for just five seconds," Arkady muttered.

"Strike lead," a voice spoke in his earphones. "This is Pigeye Lead. We have target in sight, and we have line of fire. Arming now."

"Strike Lead to Pigeye," Arkady acknowledged. "Stink 'em up. Let 'em have it all, but watch your ass. This is going to be hot."

The Pigeye flight swept into the vision field of his NiteBrite visor, the pair of non-lethally armed SPEED Cobras marked not only by the thermal trails of their exhaust plumes but by the glowing blue ID hacks generated by the Identification Friend or Foe system.

They were carrying unguided 2.75-inch rocket pods with Pigeye gas warheads. They had no option but to dive right down the throat of their target, walking their salvos down the length of the street and the armored column.

Tracer streams whipped back at them.

The string of airbursting rockets exploded down the length of the rebel column, smothering it under a blanket of swirling riot gas. But from out of the gas cloud another fire trail lanced upward.

"SAM! SAM!" Arkady yelled into his mike. "Break! Break! Break!"

The two non-lethal SPEED Cobras obeyed, snapping their wings vertical in minimum radius turns, left and right, trailing streams of anti-IR flares.

The warning had come too late. One of the banking helicopters caught the missile full in its belly.

Rotors flailing, the maimed helo staggered through the sky trailing a streamer of flame. Rolling inverted, it plunged through the roof of an apartment complex two streets over from the path of the rebel force. The walls of the building bulged outward, collapsing as a fireball of exploding jet propellant burst within it.

*Non-lethal warfare, my ass!*

"Strike Lead to Star Child. Pigeye Flight Lead is down. Do not, I repeat, do not commit crisis flight. Nonsurvivable event. Gas is deployed. Assessing results."

The chemical reactions taking place within the gas cloud that filled the street below blurred the thermal signatures into indistinction. Then the lead tank tore out of the cloud, still churning purposefully ahead, its teammates following.

"Shit!" Pink Pinkerton commented over the Talk Between Pilots. "We didn't even slow them down!"

"I can see it, Pink. Star Child, this is Strike Lead. Pigeye ineffective. Totally ineffective. They must have chemical warfare gear. Column ETA to Merdeka Square now four minutes or less!"

"Air Boss! Status on the last lift flight?"

"SPEED Hawk Foxtrot is just touching down now, ma'am. We're going to make it!"

"If nothing breaks. Crisis flight, this is the Lady. Move up to final phase check line! Arkady, I want you to position on that armored column and stand by!"

The Intelligence detail was gone, as were the members of the FAST platoon; only the single squad of the Embassy Marine garrison and one mildly terrified Naval Intelligence officer remained, hunkered against the inner facing of the perimeter wall.

Christine Rendino couldn't draw enough air through the filters of her chem war hood to ease the strain in her lungs. She tore off her helmet and the gas mask and took a deep wheezing breath. Only a faint burning coolness around her eyes hinted at a lingering residue of teargas. The rotor blast of the incoming lift ship helped to disperse the last rags of the smoke screen.

The SPEED Hawk settled toward the helipad. While its undercarriage wheels were still a man's height off the tarmac, the Marine garrison commander yelled, "Let's go! Load up!"

For a single hideous instant, Christine Rendino thought she was paralyzed, that somehow she couldn't move and that she was about to be left behind. Then she lost all choice in the matter. Callused hands closed on the straps of her interceptor vest. Two brawny leathernecks flanked her, yanked her to her feet, hauled her across the pad to the helicopter and hurled her bodily through the SPEED Hawk's gaping hatch. On her hands and knees, she scrambled across the helo's deck, getting out of the way as the Marine squad piled in after her.

The landing gear bounced on the ground once; then the Air Commando Pilot had his throttles firewalled climbing back out of the compound. Kneeling on the deck, Christine could see the flagpole drifting past the open side hatch, the stars and stripes still flying and backlit by the burning city.

There had been some discussion about lowering the embassy flag – but Ambassador Goodyard had insisted that it remain flying, a reminder to whom it may concern that the United States intended to resume residence.

The SPEED Hawk nosed down, gathering speed as it swept across Merdeka Square. In another ten seconds it would be clear and away.

Corporal Jambul Hadiah took a cautious peek over the roof parapet. The storm of fire from the walls of the American embassy that had killed the other three members of his heavy weapons team had ceased. Why Allah had allowed him to live while the others had died, he did not know. He could only recall lying tightly curled in a fetal position behind a roof ventilator while the sniper fire had picked off his teammates one at a time. Hadiah, a brave man by his own estimation, had been terrified – as the urine-soaked crotch of his fatigues could testify.

However, he was also the kind of man within whom fear could swiftly turn to anger. And now, as he watched the odd-looking helicopter climbing out of the American embassy, he was filled with a searing, white hot rage.

A few feet away, his friend Lelang lay sprawled over the tube of a French-made ACL-STRIM anti-tank weapon. Hadiah lunged for it, dragging the rocket launcher out from under the body. Whipping it to his shoulder, he took half a second to aim and squeezed the trigger.

What Hadiah hadn't thought through was the possibility that American snipers had had been positioned elsewhere in the city, outside of the embassy walls. The Indonesian never experienced the triumph of seeing his rocket slam into the tail of the fleeing helicopter before an explosive .50 caliber bullet, striking from above and behind, tore him in half.

*

At Sky Island Alpha, Stone heard the Special Forces sniper swear as he failed to get his shot off in time. In horror, the Marine watched as the fire trail of the AT rocket streaked through the night sky to kiss the tail duct assembly of the Air Commando SPEED Hawk. The entire back end of the compound helicopter dissolved, the loss of anti-torque thrust tossing it into a wild, flat pinwheel spin.

"Foxtrot is down! Foxtrot is down! We lost one!" Stone was yelling into his headset even before the doomed helo slammed into the ground.

*

The same view was being seen from overhead in the *Shenandoah*'s Landing Force Operations Center – and, for perhaps the first time in her life, Amanda Garrett had no words to speak, no orders to give. A single soft animal noise of despair and agony rose from somewhere within her as one of her darkest, deepest nightmares unfolded before her eyes.

Then there was a strong arm around her, in the darkness, keeping her knees from buckling and Elliot MacIntyre's bellow rang in her ear, "Commit the crisis flight! Get those people out of there!"

*

The first thing Christine Rendino noted was how quiet everything had gotten beyond the ringing in her ears. All that could be heard was the occasional human moan and distant gunshot. She popped her eyes open and shook the sparks from her vision, finding with some amazement that she was still alive.

The evac helicopter had been stripped of its passenger seats to gain greater payload capacity, and no one in the cabin had been strapped down. Fate and centrifugal force had intervened in her favor. She had been crouching directly beneath the rotor hub when the compound helo had gone into its death spin. Thus, she had been the last thrown onto the mass of humanity piled up behind the pilots' seats and her fellow evacuees had cushioned the impact of the crash.

The air smelled of burnt insulation, kerosene and blood – and she felt faint movement beneath her. She rolled off the bodies of the Marines and got to her hands and knees. Everything hurt but nothing seemed completely broken.

Instead of being flipped on her side by the residual torque of the

358

rotors, the SPEED Hawk's wings had kept her upright when she had pancaked. In the faint light leaking in from outside, Christine could make out that the side hatch had sprung open in the crash. She crawled to it and, using the bent door gun mount and the unconscious body of the gunner strapped behind it, she pulled herself to her feet.

They'd piled up against the base of the MONAS spire. Everything in Merdeka Square was so deathly still; only the dancing flame light from the burning buildings moved. Then, dimly, Christine heard the chatter of tank treads – distant, but drawing closer.

"We are so totally screwed," she murmured with no one to hear her.

There was no fireball. The overhead NiteBrite imaging from the circling drones showed an intact fuselage and not a scattered debris field at the crash site. Even that wisp of hope was all that Amanda Garret needed.

A single glance at the Alpha tactical display revealed that the Rebel armored column had entered the free-fire zone of the government district. Rolling down Jalan Veteran's Avenue, the enemy vehicles were on the verge of entering Merdeka Square.

Amanda smashed down the send key on her command headset. "Arkady!" she yelled. "I need you! Now!"

\*

Orbiting at ten thousand feet, Arkady had been tracking the Indonesian convoy, mentally setting up and knocking down a series of strike templates for taking it down. He and Pinkerton had arrived over Merdeka Square in time to see Foxtrot Flight crash and he was already coiled and posed when Amanda's release call rang in his helmet phones.

She had been right in her call as usual. He had been needed for this one specific moment. Arkady kicked his SPEED Cobra up and into a screaming split-S, rolling three-quarters inverted as he pitched through into his dive.

The laser-guided missiles under his wings were useless. He could not kill enough fast enough with them. Nor were his pods of Hydra rockets. Where he was going, he'd die in the back blast of his own warheads. This would be gun work. As the Jeannie II accelerated in her mad dive, he rolled the coolie hat controller under his thumb, calling up both his integral 20mm tri-barrel and the 25mm grenade launcher pod on his centerline hard point, mating both weapons to his main stick trigger.

Nor was what he was about to do something that could be plotted out and acted upon with deliberation. Instead, it had to be *felt* through, using earned and inherent instincts – and a combat aviator's experience-sharpened eye.

Arkady felt a mirthless grin tighten his face. *Use the Force, Luke!*

Arkady bottomed out of his dive over the center of the Square at a bare hundred feet. The MONAS spire blurred past his right wing while, ahead and to the left, lay the battered Presidential Palace complex. Directly ahead lay the mouth of Jalan Veteran Avenue and the inbound armored column.

The column commander had been canny, first keeping to the residential streets and then snaking his force between the high rises to mask them from air attack. But now, wedged in between the concrete wall of the Palace grounds and a row of stacked office buildings, his tactics backfired. He was trapped in a road column, unable to disperse his vehicles in the face of the berserk flying buzz-saw roaring in on him from the night. Nor could his vehicles clear their forward firing arcs to shoot at their ground-hugging attacker without hitting their own comrades. They could only perish with a great suddenness and violence.

As he swept down the length of the convoy, Arkady held down the primary trigger, emptying his magazines in a single, barrel-melting burst, the buzzing roar of the Gatling gun blending with the heavier, hoarser chug of the grenade launcher. With night-vision enhanced eyes, he saw the blocky greenish outlines of the enemy AFVs flashing under his aircraft's nose, the dazzling white fire of his shell bursts flowing over them. Without seeing, he was aware of the glass office fronts blurring past a mere arm's reach from his starboard wing and rotor tip.

Holding his strafing line, he ignored the imminent possibility of a ground strike that would snap him out of existence in an instant.

He felt the buffeting of explosions and the flicker of tracers out of the corners of his eyes, but knew they came from bursting fuel tanks and ammunition magazines. The enemy was dying too fast to shoot back.

Then the grenade launcher thermal-jammed and the Gatling's power drive clattered on empty chambers. All of his ammo was gone.

A cliff of darkened glass and steel glass rose before him. Jalan

Veteran's Avenue dead ended at a T intersection beyond the Haji Juanda canal; there was no way out but up.

Arkady hauled back hard on the stick. The Jeannie II's nose went vertical – but the residual energy from the dive and strafing run still carried her on toward the building. Arkady overrode the flight management system and slammed a massive burst of power into the rotors. A surge of horizontal ground effect reflected off the building face, the rotor blast imploding windows on the upper storeys as it shoved the Jeannie II away from a collision.

Then he was pulling through the upper half of the Immelman loop reversal and rolling into conventional flight. Below, Jalan Veteran's Avenue was a river of flame. The rebel armored force had been cut in two ... lengthwise. *No kill like a gun's kill, Babe!*

"Well ... that was fun," the conversational voice said over the TBP channel.

Arkady looked over to find Pink Pinkerton holding in his usual wingman's slot aft and above his starboard side. The burned-out barrels of Pink's Gatling glowed in the dark. In his total focus on his attack, Arkady had lost situational awareness of his wingman. Now he realized that the Marine must have followed him through the strafing run.

"Strike Lead to Strike Wing. I told you you'd be doing crazy stuff flying for the Lady, Pink."

"Negative, Strike Lead. This one was entirely your insanity."

"Strike Lead, this Crisis Lead," a new voice intruded on the Talk Between Pilots. "We are on approach to Foxtrot Crash site. Can you call status on the landing zone?"

The shimmering rotor halos of the rescue Hawks could be seen sweeping in from the check line and Arkady and Pink circled back to assume the escort slot.

"Crisis Lead, this is Strike Lead. The primary ground threat has been eliminated, but you may assume we've still got at least a warm LZ. Call any targets and we'll cover you in."

"Breaker, Crisis Lead," Stone Quillain's ground-based voice interjected. "This is Sea Demon Six. We got the approaches to the crash

362

site covered and we have survivor activity at the crash site. We got no enemy movement and we're not seein' any ground fire. You busted their wagon and pissed in their sandbox and I don't think these ol' boys want to play any more."

"Roger D, Sea Demon Six. Let's bring our guys home."

*

A bemused Christine Rendino found herself capable of giving orders and rational thought. She had witnessed the devastating air strike on the Indonesian convoy and, with that rebirth of hope, she had started organizing the crash site.

Those aircrewmen and Marines conscious and able to move were used to set up a perimeter around the wreck, while first aid was administered to those who couldn't.

So far, the flimsy security screen had gone unchallenged. No hostiles had approached the downed helo and they hadn't received appreciable ground fire. It was as if the devastation of their reinforcement column had knocked the last of the fight out of the rebels surrounding the square. Like the crash survivors, the Indonesians lay panting and exhausted in the humid night.

Then, with miniguns extended, the crisis ships came roaring out of the dark. Settling on either side of their downed sister, Air Force Pararescue teams poured out of the open hatches, some carrying basket stretchers and medical kits, others with carbines ready at port arms.

Overhead, a pair of SPEED Cobra gunships growled threateningly, promising instant retribution for any interference.

The Senior Pararescue man knelt down beside Christine as she sat slumped against the wreck's fuselage. "Are you okay, ma'am?"

Christine found her warped sense of humor coming back. "Not quite yet, but things seem to be improving."

"Good deal, ma'am. We'll be getting you loaded in just a second."

"I just hope you guys are a direct flight. I don't mind flying tourist, but having to change planes sucks."

From atop the Hotel Sriwijaya, Stone Quillain watched the rescue flight helos lift off and head north for the sea, their escort gunships trailing. Elsewhere in the sky above the city, the other strike helos and RPVs were withdrawing as well.

"This is Sea Dragon Six to Star Child. Be advised rescue flight is airborne. Looking good. Clean extraction."

Below, at the base of the spire, there was a sudden blue-white flare. Timer-fused thermite demolition charges blazed alight inside the fuselage of the wrecked SPEED Hawk, the exploding fuel cells joining in the immolation a few moments later. Phantom Force was leaving behind no secrets for an enemy to exploit.

The stillness was deepening over the maimed and exhausted city. Nothing moved, save for the boiling smoke plumes ruddily underlit by burning buildings and the distant flashing lights of a brave ambulance.

They were finished here. It was time to leave.

"Acknowledged, Sea Demon." Captain Garrett sounded tired too. "This is the Lady to all Sky Island teams. Extract!"

"Sea Demon Six to the Lady," Quillain replied to the distant voice. "Acknowledged. We're outa here." He lifted his own voice over the twirl of their waiting Little Bird. "Saddle up! Let's go!" As the sniper team retreated to the AH-6, Stone fell back to the door house and its guardians. "Get going, boys. I'll plug up the rat hole."

Stone pulled a pop-can-sized canister from a harness pouch. Slinging his carbine, he pulled the pin on the canister and rolled the incendiary grenade down the bullet-scarred stairwell, ducking back to avoid the searing sparklets of white phosphorous and the billowing cloud of metallic-tasting smoke. Below, someone hadn't ducked and a scream and a burst of unintelligible profanity echoed up the shaft. No one would be dashing up that set of stairs for the foreseeable future.

The Little Bird was already powering up for flight as Stone took his seat on the edge of the deck, latching the monkey strap carabineers onto his harness. Then the AH-6 broke contact with the roof with a jerk, leaving Sky Island Alpha behind. As they spiraled clear, Stone picked up the rotor halos of the other Army Little Birds lifting off from the other Sky Island sites and he heard their pilots calling their lift-offs. Off to the west, a single stream of small caliber tracers arced into the sky, falling well short of the departing helicopters.

The final shots of the Jakarta siege had been fired.

Amanda took a deep breath. She was tired, very tired, but that was irrelevant. She keyed her command headset into the 1-MC. "Attention on all decks. This is the Captain. All aircraft are feet wet and all landing force elements are off the beach. We are commencing recovery operation. Casualties have been minimal and all Phantom personnel are accounted for. All mission objectives have been met. Secure all Trick or Treat timelines. Well done, all hands. Exceptionally well done."

Amanda slipped off the headset and closed her eyes for a moment. Soon, someone in the Op Center started to clap. Whistles, cheers and exuberance radiated outward through the commando carrier as her crew vented their tensions of the past few hours.

She felt a warm grip on her shoulder, strong but almost hesitant. "I asked you to pull another loose handful of fingers into a fist, and by God, you've done it!"

She opened her eyes and looked up into MacIntyre's shadowed face. "I've just been lucky, Elliot. Very, very lucky."

She thought once more about Christine's revelation on that last day aboard the *Carlson* and decided that maybe it wouldn't be such a bad thing at all.

Self-consciously, MacIntyre turned the grip on her shoulder into a light slap. "How about a cup of coffee in the wardroom?"

"I want to see Chris and the other wounded in sickbay first – and I need to have a few words with the plane crew of the Cobra we lost – but then I'm your girl. Only, let's make it the salon in the stern section. I think I could use a drink."

Lake Toba, Sumatra
0031 Hours; Zone Time, December 1, 2008

"If you do not know, Captain, then find out!"

Admiral Ketalaman caught himself, forcing impassivity into his face, drawing the coldness of the mountain stone up through his legs. He had been summoned from the estate mansion to his cavern command center upon the report of an attack on Jakarta by some outside force – but, since the sounding of the initial alarm, follow-up reports had been sporadic and fragmentary at best.

The duty officer's face was wet with sweat, even in the cool interior of the cave. "17th Brigade headquarters and Brigadier Tagang are still not replying, sir. We have no explanation."

The likeliest explanation was a simple one: the 17th Brigade headquarters and Brigadier Tagang no longer existed.

"What about Halim Air Force Base? Are we through to them?"

"No, sir. They're failing to reply as well."

"We had a guard ship holding off the port? What are they reporting?"

The duty officer swallowed. "The frigate Wiratno does not reply, sir. But one of our shore stations is picking up a signal from one of her emergency locator beacons."

It must have been a massive attack, launched with both great speed and precision.

"What of the Americans? What have we got on their operations?"

"Air elements of the Regional Intervention Force were detected departing from their carrier ships at Benoa Port. They followed a radar-evasive flight path and tracking was lost over northern Bali. There was also a degree of northbound traffic from the Northern Australian bases – but nothing that could be developed into a coherent plot. We've lost a great degree of radar coverage from the Javanese and Balinese stations ..."

Ketalaman waved away the excuse. He was well aware of the breakdown in the Indonesian air defense net. He was also well aware of the only reason there could be for an American intervention in

Jakarta on this scale. The questions were: where had it come from and had it succeeded?

A fax machine hissed out a sheet of hardcopy at the communications desk. Ketalaman froze himself in place beside the main map table, requiring that the duty officer bring the information to him.

"It's from the commander of the Bekasi police garrison. His road patrols have reached Jakarta and established contact with the surviving tactical elements of 17th brigade."

"Surviving elements?'

"Casualties have been very heavy, sir. The headquarters and support battalions of the brigade have been wiped out. Brigadier Tegang is missing and presumed dead."

"And what of the American Embassy?"

"Empty, sir. The Americans have successfully evacuated, and they've taken President Kediri with them. Our garrison forces report shooting down two American helicopters and a number of remotely piloted vehicles."

"I daresay the Americans can spare them, Commander," Ketalaman replied, acid in his voice.

The Admiral turned away to stare at the shadowed basalt of the cave wall. *In disaster, imperturbability.* The lesson of the mountains. He was facing a catastrophic reversal just at the moment he must most appear invincible. Kediri had escaped him and the world and Indonesia still had an option. Beyond that, a major, precious military unit had been badly mauled.

Before turning around again, he had to annihilate the surge of fear and uncertainty welling within him. It was now a matter of triumph or perish.

Once more, he faced the silent operations staff. "We will need to consider replacements for our losses in the Jakarta area. Allocate one half-hour in the morning briefing schedule to discuss troop redeployments. Also, what is the latest word on Surface Action Squadron One?"

It took a moment for the Duty Officer to adjust his thinking. "Uh, at the last position check, the squadron had cleared Laut Kecil and were proceeding to the waters off south Sulawesi peninsula, as per your orders."

"Very good. Contact the squadron commodore. He is to proceed at once with the Port Paotere operation."

He had to get Harconan under his thumb. With Harconan's assets, there would still be a chance. Even with Kediri in the American's hands, there would be a chance.

"Very good, sir," the duty officer replied. He was already steadying down, regaining heart with his leader's show of strength.

"I am returning to my quarters now, Captain. Notify me of any further developments."

*As the mountains.*

Called by Alfred Wallace "prettier and cleaner than any I had yet seen in the east", the city of Ujung Padang made a fetish out of thriving.

First it had served as the capital of the ancient Bone Empire during the golden age of the Bugi sea clans. Then, during the days of Dutch Colonialism, it had been a booming maritime trading hub, a transshipment and exchange point for the manufactured goods of Europe and the spices and sandalwood of the East Indies.

By the twenty-first century, it was the largest city on Sulawesi and the fifth largest in the entire archipelago, its potent commercial engine still thrumming.

At the heart of Ujung Padang's success were its harbors: Sokarno, the deep-water facility that handled the modern merchant shipping, and Paotere, the shallow water port northward up the coast.

Here, the Bugi still ruled.

The piers of the port were jammed with inter-island traffic, scores of *pinisi* loading and unloading from the close-ranked warehouses, the cargoes being borne on the backs of Bugi stevedores as it had been done for centuries.

Here also, as it had been for centuries, the Bugi fleet was born. On the slipways of the port's shipyards, the *pinisi* schooners were crafted from the superlative hardwoods from the heart of Kalimantan.

Some things had changed – the *pinisi* were now constructed with metal hardware instead of being pegged together as they had been done in centuries past, and engine beds were installed to accept auxiliary diesel – but each ship was built as it had always been, by hand and without blueprints or schematics. The design for each sleek hull existed only in the mind of a master Bugi shipwright with a millennium of tradition behind him and an understanding of the sea branded into his genes.

On this morning, no trace of the disintegration of the Indonesian nation was apparent on the Paotere waterfront. Obedient to the will and command of the Raja Samudra, the sea peoples were staying out of the chaos and conflict, keeping to themselves and keeping their own peace.

Men bartered, women chatted, children laughed. Lines creaked as the ranked schooners tugged at their moorings, impatient to be free. Hammers rang along the slipways of the boat yards. The only hint of the modern world was the occasional cheerful burst of Indonesian *dangdut* pop music from a tape player.

The whirring buzz of a light helicopter cruising slowly down the coast at a high altitude was ignored as a manifestation of the dying Jakarta government. Also ignored were the three blockish silhouettes on the western horizon, their gray camouflage paint blurring them into the thickening heat haze.

The intruding ships were the "strong squadron" of the Indonesian Navy, the Fatahillah Class frigates: Fatahillah, Malahayati and Nala, the newest, the best-maintained, the most powerful. Beyond a potent battery of Exocet surface-to-surface missiles, torpedoes, and ASW mortars, the Fatahillahs mounted the heaviest gun armament of the fleet: Swedish-built Bofors 4.7-inch cannons.

This point of nautical trivia mattered little to the Bugi tribespeople going about their affairs dockside. They could not hear the forward observer in the helicopter speaking into his radio headset or see the turrets traversing shoreward, the heavy gun tubes elevating.

Aimed by the spotter helo and the frigate's fire control radars, the first three-round salvo screamed in with no warning, a triple mushroom cloud roiling into the air. The second followed precisely three seconds later, the cannon auto-firing at twenty rounds per minute, every third shell a white phosphorus incendiary.

With computer-guided precision, the shell bursts walked down the length of the waterfront. Buildings, docks and ships disintegrated, fire leaped into the sky and rained down again, the air filled with a murderous spray of wood splinters and shrapnel. People looked up, stunned, horrified, paralyzed as the wave of devastation rolled down upon them.

The holocaust ended as the three bombardment ships reversed course. Running southward, they again hosed the length of the waterfront area with a firestream of fifty-pound shells. It was an act of barbarism – but it was also stark proof that, in an age of cruise missiles and precision guided munitions, concentrated naval gunfire can still be devastating.

With a hundred rounds per ship expended, the cannon fell silent and the naval squadron sheered off into the open waters of Makassar Strait, turning away from the smoke enshrouding the fires and wreckage of Port Paotere. Left behind were dead ships, dead people, and a devastated way of life.

Those survivors who were not screaming in agony or weeping in sorrow raged at Jakarta for this savagery. The Bugi had no way of knowing that the Admirals at the Indonesian Naval Ministry had not only not authorized the attack, but that the majority of them were already dead.

"Oh, and Frank, in the final draft of the post action report, be certain to include numerous hearts and flowers for NAVEX 7.2's willing assistance, exemplary performance of all hands, etc. etc. etc. It's not only true for the most part, but we may have to work with Sorenson again one of these days. It may sweeten his outlook a little."

"Aye aye, sir." MacIntyre's Chief of Staff looked out from the screen of the laptop positioned on the corner of the cabin's desk. "Will do."

"Now, what about press control? Are we seeing any hint of a Phantom leak?"

"Not so far, sir. Media Psyops is pushing the responsibility for the Embassy evacuation onto the Regional Intervention Force and the North Australian bases, served up with a heavy side order of doubletalk. That should improve Sorenson's disposition as well."

MacIntyre leaned on the desk edge. "How about the awards list I dispatched, Frank?"

"Essentially no problems, sir. We'll have to clear Captain Quillain's battlefield promotion to Major through Quantico, but with his record I can see no difficulties."

"Excellent. That will give Stone the beef he'll need to better handle the Sea Demon command."

"Uh, sir. There will be one difficulty though – the Legion of Merit you proposed for Captain Garrett. At the moment, her position within the Navy is rather ambiguous. How are we supposed to give a medal to someone who isn't supposed to be in the service?"

"Hire her a good sea lawyer, Frank," MacIntyre replied flatly.

"Aye aye, sir." The CoS hesitated for a moment. "If I may say so, I agree. It appears to have been an outstanding operation. The damn thing apparently works."

"Phantom Force? So far, yes," MacIntyre replied, slowly pacing the length of the desk. "But we still haven't figured out a way to unlock the over-all situation down here. What are your people seeing? Are we missing anything?"

The CoS scowled out of the screen. "It's like Captain Garrett's status, sir. Ambiguous. We're seeing sporadic land and air engagements between declared Government and Rebel Forces on both Java and Sumatra – and a large-scale but seemingly uncoordinated coastal bombardment on Sulawesi that we're still trying to figure out. Beyond that, things seem fairly quiet on the outer islands. We're not seeing anything in the way of a major coordinated offensive developing from either side yet."

"I suspect both sides are still in a state of shock, thank God," Macintyre growled. "Things aren't going well for anyone down here."

"There is one thing that might be working in our favor, Admiral. Things seem to be quieting down on Bali. The island's religious leaders seem to be trying to put the brakes on the bloodshed and restore a degree of order – or at least that's what RIF tactical Intelligence is picking up."

"That is favorable. Now, what about the rest of the world? Is there anything else we need to be worried about?"

"Yes sir. The eastern Med."

"Oh, Christ." MacIntyre sank into the desk chair and turned the laptop to face him. "Who's mad at who now?"

"The usual. Greece and Turkey. The diplomatic venom coming out of both Athens and Ankara has been ramping up steadily for the past week."

"What's the point of contention this go round?"

"Again, the usual. Air and sea transit rights and national waters conflicts in the Aegean Sea. It's reached the point where the President of the European Commission has called on all involved parties to display restraint and take part in a meaningful diplomatic dialog."

MacIntyre grimaced, "I'm sure that's helping the situation no end. What are our analysts saying? Are the Greeks and Turks making their usual monkey faces at each other, or is this something more serious?"

"We're not sure, sir. The Greeks and Turks have been engaged in a major naval arms race for the past couple of decades, and they both could be about ready for another try at each other. Beyond that, a couple of wild cards have just shown up in the deck."

"Turn them over."

"Greece has recently declared a series of joint defense exercises with Bulgaria outside of the command structure of both NATO and the European Union. On the other side, Israeli naval units have started to pop up in the Aegean, apparently operating in co-ordination with the Turkish fleet."

"Christ all Friday! Are we receiving any deployment or alert-to-move orders from the National Command Authority yet?"

"Not overtly, sir. We don't want to insult our gallant NATO allies. But CinC 6th Fleet has been instructed to find reasons to keep his Surface Action Group in the Eastern Mediterranean and all US bases and military missions in the involved states have been ordered to keep their ears to the ground for any unusual military activity."

"Keep me posted, Frank. Let's hope they give us enough time to clean up this mess before something new gets dumped on us."

"We can hope, Admiral. Will there be anything else today?"

"Negative, Frank. Let's make it the same time tomorrow. *Shenandoah*, out."

MacIntyre broke the circuit and tilted his chair back, making himself a mental note. At tomorrow's briefing, he'd give Frank a message to relay to Judy. It couldn't be much, just an acknowledgement that he was alive and well, but hopefully it would be enough for his daughter. Phantom Force's draconian security restrictions would apply to him for as long as he was aboard the *Shenandoah*.

To make up for it, the *Shenandoah* was certainly the most comfortable vessel he'd ever flown his flag. He looked appreciatively around his airy, cruise ship quality cabin. Apparently, the shipping line owners of this world were expected to do pretty well by themselves.

There was a hesitant knock at the door. "Enter."

Christine Rendino entered the cabin. She had an elastic bandage snugged around a sprained wrist and a couple of Band-aids apparent, but she appeared otherwise recovered from her recent helicopter crash.

The Intel was also looking unusually somber and somewhat nervous.

She came to attention before his desk, saluting crisply. "Begging the Admiral's pardon, but may I have a word with him?"

MacIntyre straightened and answered the salute. He too had learned that, when Christine Rendino started acting like a military officer, it inevitably meant trouble. "Of course, Chris. At ease and have a seat. What can I do for you?"

"It's a ... personal matter sir," she replied unhappily, sinking into the offered chair beyond the desktop. "Something kind of off the record."

A personal matter? He leaned forward. "How can I help?" Over the past couple of years, he had come to both appreciate the insights of this eccentric little character and to grow fond of her in a fatherly fashion. If she was in some difficulty ...

She read his mind as she had the uncanny knack of doing. "Uh, no sir. It's not me with the personal problem. It's you."

Eddie Mac's brows came together. "Me? What do you mean?"

Christine took a deep breath. "You see, Admiral sir, it's kind of like this. Back when Captain Garrett seemed to be in a lot of trouble with that Board of Enquiry – you know, before I was brought into the loop on Phantom Force – I sort of made an erroneous assessment of the situation ..."

Two minutes later, MacIntyre's swivel chair crashed back against the wall as he launched out of it. "YOU TOLD HER WHAT?"

Christine Rendino cringed down in her seat, her words escaping in a rapid fire squeak. "Like I said, Admiral sir, it was an erroneous assessment of the situation – and, if you'll give me a choice between fifty lashes and being keel-hauled, I'll take the lashes because I have really poor breath control."

Elliot Macintyre couldn't think of anything adequate to say, so he said nothing. He sank back into his chair. Bracing his elbows on his desk, he cradled his face in his hands.

"When the truth of the situation became clear, I realized that I'd made a hideous mistake talking with Captain Garrett about you like that," Christine continued miserably. "I figured I owed it to you to tell you what I'd done. I'm sorry, sir. I'm really, really, really sorry."

MacIntyre looked up to see tears glistening in her eyes. "Oh, Good God Almighty, don't cry on top of everything else," he said, pushing a box of Kleenex across the desk. "Things are bad enough as it is. Besides, you were only doing what you thought best. Damned if I can condemn you for standing by your captain. The fault here is entirely mine."

"I don't think it's a matter of fault, sir," Christine replied, dabbing at her eyes. "I mean, Amanda is a very neat lady. It just shows that you've got great taste to fall in love with her."

"I've never said I was in love with her, commander! I've just maybe indicated that ... I've been greatly concerned about her at times."

"Sir, you're fudging." Christine helped herself to a second tissue. "If I may be so bold, I've seen you around Amanda. The signature is unmistakable."

MacIntyre winced and heeled his forehead with his palm. "I believe I've had this conversation with another young woman in the not-too-distant past. Tell me, Comm ... Christine. Am I really that transparent?"

"It depends, sir. Around most men, you're probably safe. Around another women, you're cellophane."

"We should *never* have let women into this man's navy," MacIntyre muttered in a deadly monotone.

"It was pretty much inevitable we'd bust in sooner or later, sir," Christine observed. "And it was pretty much inevitable that, once we were in, that men and women in the navy would get together and manage their interpersonal relationships in pretty much the same way men and women have been managing their relationships for centuries. Poorly."

"Thank you very much, Commander. I appreciate that insight. Now, how about telling me what I'm supposed to do now?"

The Intel looked uncomfortable once more. "Sir, that's not for me to say."

"Commander, you instituted this crisis. The least you can do is help me get out of it."

Christine Rendino hesitated before replying, as if weighing her words carefully. "Sir, I believe the real core question here is: do you want out of it?"

MacIntyre frowned. "What do you mean?"

"I mean, if you want to give this whole thing a pass, it won't be a problem. To put it bluntly, Amanda is the kind of female who is used to having men act just a little bit peculiar around her on occasion. If you just let it go and don't say anything to her about it, she probably won't either and that will be it. She's that kind of straight edge."

"I see," MacIntyre said slowly. Then he had to ask the next question. "What happens if I *do* choose to say something?"

Christine studied him for a moment more before continuing, a shrewd and distinctly feminine consideration that made MacIntyre somewhat uncomfortable. "I couldn't say for certain, sir," she said finally. "But, if you'd want a good sitguess, you'll probably find it real interesting."

Even with the successful operations off Bali and the battle of Jakarta to their credit, Amanda still knew she had a long way to go to hammer the diverse elements of Phantom Force into the coherent whole she wanted. Tonight's formal dining in the main salon had been another step down this path.

Theoretically, the dinner was to welcome aboard the Marine officers commanding the FAST Platoon and the Jakarta Embassy security force. Their units were being absorbed by the Sea Demons for the remainder of the cruise, their skills and numbers a welcome reinforcement to the number of boots the commando carrier could put on the ground.

It was also an excellent opportunity to bring the ship's diverse officer cadre together "outside of the box" – to get them to know each other on a personal level and to erode the interservice rivalries that might linger. What she desired was a crew that did not think "I am Navy, Air Force or Army" but "I am *Shenandoah*."

Accordingly, the best the officers' mess could provide was served on sparkling white tablecloths and the ship's formal crystal and table wear was used for the first time. All shop talk and references to the current mission had been absolutely forbidden as topics of conversation.

There was another advantage to the *Shenandoah*'s unique status. From the cargo bulkheads aft, she was a civilian vessel, equipped and accounted for as such. Accordingly, Amanda had deigned that the 'dry ship' policy inflicted upon the United States Navy by Josephus Daniels did not apply. Thus, a cocktail was acceptable before dinner, wine could be served and toasts proposed and properly delivered afterwards.

"Ladies and gentlemen," Amanda began, "I believe we have successfully integrated the Lieutenants Trennan and Bergstrom into our band of brothers. May you find the remainder of your cruise with us an interesting one."

"Thank you, Captain," the senior of the newcomers relied. "But we have to say it's already been pretty damn interesting."

As the best her Marine guests of honor had been able to manage were borrowed tropic khakis, Amanda had kept the dinner's dress code semi-formal. She herself had opted to enjoy civilian garb, a favorite green silk cheongsam that she knew suited her eyes and hair well, a naval command insignia glinting at its high collar. Amanda had been feeling rather dragonladyish since assuming command of Phantom Force and the exotic clothes suited her mood.

Now she lifted her slender-stemmed glass. "Ladies and gentlemen, if I may." She didn't rise from her chair, a tradition inherited from the Royal Navy. A shipboard toast could be offered sitting, a holdover from the days of low frigate overheads. "To the ship, to the flag, and to fallen comrades."

Soft acknowledgements rippled around the table. At its far end, Admiral MacIntyre lifted his own glass and countered, "And, if I may, ladies and gentlemen – to a clean victory, well won, and to those who brought it to fruition."

Elliot and the others were looking at her and she flushed at the sentiment. Couldn't they see it wasn't her? It had never been her. It was them. Always them.

MacIntyre spoke again, "And now it seems that that dose of trans-Pacific jet lag is finally catching up to me, so by your leave, Captain."

As the senior officer present, it was MacIntyre's call to end the evening. Amanda tilted her head in reply. "Of course, Admiral. In fact, I believe we all have another heavy day ahead of us. Ladies and gentlemen, it's been a very pleasant evening."

The grouping around the long table broke up, conversations flaring up again as the party started to disperse. Stone Quillain was enthusiastically discussing handgun hunting with the Air Commando group leader and Dix Beltrain was amiably arguing the 1998 NFL season with Captain Montgomery.

Christine Rendino and Vince Arkady had been seated next to each other through dinner and now, still talking about old days in California, they were leaving the Salon together. To her amazement, Amanda felt a sudden flash of jealousy. Then she mentally slapped herself.

A long time ago, Chris had hinted that she found Arkady decidedly attractive. If it was her turn with him now, she could only wish her friend all of the best. She lightly bit her lower lip and considered some intriguing mental images.

"What are you smiling about?"

MacIntyre was standing beside her chair, looking at her quizzically.

"Oh, nothing really. It's an extremely long and complex story."

"There seems to be a number of those going around lately." Elliot was looking at her with the same hint of that discomfort she'd sensed a couple of times since his coming aboard. "Amanda, may I talk to you about something? Alone?"

She lifted her brows and pushed her chair back. "Of course. Why not?" The lifeboat weather decks were on the same level as the main saloon and would be unoccupied at that hour.

Outside, the *Shenandoah* was running through a mixed bag of weather. To port, a thunderhead pulsed intermittently with its own internal illumination while, overhead and to starboard, the stars glittered wetly in a clear, humid sky.

The *Shenandoah* had resumed her civil guise and she was steaming slowly with her deck and running lights full on. Still, the illumination was low enough to allow the bioglow of the wake to be visible. The night smelled of jungle, sea and ozone.

"Looks like that storm will be cutting across our course line," MacIntyre commented.

"Mmm." Amanda leaned against the rail, looking out at the night. "The wave height shouldn't be too bad and the rains will cool things down a bit. I'm planning to alter course east northeast toward Makassar Strait under the storm cover. We'll ride under it for a while and get lost for a little bit."

"Are you going to try an identity change on the ship?"

"Not yet. I intend to hold that in reserve for a while longer," she replied, coming to lean against the rail next to the boat davits. "As it is, nobody seems to be paying any excessive attention to us. I think our luck's still holding."

"Pretty much." Elliot still sounded distracted. It was unusual for the CinC of NAVSPECFORCE to be indecisive about anything. What was wrong? Something personal perhaps? Maybe something with Judy?

"Amanda, have I ever told you very much about my late wife?" MacIntyre had joined her at the rail, brooding out at the looming squall.

"A little bit now and again. Why?"

"Because Anne was a very special lady," he replied. "She and I were quite literally childhood sweethearts. We were navy brats, brought up together, and she was my best friend before she ever became my girl, or my fiancée or my wife. She was always my best friend."

"That's something to be envied."

"I was extremely lucky," Elliot agreed. "When I was in high school, I never dated many other girls. I didn't need to. There was just Anne and an understanding. I married her the day after I graduated from Annapolis. After that I never … considered another woman. I had my wife and I loved her unreservedly through our three children and to the day she died." He voice buckled slightly. "I still love her and I intend to keep on doing so."

Amanda looked up at his set face and said nothing. She didn't know what to say. She sensed something extraordinary was happening here.

He continued almost impatiently, "I'm dragging out all of this emotional baggage to try and explain something, or maybe justify it."

"What?"

"I had a discussion with Christine Rendino this afternoon, a discussion concerning you."

Amanda lifted an eyebrow. "Something favorable, I hope."

Elliot's responding half-smile had a great deal of self-derision in it. "The problem wasn't really with you but with me."

"How so?" Amanda asked, puzzled.

"I've discovered that I have rather stunted social skills in certain areas," he replied. "I never developed a real capacity for saying the appropriate things at the appropriate times to another woman. With Anne around, I never needed to … until now."

At last, Amanda understood. What Chris had told her back on that last day aboard the *Carlson* was true – and now this big, strong, decisive man was breaking down an entire lifetime of conditioning and isolation to reach out hesitantly to her.

Amanda felt a tremendous upwelling of warmth, happiness and humility. She smiled up into his face. "Maybe so, Elliot. But if you want one woman's opinion, you're not doing so badly."

That pulled a short, sheepish chuckle out of the man. She felt a callused hand rest on hers on the railing. "I'm pleased to hear it. The question is, what should I say next?"

Amanda could have made some suggestions but she didn't get the chance.

"Begging the Captain's pardon?"

Christine Rendino's voice was a soft and urgent intrusion. Amanda and MacIntyre both started and turned away from the rail as the Intel hurried up to them.

"I'm really sorry but something kind of strange has come up."

"What is it, Chris?" Amanda inquired, more than a little annoyed.

"We've just had a call down from the stern section radio room. A call is coming in on the ship's commercial service satellite phone. The guy on the other end is asking to speak with Captain Garrett, in person."

"Well, who is it?" Amanda asked.

"We can't be absolutely certain yet, but he says he's Makara Harconan."

\*

The *Shenandoah*'s civilian radio shack was exceptionally well equipped but cramped. Amanda sat beside the duty sparks at the main console, MacIntyre and Christine squeezed in behind them in an environment stuffy with electronics waste heat. Both the Intel and the Admiral wore headsets that had been tapped into the satphone circuit, while Christine's also served as a live link to Signal Intelligence.

The radio operator nodded to her and, much to her own anger, Amanda found her throat dry. She forced herself to swallow before lifting the receiver to her ear. "This is Captain Garrett."

"Hello, Amanda, this is Makara Harconan." There could be no question; the voice was unmistakable and inescapable. "It's good to speak with you again."

How to react? What mask to don? What to say? "I wish I could say the same, Makara," she replied, keeping her voice steady.

"That's not a very warm greeting between old shipmates." The taipan sounded faintly amused and there was just a hair's weight of emphasis on the "shipmates."

In spite of herself, she felt herself flushing. "What do you want me to say, Makara? You've ruined a nation and you've ruined me. What more do you want?"

Christine Rendino leaned down and whispered into Amanda's free ear, "An Iridium II sat phone, in the archipelago but somewhere at sea."

Amanda nodded, staying with the voice on the phone.

"I want from you only what I have ever wanted from you, Amanda. The truth. We worked together to save the refugees at Singaraja. Now I want to work with you again."

"Singaraja? I have no idea what you're talking about."

"Of course you do," he replied equitably, "although I understand the sophistry in play. Top Security and all of that. I'm well acquainted with the mechanisms. But I still need your help."

"My help?" she probed back. "To do what?"

"To save all of Indonesia."

"Makara, the entire goal of your life has been the destruction of Indonesia, and apparently you've succeeded. It seems a little late for a change of heart."

His voice hardened. "Possibly, but I want to try. I'm quite aware that I started this disaster. Now I want to stop it. I have my reasons and I'm more than willing explain them to you – but only in person. We must talk, Amanda, and we must do it quickly, while there is still a chance."

She injected a hint of scorn into her voice. "A chance for what? What have we to talk about any more, and what do I have to do with any of this? I'm nothing but a freighter captain now, thanks to you."

Annoyance tinged Harconan's voice. "Damn it, Amanda. Will you

384

please stop this preposterous play-acting? We don't have the time for it! We both have a far greater problem to deal with. I want to offer an alliance against our common enemy. The same enemy we were fighting at Singaraja. The enemy trying to set the peoples of Indonesian at each other's throats!"

Amanda gave herself the duration of a single breath to think. Logic said this must be some kind of ploy. Instinct said he was telling the truth. "What are you proposing, Makara?"

"I'd like to discuss an alliance, an alliance between the Bugi sea clans and your command against the true common enemy. You and I, Amanda, we have to do this thing! We don't have the time to muddle about with diplomats, potentates and the powers that be. We must talk!"

She made her call. "Where?"

"My island, Pulau Piri. Our beach. Tomorrow at sundown. I will come alone. You may bring whomever you wish. I ask only that you give me your word that the two of us can have a chance to talk."

Could this be some kind of incredible trap targeted against her? Either this made perfect sense or it made no sense at all. It was a lie or it was truth. And there was no one else in the world who could judge it.

"What guarantees are you offering, Makara? Because I'm asking for them."

"The best I can possibly offer. The Raja Samudra as your hostage. It is my intent to surrender to you."

Christine Rendino trotted at Amanda's heels, protesting every inch of the way down the length of the hangar deck. "I don't know about this, Boss Ma'am. Fa'sure this could be a stupendously, catastrophically bad idea!"

"Come on, Chris, tell me what you real opinion is?" Amanda replied, ponytailing her hair with a rubber band.

Christine considered ripping out a couple of handfuls of that hair, or possibly her own. "This has got to be some kind of trick on Harconan's part. One he's using to get his hands on you."

"Makara doesn't build his universe around me, Chris. He has far more important concerns at the moment than a former lover. Admiral MacIntyre agrees that it's worth investigating."

The Intel frowned and shook her head. "It just doesn't seem logical that he'd be willing to just hand himself over like this."

"Logic comes in a number of different flavors, Chris."

An Air Commando SPEED Hawk sat spotted on the number two lift, the plane crew primping it through preflight. Sidewinder X air-to-air missiles were slotted onto the wingtip launch rails and its door gunners were lifting their 7.62mm Miniguns into their mounts. Nearby, a four-man Force Recon fire team stocked their MOLLE harnesses before boarding the aircraft.

Amanda lifted her hand toward the bristling array of firepower. "Besides, it's not as if I'm going in there naked."

The Intel glared and whispered, "That's what you thought last time."

"Relax, mother. The Admiral is making sure I'm well chaperoned."

Stone Quillain and Vince Arkady emerged from around the far side of the aircraft, flight and combat gear slung over their shoulders. "We takin' an airplane ride or what?" the Marine inquired.

"What are you seeing?" Amanda keyed the headset of her cranial helmet, speaking over the howl of the turbines and the steady state roar of the slipstream.

"No situational changes on the island, ma'am," the Air Commando systems operator replied, hunkering over his tactical access terminal. "The Bugi schooner is continuing to pull away to the northeast. Thermographic scans indicate only the single human-sized heat trace on the entire island. No signal or emission activity at all."

The SPEED Hawk had an Eagle Eye recon drone flying point for it. The RPV was already circling the target area and, so far, nothing in the way of a trick or trap had been indicated. They would know for certain shortly.

Arkady interjected over the interphone, "Traffic on the voice channel for you, Captain. It's the Admiral."

"Hang on, I'm coming up." Amanda squeezed forward past the system operators station to crouch behind the pilot's seats. Arkady looked back at her from the co-pilot's station. "Put me through," she said.

The aviator lifted a hand to the overhead commo panel, "You're on with the man."

"Gray Mare Lead to Star Child," she said into the lip mike. "This is Garrett. Over."

"What's your situation, Amanda?" MacIntyre's filtered voice came back to her.

"Everything still seems legitimate. As per Harconan's promise, he seems to be the only person on the entire island – and, if it isn't him, there's no reason anyone should be there at all."

"Christine's still insisting that he's got to be setting us up for something."

"Of course he is, Elliot," Amanda replied patiently. "But it may be a

387

set-up we can use just as well as he can. Harconan's revolution has been co-opted and he can't get it back on his own. We're trying to stave off the collapse of Indonesia and we can't do it on our own. We each have assets in place that the other doesn't – and a little mutual hand washing might be in order. 'My enemy's enemy is my friend' has been the basis of many a successful alliance."

"Possibly. But he has got to know that, if the Kediri government survives, we're going to have to hand him over to them in the end. He's wanted for everything from high treason to littering. Is he eager enough for an alliance to be suicidal about it? Especially since, in effect, he'll be fighting for his former enemies?"

"Makara is anything but suicidal, Elliot." Amanda couldn't prevent the chuckle. "I can tell you right now that he doesn't intent to be handed over to anyone. Either he's planning to swindle some kind of a deal or he figures we're not going to be able to hold onto him when he decides it's time for to take his departure."

The grunt at the other end of the circuit was noncommittal.

"Trust me on this, Elliot. Working with Harconan may be our best chance to pull this out of the fire. In fact, it may be our only chance."

"I don't know, Amanda. I'm not sure this situation is salvageable, even with Harconan as an ally. Everyone has to lose one sooner or later."

"Maybe so, Elliot," Amanda replied. "But I don't intend to lose it today."

"Very well, Captain. Carry on."

"I'll keep you advised, sir. This is Gray Mare, out."

Someone rapped on the side of her helmet with a knuckle. Amanda looked up to find Arkady pointing forward through the cockpit windscreen. "There she is."

Ahead, the Island of the Princes was swimming away from the Balinese mainland, a green low riding shape outlined in the fiery sunset.

*

388

The SPEED Hawk translated back to helicopter mode and the door gunners slid open the side hatches, training the multiple barrels of their weapons outboard. Warily they circled, first the entire two-mile perimeter of the island and then the targeted landing zone at its southern rim.

In the fading light, it was just as Amanda had remembered: the snowy surf breaking over the reef line, the black sand beaches, the dense tropic forest. Pulau Piri had theoretically been a nature preserve, and the only bite in the tree cover encompassed what had been the Harconan compound.

The helipad, the seaplane hangar and ramp, the pier and boathouse, all were untouched. For the most part, the over-growth of the tropics was only in its earliest stages. But the main buildings, the sprawling, single-storey mansion, the offices, the staff quarters, all of these were gone, burned to the ground at Makara Harconan's orders. Pulau Piri had been his island, his home and the seat of his empire. He had made sure that no other would occupy it or steal its secrets.

The big compound helo popped its landing gear and set its approach. Settling onto the paved helipad, the pilots powered back and the gunners swiveled their miniguns to cover the shadows under the forest cover.

"Set your perimeter!" Stone Quillain yelled over the fading whine of the engines.

The Force Recon team followed Quillain out of the side hatches, each Marine fully armored and armed with his personalized variant of the M-8 assault rifle. Radiating out from the helipad, they dropped behind whatever cover they could find. Intently sweeping the deepening dusk, they alternated between the naked eye, NiteBrite vision visor, and thermographic gun sights.

Minutes passed and the rotors spun down into silence. Finally, Stone rose to his feet and lifted a hand in the "stand on" gesture. Amanda disembarked and moved up to his side.

The air was sweet and salty with the blended scents of the jungle, the sea, and a faint lingering tinge of burning.

"Seems pretty much quiet," Quillain begrudged, lowering the impressive piece of ordnance he was carrying. He'd equipped his M-8 with the extended length sniper's barrel and a long-range night sight, his favorite snub-barreled combat shotgun module riding the lower grab rail. Full magazines were in place in both elements of the compound weapon.

Vince Arkady dropped from the cockpit door of the SPEED Hawk and came up beside them. "The Eagle Eye still reports no activity. There's only that one contact on east beach." He'd exchanged his flight helmet for a baseball cap and carried an FN P-90 Personal Assault Weapon balanced in one hand, spare fifty-round clips of 5.7 mm slotted into the front of his interceptor vest.

Amanda nodded, her thoughts already distant. "Thank you, gentleman. Maintain the perimeter. I'll be back shortly."

"You figure on goin' over to that beach by yourself, skipper?" Quillain asked.

"Yes."

The Marine cut a sideways glance at Arkady. "Then I expect you figured wrong, ma'am. The Commander and I have discussed this matter to some extent and we figure on coming right along with you."

Diverted and annoyed, Amanda looked back. "You have my orders."

"Yes, we do, Captain," Arkady interjected. "And we intend to disregard them."

"That could be construed as insubordination, if not mutiny, gentlemen."

Arkady and Quillain looked at each other. "You're absolutely right, Captain."

Amanda started to explode, then caught herself. "Alright then," she smiled wryly, "but I certainly don't know what I've done to deserve so much personal concern on the part of so many people."

Quillain chuckled lowly. "Oh, we'll explain it to you as we go along."

The path to the east beach began behind the main house, where the jungle was starting its reclamation. Still Amanda remembered it well: the orchid scents, the softness of the air, the looming presence of the trees. The last time she'd passed this way it had been a bright hot afternoon and she'd been wearing a swimsuit instead of camouflaged utilities. She'd also been a person surer of herself and more confident in the self-mastery of her soul.

Ten minutes later, they emerged onto the beach, the low inshore waves hissing up the broad sheet of black sand. She vividly remembered this place as well; she'd abandoned her swimsuit here as a needless burden on a perfect afternoon.

The bolt on Arkady's P-90 rasped back. Wordlessly, he turned and dropped to one knee, covering the forest behind them. Quillain lifted his M-8 and scanned the beach through his night sights, the faint circle of green light projecting back from the aperture illuminating his narrowed eye.

"He's out there," he murmured. "About seventy-five yards down. Just at the tree line at the top of the beach. I'm only seein' the one heat source."

"Thank you, Stone. And now gentlemen, I *will* take it from here."

She caught the flash of Arkady's rogue's grin. "Anything you say, Captain."

She had started to move off when a soft whistle from Quillain caught her, "It's not doin' you any good in your holster, ma'am."

She slid the SOC Model Colt .45 out of her belt and drew back the slide, jacking a shell into the chamber. As she walked up the sand, she could feel the invisible eye of the Marine's rifle sights peering over her shoulder. She had to confess, albeit only to herself, that the presence of her two roughhewn guardian angels was something of a comfort.

Her boots hissed thinly through the dry sand. She was careful of her distance, and of keeping her dark-adapted eyes on the shadows, yet Harconan still took her by surprise.

"I think I prefer you dressed as you were the last time we met here."

Startled, she looked down to find Harconan sitting cross-legged on the beach. From the angle of his silhouette, he had been looking out toward the sea.

"I'd prefer it myself," she replied, recovering. "But nudity is not entirely practical at times." She sank down six feet away, tucking her feet underneath her but keeping the automatic balanced on one knee.

"Practicality frequently does get into the way of good living," he agreed. There was enough lingering horizon glow to make out the fine planed angularity of his features, and she felt the elemental stirring within her that his presence always triggered.

"You don't need the gun, Amanda," he continued, his voice lifting just over the roll of the surf. "There's no trick here. No gambit is in play."

"I've got to be sure of that, Makara." In spite of all her assurances to Christine and MacIntyre, she maintained her personal wariness. "After all, you're a masterful liar. One of the best I've ever seen."

"I will accept that as a compliment," he chuckled. "But you are not entirely unskilled in the art yourself. I recall a parole that was given and thoroughly violated at my base at Crab's Claw Peninsula."

Amanda shrugged. "I didn't owe you anything, Makara. I was being held against my will and I'd given my oath to the navy and my country a long time before I ever made any promises to you."

"I quite understand. Honor can take several different formats. That's why I hope you will accept this liar's word when he says he tells you he's speaking nothing but the absolute truth now. You can't afford to not to believe me."

"A liar's word of honor? That's an oxymoron applicable to both of us."

"Then may I offer this as a pledge to honesty?" He took something from the pocket of his shirt and tossed it across to her. She caught it with her free hand and found that it was a CD case.

"I've already halted my arms shipments to all of the different insurgent groups. On that disk you will find the GPS co-ordinates and inventories of all of my remaining arms caches in the archipelago. Its accuracy should be easy enough to verify. The only exceptions are the weapons stores being used by the Morning Star Separatists in New Guinea. They are too close to their independence for me to give them up."

Amanda stowed it in a cargo pocket of her utilities. He was right; it would be easy enough to verify. But somehow she already knew that the disk would be just as represented. "All right, pledge accepted. But why, Makara? Just why?"

She suspected she already knew the answer, but she had to hear it from his own lips. She had to sense and learn the nuances of the exact scenario to judge the extent she could trust this man.

"I find I have an excellent reason, Amanda, the best possibly conceivable. The simplest as well. Unfortunately, it will be the one most difficult for you to believe."

She tilted her head. "I'm listening."

"Very well then. I was wrong." Harconan scooped up a palmful of dark sand, letting it flow through his fingers. "I was wrong and you were right. One bright clean slash of the sword resolves nothing in these complex days. It only spills more blood."

He caught up a second palmful, this time crushing it in a clenched fist. "I was wrong. I'm sorry now that I ever started this insanity and I want it stopped." The taipan forced his hand open and poured the sand back onto the beach. "God, it sounds so incredibly puerile and pathetic when one says it that way."

"It does seem to come rather late in the game," she replied dryly. "Right when you're on the verge of achieving what you've always wanted for Indonesia."

"Damn it, Amanda, this is not what I wanted! I wanted the Indonesian peoples out from under Jakarta's thumb, not set at each other's throats. I didn't want an oppressive government replaced with a total dictatorship. I didn't want Bali!"

She let him wait for a few seconds before answering, "All right. I can possibly buy that. Do you know about the man who does want all of this? This Admiral Ketalaman?"

"Oh yes." She could hear the bleakness in his voice. "I suspect that I helped to create him. Admiral Merpati Ketalaman, the commander of the Indonesian Western Fleet Area, was one of my more useful tools in the days of my piracy cartel. I recall I was rather smug about his purchase. He was my prized shadow puppet within the Indonesian military – but, in my smugness, I never calculated that my little *wayang kulit* might take on a life of his own. His military coup against the Kediri government was no doubt partially financed by my bribe money."

"What did you ever expect, Makara?" Amanda mused. "Did you actually think that that you were the only man with grand ambitions? Didn't you realize that such men always come out from under the rocks when someone lets loose chaos and anarchy?"

"I'm afraid I couldn't be bothered with such details," Harconan mocked himself bitterly. "I had my eye fixed on greater things."

"Marvelous! Well, now that you've let the genie out of the bottle, what do you want me to do about it?"

"Help me to stop him. Or rather, let me help you."

Amanda snorted. "You mean you want to come over to the side of the angels at this late date? Admitting you're a damned fool is a gesture in the right direction, Makara, but it still doesn't make me believe you."

Harconan's head came around angrily. "You want more proof? You can have it. You must know about the shelling at Port Paotere on Sulawesi. That was aimed at me, Amanda, personally, to bring both my organization and myself under Ketalaman's heel. He's putting his knife to the throat of the Bugi people. My people, Amanda! He's threatening to make them a hate target along with the Balinese unless I support him!"

"The puppet seeking to control the puppet master. I can appreciate that you could be a useful individual to have on a leash, Makara." She kept her reply casual, almost airy, goading at the taipan's frustration level. "But it's still not enough."

"Damn it, Amanda! What do you want me to say?"

"Why!" she demanded mercilessly. If she wished, she could call this her revenge for what had happened to her on this self-same beach a few months ago.

Harconan personalized his leadership. He saw the people he ruled and commanded as people, not as a faceless group or organization. It was a far more difficult mode of leadership, especially when one's trade was war – Amanda understood this full well for this was her brand of leadership as well.

To flip his switch so radically, there must have been a personal reason, a blood reason, beyond mere strategy, tactics or clan alliances. If there wasn't, then Elliot and Chris were right and this was all some elaborate scheme.

"Why, Makara?"

"Do you remember my factotum, Mr. Lo?" Harconan's voice was toneless.

"The little Straits Chinese gentleman I met here on Pilau Piri?"

"Yes. Lan Lo was a servant in my parent's house before I was born. He was my personal tutor and oversaw my education from my earliest days. When I entered the family businesses and began to rebuild the Harconan Empire, he was my counselor, my assistant, my guide and the one individual whom I could totally and without question trust in all things. He was a brilliant man. Brilliant! He could have effortlessly become a man of wealth and power in his own right, but instead he chose to serve me." Amanda felt the brush of something cold. "What happened?"

"I had a concealed command base in the Spice Islands. Ketalaman located it. His people moved in to seize me, but it happened that I wasn't present. I'd left to oversee the evacuation operations in Bali, leaving Lan Lo in charge." Harconan paused. "Lo died, Amanda. I don't know if he was killed or if ... something else happened, but he died." That coldness and an echo of some vast internal pain were in Harconan's voice now. "I have loved two men in my life, Amanda. One was my mother's father, the Bugi clan chief who taught me about the sea and ships and about who I am. The other was my friend, Lan Lo." Once more, he dug his fingers into the sand. "For Lo, I will end the madness I have started – and destroy the man who killed him. Please help me do this thing, Amanda. I can't do it alone."

Amanda uncrossed her legs and got back to her feet. Snapping on her pistol's safety, she slid it back into her belt holster.

"Now I can believe you," she replied, holding out her hand.

Hydraulics moaned as the aircraft elevator sank to the hangar deck level, the MacGregor hatch sliding closed over the recovered SPEED Hawk.

The interior of the bay went to white lighting, and Christine Rendino and Elliot MacIntyre looked on as the side hatches of the helicopter slid open, the Intel with interest, the Admiral stone-faced.

Amanda hopped lightly down to the deck, Stone Quillain following a few moments later. The third figure followed with greater caution, hampered by a blindfold. Amanda led him across to the small reception committee. "Admiral MacIntyre, I believe you remember Makara Harconan."

Still blindfolded, Harconan extended his hand. After a hesitation, MacIntyre positioned himself to accept the handshake. "I remember Mr. Harconan quite vividly," he said.

"As I remember the Admiral," Harconan replied with a slight smile. "Especially our meeting at Crab's Claw peninsula. Your application of the Campbeltown maneuver was most masterful. I look forward to working with you."

"Thank you, Mr. Harconan," MacIntyre replied grimly. "As for the rest, that's yet to be seen."

Amanda turned to Stone and the assembled Force Recon Marines. "Captain Quillain, would you see about appropriate quarters for our guest, please?"

Stone already knew what she meant by "appropriate." Harconan would be given a guest cabin within the hold section, but there would be a Sea Devil sentry at his door at all times and he would be held isolated and incommunicado from the rest of the ship until further notice.

Quillain nodded and clamped a massive hand on Harconan's shoulder. "Yes, ma'am. If you'd come this way, sir."

"It's unlikely I could refuse the invitation, Captain. Good evening, Amanda ... *Admiral*."

MacIntyre waited for a few moments until Quillain and his charge were out of hearing range, then turned on Amanda. "Captain, you're with me. We need to talk."

"Yes sir," she replied, returning his gaze levelly. "We do."

Christine Rendino, who had been fervently trying to imitate a patch of paint on the bulkhead, took a deep breath. With his flight helmet cradled under one arm, Vince Arkady came to stand beside her. "Why do I think there's a lot more going on here than I know about?" he asked, looking after the two departing senior officers.

"Fa'sure, you don't even want to know," Christine replied, claiming his free arm with her own. "Take me to the geedunk shop, Vincent. I urgently require a chocolate cherry fudge milkshake and let's make it a double."

*

MacIntyre held off until the soundproof door of the owner's cabin closed behind them. "I don't know about this, Amanda. We've just gone through some the most elaborate security evolutions since the Manhattan Project to build the *Shenandoah* and here you are, dragging the enemy right back to our decks!"

"His people have no idea where he is," Amanda replied, turning to face him, her hands braced on her hips. "Neither does he for that matter. He's been blindfolded ever since we departed Pulau Piri. As long as we keep him below decks in the hold section, all he can ever say for sure is that he was held aboard a large US man of war."

"Given your presence, I'm willing to wager he'll be able to make a pretty good guess."

"A guess isn't knowing, Elliot. Besides, when we're done with him, we have the sanction to kill him if needs be." The stark practicality of her words stalled MacIntyre, as did the level frankness of her gaze. A quote bubbled unbidden to the surface of his mind: *the female of the species is more deadly than the male.*

"Until we have to make that call, we can use him," Amanda continued. "And I intend to just use the hell out of him."

MacIntyre couldn't help but note a certain undertone of satisfaction creeping into her voice. She reached up and unbanded her hair, shaking the amber strands down around her shoulders. "Would you mind if I changed while we talk?" she continued, indicating her sand dusted utilities.

"Uh no, go ahead," MacIntyre replied, nonplussed. "And just how do you intend to use him?"

"Here's the situation as he presented it to me," Amanda said over her shoulder as she unlocked the connecting door to her cabin. "As we know, the man behind both the Bali jihad and the attempted coup against President Kediri is Admiral Merpati Ketalaman, the Western Forces Fleet commander of the Indonesian navy." Amanda disappeared through the door, leaving it ajar. "According to Harconan, Ketalaman was also one of his bought men inside of the Indonesian military, back when he was running his piracy operations within the archipelago. Apparently, through this connection, Ketalaman picked up on Harconan's plans to disrupt the Indonesian Government and elected to piggyback his own coup on top, with the intention of assuming power on the core islands of Java and Sumatra."

MacIntyre leaned back his desk. "And why should Harconan object? Wasn't the breakup of the archipelago into separate independent states his goal from the beginning?"

Discarded boots thumped onto the deck in the next cabin. "Not exactly. Having an aggressive military dictatorship as a major player in his revived Bone Empire wasn't quite what Harconan had in mind. Beyond that, Ketalaman is not merely attempting to co-opt Harconan's revolution but his organization as well. Ketalaman wants Harconan's sea lift and his arms distribution network. If Harconan and the Bugi refuse to assist him, Ketalaman is threatening massive retribution against the sea clans. That mysterious bombardment at Port Paotere was a demonstration by Ketalaman of what might happen if Harconan refuses to play along.

"Ketalaman is also responsible for killing some of Harconan's personal staff, including one individual who was very close to Harconan. That's what pushed Harconan into coming to us. Well, 'my enemy's enemy is my friend' after all. He wants friends to use against Ketalaman and in the worst way." Amanda paused. "Excuse me a second."

MacIntyre heard a faint intercom filtered voice from the far room and Amanda's replies to it. "This is the captain ... Have we seen any major situational changes on the threat boards or in the theater sitreps over the past couple of hours? Very good, Dix. I want to call an O Group for the primary planning staff in two hours and I want our guest, Mr. Harconan, to be on call should his presence be needed. Understood? Carry on."

"Apparently you think Harconan is giving you the straight dope?" MacIntyre said as she hung up the phone.

"It fits with everything we're seeing on the boards and it fits what I know about the man."

MacIntyre scowled. Damn, she would have to bring that up.

"Makara Harconan can be a focused planner, but he's also mercurial and essentially egocentric. He has no government or set national policy to answer to, no bureaucracy to turn around. He is a king with a king's prerogative to change his mind in a heartbeat. Now he's been attacked, he's angered – and he's turning on his attacker. That opens a window of opportunity for us."

Harconan was not the only mercurial figure in the equation. MacIntyre had to struggle to keep pace with this drastically altering scenario. There were also the diverting sounds of zippers opening and clothes slithering from the other room. "To do what?"

"To turn the entire Indonesian situation around," she replied. "To regain control on our terms."

MacIntyre glanced up toward the gap in the door, just in time to catch a momentary flash of golden tanned skin. *God damn it to hell, MacIntyre, not now!*

"That would be quite a trick," he fired back. "The entire archipelago is in chaos."

"Exactly, Elliot." Her purring alto grew more distant, lifting over the sound of water hissing from the shower. "For the first time, we know who we're fighting and, for the first time, we have a level playing field. Ketalaman's intervention has thrown Harconan's plan into chaos. But our successful evacuation of the Kediri government from Jakarta has also thrown Ketalaman's plan into chaos. Nobody has a viable plan in play and the first people to develop one wins."

"You're sounding like you have one."

"I think I do. But it all depends on two factors. One, we have to keep our alliance with Harconan a secret. Nobody – and I mean nobody – can know he's actively working with us. That's why I brought him out to the *Shenandoah*. Here, we have full control of him and of the situation.

"Next, the trick will be to bring together a widely diverse group of factions. You're still a fishing buddy with the Secretary of State, aren't you?"

"Yes."

"Great. You can deliver him, and through him, the State Department." The water shut off. "Beyond State, we'll need to bring on board the Kediri government, the Australians, the Bugi Pirate clans, the Morning Star revolutionaries in New Guinea and the Balinese religious leadership."

MacIntyre turned to fully face the door. "Damn it, Amanda, that wouldn't be a trick, that would be a canonizable miracle!"

Amanda appeared in the doorway, wrapped in a thigh length beach jacket and vigorously toweling her hair dry. "Don't I know it," she said, smiling wryly. "What's more, we only have a matter of days, if not hours, to make it happen."

Harconan found himself amused. The situation was strikingly novel, the shark surrounded by the pod of killer whales. The group of uniformed men and women gathered around the big briefing table were all eyeing him with the same baleful wariness as the two side-armed Marines at the compartment door.

It was something of a compliment to be considered so formidable, but it was also going to make his eventual disengagement from this situation something of a challenge.

But that was a matter to be dealt with later. For now, he was where he wished to be.

"Ladies and gentlemen, allow me to show you what I can bring to the table." From his position at the head of the briefing table, Harconan gestured at the large screen display. It glowed with a map of western Indonesia, the islands dotted with several score position hacks paired with geographical co-ordinate sets. "With certain previously mentioned exceptions, these are my untapped weapons caches in the archipelago. The Indonesian government forces should find them useful. I trust that, by now, you have proven their veracity?"

"We've been in communication with the Indonesian Army command on Java," Admiral MacIntyre replied. "They've already investigated a couple of your cache sites. The arms were there and the inventories match. We're willing to concede you're delivering the goods in this instance."

"As I can in a number of other areas, my good admiral," Harconan replied. "I can give you Intelligence contacts in every major and the majority of the minor ports in the archipelago, as well as a major coast watcher network. For example ..." Harconan stood and turned to the screen, then tapped a port symbol at the Northwestern tip of Sumatra. "Here at Banda Aceh, you have the primary concentration of rebel naval forces. Currently in port and ready for sea you've got the frigates Slamet Riyadi and the Silas Papare, a Van Speijik and a Parchim conversion.

You've also got two major amphibious warfare vessels, the LSM Teluk Hading and the Indonesian Fleet flagship, the Teluk Surabaya.

"You also have a light forces group: a dagger missile boat, two Lurssen FPB 57 gunboats and two Kondor class minesweepers." Harconan swept his hand to the eastern entrance of the Malacca Strait. "Here you have – or at least you had – their first-string force: three Fatahillah class frigates and another dagger boat inbound to Banda Aceh from their patrol stations. The port facilities at Banda were making preparations to refuel and restore them upon their arrival."

At the other end of the table, Amanda glanced at her little golden-haired shadow, Christine Rendino. The younger woman nodded.

"We've known you've always had a handle on anything moving by sea in these waters, Makara," Amanda replied. "Point taken. Continue."

"All right, I can also provide you with armed commando and Intelligence gathering teams on a number of the islands, including Java and Sumatra. I can provide you with names and targeting data on a number of the Islamic radicalist cells that are likely supporting the Ketalaman coup, and I have contacts with a number of the prominent Hindu religious and community leaders on Bali. I've already urged them in the strongest possible terms to reign in the anti-Muslim violence there.

"Most importantly, I can give you littoral sea control and shallow draft sea transport. I can mass dozens of armed *pinisi* wherever you want them, and I can give you a couple of hundred inter-island coasters and schooners ready to sail and deliver troops, passengers or cargo wherever needed." He stopped and quietly considered them all. "But I will require a few things in return."

"Such as?" MacIntyre replied.

Harconan noted that the Admiral's stare had the truculence of a displeased bull water buffalo.

"For one, I'll need communications facilities. Ketalaman took out my own headquarters. Your fine ship here, the Galaxy *Shenandoah*, should be able to provide what I need admirably."

Not an eye blinked around the table. There was not the least whisper of reaction to his probe.

"Or wherever it is that we are," Harconan went on. "I will also need some promises."

"Such as?"

Harconan leaned against the edge of the briefing table, putting emphasis on each word. "I want your word, Admiral, and that of Captain Garrett, that my people will be protected, my captains, my crews, my clan chiefs, my agents. They will fight under your command, not Kediri's. You will, in turn, guarantee them anonymity. Their identities will not be handed over to the government."

Amanda and MacIntyre again engaged in a silent visual conference. "Accepted," MacIntyre replied. "What else?"

"If I actively begin assisting you, Ketalaman will know about it. He will retaliate against the Bugi colonies within his reach. I want your guarantees that, to the fullest extent of your capacities, you will assist in the protection of my noncombatants."

This time it was Amanda who replied. "You have my promise."

"That will be satisfactory."

"You don't mention anything about immunity for yourself," MacIntyre said.

The taipan shrugged and grinned. "A minor matter to be discussed at a later date."

Amanda's eyes narrowed and the faintest hint of a rueful smile tugged at her lips. "I've got one more question for you, Makara. I know you're in very deep with the leadership of Morning Star Liberation Movement on New Guinea. Just how much so?"

"I've supported their cause and they've supported mine," Harconan replied with caution. "I've delivered them arms and I've done them other favors here and there."

"Will they listen to you? Can you influence them?"

"I can put you in contact with certain of the tribal counsels. And, if my advice is asked for, I will give it."

Amanda and her Admiral exchanged another protracted look and

MacIntyre nodded minutely. Then he looked back to Harconan. "All provisions accepted, Mr. Harconan."

Harconan returned to his chair at the briefing table. The Admiral had spoken. Provisionally, he was on board and a member of the team.

But the Marine sentries still remained at the door.

"Captain Garrett," MacIntyre continued. "This is your package. Bring the Operations Group up to speed on what we've been looking at."

"Yes, sir." She rose from her chair and walked the length of the table, brushing past Harconan without looking at him.

"Go to full map view, please."

The large screen display flicked to a full imaging of the Indonesian Archipelago. "Ladies and gentlemen, as you know from our sociopolitical database on Indonesia, a key aspect of national discontent has been a perceived Java-centricity within the Jakarta government. In this instance, it's valid. The island of Java and the capital of Jakarta are at the very heart of this conflict. The side that controls Java and Jakarta will win.

"At the moment, the question who exactly controls what is still up in the air. The rebels are in nominal possession of the capital city, but fighting between rebel and government forces is ongoing across the rest of Java. Our assessment is that neither side has an adequate block of ground forces on the island to secure it. The classic doctrine of 'Who gets there fustest with the mostest' will decide the outcome of this battle.

"In this, the rebels currently have the edge." Amanda's hand drifted from Java across the Sunda Strait. "Their primary base of power and the bulk of their reserve formations on Sumatra, right next door, while the government's loyal troops are scattered throughout the islands, especially on New Guinea at the far eastern end of the archipelago.

"The basic strategic equation is simple. We must use the assets available to us to slow the rate of rebel reinforcement while accelerating that of the government. The distance factors can be leveled by outside airlift, ours and that of the other Regional Intervention Force powers. That will not exceed our existing rules of engagement.

"As for the rest? That will be up to us."

Washington D.C.

0452 Hours; Zone Time, November 5, 2008

Secretary of State Harrison Van Linden didn't much enjoy diplomacy by video. He was both a statesman and a poker player of the old school. He preferred direct eye to eye contact with his opposite number.

Modern telecommunications also put you at the mercy of time zones. Diplomacy and discretion dictated that one had to give the other fellow the decent night's sleep.

Van Linden had elected to conduct this video conference from his own office at the State Department. Per force, it must be an off-the-cuff piece of work, if for no other reason than President Kediri's "Capital City" was now the USS *Pelelieu* holding at anchor in Benoa Port.

"Mr. Secretary, the President of Indonesia is standing by on-line," the communication officer's voice issued from the speaker of his desk videophone deck.

Van Linden snuck a last sip of strong black coffee and passed the cup and saucer to an aide outside of the camera. His Chief of Staff was present in the room as well, as well as a staffer with a networked laptop balanced on her knees, ready to call up and feed him any required information from the crisis database.

There would be another observer as well, one not physically present. President Childress would be monitoring both ends of the call from the White House.

"Put President Kediri through, please, and record."

"Very good, Mr. Secretary."

The phone's small flat screen flicked over from the State Department seal to an image of a briefing room aboard the Regional Intervention Force flagship.

President Kediri sat stony-faced in the foreground of the screen. The Indonesian Foreign Minister and the Golkar Party Chairman flanked him, each man wearing translator headsets. A handful of other Indonesian officials and senior military officers occupied the other seats in the briefing room, refugees rallied from locations outside of Jakarta.

405

This was the only remnant remaining of the standing national government. The question was: was it enough of a seed to grow again?

"Good day, Mr. President," Van Linden began. "I hope that you are well and that our accommodations and facilities have been adequate."

"Your military has been most helpful, Mr. Secretary," Kediri replied stiffly. "We have been able to re-establish communications with those elements of our armed forces still faithful to the true government. We survive, but the situation is critical."

"We are well aware of that, Mr. President, and we are doing everything within our power to assist you in this crisis."

"Does this course of action include more troops to assist my government in putting down Ketalaman's coup?" Kediri demanded.

"It does not, Mr. President," Van Linden replied levelly. "The commitment levels and the mission of the Regional Intervention Force will remain as they are now. However, we are fully prepared to give your government full support in the areas of Intelligence-gathering, logistics, transportation and communications. Indeed, we are already giving you that support. We will back you to the limit, Mr. President, but that limit is any active involvement in your civil war."

"But we are losing the war on the three principal islands, Java, Sumatra and Bali!" Kediri protested. "The damn Hindus have driven all government authority from the island, save for that which is supported by your peacekeeping troops. Ketalaman holds Jakarta! It's only a matter of time until there is a total collapse of resistance!"

Van Linden nodded gravely. "We fully agree, sir, and we have been working to develop a resolution to this situation. We have entered into negotiations that we feel could produce such a resolution."

"Negotiations?" Kediri stiffened. "What manner of negotiations and with whom?"

"With a number of the involved parties, Mr. President," Van Linden said, sidestepping the question. "We believe we may have come up with a course of action that could lead to a favorable outcome for your government."

"Why were we not advised of these negotiations?" It was a demand from the Indonesian, not a mere question.

"We weren't certain how events would develop, sir, and we desired to provide you with a concrete package before we brought it to your attention," Van Linden replied. *And I didn't need you jiggling my elbow, Mr. President. Things are difficult enough as is.*

"We've developed a two-phase plan actually," the Secretary of State continued before he could be interrupted. "A Balinese resolution and a Javanese-Sumatran resolution. The Balinese resolution can be solely diplomatic and can be in play very rapidly.

"We have opened channels of communication with a number of the most powerful and respected pedanda of the Agama Tirta leadership. We have explained to them the true source and intent of the acts of desecration against their religion and we have provided them with evidence in this matter. So far, they've proved receptive to our contacts and they're willing to use their influence to stop the violence against the Balinese Muslim population. The Balinese are essentially a people of peace, and this outburst of bloodshed has become appalling even to them. They are willing to work with us, Mr. President."

"In the name of sanity, I should hope so!"

"But," Van Linden said, "there is also a list of their concerns that they wish to be addressed."

Kediri's eyes narrowed. "Concerns? Of what nature?"

"They desire – no, they require – an increased Hindu representation within the National Government and a semi-autonomous Balinese island administration. They desire that Bali be led by the Balinese."

"That is a blow against the central government," Kediri protested. "That is totally against the spirit of our national policy of Bhinneka Tunggal Ika!"

"The Balinese leaders that I conferred with brought that subject up." The corner of Van Linden's mouth quirked slightly. "They stated that if 'we are many but all are one' is indeed the law of the land, and if the Javanese desire to administer Bali's internal affairs, then perhaps a just solution would be for the Balinese to administer Java's internal affairs. Thus, symmetry would be established."

Kediri's jaw tightened.

407

"However, Mr. President, the Balinese also state that, if their proposals are unacceptable, they are quite willing to consider independence."

Van Linden adjusted his glasses and looked to the papers on his desk, not giving the Indonesian an opportunity to reply. "To move along to the greater problem of Java and Sumatra. The situation continues in a state of flux on both islands, with scattered elements of the government and rebel forces clashing with no clear-cut dominance as yet established and no fixed territorial lines yet drawn. Some governmental forces are continuing a resistance even around the Jakarta area.

"To date, Ketalaman has established no true dominance over either island. At this juncture, our military leaders feel that an infusion of fresh government forces could very well turn the tide and lead to a collapse of the anti-government rebellion."

"But we have no fresh governmental forces," Kediri protested. "We're fully committed. We have nothing left!"

"Yes, you do, Mr. President. You have a very large force pool, including some of your best and most reliable ground combat units that can be immediately committed to the fighting on Java and Sumatra. Your garrisons on New Guinea."

Kediri shot to his feet. "That's impossible!"

"No, it is not, Mr. President." The Secretary of State refused to understand Kediri's meaning. "The Air Forces of the United States and Australia are standing by to provide all of the required airlift. The first transport missions can be launched within a matter of hours."

"It cannot be done!" Kediri insisted. "Our people are fighting for their lives on Irian Jaya against the Morning Star revolutionaries. If we withdraw our troops, those savages will butcher our citizens!"

"We are currently in communication with the leadership of the Morning Star Movement," Van Linden replied slowly. "They have agreed to an immediate cease-fire and they have guaranteed the safety of all Indonesian citizens currently on Irian Jaya. You may withdraw your forces to deal with the Ketalaman situation without any concern of a massacre. They've given us their word and we feel they can be trusted."

"And how can you be so sure the word of those barbarians is good?"

"Because they expect something in return, President Kediri. A withdrawal of all Indonesian garrisons, transmigrasi and government administrators. Also, the recognition of a free and independent Papuan republic under the Morning Star flag."

It took Kediri several sputtering seconds to regain his English. "Unthinkable! Unthinkable! That is beyond all possibility, Mr. Secretary. Do you realize how many Indonesian patriots lost their lives liberating Irian Jaya from the Dutch colonialists? That is a sacred island."

"The Morning Star Movement feels much the same way, Mr. President." Van Linden lowered his voice. "They have lost a great number of lives as well, seeking to drive out what they perceive as an Indonesian colonial government. We do not sit in judgment of you or Indonesia, President Kediri, but the age of colonialism is over, for everyone."

"May I ask how you have managed to make these agreements with these ... Morning Star leaders?"

"No, Mr. President. You may not. Suffice to say that we have been able to make these arrangements. They are yours if you chose to accept them. We – that is, the governments of Australia and the United States – believe you should. We desire to see a unified Indonesia survive. We believe that this is in the best interests of the Pacific Rim nations and of the world as a whole, and that this may be the best, if not the only, means of rectifying the current situation. But be advised, sir, should you choose not to accept this option, we may be forced to accept the dissolution of the Indonesian State as a fait accompli. Out of national necessity, we may have no choice but to commence the recognition of the independent island governments of the archipelago."

President Kediri stared down at the tabletop for a long time, then looked up, his worn face expressionless. "It seems I am being left with few options."

"We have very little time in which to act Mr. President," Van Lynden said without remorse, "and you have a choice to make. You can lose New Guinea or you can lose Indonesia. As we say in my country, 'take it or leave it'."

409

"KGKR calling KGGX, on sched Zulu ... KGKR calling KGGX on sched Zulu ... The words are Honor ... Apple ... Tin Pot. I repeat, Honor ... Apple ... Tin Pot."

"KGGX replying to KGKR on sched Zulu. I hear the words. I reply Glory ... Papaya ... Kettle. I reply Glory ... Papaya ... Kettle."

"It's good to hear your voice again, my father Akima. I am pleased to see things go well for you and the Morning Stars."

"We gain ground daily, my son Harconan. We gain hope as well, thanks to you. I trust things go well for you in turn."

"No. Things do not go well for me, my father. My friend Lo is dead and my cause has failed."

"I cannot see my son failing. How may the people of the Morning Star help you?"

"My failing is of my own doing, father. I have let others steal my dream and I must end my fight. But my defeat can be the victory for the Morning Star movement and an end to your fighting. There are two other men standing by on this channel who wish to speak with you. Will you listen to their words?"

"If that is your wish, my son."

"It is. May I present to you President Kediri of Indonesia and Secretary of State Harrison Van Linden, the senior diplomat of the United States of America. Gentlemen, this is Chief Akima of the Asmat people, a member of the ruling council of the Revolutionary Government of the Free Papuan Republic. Mr. President ..."

"I greet you, Chief Akima."

"I greet you as well, Mr. President. I have wished to speak with you for a long time."

"Perhaps we should have spoken long before. Chief Akima, I wish to negotiate a cease-fire on Irian Jaya between the Morning Star Republic and Indonesia and the withdrawal of all Indonesian military forces and governmental administration. This withdrawal to commence immediately."

"I see, Mr. President. And you, Mr. Secretary?"

"Chief Akima, the United States wishes to discuss its formal diplomatic recognition of the Free Papuan Republic. We are also prepared to discuss sponsoring your membership within the United Nations."

Dead air.

"KGKR calling KGGX ... did you copy that, my father?"

"I am still here, my son. Give an old man a moment to weep."

The Army of God's Sacred Vengeance set sail aboard two fishing luggers and a dive boat stolen from the Turtle Beach resort.

Fate had been alternately kind and cruel to Mohammed Sinar. First there had come the money and arms from his mysterious benefactor and Sinar's star had ascended once more. He had all of the power and respect that could be purchased with a handful of rupiahs and a truckload of AK-47s. His foes, at least his immediate ones, had fled in terror and throats had been presented for his heel to rest upon.

For a time, being the Flaming Sword of Allah and a Liberator of the People had been a pleasant mode of existence. But the gifting of arms and funding had not been repeated and money, ammunition and ideas again ran low.

Events on Sumatra had also taken an ominous turn. The war had become a true war between true armies. Ketalaman the usurper and Kediri the ruler had their jaws locked in a death struggle, and there was no room left on the island for pretenders to power. To side with the old government meant being stoned to death, yet to side with the rebels meant actually having to fight. Neither alternative was particularly attractive to Muhammad Sinar.

As a foreign wise man had once phrased it, "It was time to get the Hell out of Dodge."

The call by the Muslim radicalist leadership for reinforcements for Ketalaman's Army on Java had given Sinar his opportunity. Backed by the bloodstained words of the Mullahs, he had rallied some threescore of his followers to battle, pledging to bring God's justice to the hated infidels and their treasure to his troops. Procuring what small craft were available, the Army of God's Vengeance had loaded the remnants of their arsenal aboard and taken off for the battlefront.

However, Mohammed Sinar had absolutely no intention of landing on Java. He had a plan of his own. On the pretext of "establishing a base", he would seek out one of the smaller, outer islands, some pleasant little place with a village or two full of helpless workers to cow and nubile women to enjoy. There, Sinar would establish his own personal kingdom and await developments in the outside world.

Tonight, Sinar's little fleet was making the dash across the Selat Sunda, the narrow stretch of sea that separated Sumatra from Java. He'd had some concern about this passage; they would be passing close to the actual zone of conflict and it would be an open water run with no convenient coastline to offer concealment and escape. Accordingly, Sinar had ordered all lights extinguished and all hands, or at least those who were not seasick, to man the rails, armed and ready for trouble.

And yet, the better part of the crossing had been made and nothing had happened. The seas were low and easy under a starlit sky and they seemed to share the strait only with the gaunt craggy bulk of Anak Krakatoa, the dim ruddy glow from the volcano's crater underlighting its steam plume.

Mohammed Sinar was just beginning to relax when, with no warning, the darkness coalesced beside his dive boat flagship. Three black-hulled *pinisi* had come sweeping out of nowhere. With their gaff rigs reefed and running on their auxiliary diesels, they paralleled the course of Sinar's ragged flotilla. Moving with an ominous lazy precision, each dark schooner kept exact pace with one of Sinar's craft, like a barracuda considering its prey.

"Who are you and where do you think you're going?" an insolently casual voice called from out of the night.

Sinar could see the eyes of his men glinting wide and frightened along the rail. At best, they were not the greatest of warriors on land, and they were less so at sea. Yet Sinar knew that he must maintain his face in front of them for they were all he had left.

"We are the Army of God's Sacred Vengeance, in the service of Allah. The Prophet has spoken and we sail to avenge the spilled blood of our Javanese brothers."

The voice in the darkness sounded amused. "No you do not. Turn about and go home, landsman. You are not needed or wanted on Java."

Sinar's hands tightened on the cockpit railing. He had an ominous

413

hunch about who he was dealing with, but he also knew that every man aboard the dive boat was awaiting his word, judging him as their leader. He must try and maintain the bluff he had built for himself, at least until he could get his feet on dry ground.

"Allah and his Prophet Muhammad say that we shall pass!"

"And the Raja Samudra says that you shall not."

Flame leaped from the bulwarks of the *pinisi* squadron. Machine guns raged, fuel tanks and rocket-propelled grenades flared – and Mohammed Sinar and the Army of God's Sacred Vengeance ceased to be a matter of concern for anyone.

The object lay in the slime of the harbor floor just off the ferry terminal docks. A great, flattened lozenge encased in a jacket of rubbery anti-echoic material, it electronically debated one of the two great pressing questions in its limited universe.

Two days prior, it had been carefully positioned by the SEAL Delivery Vehicle *Remora*. But it had rested inert until prodded to life only an hour before by a protracted and complex sequence of events.

At the port of Bakauheni on the Sumatran side of the trans-straits ferry run, a Bugi stevedore had noted the equipment and personnel of a Rebel armored reconnaissance company being loading aboard the commandeered car ferry, Bukit Barasan.

A phone call was made and, after that, a brief transmission from a concealed radio transmitter to the USS *Shenandoah*. From the commando carrier, another transmission was made, a digital activation code sent on a carrier frequency pitched to penetrate the shallow water of Marak harbor.

Now the debate began. The object's passive hydrophone system scanned the surrounding maritime environment, comparing the sound signatures of passing watercraft with one specific signature pre-loaded into its computer memory. Previously captured by an air-dropped sensor buoy, it was the sound pattern produced by the motor ferry Bukit Barasan, as distinctive and unique as a human fingerprint.

An outboard powered water taxi buzzed past. *That's not it!* A fishing lugger chugged out into the Straits. *That's not it!* The beat of a heavier screw drew closer. The object's idiot savant brain minutely assessed the sound pattern, matching the chirp of the nicked propeller blade with the vibration of a coolant pump and the rumble-swish of the water flow around a blunt-bowed hull.

*That's it!*

One of the two great questions had been answered. Safety interlocks disengaged and secondary sensor systems came on-line.

The Bukut Barasan slowed and eased in toward the dock. The tide was out and the hundred-and-eighty-foot-long ferry was heavily burdened with some score of armored fighting vehicles on her car deck and a hundred odd troops in her passenger spaces. Her keel passed a bare ten feet over the object on the harbor floor. The object's pressure sensors and magnetometers reacted to the displacement and steel of the ferry's hull and the object answered its second and last great question.

*Now!*

Firing impulses flashed to the detonators buried within half a ton of PBXN high explosive and the smart mine fulfilled its destiny.

The Lockheed C-130 transport had been dubbed the "Hercules" – but perhaps the aircraft would have been better named the "Storm Crow" or the "Stormy Petrel" for, after fifty years of continuous production and service in the world's air forces, she was the omen of war and disaster.

For fully half a century she had been the world's premier tactical military airlifter; absolutely necessary and apparently immune to obsolescence. Like the KA-BAR knife, the model 1911A Colt .45 and the "Ma Deuce" .50 caliber machine gun, the only thing that can replace a C-130 is another C-130.

The field at Bengkulu was lined with them, bearing different camo-patterned paint and different national insignia: Australia, New Zealand, Japan, Indonesia, Singapore, the United States. Ground crews swarmed around them and a steady stream of vehicles and equipment flowed up their tail ramps to vanish within their commodious bellies. Every few minutes, a Hercules would lift into the sky with a moan of racing turboprops, only to be replaced a few minutes later by a sister plane, an empty "bucket" returning on the air bridge to Java.

Aboard the departing aircraft, Indonesian soldiers lay across cargo pallets or squatted in odd corners of the cargo bay, their eyes closed, not seeking to speak over the deafening song of the propellers. They were leaving the "Land of Lapping Death" behind.

This was no escape from conflict – they were flying from war to war – but at least, if they fell, they would die on home ground.

On the hills overlooking the airfield, black-skinned men looked up at the sky and watched the airplanes bearing the brown-skinned men away. Soon, this land, their land, would belong only to them once more, for better or worse, to make of it what they could.

They looked on with an ageless patience. They had waited a long time for this moment. They could wait a little longer.

Pangkalpinang Airfield
Banka island
0716 Hours; Zone Time, November 14, 2008

It was a cool and showery morning but Captain Raya Sukawate, former Garuda airlines pilot – and now rebel Air Force officer – was sweating as he argued on the edge of the parking apron.

"Damn it! The airplane doesn't know about your bloody orders!"

Sukawate's de Havilland Dash-8 300 turboprop airliner had been converted into a military transport by the fast and dirty gutting of its interior. Now it was being loaded for another shuttle run to Java. Loaded and *overloaded*. The oleo legs of the Dash-8's undercarriage sank as case after case of artillery ammunition was shoehorned through the passenger hatch to be sketchily lashed down within the stripped aircraft.

"We're already over our maximum safe payload weight! We could lose the aircraft if we try a take-off like this."

"We are at war," the stone-faced logistics officer replied. "Risks must be taken for the victory. These munitions must be delivered to our forces in Java. We must increase the tonnage we airlift!"

"Destroying your aircraft and killing your pilots won't get it done!"

The Army man's expression didn't change, but his hand drifted toward the holster at his belt and Sukawate yielded. There were a growing number of reports of men being shot for "defeatism."

The pilot turned back toward the airliner, recomputing his fuel load once more. If he dumped another hundred gallons, he might be able to scrape into Jakarta on fumes.

\*

The logy turboprop lumbered out to the very end of the main runway, Sukawate wanting every last inch of the tarmac working in his favor. He and his copilot rushed through the preflight checklist and engine run-up, balancing the need to make sure of the power plants with the consumption of precious kerosene.

418

Finally, there was nothing for it but to take a deep breath and firewall the throttles. Sukawate held her back on the brakes as the twin Pratt & Whitney 123 Turboprops screamed up to full, shuddering power. Then, when the tires finally started to walk, he let her go.

The de Havilland gained speed far too slowly. When she thundered through the Point of Decision, she still rested firmly on her landing gear. With the thought of that Army logistics officer and his pistol lingering in his mind, Sukawate gritted his teeth and continued the take-off.

As the end of the runway rushed toward them, Sukawate eased back on the yoke and coaxed every last ounce of lift out of the wings. The De Havilland danced on her toes for a long breathless moment and edged into the air.

"Gear up!"

The air speed needle crawled upward and they barely cleared the tree line beyond the airport. Beyond was the beach and the beautiful, flat waters of the bay, a lone schooner cutting across them.

The Dash-8 began to climb with more authority and Sukawate let his breath out. They were going to make it.

*

Out on the bay, the captain of the pirate *pinisi* tracked the airliner with his binoculars. He and his ship had been loitering under the airport's offshore traffic pattern for an hour, waiting for a decent prize and this low-flying twin-engined transport looked promising.

"Gunners load and stand ready ... ready ... shoot!"

The firing teams dashed out of the deck shelter to the bow and stern. The gunners lifted Stinger MANPAD surface-to-air launchers to their shoulders and acquired the target. An instant later, a two-round missile salvo screamed away.

The explosion that followed almost laid the Bugi raider over on its beam ends.

"We have positively identified elements of the 9$^{th}$ Infantry brigade, the *Polici* Mobile Brigade and the 1$^{st}$ Armored Cavalry on Java." Ketalaman's Chief of Staff was being hesitant with his words. "And the Government garrison at Palembang has been re-enforced by an as yet unidentified airborne unit."

Ketalaman did not answer. The silence in the cavern command post stretched out to a dangerous degree, forcing a staffer to blurt out, "The only way Kediri could produce these reinforcements would be if he's abandoning Irian Jaya altogether."

"That's easy enough to ascertain," Ketalaman replied, his voice low. "What are we hearing from our sources in Jayapura?"

"As before, sir. The garrisons are being airlifted out by the Regional Intervention Force and the transmigrasi are being brought in from the outlying villages to the major population centers. No official statement has been issued by the island administration yet but the unofficial word is to prepare for an evacuation."

"And the Morning Star Separatists? How are they reacting?"

"They're not reacting at all, Admiral. Separatist military operations have come to a complete halt. Again, there's been no official notification of a cease fire – but it's obvious that one is in effect."

Ketalaman nodded. "Kediri and the Americans are sacrificing New Guinea to save the remainder of Indonesia. And I suspect I know the intermediary who made this accommodation with the Morning Stars possible."

Again, silence settled in the command center. General Tiamatu, the Islamic Militia Group commander, broke it this time. "What's our air force doing about this troop airlift? Can't it be cut off? The planes shot down?"

"Not without bringing the damn Americans and Australians down on us," the air force liaison replied. "The majority of the transport aircraft involved belong to them. Beyond that, the air convoys are being escorted by Australian Air Force fighters and the flight routes are being covered by American Aegis guided-missile cruisers. Any attempt at an intercept would simply lead to the annihilation of what air assets we still possess."

"What about bombing the government airfields on Java then? That would be something, at least."

"We're doing the best we can with what we have!" the aviation commander snapped back. "Kindly recall that the Air Force's best strike group, the F-16 squadron, did not side with us. The enemy has the air superiority."

"Enough!" Ketalaman barked, reining in his subordinates. "As long as we don't directly involve the Americans or the Australians, neither side in this conflict will have the air assets to decisively affect the outcome of this conflict. This war will be won or lost on the ground in Java. What's the current situation there?"

"The fronts appear to be stabilizing, sir," the Chief of Staff replied. "We've secured the Jakarta area and, barring one or two pockets of resistance, we hold all of the power centers in the western third of the island, from Cerebon on. The government forces still hold the eastern two-thirds. Certain regional military commanders in eastern Java whose support we had counted on apparently had a change of heart when Kediri survived."

"They'll sway back in our direction soon enough if we can regain the initiative." Ketalaman's finger dropped to the map of the archipelago, sweeping from one end of Java to the other. "It's elementary. We are here. They are there. Sumatra is secondary. We can hold what we have and claim the rest with ease if the Kediri government falls. The battle of Java will decide this war and the side that develops the superiority and attacks first will win that battle. What is the status of our force build up?"

"We're doing the best we can, sir," the Chief of Staff murmured.

"That sounds like the start of an excuse, Captain," Ketalaman snapped. "Our enemies are having to redeploy across two thousand kilometers of ocean. We only have to move them across a twenty-kilometer strait. Why are they succeeding while we are not?"

"We're having great difficulty in coordinating shipping for troop and equipment transport. Many coastal vessels have left the ports we control. Other craft have been sabotaged, some of them we believe by their own crews. Some captains have even accepted munitions cargos from us, only to deliver them to the government forces."

"Conscript the vessels and their crews and place guards aboard them," Ketalaman responded.

"We are doing so, Admiral, but we're also being interdicted. Our ships and ferries are being attacked in transit and the harbors under our control are being mined. Even transport aircraft have been shot down."

"And the cause? Who's behind it?"

"Some of it's being done by government patrol forces. Other acts have been done by naval guerillas."

"The Bugi?"

"Yes, sir. So it appears."

"And could there be any involvement by the Regional Intervention Force?"

The Chief of Staff hesitated. "There appears to be no overt involvement, sir. They've completed the evacuation of the foreign nationals and all of their ships have withdrawn to the waters off southern Java. Beyond their support operations to the troop airlift and their logistical aid to the Kediri government, there has been no active involvement in the war since the Embassy incident in Jakarta."

"You prevaricate, Captain." Ketalaman said.

"Some of our Intelligence analysts feel that there are certain ... sophisticated aspects to this interdiction campaign that are beyond the capabilities of either the Bugi or the Kediri government."

"But American naval or air units are not directly operating against us? There are none of their ships in the Karimata Straits or the Java Sea?"

"No, sir."

"Undoubtedly the Americans are providing advisors and Intelligence to Kediri – but, as long as their combat units are not involved, we'll cope." Ketalaman tapped the map at the Northern tip of Sumatra. "The classic and most successful methodology to break a naval interdiction campaign is the convoy. Our naval strength is massed here at Banda Aceh fleet base – our large ships, our amphibious and mine warfare forces and most of the heavy merchant vessels we have under our direct control. They will load the 4th Infantry brigade and its supporting elements, the best of our Militia Cadres and enough stores to provide for a major offensive operation. We'll run them through to Jakarta in a single convoy, massive enough to brush aside any pirate interdiction. We can utilize these troops to launch our finishing offensive before Kediri is ready to launch his."

"The 4th constitutes our entire strategic reserve," the Chief of Staff murmured uneasily.

"Kediri is sending in his Old Guard. We must counter with our Grenadiers. If Kediri wishes to block us, then he must counter with his remaining naval forces – and we have the decisive advantage in sea power. Either way, he will be crushed. Gentlemen, I want this troop movement ready to launch within forty-eight hours. No excuses will be accepted." Ketalaman began to turn away from the map table, but then turned back. "General," he said, addressing his Air Force commander. "There's something else. Do you recall that special targeting template I had you prepare when we were negotiating with Harconan?"

"Yes, sir," the airman replied uneasily.

"Put it into effect immediately. Maximum effort. Maximum sortie rate."

The Air Force general – who was a political animal, but also a human being –grasped for a straw. "Admiral, that would be a critical diversion of our limited resources away from far more vital military objectives."

"General." Ketalaman's voice was soft, almost gentle. "Start hitting the Bugi population centers now and keep on hitting them until you're ordered to do otherwise. Someone must be reminded that I keep my promises."

Off his left wing, the Java Sea glinted in the hot sunlight. Off his right, the verdant slopes of Madura's central mountain range rose out of the island's narrow coastal plain. Ahead and below, the pale surf-and-sand snake of the beach line writhed. Flying in the last slot of the four-plane stacked echelon formation, the rebel pilot was somewhat bored.

He took a degree of pleasure in that boredom as well.

He had no idea why his strike flight had been diverted to these village bombardment mission – the objectives were well away from the fighting lines and didn't appear to be conventional military targets – but the decision had been made by higher-ranked heads than his.

The Indonesian flier was simply pleased that these new targets appeared to be more lightly defended than the Government columns his group had been hammering. The damn Americans were becoming far too generous in handing out their Stinger SAMs.

Not that these village strike missions were an entire walkover. They'd encountered furious small arms fire over the first village and his aircraft had come home with bullet holes in its skin.

For this go-round, they'd devised a crude stand-off tactic. Their BAC Hawk strike/trainers carried four-round HVAR rocket pods under their wings, four pods per aircraft, fully the equivalency of a field artillery barrage.

As they'd been given no specific targets, just the leveling of the village as a whole, they would roll in and launch their rocket salvos at long range, shotgunning the target with a dispersed fire pattern. After that, they could pitch out again before coming into the effective reach of small arms.

"A piece of cake," as the Australian pilots would say.

Ahead, the coastline indented into a cove, and the click and hiss of a carrier wave sounded in the rebel pilot's helmet phones. The words of the flight leader were curt. "Rakshasa Flight. Target ahead. Arm and prepare to follow me in."

The rebel pilot flipped his armament switches, heating up the HVAR pods. The captain was a man of few words: get in, get out and get back to base.

He could make out the target at two o'clock. A narrow crescent of huts and buildings following the apex of the cove. A number of piers and slipways extended across the beach and into the pale blue-green waters. The other village they had hit had possessed similar boat building facilities. Was that why rebel command was having them bombarded?

"Rakshasa flight. Engage!"

With the snapped command, the wingtip of the flight leader's aircraft whipped up in a sharp right-hand break, the other Hawks peeling off after him at precise two-second intervals, diving in on the objective.

As his speed grew, the rebel pilot pushed his focus and awareness out ahead of his aircraft, selecting the launch point for his weapons. It would take a second or two for his pods to empty, so it had to be within the narrow range band that would allow his unguided rockets to reach the target but still allow him to evade the ground fire. As last man in he'd catch the worst of it.

He was wrong in that estimation.

He saw the lead aircraft fire its warloads, the smoke trails of the big five-inch HVARs snaking out toward the village. Then he had a split-second's awareness of something odd. It was as if there were other smoke trails entwining with those of the flight leader's weapons: trails streaming outward from the coast. Then his flight leader's aircraft dissolved in a smear of black smoke and orange flame.

The pilot of number two started to scream a warning as he tried to pull out of his dive, but both acts were cut short by the vaporization of his own plane. The rebel pilot had no chance to see what happened to number three as he simultaneously chopped his throttle, cranked hard right and jettisoned his ordinance load, utilizing the third arm all aviators can grow in an emergency.

The gee load hammered him as his aircraft stood on its wingtip in a minimum radius turn. Looking down from his cockpit toward the sea, he saw two slender dark shapes flash past beneath him.

Helicopters! Black helicopters, moving faster than anything with rotors had any right to move! They were what had killed his flight leader and his wingman and, no doubt, they were going to try and kill him too. He had also caught the fragmentary flash of ominous white, beneath their bizarre, swept-back wings. Air-to air missiles! Sidewinders! From the way his flight mates had died, no doubt these were an advanced all-aspect homing variant.

Firewall the throttle! Arm cannon! Reverse the pitch out and try and drop in on their tail! His little British-built strike/trainer could be a vicious dogfighter when she had to be. She swapped wingtips and pivoted into a pursuit curve behind the mysterious interceptors. The cartwheel sight in his heads-up display brushed across the tail of the lead helicopter.

Before his finger could tighten on the stick trigger, his target's nose snapped into the vertical. With the wingman holding precise station on the leader, the two helicopters screamed into a half-looping Immelmann reversal. With rotors flickering in inverted flight, the two weird intruders flashed over the top of his canopy.

The rebel pilot's instinct was to dive for the sea and run for it – but his training made him haul around in another minimum radius turn. 'Keep your nose pointed toward the enemy' was one of the oldest but truest axioms of air warfare. To attempt to extend out and disengage would be an act of suicidal futility, especially given the reach of those Sidewinders and the way their launching platforms could writhe across the sky.

But maneuvering against those black monsters might be an act of futility as well. This wasn't the distant cut and thrust of jet combat; this was the "knife fighting in a phone booth" of World War Two vintage air warfare and his Hawk wasn't built for it. No jet was. He was bleeding energy in these steep turns faster than his engine could replace it. Another violent maneuver or two and he'd be running out of airspeed and life.

As he came about, he heard the other flight survivor yelling for help over the radio band.

The number three Hawk had tried to run, breaking away east along the coastline. The helicopters, still moving with that unnerving, unnatural speed, were now hooking in behind number three. He caught the flash and fire streak of the missile launches, the supersonic bolts reaching across the gap between the hunted and the hunters.

"Eject!" the rebel pilot screamed into his oxygen mask mike. "Eject!"

The targeted Hawk twisted madly, belching a fireball. Shedding its wings, it tumbled from the sky. Again there was no parachute.

But in his death, his last flight mate had given the rebel pilot his chance. Once more he set up a pursuit curve, closing the range to engage the helicopters. If only they remained distracted for a few seconds longer ...

He swept in behind the dark copters, regaining his speed advantage as he brought his sights in on the leader. The enemy wingman must have spotted him coming in and panicked. He broke hard left, cutting behind his flight leader, passing through the rebel pilot's crosshairs.

The Indonesian shifted to the closer target, tightening his turn to engage the new, more vulnerable enemy.

He had range!

The enemy copter dancing tantalizingly just outside of the targeting reticle, he strove to force the Hawk's nose around those last few degrees to give him a firing solution.

Tracers suddenly streamed by the Hawk's cockpit and a hideous racketing vibration tore through its airframe. The rebel pilot got a single, fragmentary glimpse in his rearview mirrors of the lead black copter riding his tail, spewing hellfire.

Then the stream of cannon shells walked up the spine of the Hawk and chewed their way into the cockpit.

*

Vince Arkady eased the SPEED Cobra's bank and came back on his velocity controller, watching the dying Hawk roll into the sea below. *No kill like a gun's kill!*

427

"Strike lead To Strike wing. You okay, Pink?"

"Yeah, Roger that, Vince." Pinkerton's SPEED Cobra faded back and dropped into its wing slot. "Nice moves, skipper."

"Roger D. Even after all these years, they're still a sucker for that old Thatch Weave. Let's go home, my man."

*

The *Shenandoah* had found a tropical squall to conceal her air operations and she was loitering deep within a solid front of gray, misting rain. Going into helo mode, the two SPEED Cobras nosed slowly through the wall of blood temperature precipitation, riding the ground effect a mere ten feet above the low wave crests.

Peering ahead through their water-streaked canopies, the two aviators watched for the trail that would lead them home. After a few minutes of nuzzling into the wind, they picked it up, orange sparks of light glowing and flickering in the haze, a string of small float flares bobbing on the surface of the sea. The two compound helos swung parallel to this flare train and began to follow it through the haze.

The flares were being dropped off the stern of the *Shenandoah*. It was a simple and reliable approach and landing technique pioneered by the Royal Navy's Harrier and helicopter squadrons in the fog-haunted North Sea.

Easing alongside their mothership, the SPEED Cobras matched course and speed. Lifting above deck level, they popped their landing gear and sidled over the helipads waiting for them. A few moments later, they were aboard and down with the MacGregor hatches shutting out the rain.

*

"Well done, Arkady, and congratulations."

"Congratulations? For what?" Arkady dropped into a chair across the table from Amanda. For the moment, they were alone in the main

428

saloon with the rattle of the gusting rain on the windows contesting with the rumble of the engines.

"For making history. Karen, a drink for Mr. Arkady, please."

A smiling stewardess emerged from the saloon pantry, bearing a tray with a pair of tall, frosted glasses and a pair of opened bottles of Tsingtao beer.

"Congratulations, Commander," she echoed softly, deftly filling each glass.

"Thank you," Arkady replied, bemused as the stewardess vanished back through the pantry door. "But I say again, for what?"

"For becoming the first navy ace since Randy Cunningham and Willie Driscoll and the first helicopter ace in history."

"Son of a bitch!" The realization caught up with him with a jolt. "Two kills today and the three over Drake's Passage ... Five down and glory! Son of a bitch!"

Amanda nodded. "You missed the opportunity to claim the first kill on a nuclear sub by giving the credit to your teammate that day off Shanghai. This will be your page in the book."

"Just a footnote in your chapter, babe."

She smiled and shrugged, lifting her glass. Arkady followed suit and the glasses sang as their rims touched.

"That goes down very easily," Arkady sighed, setting his half-emptied glass down again. "You know, serving aboard this beast does have certain amenities above and beyond what you get aboard a conventional navy bird."

"Indeed," Amanda agreed. "If I'd known that merchant skippers had it this good, I'd have crossed over long ago."

The aviator only lifted an eyebrow. "Tell me another one, Admiral."

"I'm not an Admiral yet, Arkady." She mused over the thought for a moment. "In fact, at the moment, I'm not exactly sure what I am. I'm not a naval officer commanding a ship that isn't a naval vessel – but I *am* captaining one of the most powerful men-of-war in existence. What does that make me?"

"Indispensable?"

Amanda chuckled and took a sip of her own beer. "Thank you, good sir, but indispensability is a myth. Seriously though, I wonder just where I do stand in the convoluted rules of warfare."

"Last time I looked, the only actual honest to God rule of warfare was 'win' – and you're good at that, so who cares?"

"Thank you again. But it's still an interesting question."

Arkady pondered, scowling at empty air for a moment. "How does 'privateer' sit?"

"Privateer," Amanda mused, rolling the word over in her mind. "I haven't heard that one for a while. A pirate with a license to commit piracy on behalf of a government."

"Nowadays they'd call you a private naval warfare contractor."

Amanda laughed out loud. "Privateer it is then. I like it."

She realized that she felt good with the relaxed comfort of an old friendship. She and Arkady had shared moments like this many times before, beyond their times of passion. It was interesting to learn that the one didn't depend on the other.

Arkady cut a quirky sideways glance at her. 'Hey, babe, you ever think about the old days?"

"Of course," she nodded. "They make good thinking."

"That they do. Do you ever think ..."

"What do you think?" she asked back levelly.

He paused for a long moment, maybe giving a long-considered thought one last examination. "I dunno," he said finally, "I guess it might be kind of a step backwards at that."

She lifted her beer once more. "Here's to steps forward, my very dear and special friend."

Again the glass rims touched and sang.

"What's the world like on the outside?"

Startled, Amanda looked up from the central chart table. She had been alone in the briefing room, involved in a private pondering session. Now Makara Harconan loitered in the doorway. "Are they still doing sunlight, rain, stars, that sort of thing?"

"So I gather," she replied ruefully.

"I wouldn't know. I haven't seen many examples recently." He ambled into the workspace, clad in borrowed Levi's and a white T-shirt. To Amanda's eye he displayed no overt indication of his semi-incarceration in the hold section. The pirate king looked as tanned and fit as ever.

His marine escort shouldered through the doorway behind him and Harconan grimaced mildly. "I'm beginning to know what a tugboat feels like, however."

Amanda hesitated for a moment, then spoke to the guard. "It's all right, corporal. Take a break for five. I've got the watch."

It occurred to Amanda that, over the past couple of weeks since Harconan's coming aboard, she'd never been alone with the man. Whether by sheer happenstance or unconscious instinct, she wasn't sure. If it was the latter, it was a hoodoo she intended to break.

"As you wish, ma'am," the Marine replied formally, eyeing Harconan for one last suspicious moment before taking his leave, the closing click of the soundproofed door isolating them from the soft duty clamor of the CinC block.

"I wish I was actually as formidable as that gentleman seems to think I am," Harconan commented.

"You are, that's the problem," Amanda said, returning her attention to the hardcopy charts she was studying.

"Compliments graciously accepted," Harconan replied, crossing to the chart table. "You still use something as archaic as paper on this technological marvel you call the *Shenandoah* Galaxy?"

"Oh, is that where we are?"

"Have it your way," he sighed. "But really, why do you bother with these old-fashioned things when you can pull a chart up on one of these wall screens with a push of a button?"

"Because these wall screens can break down," Amanda replied patiently. "And because I simply like to use them. They help me think."

"Ah! I've always known you were more anachronistic than you let on. If you had your true choice, it would be back to cutlasses and carronades – and you'd lust for the command of a ship of the line."

Amanda suppressed her smile. "A good sloop of war actually, but that's the difference between us, isn't it? I know I live in the twenty-first century. I don't try and live out my fantasies or force my fantasies on other people."

Harconan lifted an eyebrow. "Touché. First blood, well drawn."

Amanda sighed and stopped working with the chart. "That wasn't really necessary, I guess. I'm sorry."

"Don't be. As it turns out, you're right. 'Here and now' cannot be denied, much to my regret." He studied her quizzically. "What about you, Amanda? What do you regret?"

"Many things," she replied quietly. "Among other things, that you ever started this."

"Again we are in agreement on a point. But you already knew that. You also know that's not what I mean."

Amanda started to pick up a pencil but hesitated. "Well, what *do* you mean?"

"I mean this is the first time we've been alone together since I've come aboard your extraordinary vessel, whatever it's called. A status quo I suspect you've been working very hard to maintain. But, since you've elected to come out of hiding for the moment ..."

"I haven't been hiding!" But with the exclamation came the realization and acknowledgement that she had been doing just that, avoiding this particular confrontation.

"Be that as it may," he continued blandly, "since I now have the chance, I'd like to assuage both my curiosity and my masculine ego with a question. Do you regret what we, albeit briefly, had?"

Amanda stacked ice into her voice. "We never had anything, Makara. At least nothing that ever mattered."

Harconan crossed his arms and leaned back against the edge of the chart table, rolling his eyes elaborately toward the overhead. "Amanda, you're one of the most honorable and trustworthy people I've ever known, save in one critical area. In anything to do with yourself, you are a flagrant liar."

Amanda slammed the pencil down. "And you are one arrogant asshole!"

He nodded. "Quite so, my dear," he said, keeping his voce low. "But at least I'm willing to confess to it. You, on the other hand, don't have the guts to admit you're a liar. Not even to yourself."

His words jolted through her like a taser shot, striking harder than mere words should. She heard an angry yip of denial and realized she was making it, her arm whipping back and then up, not in a slap but in an infuriated damaging blow, her knuckles aimed at Harconan's vulnerable throat.

He'd been waiting for it. His hard sailor's hand closed around her wrist, braking the punch before it could land. "The fact is that Captain Amanda Garrett thoroughly enjoyed losing control of herself. That, just for a little while, back on Pulau Piri and at Crab's Claw, this officer and lady had a marvelous time being a pirate's slave girl."

The cry of denial was torn out of her just as she tore her hand out of his grip.

"That is what you really regret, isn't it Amanda?" Harconan continued with a remorseless smile. "That and the fact that you can't hide it from me. It's a piece of you that I possess and that you can never get back, not even when President Kediri stands me up in front of his firing squad."

Something broke inside her and, to her shame, it manifested in a hot silent gush of tears. "All right, all right! I'm a liar! Are you satisfied now?"

"Yes, I am." The Raja Samudra reached into the back pocket of his dungarees and removed a clean white folded handkerchief. Very gently, he patted her tears away. "My dearest Amanda, the lies we tell ourselves are frequently the most corrosive. If you can own up to yourself, I will truly become an irrelevancy and you will be able to go on with your life – and with your big protective bull of an admiral."

She finished wiping her eyes with the back of her hand. How in hell could Makara have known about the decision she'd already made about Elliot? "What about that piece of me you're taking away?"

He smiled down at her. "Since you'll be bearing off a large, bleeding chunk of my soul as well, I consider it fair exchange. Please, my queen, we both recognize that what has been is all that will ever be. Accept those memories as a momentary, pleasant insanity. Don't muck them up with guilt."

Oddly enough, Amanda felt the presences of Arkady and Elliot in the room with them, along with that of another who had passed through her life long before. She took a deliberate breath, releasing it slowly – and something that had slightly warped snapped back into perspective. She was wondering what words she should say next when there came a quiet rap on the briefing room door. The handle turned and Christine Rendino peered cautiously into the briefing room. "Uh, may I come in?"

"Of course, Chris," Amanda replied, her voice perfectly level. "We were just discussing recent events and what may happen next." Which, on consideration, was only the perfect truth.

"Oh." The Intel looked relieved. "What have you come up with?" she asked, joining them at the chart table.

"You may expect desperation," Harconan replied, turning to the deployed charts, his own voice not hinting at anything beyond professionalism. "I have had a degree of exposure to Merpati Ketalaman. I can tell you that he gives the impression of being a man very much in control of himself. In reality, however, I suspect he is a man who is merely afraid of not being in control." He glanced in Amanda's direction and one eye flicked in the briefest of winks. "But this makes him brittle. When the load grows too great on such an individual, they break. The aftermath is usually impetuous."

"So we can expect a Hail Mary play out of Ketalaman?" Amanda said, a slight edge to her voice.

"Exactly." Harconan's hand swept across the chart of the archipelago. "If your intelligence is correct, the interdiction campaign is working. Kediri's forces are gaining the initiative on Java and Ketalaman's are losing it. It will not be in Ketalaman to fight out a war of attrition while awaiting developments. He'll put it all in one last throw. Block that and you've won your war."

"You think so?" Christine asked, dubiously. "Fa'sure, Ketalaman has shown a heck of a lot of patience and deliberation so far."

"Quite so, my good commander," Harconan replied. "But a man is like a ship's mast in a typhoon. They always stand, right up until they break."

After the weeks spent in his cavern command post, the piercing brightness of the morning sun stabbed painfully at Admiral Ketalaman's eyes.

On the long drive down the coast from his headquarters at Lake Toba, he tried to keep his focus on the trials ahead. He could see the trend developing. Kediri's escape from Jakarta had opened the door to disaster and the outside interference of the regional intervention powers was steadily tilting the odds against the coup. Mistakes Ketalaman had counted on were not being made. Allegiances that should have been shifting were remaining fast within the Kediri government. Men he had trusted were beginning to look upon him with distrust. Defeat could be tasted in the air.

The reinforcement convoy to Java was the last realistic chance he had to regain the initiative. Ketalaman could not risk leaving its command to an unsteady subordinate. He must demonstrate his resolve. He must show that he still commanded.

Seated in the rear of his staff car, he once more closed his eyes against the brightness and tried to project coming events. It was useless. The past kept intruding. Parents long dead. Siblings distanced. Old comrades recalled. An approximation of a love affair. Memories of simpler times and simpler desires.

The supernatural still exists close to the heart of even the most modernist and pragmatic of Indonesians. These inescapable thoughts of the past seemed to be portents, dark omens against his future.

Even if there were any validity to these fears, they were irrelevant. Merpati Ketalaman had committed himself to a long, last reach for his destiny.

At Banda Aceh Fleet base, the Java convoy was loading and arming. Transports were boarding troops and supplies, the warships drawing on the dwindling munitions reserves, all vessels emptying the modest tank farm of bunker fuel.

The ten thousand men being embarked might have been called an infantry division if the loosest possible connotation of the term were to be employed. Only a single brigade, the Indonesian 4th Infantry was a fully trained and equipped combat unit. The remainder consisted of a hodgepodge of the more fanatic Islamic militia units, equipped only with small arms.

There was no commonality of force structure or of ordnance. The ad hoc chain of command was wracked by the politicking and jealousies of the various Imams. There had been no chance for the units to work up or train together. There were major insufficiencies in artillery, motor transport, command-and-control and logistics.

Still, if it could be delivered intact to the Javanese battle zone and launched as the blow of a single fist, it might be enough to shatter Kediri's own tenuous force and win the day. Or so Ketalaman deigned to believe.

The operative words in the equation were "delivered intact". To perform the delivery, the anti-government forces had accumulated a task group of four transports. Two were big inter-island car and passenger ferries commandeered for the cause from the PELNI State shipping line. One was a small elderly Frosch class LSM acquired by Indonesia during the mass sell-off of the East German navy after the fall of the Berlin wall.

The last was Teluk Surabaya.

She was the largest ship in the Indonesian Fleet, the flagship of the Indonesian navy, and a freak of nature. Purchased from the imploding Russian navy following the collapse of the Soviet Union, she too was an amphibious warfare vessel. For all intents and purposes, the Teluk Surabaya was an LST – but, with a displacement of fourteen thousand tons and a length of five hundred sixteen feet, she was a behemoth of the breed, over three times the size of any other beaching class amphib ever to sail. She and her sisters of the Ivan Rogov class had been built under the old school Soviet philosophy of "if it's bigger, then it must be better."

Unfortunately for her, she had also been built at a time when military doctrine and technology were turning against the beaching ship. Even after the partial modernization and westernization of her systems, the Teluk Surabaya was hopelessly obsolete – but, with her towering castle-like deck house and her bristling gun and missile defense batteries, she was impressively obsolete.

She would be carrying the bulk of the 4th Brigade's heavy equipment and combat support elements to Java. She would also be carrying Admiral Ketalaman and his staff to Jakarta. No matter what the outcome, Ketalaman intended to sit in the Presidential palace at least once.

The boatswains' pipes trilled, and the crew of the Teluk Surabaya manned the rail, holding their salutes as Admiral Ketalaman climbed the gangway with stately deliberation. Few people noted how he had one hand slipped into the pocket of his uniform jacket. None other knew of the fragment of mountain stone that he clutched tightly in his fist.

"Here's the latest word from my people in Banda Aceh," Harconan said, studying his handwritten notes. "You've got fifteen ships preparing to sortie. The transport group and a two-division escort force. You'll have five frigates in the heavy division: the three Fatahillahs, one Van Speijk and a Parchim. With the light division, you'll have two dagger missile boats, two Lurssen gunboats and two Kondor minesweepers."

Christine looked up from her laptop. "I can confirm on all points."

"Thank you, my redoubtable Miss Rendino." Harconan gave her a courtly nod. "Combat loading of the transports is well underway and large numbers of troops are embarking. Waterfront rumor is that the convoy will sail tonight. Knowing those harbor approaches and tonight's tides, they'll probably be clearing the harbor sometime between ten and eleven thirty."

"I'd say that's a good call," MacIntyre said.

"And I'd agree," Amanda replied. "Do your people have anything else for us, Makara?"

"Indeed they do." Harconan tossed the notebook onto the chart table. "I've been saving the best for last. A large group of senior rebel officers has been observed going aboard the fleet flag ship. Given the level of ruffles and flourishes involved, Admiral Ketalaman may very well be among them." Harconan hesitated before going on. "If you would desire this humble pirate's opinion, my friends, then this is that last throw of the dice I have been talking about. The fattest prize conceivable is about to drop into our laps."

Harconan's usage of the words "friends" and "our" no longer had the tinge of irony to it. Two weeks of jointly confronted adversity had bonded him firmly into the *Shenandoah* command cadre. Amanda wryly noted that the taipan also had his dynamic personality cranked up to its fullest degree. As she could testify, it was one of his most potent weapons.

"Possibly," Amanda agreed. "But a great deal depends on the size of the lap available to catch it. Chris, what does the Indonesian Government have in position to intercept with?"

The Intel called up the Indonesian deployment listings. "Currently, they've got a single small task group covering the Jakarta approaches," she replied. "The fleet training frigate Ki Hajar Deweantara, a single Parchim class frigate and a single Lurssen gunboat."

Amanda shook her head. "Not enough. Not even close to enough. Elliot, maybe Ketalaman has come out of his hole, or maybe he hasn't. It doesn't really matter. This has got to be the decisive event of this conflict. We can't let this convoy through. This is going to require our going hands on."

MacIntyre scowled and used the remote pad to call up the western Indonesia theater chart on one of the wall displays. "I agree about the event status and about the necessity of intervention – but, whatever we do, it's going to be dicey. Eleven escorts, Amanda, seven of them missile carriers packing a mixed bag of both late mark Exocets and Harpoons. If they keep it simple, stupid, and ram the entire force down our throats ... Commander Arkady, what do you think?"

Flight suit clad, Arkady had been doing his lazy leopard slouch against the rear bulkhead of the briefing room, listening. Snapping his spine straight, he circled the chart table to join the group at the wall display. "The air group can do it. We can stop them for you, just not all at once. We're limited with our naval attack ordnance. Penguins and Hellfires are the heaviest anti-ship stuff we can deliver. The Penguins are kind of dumb and the Hellfires have short legs. It'll take a series of strikes. We'll have to peel the escorts layer by layer to get at the core elements."

Amanda glanced back at Christine Rendino. "Chris, what kind of anti-air can we expect?"

"Ferocious, Boss Ma'am. Just about any kind of radar and optronics guided gunfire you could want, 20s, 40s, 57s, everything up to and included 4.7 inchers. Also, all of the Reb ships will probably be carrying Mistral infra-red homing missiles in either the shoulder-fired format or in two, four or six round SADRAL cluster mounts.

"They've also got at least one area defense missile system. The big guy, the expat Ivan Rogov, mounted an SA-N-4 when she was built. However, when the Indonesians picked her up, they decided to go with their French motif in air defense and they swapped out the Gecko launcher for an octuple-mount Naval Crotal: NATO standard issue, eighteen klick range, line of sight command guidance with supplemental infra-red targeting." She looked up from the laptop to the aviator. "You can work wonders, flyboy, but if you take on this package with helicopters, even with your cool cat compound birds, you're going to take hits and you're going to take casualties. Possibly a lot of them."

"That's why they call it war," Arkady said, his voice flat.

"No," Amanda said sharply. "My policy now is just as it was on the Duke, Arkady. There is no such thing as cannon fodder in Phantom Force! We've done this kind of thing before. We've just got to wait for our shot. Convoy killing is just a matter of opportunity."

"And position." Harconan had joined them at the wall screen. "If you want to do this thing and keep your people alive, you're also going to need a favorable position to stage your attack from."

"What would you suggest?" Amanda asked.

"Here." Harconan stabbed a finger at an extended cluster of islands at the eastern mouth of the Straits of Malacca, immediately to the southeast of Singapore. "The Riau and Lingga island groups. We call them the Thousand Islands. That's where you need to engage Ketalaman."

"What's so special about those particular islands?" MacIntyre said curiously.

Harconan shrugged and stroked at his moustache with a fingertip. "My people have been sinking ships there for centuries. Why argue with success?"

"I can see what he's talking about, sir," Arkady added slowly. "If we had a little terrain cover, some radar shadows to work with, we could do some good business."

"And if we could catch him in restricted water ... like in a narrow channel," Amanda mused aloud, her thoughts already projecting ahead, merging with that of her CAG and the taipan.

"Uh, excuse me," Christine said, squeezing closer to the chart. "At the moment, all of the bad guys are still way up *here*." She pointed to the northwestern tip of Sumatra. "How are we going to make sure they go down *there*?"

"Oh, that's quite easy, my dear," Harconan replied, dropping an arm companionably around the Intel's shoulders. "Convoys are like cattle. You merely have to know how to herd them."

The oceanic horizon was empty and the sea rolled undisturbed, save for the occasional flash of a whitecap. Then, a broad 'v' of submarine turbulence smoothed the wave tops. At its apex, a periscope broke water. Trailing a narrow feather of wake, it rotated with deliberation, surveying the local environs. A few moments later, an electronic warfare pod and a communications mast broke surface as well.

Sixty feet down, the USS *Hampton* swam close to the surface to "answer the phone."

The "bottom gun" patroller of NAVEX 7.2, the Los Angeles class nuclear attack submarine, had been covering the westward flank of the Regional Intervention Force. Then she had received a coded signal by water penetrating ultra-low-frequency radio, ordering her to periscope depth to accept a new tasking.

In her control room, the *Hampton*'s Captain and Executive officer each read and reread the message. By the philosophy of the submariner, they were being asked to commit the rankest heresy.

"Proceed northward toward the Sumatran coast at periscope depth with masts extended. Transmit intermittently on standard radio bands." The exec looked up from the hardcopy. "I don't get it, skipper. Transmit what to who? What's going on?"

"I don't know, Don. It's almost as if they want someone to know we're out here."

The stream of orders rolled over the 1-MC circuit. "All sea and anchor details, lay to on the double! Power rooms, light off all turbines! Stand by to answer bells! All hands, set Condition Zebra in all compartments! Make all preparations to get underway! Expedite!"

"Status, Mr. Winfield?" Captain Ken Hiro strode onto the Duke's bridge, settling his command headset over his short brush of hair.

"Capstan room standing by to heave 'round, captain. Ready to maneuver in ..." Hiro's exec checked the Lee Helm power displays, "... four minutes."

"Very good. Any word yet on where we're supposed to be heading?"

"No, sir. Just the emergency sortie order from the *Carlson*. Wherever it is, though, the *Shiloh* must be going with us."

Across the anchorage, dark smoke was jetting from the stacks of a Ticonderoga class Aegis cruiser. One of the escorts assigned to the NavEx 7.2 Group, she was obviously powering up to get underway as well.

Hiro's headset activated. "Captain, this is communications. Signal incoming from the *Carlson*. It's Captain Carberry."

"Put him through."

A few moments later, the voice of the Sea Fighter's new TACBOSS sounded in Hiro's earphones. "Captain Hiro, this is Carberry. What's your situation?"

"Emergency sortie order received, sir. Ready in all aspects to get underway. What are your orders?" Hiro knew that Carberry was a man who preferred brevity.

"You are being temporarily detached from the Sea Fighter Task Force, Captain. The USS *Cunningham* and the USS *Shiloh* are being formed into an independent Surface Action Group under your command. You are to proceed to sea immediately and you are to conduct a high-speed anti-shipping sweep inshore to the westward, paralleling the southern coasts of Java and Sumatra."

444

Hiro frowned. "Is that it, sir? I mean no further information on objectives, mission duration, rules of engagement, anything?"

"You've been given as much as I have, Captain," Carberry replied dryly. "We both must presume that further orders will follow. Pending their arrival, proceed and good luck with whatever it is that you're intended to do."

"Aye aye, sir."

The link broke and Hiro muttered, "Christ," under his breath.

Almost immediately, the voice of the duty sparks came on-line. "Skipper, another 'Captain's ears only' coming in for you."

"Put it up."

"It's one of those special 'Ladyline' calls, sir."

Hiro hesitated only an instant. "Right, I'll take it in my quarters. Mr. Winfield, take us out of the harbor. Make a signal to *Shiloh*. 'Form up with us in line astern. Further orders to follow.'"

Hiro dropped down one deck from the Duke's bridge level into officer's country and to his cramped cabin. This had to be those "further orders to follow." The *Cunningham*'s stocky Japanese-American captain found himself moving faster than his personal decorum usually permitted. Not only would this be his first Task Group command, but it was apparently a job involving Amanda Garrett.

There was a winking green light on his communication deck. He scooped up the handset and hit the hotline button. "Hiro here, Captain."

"Hello, Ken," the faint but familiar voice replied. "It's good to have you back under my command again."

"Ha, I knew it!" Hiro slapped the desktop. "What's the dope, ma'am?"

"I presume that, if you're not underway, you will be shortly?"

Hiro felt a faint vibration rippling through the Duke's structure. "Anchor coming up now, ma'am."

"Excellent. Neither of us have any time to loose. This probably won't be a fangs out job, Ken, but it is critical. You've been informed that you're to conduct an anti-shipping sweep up the southern coasts of Java and Sumatra?"

445

"Yes, ma'am. But who am I sweeping for?"

"Hopefully for no one who's going be there. This is not any kind of stealth job. You're trailing your coat, Ken. Keep all of your radars cranked up to full power. Go active on your sonar. Maintain a lot of TBS traffic with the *Shiloh* and chat up the attack sub *Hampton*. She's somewhere out to the southwest of you with her radio masts up. Fly off your helos and intermittently drop within visual range of the Indonesian coast. Be obvious!

"Also – go like hell! Best maintainable speed. I want the rebels to know that a powerful US Surface Action Group is tearing up the coast to the westward, looking for blood. Can do?"

"Can do, ma'am!"

\*

Across the harbor, aboard the Indonesian "capital city," the USS *Pelelieu*, President Kediri and his military advisors scowled at the presentation being laid out before them.

"But we lack even a fraction of the ships in position necessary to contest Ketalaman's fleet," the senior surviving government naval commander protested. "It would be suicidal."

With vast patience, Ambassador Goodyard repeated his explanation. "Your ships will not be required to actually contest the passage of Kediri's task force. We merely require that your naval forces make a strong demonstration in the face of Ketalaman's advance. They'll never actually engage the enemy until after the majority of their forces have been eliminated."

"How is this elimination to take place, Mr. Ambassador?"

Goodyard tugged at his earlobe. "I'm not really privy to that information myself, Mr. President. I can only assure you that it will happen ... somehow."

The sharp edges of the stone in Admiral Ketalaman's pocket bit into his palm as his fist clenched around it.

The feeble Russian-built air conditioning had faltered and the flag plot of the Teluk Surabaya was sweltering. The workspace was tightly packed with both Ketalaman's personal staff and that of the task force commodore.

A steady stream of reports were flowing in from the flagship's communications center: ship's sortie readiness, loading status – and, as now, Intelligence updates.

"We have a confirmation from coast watcher outposts on both the Blambangan Peninsula and on Barlung Island. A powerful task group of at least two American guided missile cruisers have left Balinese waters and are proceeding westward at a high rate of speed. Radio Intelligence units in southern Sumatra have also detected radio transmissions from what they believe to be an American atomic submarine in the Indian Ocean somewhere to the south. The submarine appears to be in communication with the surface force and is closing the range with the coast."

The sharp edge of the stone cut into Ketalaman's flesh until he could feel the blood. "Is it the assessment of the Intelligence section that this activity is in reaction to the formation of this convoy?"

"We can project no other explanation at this time, sir."

"Have there been any American force deployments northward into the Java Sea?"

"None noted at this time, sir."

"What about the other Regional Intervention Powers?"

"No unusual activity by the ANZAC nations outside of their support operations for the Kediri government and their peacekeeping duties on Bali. Singapore and Japan continue their routine patrol operations in the Straits of Malacca."

"And Kediri? What is Kediri doing?"

447

"We've observed only one possible overt response. The three-ship government squadron blockading Jakarta has taken departure from its patrol station and is steaming to the north toward Karimata Strait. But there have been other events on Java, sir. The government's offensive along the north coast highway is continuing to gain momentum. Our force commander in Ciribon is reporting that his flank has been turned and that his situation in the city is becoming untenable."

Ketalaman felt the corner of his mouth twitch. He did not reply until he was certain his voice would be steady. "Inform Colonel Trabruk that the Ciribon line must be held. He may expect major reinforcements within seventy-two hours – but he must hold!"

"Yes sir." His Chief of Staff was not meeting his eyes. *Why was he not meeting his eyes?*

Ketalaman jerked his head around to look at the brooding naval officer at the far side of the chart table. "Commodore, when will the task force be ready to sortie?"

"All major ships are prepared for sea, Admiral," the Task Force commander replied. "The minesweeper division is already underway, conducting an ASW and mine sterilization sweep of the harbor approaches."

"Very well. Commodore, you may get underway."

"What course are we to set, sir?" the Commodore inquired slowly.

Ketalaman had been shoving that decision aside for the entire day, hoping for the situation to clarify. Now his procrastination was flashing back upon him. This was a call that he should have made sooner. His eyes flicked down at the chart with the Perspex spread over it for a final moment's debate.

"Turn east for the Straits of Malacca and the Java Sea. The shorter inner route through the archipelago."

"Sir," the commodore said, "may I point out that that course will take us through a great deal of constricted water, especially around the Riau and Lingga island groups? The outer passage to the west of Sumatra through the Indian Ocean and back through the Selat Sunda will add a few hours to our steaming time, but it will give us far more sea room for maneuver."

"The Americans are in the Indian Ocean!" Ketalaman's voice almost broke and he furiously reigned himself in. "The Americans have been the wild card in this battle from the beginning. On the inside route we'll be facing only the forces of Singapore and Japan. These governments are not risk takers. They are not cowboy warriors like the Americans. We will take the inner passage!"

Why was he justifying himself to his junior officers? This was his decision to make! His command to issue.

And had he just admitted that he was afraid of the Americans?

"Carry out your orders," Ketalaman finished curtly. "Get us underway."

He turned abruptly and left the operations center, keeping his hand in his pocket. His palm was filled with the hot sticky wetness of blood, the stone shard having pierced his flesh.

"Okay, kiddies, here comes the big one." Christine Rendino shoved her glasses up onto the top of her head and moistened her throat with a sip from a bottle of flattening Pepsi. She and the others in the center focused all attention on the overhead view playing out on the master display.

The image was downlinking from the cameras of an Oceanstar Naval reconnaissance satellite arcing high over the western Pacific Rim in its orbit over the poles. The satellite was cruising at better than five miles per second, a hundred and twenty miles above the night side of Earth – yet its black and white imaging might have come from five thousand feet on a bright sunlit day. At that, the reconsat wasn't really trying. If Christine had desired it, the Oceanstar could have read the ratings badges of the Indonesian bridge lookouts.

The Intel was far more interested in the larger view, however, and in the answer to a single question. Port or Starboard. East or West.

The two Kondor class mine hunters came first, probably conducting a sketchy sweep of the main channel with their low frequency sonars. As they cleared the channel mouth, and got the water depth, they turned to starboard.

Eastward.

The angle of the imaging changed as the satellite continued along its trajectory. The fighting team, the distant escort of the three Fatahillah class frigates, was next. Running in line, astern with the squadron's flagship, the Nala was in the number two slot. She was easy to make out because of her distinctive helipad and hangar.

And the Fatahillah's turned to the right, following the minehunters.

"Two down," Christine murmured.

The Oceanstar was edging lower in the sky, but they still had a valid oblique angle as the transport group cleared the mouth of Banda Aceh. The simplistic angularity of the elderly Van Speijk frigate sailed point, then the transport line with the smaller LSM leading, followed by the curved bow and massive, blockish upperworks of the Teluk Surabaya. Last of all came the two more streamlined silhouettes of the PELNI ferries. The smaller missile and gunboats were out on the convoy flanks and the Parchim corvette trailing behind the formation covered the six slot.

Slowly, the outline of the ex-Dutch frigate in the point slot began to shorten. She was turning to the east – through the Straits of Malacca between Malaysia and Sumatra and on to the Java Sea.

By way of the Thousand Islands.

Christine chuckled and took another sip of Pepsi. "Git along you little dogies," she murmured.

Amanda's desk phone buzzed over the Prince and Princess movement of Rimski-Korsakov's Scheherazade. Barefoot and still clad in a rumpled white uniform shirt and shorts, she rolled off the bed and was across the cabin in a moment. Switching on the desk lamp, she lifted the receiver. "Captain here."

"This is Chris down in Joint Intel. We've bluffed Ketalaman, Boss Ma'am. The reinforcement convoy is turning east for the Straits of Malacca. We got the bastards!"

"We've possibly got a shot at them, Chris," Amanda corrected. "Stay on them and keep me posted."

"Will do."

She was just hanging up the phone when a soft knock sounded on the connecting door to the owner's cabin. MacIntyre must have received essentially the same call. The Admiral had turned in at the same time as she had, and for the same reason, to try and snatch a couple of hours of sleep before the next round of decision making.

Given the uninterrupted bar of light from under his door, he hadn't been having any more luck at it than she had.

"Come in, Elliot," she said, lifting her voice.

Macintyre pushed through the unlocked door. He was in crumpled khakis and had a good start of a new beard. "I heard your phone ring. No doubt you've been passed the word?"

"Yes," she nodded. "That was Christine."

"It looks like Harconan is getting his wish. They're heading down the Straits of Malacca and through his Thousand Islands."

"Give the man credit, Elliot. He's right. The Bugi pirates have been targeting ships in the Riau and Lingga groups for centuries. It does make an excellent killing ground. I've been lying in here thinking about it."

"So have I." Macintyre ran a hand through his hair, trying to smooth

452

it into some kind of order. "The problem keeps breaking down into a three-sided equation: the need to destroy Ketalaman; the need to minimize our casualties; and the need to preserve the anonymity of Phantom Force. The best I've been able to manage is two out of three and that's not good enough."

"I know," Amanda replied. "My thoughts have been running in the same circles. As I see it, the key is to hit Ketalaman hard enough and fast enough to take his entire force down in a single strike. The problem is that neither the *Shenandoah*, nor the air group, can deliver an adequate volume of fire to do the job alone. It's going to have to be some kind of composite air and sea engagement. The ship and the air group are going to have to hit the target at the same time."

"Composite strikes are tricky to coordinate, Amanda."

"I know. And what's going to make it really interesting is that, while the air group has reach, the *Shenandoah* doesn't. It's going to have to be a close action. Very close."

MacIntyre leaned back against the desk beside her. "How close are we talking about?"

"I think the bow might be our leveler in this scenario."

He whistled lowly. "Possibly. But Good God, you really are talking about a knife fight in a phone booth."

"I know – and Harconan was right again. It's all going to be about position." She straightened and started to turn on her laptop. Then, with a grimace, she flipped the screen lid closed and went to the chart rack on the bulkhead, taking down the admiralty number for the western Java Sea. "Here are the Lingga and Riau island groups," she said, her face underlit by the desk lamp as she spread the hardcopy chart across her desk. "There are three deep-water channels Ketalaman's force could take to transit the Thousand Islands: the northern channel between the Riau and Lingga groups; the central channel through the Lingga group between Sebangka and Lingga islands, Sebangka Strait; and then there's the wider southern channel, Berhala Strait between Singkep island and the Sumatran mainland."

"I don't think Ketalaman will use the northern channel. That would swing him off his course and add several steaming hours to his transit to Java, hours that he can't spare. Berhala Strait to the south would be his best, safest bet."

Amanda tapped the central channel with the nail of her forefinger. "Somehow we've got to play cowboy again and herd Ketalaman into this narrower central channel, into Sebangka Strait. I think that's going to be our best killing ground."

MacIntyre leaned over the chart with her, his chest lightly brushing her shoulder. "That's the least likely of the three. Sebangka Strait looks to be barely ten miles wide at the throat. And with shallows, reefs and those smaller secondary islands lining the passage, the blue water shipping channel will be more confining yet."

"It's a meat grinder. Once he's in there, he won't be able to turn away. He'll have to keep coming."

MacIntyre glanced at her. "That'll apply to us as well."

She shrugged. "You know what the Eskimos say about hunting polar bears. The bigger he is and the more scared of him you are, the closer you get before taking your shot."

*

At a word from her captain's cabin, a metamorphosis was launched aboard the *Shenandoah*. Not of caterpillar into butterfly, but more caterpillar into a different caterpillar.

Air horns blared, topside work lights blinked out and night-vision-equipped work crews sprang to their carefully orchestrated tasks.

The *Shenandoah*'s jackstaff mast disappeared, retracting into its recess in the hull. Power wrenches buzzed at a score of locations around the decks. Panels were reversed along the edges of the MacGregor hatches, changing the hatch trim from black to yellow. Hatch access ladders were unbolted and shifted to new hard points. Mock-up fiberglass ventilators and deck fittings were stricken topside and tacked down on empty deck areas.

Around the superstructure, the blue and white galaxy funnel badges were replaced by a yellow and green winged horse. False structural panels folded outward or were lifted and bolted into place. The two side-by-side exhaust stacks merged into a single squat funnel. Deckhouse windows became portholes and portholes and exterior hatchways disappeared altogether.

Yellow decal strips were applied around the boot tops of the lifeboats, while atop the wheelhouse a large white plastic bubble was inflated into a distinctive but phony radome.

With the physical modifications complete, the wash crews took over with their pumps, hoses and chemical compounds. Streaks of artificial rust drooled down from the hawse holes and a layer of dinge was added to the white upper works.

Many of the false and reversed panels had been coated with radar absorbent Retinal Schiff-based paint. The *Shenandoah* would now produce a somewhat smaller radar return. She also became a single screw ship, with one of her propellers stopped and feathered. Underwater hull speakers scrambled her audial pattern to any listening hydrophone, and intermix blowers in her engine exhaust system altered the density of the thermal plume streaming behind her.

Lastly, the name boards at her bow, bridge railing and stern were changed – and a new national flag rose to her masthead.

As this conversion took place, an odd ripple radiated outward through the global internets from an obscure location somewhere in the western hemisphere. It was a computer virus, a carefully crafted but minute affliction that invaded only a few dozen systems worldwide and was of such a trivial nature that it would be disregarded and eventually corrected as an annoying but minor data glitch.

But for the next forty-eight hours, should an internet inquiry be made about a certain, specific merchant vessel, said vessel would be listed as being somewhere in the Java Sea instead of placidly loading cargo in a Chilean nitrate port.

By morning, the grimy Greek bulk carrier Andronicus, sailing out of Athens under the house flag of the Pegasus Shipping Combine, plodded slowly westward toward the Straits of Malacca.

The thin gray light of dawn slotted through the blinds. Both the Captain's and owner's cabins displayed the wreckage of a marathon planning session: charts, reference books, ruffled stacks of hard copy and a multitude of empty tea and coffee cups.

From his position sprawled on the cabin settee, MacIntyre looked on as Amanda spoke into his desk phone.

"Any situational updates, Dix? Very well then. Tie on a full Operations Group for one hour from now. All division heads and Mr. Harconan. You may also pass the word that we are heading into a big show tomorrow night. As of right now, we are on maximum effort. All divisions are to set taut and stand by for orders."

She returned the phone to its cradle and stretched a luxurious dancer's stretch, lifting her arms over her head. "Lord but I'm getting too old for this."

"That's my line," MacIntyre replied.

She came out of her stretch and padded across to the settee. Dropping into it beside him, she tucked her bare feet under her. In last night's explosion of activity, she had never gotten around to donning shoes; she still wore her rumpled merchant mariner's uniform, her hair tousled out of its usual impeccable neatness and her face untouched by makeup.

And yet she still managed to be infinitely desirable.

That connecting thought triggered the return of the complex emotions he'd been dealing with lately, his concerns, his embarrassments, his determinations. But somehow, possibly because of his adrenaline inspired lack of sleep, it all seemed detached, a separate kind of thing. What was real and immediate was that, for the moment, he was alone with this unique woman, seated a mere foot away.

They had worked together at their grim, demanding craft all through the dark hours. And now, for a time, that work had been cut off, leaving them suspended with nothing but the bond they'd created.

What in hell was she feeling? For the moment, she seemed to be studying him thoughtfully with those striking golden eyes, as if she was content to simply look at him.

Somehow, they had been granted this one quiet bubble of time and intimacy. *Get on with making a fool of yourself, MacIntyre.* He knew he ought to end it, one way or another, before the world intruded again. "Amanda ..."

"Why not, Elliot?" she smiled.

Her statement derailed him. "Why not what?

"Our having a relationship could be a perfect adjunct to the whole Phantom Force security program," she replied practically. "Everyone knows that male and female officers in the same chain of command are not permitted to become romantically involved. Such a relationship could only publicly emphasize the fact that I'm no longer in the Navy or serving with you in any capacity."

"Amanda ..."

"Of course, we'll have to be rather flagrant about the whole thing," she continued, her smile deepening. "We'll have to see a lot of each other whenever we're in the same port. We'll have to spend leave time together – and there must be numerous public displays of affection, kissing, hand holding, that sort of thing."

"Amanda!"

"And presents, of course. I'll have to be sent lots of presents, on the lavish and intimate side. Perfume, jewelry, lingerie. I'll give you a list of sizes, colors and so forth. That won't be a problem."

MacIntyre sat up straight. "God damn it to hell, woman!"

Amanda exploded with laughter, collapsing against him. "Oh, Elliot, you have to admit, it's going to make a wonderful excuse."

His arms were around her then and he was gathering her close as he had wanted to do, holding her as he had not held anyone in such a painfully long time. He felt her head settle on his shoulder in a comforting nestle and his hand ranged down her warm, strong flank. MacIntyre felt his self-built barriers begin to collapse.

"God, I feel incredibly stupid at the moment," he said after a time.

"Why's that?" she murmured, her eyes closed.

He looked down at the head of sun-streaked amber hair. "Like I'm a little out of practice with saying the right things to a beautiful woman."

Amanda lifted her head, her eyes opening. "Who, me?"

"Yes damn it! You and you know it!"

"If you insist." She plopped her head back onto his shoulder and stretched once more, climaxing with a contented kind of sigh. "I've already told you, you haven't been doing badly so far. We'll get you up to speed soon enough."

"Thank you ... I think." He looked into her amused expression. "You've been enjoying yourself watching me suffer over this, haven't you?"

Her brows came up. "Well, no more than any other woman – but I've been getting a little impatient for you to get on with it."

MacIntyre shook his head. "It is totally insane to be talking about this. Especially now!"

"Quite possibly," Amanda was forced to agree, "but – as a friend pointed out recently – sometimes being too much in control doesn't necessarily make you stronger."

"Amanda, all of the smoke and mirrors aside, you *are* still under my chain of command."

Her brows knit. "And that's something else I'm getting fed up with! I don't know about you, Elliot, but I'm getting a little bit tired of the Joint Chiefs of Staff telling me who I can and cannot sleep with. I've been saving western civilization from certain destruction for some time now and, if someone wants to say I'm not emotionally mature enough to manage my own relationships in my own way, let 'em prove it!"

Lord God Almighty, what was he getting himself into? For certain, it was going to be interesting. But he was also certain now that it was what he wanted. She was right. Let 'em prove it.

He kissed her.

It was a good kiss. An excellent one in fact. Different than Anne's, but that was as it should be.

"This is going to be one hell of a peculiar courtship," he commented, nose to nose with her.

"We're peculiar people, Elliot," she replied softly. "I'll admit, it would be nice if we could waltz 'neath the harvest moon 'til dawn and gaze deeply into each other's eyes for hours on end – but I'm afraid we're going to be too busy. We have too many places to go and too many important things to do, and what we would like or want really isn't very important in the greater scheme of things. So, whatever bits of the sweet life we're ever going to have together, we'll have to grab as the opportunity presents."

"Very true, Captain," Macintyre replied wryly. "Like right now. We have an Operations Group in an hour."

Amanda's grin became impish and she consulted the old Pusser's Lady Admiral wristwatch strapped to her wrist. "In forty-seven minutes to be exact. Granting fifteen minutes to shower, dress and get our notes together and get forward, that gives us exactly thirty-two minutes."

She clicked the alarm on her watch, then squirmed out of the curve of his arms. Clothes rustled, a zipper whispered open – and, in only moments, a wad of discarded clothing lay on the blue carpet. Amanda knelt on the settee, sleek, bare and golden tanned. "You may be a little out of practice, Elliot, but two people can accomplish quite a lot in thirty-two minutes."

"Fighting ground and ships, Makara," Amanda said, leaning across the chart table. "That's what we need. We require an isolated hide site for a squadron of helicopters overlooking the passage between Sebangka and Lingga and a small, totally deserted island within the passage itself. We also need a Bugi squadron down here in Berhala Strait. Can you give them to us?"

The Operations Group was forming up in the main briefing room, but Amanda and MacIntyre had called the taipan aside into what once would have been called the chart room. Now, though, it was referred to as the ship's Geo-Intelligence Center, and it placed the complete cartographic database of the US Defense Mapping Agency at the disposal of Phantom Force.

"It depends," Harconan frowned. "Let's take the ships first. If you're talking about armed Bugi raiders, I don't have anything anywhere that could stand against Ketalaman's blue water warships."

"They don't have to fight," MacIntyre replied. "They don't even have to be armed. They just have to be able to maneuver under power, and they've got to have crews with nerve enough to stand. And they have to be in the gut of Berhala Strait by nightfall."

Harconan consulted his mental listing of Bugi assets in the region. "I'll have to talk with some of the local clan leaders, but that should be easily enough done. Three or four at least. Maybe half a dozen. They'll be powered fishing luggers and small coasters. Will that be adequate?"

"It should be," Amanda said. "We'd be putting small teams of our personnel aboard those craft and their captains would have to follow the orders of the team leaders. Will that be acceptable to your people?"

"If I tell them it's to be acceptable, it will be."

"Excellent. Thank you, Makara."

There was something odd about Amanda this morning, Harconan noted, a certain difference. There was a brightness to her eyes beyond a lack of sleep and a certain vibrancy, as if she had been tuned to a higher level. He had seen her so before, under pleasanter circumstances.

Amanda Garrett was, beyond her self-discipline, essentially a woman of passion. Like a gemstone, she glowed after the polishing of physical love.

And this craggy man with the three stars on his collar, this Admiral Macintyre. Wasn't he standing just an inch or two closer to her this morning? And wasn't he allowing his eyes to linger on her a little longer for each glance?

These hints were indicative. Somewhere in this past night, the dam had broken.

Makara Harconan felt a pang of sadness. He'd lost a great deal lately. *Still, my queen, I shall be man enough to wish you and your Admiral good fortune and much happiness.*

Words were spoken that he didn't hear and he snapped his attention back to the real world.

"The islands, yes. The Riau group is especially involved in the tourist and vacation trade out of Malaysia and Singapore. Beyond customs personnel, you won't find a large government presence ..."

The usual scattering of tropic squalls rode with the trade winds through the Java Sea, each a few square miles of mist and blood-warm rain that materialized randomly, blotted out the sea and sky for a few hours and then dissipated, ghostlike.

The bulk carrier Andronicus, a.k.a. Galaxy *Shenandoah* disappeared into one such squall and did not emerge again. Instead, from the heart of the squall, flights of sea-skimming helicopters fanned out, preparing the battlefield.

*

The low, forested ridge on Sebangka island overlooked both its verdant sister island, Lingga, and the deep-water channel that separated the two.

One isolated section of the ridgeback had been scalped by hardwood logging and this pale patch of sun-bleached scrub drew in two Air Commando SPEED Hawks. Flying in the nape of the Earth on the inland side of the ridge, one of the helos dropped off a sling-loaded cargo pallet, while a Green Beret A-Team fast-lined down from the second.

Under the direction of the team's Engineering and Demolitions Sergeants, det cord was used to blast out stumps that might interfere with a landing zone and camouflage nets and anti-IR tarps were rigged to receive and conceal aircraft.

Lower on the ridge, where the old logging road fed into the cut area, other members of the A-team established an interdiction and capture site. Any curious individuals coming up that road to investigate the unusual activity along the ridge wouldn't be returning for a while.

*

Some eight miles to the south and slightly to the west of the hide site, a tiny island lay close to the Lingga shoreline on the southern side of Sebangka Strait. It was too small to warrant a population or even a name on the charts. Just a meager few acres of coral sand, salt grass and mangrove, it served no purpose beyond being a navigational hazard to passing ships.

Nonetheless, another flight of half a dozen sea-skimming SPEED Hawks invaded it. More cargo pallets were dumped in the heart of the mangrove patch, Marines and Army Rangers slithering down the fast ropes after them.

The helos departed with all speed and the labors of the firing detail began. Mortar tubes, base plates and shell cases were wrestled into firing positions. Stable weapons platforms were improvised on unstable soil. Sighting and designation platforms were established in the tops of the tallest trees. Sand flies and mosquitoes were swatted and cursed.

And above all, meticulous care was taken not to disturb the vegetation cover or to put a single boot print on the islet's perimeter beaches.

*

A hundred miles to the south, an Army AH-6 Little Bird went to hover over the stern of a Bugi Coaster. One after another, an Army Intelligence linguist, a Navy Special Boat Officer and an Air Force electronics technician were lowered by sling to the small vessel's rear deck, a heavy aluminum equipment case following them down.

A Bugi captain awaited them on the deck of the coaster, stony featured until they presented him with the introductory envelope they bore. The Bugi read its contents, then smiled a gap-toothed smile and welcomed them aboard his ship.

*

Thin drizzle filtered down through the gap left by the retracted elevator pad, the water pooling up on the antiskid.

"Did you check to make sure all onboard batteries were replaced and fully charged? We're not going to have the luxury of a starter cart out there."

"Checked, checked and double checked, Vince." Pinkerton looked up from his data pad. "We got it covered. Push the button and we're gonna go."

Around them the final phase of pre-launch was underway, the ordnance teams shackling stumpy, multi-finned shapes onto the hard points of the strike group.

"Just doing some of that commander's shit, Pink," Arkady replied, taking the pad from his exec and checking the figures display. "How are we doing on aircraft availability?"

"They've got oh-six put back together. It looks like we'll be able to launch all eleven. But that leaves us another problem. With Murph gone, we're going to be putting a singleton up if we launch a maximum effort strike. Somebody's not going to have a wingman and that's not good."

"I know it, Pink," Arkady agreed, handing the pad back. "But we're going to have some big hulkin' ships out there tonight. We're going to need to put every round on target that we can."

"I'm aware of that, sir," Pinkerton said formally. "I'd like to suggest that Ensign Rollins fly your wing tonight. I'm volunteering."

"Forget it!" Arkady looked levelly into Pinkerton's eyes. "You'll lead Echo flight. Cheryl is on you. I fly the singleton. The matter is not open for further discussion, Lieutenant."

"Shit ... sir."

Arkady slapped his friend's shoulder and grinned. "I'll be fine, Pink. It'll do me good to watch my own ass for a change. Don't sweat it."

"Is that an order or a request?"

*

It came time to saddle up.

Arkady donned his flight and survival gear. Reaching up, he patted the SPEED Cobra's pretty genie nose art in a personal luck ritual. Then, swinging himself into the cockpit, he harnessed in and started to work down his preflight lists as his plane crew trundled his aircraft onto the deck lift.

"Good luck." Arkady looked up to find a pair of blue-gray eyes regarding him from close range. Christine Rendino was standing on the fuselage step, her arms hooked over the canopy rail.

"I've always got good luck, sis," he said, puzzled but pleased. "What are you doing down here?"

"Oh, nothing better to do for the moment," she replied airily, the rain starting to slick her blonde hair. "By the way, how come you always call me 'sis'?"

"Heck, I dunno. I have to call you something I guess."

"Come up with something else. I don't want to be a sister."

\*

Back aft, Amanda caught herself just as she was rounding the tail of a parked utility copter. She'd been coming down to see Arkady off herself. Taking a step back into the shadows, she watched Christine standing on the fuselage step of the Jeannie II, speaking animatedly with its pilot.

Again Amanda felt that momentary surge of jealousy. Then she smiled at herself and the universe. One of the most important skills a good officer had to learn was the delegation of authority. From the look of things, taking care of Vince Arkady was going to be someone else's duty from now on.

Harconan glanced at the bulkhead clock. "It must be getting dark topside. I would say it's time to start the performance."

MacIntyre nodded. "Likely you're right. If he's going to put scouts up, it'll be soon." MacIntyre keyed his headset. "This is MacIntyre to communications. Advise the Berhala Straits group to begin the fake-out package."

They were alone in the briefing room, Harconan's guard on station outside of the door. Given the circumstances, Elliot MacIntyre found it to be an odd and slightly uncomfortable feeling. He had no idea that Amanda had felt much the same way in this same space only the day before. "I hope this bluff works," he said, more to end the silence than for any other reason. "There's going to be hell to pay if it doesn't."

"I'd say the odds are in our favor," Harconan replied. The taipan had a chair drawn up to the chart table. His arms were crossed on its surface, an ashtray with a thin, smoldering cigarillo resting at his elbow. "I think our friend Ketalaman might be very susceptible to a bluff at the moment."

"Why so?" MacIntyre challenged.

Clinching the cigarillo between his teeth, Harconan rose and circled the chart table to the strategic display. On the great glowing wall chart, the position hack of Ketalaman's convoy could be seen approaching the Lingga island groups. The turning point for the northern passage had been passed and the point of decision for the central or south passages was approaching.

The Indonesian government task group guarded the eastern entrance to Berhala Strait. The *Shenandoah*'s hack, her name blanked out, hovered off the eastern tip of Sebangka Island.

"Tell me, Admiral. Let's say you were commanding Ketalaman's task group and you saw the government fleet waiting to challenge you and our people doing their little performance in the southern passage. What would you do?"

MacIntyre frowned and joined him at the chart. "I'd make note of them certainly and I'd try and assess their actions, but I'd still stand on. Berhala Strait is still the best choice. I'd trust in my numeric superiority and in the extra sea room the southern passage would give me in a fight. I wouldn't be bluffed."

"Ah, but that is where you would have the edge over Ketalaman. You would trust in your ships and your crews and in yourself to see you through any eventuality. Ketalaman will not. He has been beaten too often and he hungers for cheap, safe victories."

Harconan traced first the northern, then southern passages with a fingertip. "Trust me, Admiral. Ketalaman will sidestep. He will scout both of these passages through the islands, and he will take the path of least apparent resistance."

The pirate sipped a lungful of smoke from his cigarillo. "You may rest assured, my friend. Ketalaman will willingly run from the ghost and into the jaws of the tiger."

The Special Boat officer consulted his hand-held Global Positioning Unit and made a minute check on a chart line. "Have the captain maintain this heading for another twenty-five minutes."

"Yes sir. Will do." The translator turned to the man at the *pinisi*'s wheel, relaying the order in Bahasa Indonesia.

The elementary wheelhouse of the coaster smelled of fish and diesel fumes and the Bugi shipmaster was holding his course with a battered car compass. Still, the engine had not missed a beat and the wake streaming behind the little vessel, north to south, was as straight as a die.

Another glaring technological exception to the ship's primitivism rested in the far corner of the wheelhouse, the open electronics case under the management of the electronic warfare specialist. Antenna wires had been strung to the peak of the coaster's mast and the SO crouched on a crude stool in front of his equipment, occasionally shifting a channel dial or an output slide.

"Just what is it you're putting out on that rig, Kenton?" the SB officer inquired.

"Pretty much junk, sir," the airman replied, ejecting a tape cassette from the module and inserting a fresh one. "Mostly random signal patterns on different frequencies, right up into the microwave. They don't really mean much of anything."

"But they might sound like they do if you don't know what's going on?"

"That's pretty much the idea, sir."

A yell came from one of the deck lookouts. "Aircraft sighting, Lieutenant," the translator reported.

The Special Boat officer leaned out of the wheelhouse window, scanning the gathering twilight. Faintly, over the chug of the engine, he made out the thin whine of high-altitude turboprops.

<u>Sebangka Island.</u>
<u>1941 Hours, Zone Time, November 20, 2008</u>

The Indonesian Navy Sea Lynx helicopter droned down the length of the ridge line, the observers aboard it dividing their attention between the terrain below and the Straits to the south, passing off the single pair of NiteBrite binoculars available aboard the little aircraft.

If the Sea Lynx had been better equipped for its mission – or if its crew had been better trained in the art of tactical land reconnaissance – they might have detected something unusual in the eleven roughly symmetrical mounds of dried grass and brush spaced out across an overgrown lumber cut.

Arkady carefully parted a gap in the camouflage netting and watched the shadowy outline of the helicopter draw away across the cloud heavy sky.

"What do you think, Vince?" Crouched under the camouflage nearby, Keith Pinkerton had instinctively lowered his voice to a near whisper.

"I dunno, Pink. He's looking but I don't think he's finding." Arkady worked his way back under the nets to the Jeannie II's cockpit. Groping over the rail, he came up with a hand mike. "This is Strike Lead at Hide Prime, calling Star Child. Contact report ..."

"Where are the government's ships?"

"Still holding off the exit of south passage, sir. No essential change in position."

"Are you certain there's nothing else out there?"

Ketalaman's Chief of Staff hesitated. "We have a Nomad Searchwater aircraft sweeping the channel now, sir. Those are the only major hostile combat units we have a fix on."

"But there is something else?" the Admiral insisted.

"There is some unidentified activity in the Straits, sir."

"Unidentified is not a valid sighting report, Captain!"

The CoS gulped. "There's a group of Bugi coasting vessels maneuvering in an unusual manner across the main channel, sir."

"Show me."

They turned to the large theater chart. The black wax marker squeaked on the Plexiglas sheet laid across it. Ketalaman seemed to flinch at the sound.

"Here, sir. Between Cape Buku and Cape Jabunk. Half a dozen Bugi *pinisi* are sweeping south and north in a regular series of narrow boxlike patterns."

"Mines," Ketalaman murmured. "They're laying mines."

"It might almost look like that, sir. The maneuvers do have a resemblance to a mine laying pattern, but the Bugi have no deep-water mines."

"But Kediri's forces have such weapons, as do the Americans."

"Sir, it is difficult to conceive of the Americans sanctioning the mining of a major international waterway."

"They've managed to conceal their meddling quite well so far, Captain," Ketalaman spat. "Their smart mines have been put to use against us already. Has our reconnaissance uncovered anything else?"

The Fleet signal intelligence officer responded to the question. "Our search aircraft are reporting unidentified transmissions coming from

470

somewhere in the straits sector. The signals are definite but there's nothing we can clearly identify as to source, intent or exact point of origin. They match up to nothing we know of in either the government or the American inventories."

Ketalaman's fist came down on the chart, the bandage on his hand smearing the crayon marks. "We know nothing of what the Americans actually have! They're setting up some kind of ambush! They intend to draw us into a minefield keyed to destroy our ships. Kediri's forces will finish off the survivors and take the credit!"

The Chief of Staff moistened his lips. "That is a possibility, sir. But we have minesweepers with the task force."

"What about the Sebangka Strait?"

"The Nala's Sea Lynx is scouting the passage now, sir. So far, they've detected no sign of enemy activity."

Ketalaman turned away from his Chief of Staff to face the Task Force Commander. "Commodore, order the task force to change course. We will proceed through Sebangka strait at best possible speed."

"Admiral, I must protest!" The commodore stepped forward from the rear of the plot room. "We won't have any room to maneuver in that channel."

"Nor will we have an American ambush waiting for us. Now order the course change, or I will have your successor in command do it!"

Admiral Ketalaman turned and strode from the flag plot. The other officers clustered there lowered their eyes, refusing to meet one another's gaze.

Ketalaman's CoS gave a shuddering sigh. In a way, Ketalaman's abrupt departure was a relief. Had the Admiral remained the Chief of Staff, sense of duty would have forced him to ask, "But what if someone desires that we go through Sebangka Strait?"

"They're doing it, Boss Ma'am. The rebel task force has committed. They're going for Sebangka."

"Thank you, Chris. Mr. Beltrain, secure from aviation stations. Bring the ship about to two six zero degrees, all engines ahead full, civil power." Amanda paused. "Attention all hands, this is the Captain. Early tomorrow morning we will be taking the *Shenandoah* into what will possibly be the decisive engagement of this conflict. In approximately one hour, we will be clearing for action. Prepare to rig the ship for close range surface engagement and special attack operations. That is all."

Sitting in the top of a tree in a rainstorm with a disgruntled Army ranger was not one of the things Stone Qullain had ever planned on doing in his life, but the Sea Demon commander was adaptable if nothing else.

"Begging your pardon, sir, but I gotta say this is just plain crazy."

"Oh hell no, sergeant." Stone hitched himself to a slightly less uncomfortable position straddling the tree branch. "This kind of deal is old business for the corps."

"You're kiddin', sir? You mean somebody's tried this before?"

"Why sure," Stone nodded, water dripping from his helmet brim. "Ain't you ever heard of Lou 'the Honker' Diamond?"

"Uh, no sir, I haven't."

"And here I thought they taught you somethin' about the military in that Ranger School of yours! Anyways, the Honker served back in the Old Corps and he was the model God used to make the Marine Gunnery sergeant. He went ever'where and did ever'thing and wore out more sea bags then most men do socks. When he was sixty years old, the Honker could still drink a case of beer at one sittin' and pitch a no-hit baseball game afterwards."

"Uh yes sir, I'm sure he could," the rather dubious reply came back. "But what does that have to do with the NATO Alliance?"

"It has everything to do with it. You see, the Honker was a mortar man. Probably the best one to ever draw breath. He used to sleep with a battery of 81 millimeters set up around his bunk. Once, durin' the Guadalcanal campaign, he saved the whole damn Tulagi landin' by driving off a Japanese destroyer squadron with mortar fire alone. Like I said, Sergeant, this is old stuff for the Corps."

"Begging the Captain's pardon, but did this Honker guy also hand-carve the Marine memorial with a bayonet?"

"Naw, Chesty Puller done that thing."

The banter was interrupted by a hissing voice issuing from a Leprechaun transceiver hung from a nearby tree limb. "OP West to

473

Director One. We have trade in the channel. Small surface warship. Heading zero niner eight degrees. Range eleven hundred meters."

Instantly, Stone and the Ranger Forward Observer swung their thermographic binoculars onto the bearing. For a moment they saw nothing. Then a glowing became apparent on the cool darkness of the sea, a misty cloud of exhaust heat hovering above it.

"I got him!" Stone commented. "Length, 'bout a hundred and eighty feet. A single stack. Three gun tubs, over 'n under autocannon, 'fore, aft and amidships."

A penlight clicked on, shielded by a cupped palm as the ranger consulted a waterproofed pocket Jane's. "It's a Kondor class minesweeper."

"He'll be one of the point men." Stone unclipped a hand mike from the Leprechaun. "This is Sea Demon six callin' Star Child. We are in contact. They're comin' through the pass."

On the ridgeline above the channel, eleven mounds of underbrush bifurcated and drew open, aviators and Special Forces troopers opening the soggy camouflage nets to reveal the concealed SPEED Cobras.

"Make sure you haven't picked up any passengers in your cockpits," Arkady yelled over the rustling of displaced vegetation. "And make sure your air intakes are clear and your ordnance safety pins are out. We'll get one shot at this!"

The aviator aimed a judgmental glance at the overcast night sky, the cloud cover being intermittently underlit by a flicker of lightning. This squall line could work both for them and against them in the upcoming fight.

"Hey, Vince," Keith Pinkerton yelled from farther down the rough flight line. "Do you want us to go right to engine?"

"Negative! Save the gas. We're light on fuel as is. We'll hold off to the last second."

The briefing room screens had gone to the tactical battle display. Ketalaman's task force was solidly in the gut of the pass. The minesweeper group was on point with a five-mile lead on the other formations. Then came the frigate force and, after another five-mile gap, the transports and their escorts. The dispersed formation was steaming southeastward at a steady fourteen knots.

The *Shenandoah*'s position hack had entered the eastern end of the angled channel between the islands and was steaming to the northwest, directly into the long column of Indonesian ships.

"I find it remarkable that Ketalaman has yet to note the presence of your ship or ships, Admiral."

"You must have heard of the Philadelphia Experiment, Mr. Harconan," MacIntyre replied dryly. "We're invisible."

With the *Shenandoah* closed up at general quarters, they remained alone in the briefing room, watching the positioning for the battle develop.

"Ah, that explains everything." Harconan paused. "Admiral, might I ask a favor? I have a certain nodding acquaintance with amateur small ship actions, but I've never seen the professionals go at it in a true world class match-up. Might it be possible for me to observe the engagement?"

MacIntyre shook his head. "I'm sorry, Harconan. That will be quite impossible for security reasons."

"I quite understand," the taipan replied. "A pity though. It would be something to see."

"Likely." MacIntyre hesitated, then continued, "Look, Harconan – on behalf of this command, I'd like to thank you and your people for the assistance you've given us. I'd also like to say that we won't forget it. When this thing is over, I give you my word that we will be interceding with the Indonesian government on your behalf."

"I thank you for the gesture, Admiral, but I fear that President Kediri and his government might not be too forgiving. Fair being fair, I must confess that I am rather responsible for this current round of unpleasantness in the archipelago."

Macintyre nodded grimly. "I won't argue that point. Nonetheless, NAVSPECFORCE pays its bills. I've talked with certain contacts I have within our State Department. Maybe we can get the Kediri government to agree to have you brought up on international piracy charges before the World Court at The Hague. It will probably mean a life sentence – but there won't be a death penalty and you won't have to worry about 'being shot trying to escape.' It's a poor thanks but, under the circumstances, I'm afraid that's the best we'll be able to do."

"That's a most gracious gesture on your part, Admiral, and I thank you for it. She chose well."

MacIntyre stiffened. "What do you mean?"

"I mean I congratulate you for having won another battle and for having stolen the prize from under my guns." Harconan lifted a finger to his brow. "I salute your victory."

Macintyre scowled like a gathering thunderhead. "She isn't a prize to be given or taken by anyone."

"Oh, I am quite aware of that, my friend," Harconan smiled. "I think you'll find that, in the end, she needs neither you, nor I, nor any man, as a necessity. But to have her with you, even for a little time, is a great joy and something of an honor."

Slowly, a wry smile returned to MacIntyre's face. "I think that is a point we may both agree on."

"That is good. Then may I ask you two further small boons?"

"Like what?'

"For one, do not begrudge me my small time of happiness with Amanda, nor hold that time against her. And for the other, believe me when I say that I wish you both well."

MacIntyre didn't speak, but he held out a hand in reply. Harconan clasped it in a strong grip, the ancient sign of pax and a bargain sealed between two men of honor.

"Attention all hands," Amanda Garrett's calm voice sounded over the 1-MC. "We are entering the primary engagement zone. All deck battery teams and Avenger crews, man your stations and stand by to strike topside. Set condition double-zebra in all forward frames. Good luck to us all."

Both men had looked up at the words from the overhead speaker. "That's it," MacIntyre said. "I'm afraid I'm going to have to ask you to return your quarters."

Harconan nodded. "Understood, Admiral. Good luck and good hunting."

"We'll keep you advised on how the situation develops. Corporal!"

Harconan's guard appeared at the briefing room door. "Yes, sir."

"Return Mr. Harconan to his quarters. Battle protocols, do not secure the door."

"Very good, sir." The Marine looked to the taipan. "Mr. Harconan, will you please come with me?"

"But of course," he replied mildly.

*

The sentry had Harconan precede him down the now familiar passageways, working their way through the series of watertight doors to the bank of guest cabins. The young Marine was gravely courteous, intent and watchful, his hand resting lightly on his holstered sidearm. But he was young.

With all hands at their battle stations, the living spaces corridor was deserted as they reached Harconan's guest quarters. Harconan was just entering his cabin when he grunted in pain, clutched at his chest, and collapsed against the door frame.

For a split second, the Marine's professionalism cracked and he took a step forward, extending a hand.

Harconan's elbow whipped back with the force of a kicking mule, driving into the Marine's stomach, folding him over with a gasp of agony. Before he could recover, Harconan straightened and landed a sharp chopping blow on the Marine's neck, angled to incapacitate but not to kill.

Harconan caught the unconscious sentry before he could collapse, hauling him through the door and laying him on the cabin deck.

"Battle protocols, my friend. I won't secure the door."

Harconan began to work his way aft, moving silently through the red-lit passageways.

*

Amanda shrugged into the combination flotation and flak vest and settled the slightly oversized K-pot helmet over her command headset, the familiar cladding-on of armor she had performed so often before.

The *Shenandoah*'s bridge had been rigged for action and a thin spat of rain licked at the windscreens. She could not have asked the ancient gods of Indonesia for better than this murky night.

Below her and forward, on the water-washed main deck, the MaGregor hatches parted and the three aircraft elevators lifted topside. Only this time they carried no aircraft.

When the *Shenandoah* was being designed, a great deal of sweat had been expended on the nature of its anti-missile and anti-aircraft defense systems. They must be highly compact, self-contained, readily concealable, rapid to deploy, not dependent on elaborate radar and sensor arrays, have a secondary anti-surface attack capacity and, if possible, be of use to the Sea Demon force on land deployment.

The answer to this complex challenge proved to be amazingly simple. Parked and tied down in the center of each deck lift was a standard Avenger Antiaircraft vehicle, an armored Humvee with a twin-armed missile launcher on its rear deck. One arm carried the standard quadpack of Stinger SAMs, the other an adapter rail that permitted the launching of navalized Hellfire anti-tank missiles.

As each lift locked into position, the Avenger it carried extended its sensor masts and a deckhand dashed across to the Humvee, jacking a coaxial cable into the vehicle, integrating it into the *Shenandoah*'s fire control matrix. The launcher arms swiveled and elevated as the gunners checked their systems. Other hands crouched beside the Avenger Hummers with cases of reload missiles.

Additional close-range weapons teams were deploying as well. Around the superstructure, railing stanchions were being lifted out of their unusually deep and heavy deck sockets and replaced with pintle mounts and monopods. The Marine heavy weapons teams further augmented the *Shenandoah*'s armament with .50 Caliber "Ma Deuce" heavy machine guns and Javelin anti-tank missiles.

On the bridge, Amanda tapped her lip mike key. "Moon Pool, you are cleared to flood down and open the belly doors. Rig and arm all drop collars, Mark 48's. Program for surface engagement."

Anything and everything that could punch a hole or even make a dent in another ship's hull would be pressed into play tonight.

Soon ... Soon ... Soon ...

Soon they would be back in open water with a clear run to Jakarta. Ketalaman felt the knots in his stomach start to loosen. He had lost himself for a time but he was regaining himself, regaining his precious control.

He had acted hastily. Out of fear. Out of stupidity. He had been stampeded into a potentially disastrous action in taking his precious ships through this narrow bottleneck of a channel. But, thankfully, Kediri and the Americans had placed nothing there to contest him.

It would have been far better to meet the government fleet in open battle. It would have made him stronger in the eyes of his followers.

*Fool!*

They were losing faith. He could see it in the sideways glances cut at him in the low-lit compartment. He could see it in the way his officers clustered in whispering cryptic clusters. In the way their eyes went to his Chief of Staff and to the Commodore first when he, Ketalaman, gave a command.

He must rebuild his stature in the eyes of his men. And he must order the Commodore and the CoS killed upon arrival in Java. That would help.

His wounded hand closed tight around the blood-stained rock shard in his pocket, relishing the pain.

In the corner of the Flag Plot, the talker straightened and pressed his headset closer. "Surface contact report from the Pulau Raas! A large surface contact in the channel! Bearing one three five relative! Speed eighteen knots! Range five thousand meters relative! Closing rapidly!"

A quartermaster leaned over the channel chart and placed an unidentified contact marker off the bow of the minesweepers running ahead of the main force. The unspoken tension ramped up in the flag plot.

"Order the Pulau to close and challenge the contact," Ketalaman said quietly.

"Yes sir." The talker repeated his command to the radio room.

*As the mountains. As ... the ... mountains!*

Minutes crawled past. Ketalaman metered each breath, keeping them steady.

"Pulau Raas reports target is a large merchant ship, bulk-carrier type."

The chartsmen replaced the unidentified contact marker with that for a merchantman.

"The captain of the Pulau Raas reports the merchantmen identifies itself as the Greek freighter Andronicus."

The MV Galaxy *Shenandoah*
2312 Hours: Zone Time 2008

"Mr. Carstairs, have countermeasures deploy their antenna arrays. Stand by to commence radar-range scrambling."

"Aye aye, ma'am."

The islands that walled the channel could only be seen as traces on the navigational radar, could only be sensed as a differing quality in the darkness of the night. Off to port, the running lights of a small ship snapped on, blurred in the mist. The rebel fleet had been running blacked out – but, as they were sharing the tight channel with a "neutral" merchantmen, they were illuminating themselves for safety's sake. Amanda thought it very obliging of them.

The lights began to pass astern. They were past the first picket line, inside the initial layer of rebel defense.

Amanda's eyes flicked to the tactical display on the laptop clipped to the chart table. The positioning was looking favorable. For the last hour, she had been carefully gauging her approach to the enemy shipping column. Tracking them via the drone net, she had been varying her speed and approach angle to place each of the rebel convoy elements in exactly the correct position in relation to her deployed forces.

"Lee helm, make turns for twenty-two knots. War Power."

"Aye aye, ma'am. All engines answering at War Power. Making turns for twenty-four knots."

"CIC, this is the Captain. Advise all attack elements. Stand by to engage."

"CIC acknowledging." Elliot MacIntyre himself made the reply. "All attack elements standing by."

"Electronic countermeasures, this is the Captain. Arm RBOC launchers. Commence range jamming. All emitters."

\*

Below the ridgeline on Sebangka Island, a long line of helicopters hovered in ground effect like a row of prancing cavalry chargers, the thunder of their rotors merging with the thunder in the skies. Taking advantage of the terrain, they were preparing a pop-up attack on the enemy convoy in the same way a flight of Army gunships might ambush a hostile armored column.

Cautiously, Vince Arkady increased power and hovered up to peer over the hill crest, careful to keep his radar return merged into the ground clutter. For several minutes he stayed there. The enemy combat force had steamed past his position. Cranking up his sighting systems to full gain, he could now make out the clustered silhouettes of the rebel group approaching the ambush point.

*

On the south side of the channel, Stone Quillain held a penlight in his teeth. It was his turn to feverishly thumb though the rain-slick waterproof pages of the pocket *Jane's*. "Okay. That lead boy in the near column. That's the dagger boat. He's got the missiles. We want to kill him first."

The rebel transport force had its outriders. The lighter, shallow-draft missile and gunboats were out on the column flanks, warily ready to absorb the first of any blow aimed at the convoy. Critical only in that they could complicate the attack on the primary targets, they had to be dealt with decisively.

"The fucker's dead," the ranger replied. He rested the camera-like laser rangefinder on a tree limb and squinted through the integral thermal sight, speaking into his lip mike. "Battery, stand by. Mission to fire."

*

High in the *Shenandoah*'s upperworks, an antenna array lifted out of the cluster of exhaust pipes in the funnel structure. Unfolding flowerlike, the ECM dish aimed to cover the forward arc of the ship. Deep within the hold section, a skilled electronic warfare technician armed with several million dollars' worth of sophisticated systemry inflicted an illusion upon the oncoming Indonesian warships.

As the Indonesian surface search radars painted the *Shenandoah*, each sweep was recorded, its frequency and wave characteristics analyzed, perfectly mimicked and then beamed back at its point of origin, delayed by a few milliseconds.

As the sweeps continued and their intervals were assessed, the ECM system began to predict the scans and project false returns a few milliseconds *before* the arrival of the actual radar beam.

Aboard the warships of the Indonesian combat formation, radar operators frowned and bent closer to their scopes. They were still detecting the large surface contact off their bows and they could get a bearing on it, but the range was blurring. It looked like a malfunction of some nature and the radar operators began to run systems diagnostics.

What they didn't realize was that the radars aboard all three frigates were suffering from the same "malfunction" simultaneously.

*

"Captain, this is countermeasures. Range scrambling is up! We have no scan variance or frequency jump. They're falling for it!"

"Very good, countermeasures. Keep it coming." Amanda looked at the figures silhouetted in the instrument glow of the helm station. "Lee helm, all engines ahead full! War Power!"

"Aye aye, ma'am. All engines answering full. War power!"

"Helm, we'll take the lead frigate. Special attack! Steer parallel approach heading. Hold target ten degrees off the starboard bow until attack commit. You have the ship!"

"Targeting lead frigate. Parallel approach heading. Steering ten off the bow and tracking!"

The deck beneath Amanda's feet began to tremble under the augmented thrust of the propellers as the commando carrier gathered herself for her charge.

Ahead, Amanda could dimly make out the aligned running lights of the frigate group. She flicked her eyes to the tactical display before her. Range was now five miles and closing. Maybe six minutes to contact, given their combined closing speeds.

*Another squall!* she thought feverishly. *Please give me just one more good rain squall!*

"Bridge, we have a problem!" It was MacIntyre from the Combat Information Center.

"What is it, Elliot?"

"Harconan is gone! His guard just recovered consciousness in his cabin."

"Damn!" Amanda spat. "I do not need this! All of our onboard security teams are tied down at weapons stations. Have Mr. Beltrain arm some of the damage control parties ..."

A hand dropped on her shoulder. "Please don't discommode yourself or your crew, Amanda. I'm right here."

Amanda nearly sprang out of her skin. "Makara!"

"Of course," the pirate replied amiably. "As I told our friend MacIntyre, this may be my only opportunity to witness a world class sea battle. My apologies to your Marine, but I simply couldn't pass on the opportunity."

He circled the chart table and stepped closer to the windscreen, enthralled with what he saw stretching out before him. "Amanda, she's magnificent. Absolutely magnificent! A modern-day Q-ship! Why didn't I ever think of something like this?"

"Amanda, what's going on up there?" MacIntyre demanded over the intercom.

"Cancel the security sweep," Amanda replied in disgust. "Harconan's here on the bridge with me, sightseeing."

MacIntyre muttered a curse. "I'll be up there personally with a detail and a set of irons."

A sudden downpour lashed the bridge windows and the lights of the oncoming Indonesian frigates faded out of visibility.

"Negative, Elliot. It's too late! The cat's out of the bag and we have more important things to worry about. Cut all deck and running lights!"

With each accelerating beat of her propellers, the *Shenandoah* was gaining speed and devouring distance. Amanda shot another glance at the tactical. "Range now three miles and closing rapidly. Advise all attack elements! Engagement imminent! Stand by to open fire!"

"This should prove most interesting," Harconan said, strolling back to stand at her shoulder. "You're taking us in to point blank range."

"And I intend to get a lot closer," she snapped back. "CIC, stand by to invert running lights."

"What do you plan to do?" Harconan mused. "Ram him?"

"That's the idea."

"What?" It was Harconan's turn to be taken by surprise. "You can't be serious?"

"Why not? When I set the design parameters of this ship, it occurred to me that the ability to stage the occasional accidental collision at sea could prove useful. The ship we modeled the *Shenandoah* on was ice strengthened for Arctic operations, so we built the concept. This *Shenandoah* has a hull like an icebreaker. She's double-framed and cross-braced and her bow plating is three inches thick, made out of DY-100 steel salvaged out of a nuclear sub hull."

"Magnificent," Harconan murmured. "Simply magnificent!"

*

On the bridge of the frigate Fatahillah, the skipper peered nervously into the night. Even with his night glasses he couldn't pick up the lights of that damn bulk carrier in this murk.

"Radar, range and bearing on that freighter?"

"Bearing zero three five off the starboard bow, angle off increasing. Range indefinite."

"Indefinite? What do you mean indefinite?"

"We have the bearing but the range keeps breaking up. We seem to have a scope malfunction, sir. Conducting diagnostic now. Target should be out at about three miles."

*Should be? About?* This was a ship handler's nightmare! Blundering about in sloppy weather with a squadron in column behind him and a Greek freighter standing on towards him and all with a dicky radar.

"Damn it, Radar. Get me a range on that merchant ship!"

By the international maritime Rules of the Road, the bulk carrier should be passing safely to starboard of him, but who could say what a crazy freighter captain might do?

By common sense, he should also reduce speed until the plot clarified, but he couldn't do that without first contacting the task force flag and throwing the whole column into disarray.

This couldn't possibly get worse.

"Radar, where the hell is that range?"

"I'm sorry, captain, but we're still getting inconsistent ranging in the forward arcs of both the surface search and navigational radars."

*Both systems?* But how could *both* systems possibly malfunctioning in exactly the same way at exactly the same time?

*

"Helmsman, now!" Amanda cried. "Turn in on him! Hard over! Set collision bearing!'

The brass wheel spun and glinted in the binnacle light. "Helm is hard over, Captain! Target ship is now bearing zero off the bow!"

They were about to unleash one of the most ancient and devastating of all naval attacks.

"CIC, this is the bridge. Invert the running lights! Sound collision alarm! Stand by to ram!"

*

"Ship off the starboard bow! Bearing zero four five!" one of the Fatahillah's lookouts yelled.

Through the water-streaked bridge windscreen, a pair of red and green ship's running lights that had suddenly become clear.

Something was wrong, the frigate's captain thought feverishly. By the

International Maritime Rules of the Road, the merchantman would be showing a red running light to port and a green to starboard.

But by her lights, the bulk carrier had suddenly turned away from the task force and out of the channel and was steaming hard for the northern coast of Lingga Island.

The frigate's commander lifted his night glasses. "Have the Radio Room hail that ..."

His binoculars centered. He could make out a shape between those lights now, an angular outline. But it wasn't a ship's stern as it should be. It was a bow.

The sanity of the Fatahillah's captain trembled. The bulk carrier's running lights were reversed. It wasn't steaming away; it was bearing down on them!

"All engines ahead emergency!" The scream tore from his throat. "Hard left rudder!"

The bow could be seen without night glasses now, an enormous axeblade of steel with a foaming bow wave at its cutwater, towering over the side of the frigate. Someone on the frigate's bridge was yanking frantically on the lever of the ship's siren. The Fatahillah herself was screaming in terror.

And in response, the bow of the onrushing ship was turning as well. Turning in ...

*Towards them!*

*

Amanda keyed the I-MC circuit. "All hands, brace for impact! Hang on!"

She had been involved in an accidental collision at sea before – but never a deliberate one. She felt an arm close around her waist as Harconan got a grip on both her and the chart table. Then steel impacted steel.

There was a thunderclap and an insane shriek of tearing metal. A dazzling double fan of molten sparks sprayed half a thousand feet into the air. Amanda had expected the bow of the *Shenandoah* to lift as she drove up and over the Indonesian frigate, but it didn't work that way. The Commando carrier displaced sixty-six thousand tons, the frigate less than two thousand. It was a rhinoceros running down a sheep.

There was a tooth-rattling shock, a long shudder, and the *Shenandoah* simply sailed through the smaller vessel, her underwater propeller guards shoving the two sundered halves of the frigate aside.

Looking to port, Amanda caught a momentary glimpse of the frigate's stern section, as if she were seeing an engineering cutaway. The compartments and passageways were torn open but still internally illuminated. Maimed and struggling crewmen could be seen toppling into the sea.

Then the inrushing waters must have killed the power systems. All went dark and the *Shenandoah* was driving clear.

"All elements open fire!" Amanda yelled into her headset. "Commence! Commence! Commence!"

\*

On the nameless channel island, Stone Quillain yelled into his lip mike. "Battery, fire the mission!"

"On the way!" the reply rang back.

Four 120mm mortar shells were released, each sliding down the throat of its tube to strike the firing pin at the bottom. Propulsive charges exploded and the shells screamed on their way, tracking on their high ballistic trajectories.

One of the strengths of the trench mortar is in its disproportionate firepower. As it is a low pressure, low velocity weapon, less of its throw weight needs to be put into its shell casing and more into the explosive charge it carries. Thus, a mortar shell can be more powerful than the equivalent round fired from a cannon or howitzer.

The shells being fired this night by the Sea Demon battery were British-made Merlin anti-tank rounds. Their infra-red precision guidance system took up a percentage of space within the shell casing

490

– but, as they pitched over the peak of their arcs and homed on the exhaust stack glow of the missile boat Rencong, they still packed a hellish punch.

Yet another advantage of the mortar is that it can be fired with great rapidity. A good mortar crew can have three rounds in the air before the first round hits its target. And the Army mortar men of the Sea Demon force were excellent.

The missile boat Rencong, the betrayer of the Karel Satsuitubun and the Teluk Berau, dissolved.

*

On the other flank of the rebel transport group, a section of SPEED Cobras popped over their concealing ridgeline.

"Flanker birds, designate your targets!" Arkady spoke carefully into his helmet mike. "Call it as you lock!"

His was a precise exercise in ammunition management. He had eleven SPEED Cobras with twenty-two small Penguin antiship missiles to be distributed among eight potential targets. He must get maximum effect out of each and every round.

"Flanker Lead, I got locks on the column leader!"

"This is Flanker Wing! I'm on the column trailer – I say again, I'm on the column trailer!"

"Flanker birds, take your shots!"

Stumpy, deadly projectiles roared from the launch rails of the flanker killers, flames streaming from their solid fuel booster rockets.

The compact Penguin anti-ship missile was unique among the world's arsenal of anti-ship weapons. Designed by the Norwegian Defense Research Institute, it had been built specifically for the unique needs of the Norwegian Navy. Designed for use along the jagged, fjord-wracked Scandinavian coast, the Penguin was short-ranged with a comparatively small 120-kilogram warhead.

But it was a nimble little monster, its large fan of guidance fins making it extremely maneuverable and difficult to evade. Its guidance package was one of a kind for a ship-killer. The Penguin was a passive infra-red homing missile. It gave no electronic warning of its coming; you learned of its presence only when it came screaming down upon you.

"Flanker flights hover down! Evade!"

The SPEED Cobra team sank back below the safety of the ridgeline. The Jeannie II held her exposed station.

"Vince!" It was Pink Pinkerton's alarmed voice over the Talk-Between-Pilots. "Get your ass down here!"

"Just calling the shots, my man," Arkady murmured. "Be down in a second."

*Flash! Flash!* It was like low set lightning through the drizzle. Through his thermographic imaging system, Arkady saw the outline of the lead missile boat distort and blaze bright. Two solid hits and a heavy topside fire! Dead meat!

*Flash!* There was only one impact on the trailing gunboat. One of the Penguins had "gone stupid" and had missed. A seventy-five per cent hit ratio. Arkady scowled. This wasn't good enough.

Something began to pulse and flare rhythmically at the bow of the damaged surviving flanker boat. Muzzle blasts. Off to Arkady's right, explosions raked along the top of the ridge. The maimed Lurssen was lashing back wildly at its attackers. Ignoring the gunfire, Arkady deliberately aligned his sights on the survivor. He keyed the arming and aiming sequence on one of his Penguins, giving it a look at its target. As the odd man out in the strike, he'd reserved his brace of missiles as coup-de-grâce shots.

He got the Penguin's lock up tone in his earphones and squeezed off the round, closing his eyes for a moment against the glare of the missile booster.

When he opened them again, it was to see a wave of tracer rounds and fire trails sweeping towards him.

\*

"Collision! There has been a collision!" the startled talker bleated in the Flag Plot of the Teluk Surabaya. "The battle force flag reports that the point frigate Fatahillah has collided with a merchant ship!"

"What?" Ketalaman snapped. "How can that be? What's happened?"

The systems operator manning the Plot radar repeater buried his face into the eyepieces of the black scope hood. "There are two unidentified targets in the vicinity of the Fatahillah!"

The task force commodore charged across the Plot room. Shoving the radar operator aside, he peered into the radar screen. "In Allah's name, there aren't two new targets out there! Fatahillah has been cut in half!"

"What happened?" Ketalaman repeated, recognizing fully how stupid he sounded.

"There's a distress call from the merchant ship!" the radio room talker interjected. "They're reporting a collision and are asking for assistance ..."

The decks of the big landing ship shuddered lightly, a series of faint multiple thuds leaking through the hull plating.

"Bridge reports missile boat Rencong is under attack! Heavy naval gunfire! Rencong is hit! Rencong is hit! She's burning!"

"Where's the fire coming from?"

Before anyone could reply to the Admiral's demand, the next layer of disaster dropped onto the task force. "Air contacts to port! Hostile air contacts! Missile alarm! Missiles incoming!"

"Commence firing! All ships commence firing!" It was the Commodore calling the desperate command. Admiral Ketalaman simply stood, staring unseeing at the chart table.

They had been waiting.

There had been a trap.

\*

"Helm, are we answering?" Amanda cried.

"We have full steering control, captain. Rudders are answering!"

"Then come hard left! Steer two seven zero!"

"Steering two seven zero!"

"Damage control, this is the bridge! Report!"

"No flooding alarms in forward spaces, Captain. Stress gauges indicate no frame displacement. We didn't even scratch the paint, ma'am!"

"Very good. Engine room, report!"

"Bridge, this is main engine control," Chief Thomson's steady voice replied. "We got a slight vibration in the starboard propeller shaft. I think we nicked a blade."

"Can we maintain turns?"

"For a while. Nothing's shaking apart yet. But slack her off as soon as you can."

"Understood, Chief. Keep it coming!"

Beyond the windscreen, the *Shenandoah*'s bow was already starting its swing across the bow of the next frigate in the battle line, the helmsman supplementing the wheel with a hand on the bow thruster controller, the big commando carrier pivoting with ponderous agility.

Amanda intended to weave an S-shaped course through the line of Indonesian frigates. It was unlikely that they could catch another of the smaller nimbler vessels in a second ramming attack, but it was still critical that they stay in close.

Amanda became aware of a credible imitation of an hysterical Greek shipmaster shouting broken English into the Talk-Between-Ships radio.

"You hit us! You hit us! You stinking bastards run us down! You sink us! We sue! We sue!" It was Harconan, the pirate adding his own useful two cents into the confusion of the moment. He was also sounding as if he were enjoying himself enormously.

Build on the panic. Build on that confusion. Every second stolen before the Indonesians could react was precious.

"Bridge, this is the CIC." It was Admiral MacIntyre, subservient to Amanda at the moment. "Flanker forces are engaging the transport group!"

One down and two to go, and they'd taken all of their free shots. Now the real fight was on.

"Very well, CIC," Amanda ordered. "RBOC launchers, fire full chaff patterns! Initiate full spectrum jamming. Stand by to clear casemate mounts! All guns and launchers train to starboard and prepare to open fire!"

Harconan clamped a hand over the mouthpiece of the phone. "You have guns on this monster as well?"

"We're a Q-ship aren't we?" Amanda replied. "What would a Q-ship be without hidden gun mounts?"

*

Stone Quillain found being perched in the treetops amidst a ferocious autocannon barrage not the most comfortable of places to be. "Goddamn! The sumbitch figured it out!"

"No shit, leatherneck?" The Ranger NCO gritted, trying to crawl into his helmet amid the flying wood and metal splinters.

The second of the convoy flankers on their side of the transport formation had also been a German-built Lurssen FPB gunboat. In the greater scheme of things, it had been rated as a secondary threat because it lacked anti-ship missiles – but it did rate a formidable battery of 57 and 40-millimeter cannon and a sharp captain and crew. When the hidden mortars on the nameless islet had opened up on its column leader, someone aboard the Lurssen had either heard the firing discharges or had made a good guess as to their point of origin. The gunboat had instantly lashed back with everything it had, making up for precision targeting with sheer volume of fire.

"Shift target!" Stone yelled. "Kill that little bastard before he chops this friggin' tree down!"

*

*Six, six, four! Six, six, four!* Arkady allowed his pilot's instincts to sidle his aircraft down the ridgeline to his next firing position, while his conscious mind feverishly chanted the numeric mantra. He liked the sound of it less each time he did so.

The strike squadron had sixteen Penguin rounds remaining, barring his last silver bullet, with three critical targets left to kill. The larger Van Speijk frigate had the battery of more sophisticated, more lethal American-made Harpoon surface-to-surface missiles. The big Ivan Rogov amphibious ship had the area-defense Crotal SAM system and was the biggest threat to Arkady's helicopters. And the trailing escort, the smaller Parchim-class frigate. had a set of Exocet tubes. It couldn't be ignored.

He had decided on a 'six, six, four' dispersion as the least-worst kill template on the three targeted missile ships. But with the little Penguins, every round would have to hit to ensure the destruction of all three vessels. And that just wasn't going to happen.

After that, he'd have only his one uncommitted missile to try and tidy up with.

"Flights call your positioning?"

"Point flight, on station, Lead!"

"Amphib flight on station!"

"Trailer flight on station!"

Had Amanda been plagued by this kind of second-guessing before she'd committed to one of her plans? She must have, yet she never hinted at it by word or gesture. It was too late for second thoughts anyway.

"All flights, hover up and engage primary targets!"

*

"CIC, this is the bridge! Clear the casemate mounts!"

On the *Shenandoah*'s fore and aft hull quarters, massive, hinged steel panels swung outward and down, hydraulic shock absorbers catching and braking their fall. Compact domed turrets were revealed within the hull pockets and slender gun barrels trained outboard with a venomous whine.

*

"Radar and communications are degrading, captain! High intensity military grade jamming on all frequencies!"

"What are we getting from task force flag?" the senior captain of the rebel battle squadron demanded.

The scene on the darkened bridge of the command frigate Nala was one of organized hysteria, demands for information flowing out over the phone and radio circuits, fragmentary and fearfully unsatisfactory responses returning.

"The transport force is under attack from aircraft and artillery fire, possibly from a ship or shore battery," his exec blurted back, pressing the earphones of a headset close. "The missile boats are being cut to pieces!"

"Do we have targeting data?"

"No sir. No valid targets are registering on any bearings."

"Orders? What about orders from the Task Force Flag?"

"Only repeated commands to engage the enemy."

Damn it! "What enemy? Where?" The squadron commander tore off his uniform cap and dashed it to the deck. "What's the status of the Fatahillah?"

"There's something burning off the bow, sir!" one of the bridge lookouts shouted.

"Radar, what do you see?"

The systems operator lifted his face from the radar hood. "I believe one of the segments of the Fatahillah has sunk, sir. I only register one contact on her last bearing. We should be coming up on her soon."

"Where's the merchant ship she collided with?"

"It's still out there, sir. Bearing ... approximately ten degrees off our port bow."

"What's the range? The heading? The speed?"

"We don't have a clear plot, sir. Jamming is intensive from multiple points and we're entering a chaff cloud."

"It could be from the Fatahillah's countermeasures launchers," the exec interjected. "They could have fired accidentally in the collision."

"And maybe they didn't! Have gunnery control train on the bearing of that merchant ship! Fire illumination flares!"

"Sir, that could illuminate us as well!"

"To hell with that! We've got to see!"

"Aye aye, sir. Gunnery control, this is the bridge ..."

"Captain!" It was the bridge wing lookout. "A ship! A ship off the bow!"

There was a shape in the rain-streaked night, a mammoth outline displacing the surface mist, riding the pale streak of a boiling wake. It was cutting across the frigate's course line, moving at a speed no mere merchantman should be able to reach.

Suddenly, flame starkly backlit the big intruder and a roaring wave of devastation swept back over the frigate, raking it from stem to stern. The decks bucked and heaved. The wheelhouse windscreen imploded in a shotgun blast of jagged glass. Men screamed and fell as bullets and shell fragments ricocheted and howled.

The Nala's captain collapsed to the glass-sharded deck, clutching at a torn thigh. "Fire! Open Fire!"

The cry was an instinctive reaction. The last thing he had seen before he had fallen had been the forward turret with its glacis plate caved in and its wrenched gun tube angling uselessly toward the sky.

"Someone radio the Flagship! Tell them it's the freighter! The freighter!"

*

Modern naval warfare was supposed to be a courtly over-the-horizon exchange of precision guided high-tech weaponry. That was why Amanda Garrett ignored the conventions. Trick your way in close where you weren't expected, she thought, then ravage them! Rip their guts out before they know you're even there! Preserve your own crew by not giving the enemy a chance to fight back. It had worked for her before and it could work again. It all rested on how fast she could deal death and destruction.

"All batteries! Guns free! Engage to starboard! Fire!"

There as a meager half-mile between the commando carrier and the

498

frigate when the *Shenandoah* lit up. The two flat-shooting OTO Melara "Super Rapid" auto cannon in the starboard casemates began to spew their eighty-five-rounds-per-minute barrage of 76mm shells, aiming low to body-blow the frigate's hull.

The Marine gunners manning the Avenger-Hellfire systems and Javelin anti-tank launchers went high. Squinting through their weather penetrating night vision sights, they steered their laser-guided projectiles in on specific targets: the frigate's bow turret and bridge. The Hellfires and Javelins had not been designed for naval war. They were intended for killing tanks, but they were also adaptable.

The machine gun teams were not meant to engage heavy surface warships either, but they served as well, their tracer streams holding on target. Battlefield multiplication worked in their favor. A .50 caliber heavy machine gun bullet can effortlessly punch through the half-inch plating of a standard ship's hull and, while one such round won't do a great deal of damage, several thousand of them can wreak a great deal of havoc indeed.

Over the course of a bare two minutes, the command ship of the Indonesian battle force was gnawed to death, hundreds of minor hits accumulating into major devastation. OTO Melara rounds ripped open her waterline. Automatic weapons fire riddled her sensor antenna, blinding her and stacking the dead up in her gun tubs. Anti-tank missiles burned out her interior one compartment at a time, wiping all life off of her bridge. Fires and secondary explosions began to flare brighter than the projectile hits.

The *Shenandoah* curved around the Nala in a foaming half circle, the hapless Indonesian held at the center of the turn, the commando carrier's fire streams linking the two vessels.

"Dead one! Drop him!" Amanda yelled into her headset as they cut across the dying frigate's stern. "Helm, steady as you go! Clear portside casemate mounts! All Batteries, shift fire! Target to port! Fire as you bear!"

She glanced at the tactical display. With the straits exploding in front of him, the captain of the third and last frigate in the battle force column, the Malahayati, had put his helm hard over, swinging to port and parallel with the turning *Shenandoah*, unmasking his own batteries.

To emphasize the point, there was a series of deeper thuds out in the night and the roaring howl of incoming heavy shells. A row of towering spray plumes from the Malahayati's 4.7 marched past the *Shenandoah*'s bow.

"CIC! Clear portside missile bays! Let's give him a broadside!"

*

All along the ridge above the strait, the line of SPEED Cobras bobbed up into their firing positions. On the Indonesian air defense radars, they registered as faint returns blending into the island's ground clutter. The row of ships registered cleanly on the infra-red sensors of the American attack helos. The only "ground clutter" the helos had to deal with were the thermal blooms of the burning and sinking missile boats along the transport column's flanks. The wrecks of the smaller vessels were already falling astern and were no longer a factor. The "peeling" portion of the fire mission had been accomplished.

"All flights, salvo fire on my mark!" Arkady commanded. "Three ... two ... one ... mark and fire!"

Far out across the waters, there was a heat pulse on the decks of the Taluk Surabaya as a Crotal area defense missile roared from its launcher cell, aimed at the line of attacking helicopters. But sixteen Penguins replied to the single Crotal, launch flame rippling down the length of the ridge.

Before the Indonesian anti-air missile could reach them, the SPEED Cobras ducked, sinking back behind the safety of the high ground like a row of prairie dogs seeking their holes.

The anti-ship salvo had been launched with as much perfection as the battlefield would allow. There was no place for the ship column to hide.

Then raw, blind fate intervened.

The Teluk Hading was the second ship in the Indonesian line, cruising directly between the frigate Slamet Riyadi and the Teluk Surabaya. The elderly LSM was the feeblest warship in the rebel fleet. It hadn't even been considered in the *Shenandoah*'s attack template, being classified as a mop-up target. But now the little ship intervened in the developing battle in a way that no one had expected or desired, especially by its crew and passengers.

The captain of the Teluk Hading had sensibly attempted to augment his ship's fixed armament of four 37mm anti-aircraft guns with whatever defensive odds and ends that might prove useful from his cargo of troops and military equipment.

But the young Indonesian soldiers he carried were by no means seamen or sea warriors.

Acting in response to frantic orders yelled down from the LSM's bridge, an Army missile team hastened to the portside rail, trying to load and prep their Mistral MANPAD launcher for firing.

The foot of the number one man of the team – the missileer who actually carried, aimed and fired the launcher tube – came down on a streak of oil that had leaked from one of the military vehicles loaded onto the amphib's weather deck. He slipped and fell and, as he did so, his hand convulsively tightened on the missile launcher's handgrip.

The weapon's external safety should have been engaged. It wasn't.

Wildly unguided, the little Mistral anti-aircraft missile screamed out of its launcher tube. Bouncing off the deck plating, it skittered under the cluster of vehicles parked in the amphib's waist. The flare of its exhaust momentarily reflected off the Day-Glo warning painted across the rear face of a tanker truck.

DANGER! PETROL!

A massive mushroom of orange flame geysered upwards and grew on the LST's deck, lighting the sea around the doomed ship for a mile in all directions. Bright as it was to the naked eye, the heat radiation it threw off was even more dazzling to the seeker heads of the oncoming wave of anti-ship missiles.

The major problem with so-called "smart" weapons is that they aren't. They can be exceedingly simple-minded when confronted with a problem or decision outside of their very limited zone of expertise. In this instance, a number of the incoming Penguin missiles caught the heat flare of the exploding Indonesian landing ship on the periphery of their guidance sensors. This was something obviously much bigger and hotter than what they had initially been aimed at, so it obviously must be more worth killing.

Three of the Penguin rounds targeted on the Slamet Riyaid skidded in flight and swarmed in on the flaming LSM, as did two from the flight launched at the Teluk Surabaya. In the end, it was, perhaps, better for those aboard the Teluk Hading.

Being blown to bits was marginally a superior death to being burned alive.

*

Of the four Penguins that did continue to home on the Teluk Surabaya, one was deflected by the ship's countermeasures launchers. Another was intercepted and disintegrated by a burst from one of the big amphib's AK630 antimissile Gatling guns. The two surviving ship-killers executed their end of run pop-up maneuvers and dove into the decks of the Surabaya.

The warhead detonations reverberated through the hull of the big ship like blows landing on an empty oil drum. The flagship was wounded, but far from slain, and the overhead speakers filled with the elevated voices of the damage control parties as the ventilation system filled with the smell of hot metal and burning paint.

"Admiral! What are your orders, sir? *Admiral Ketalaman, what are your orders?*"

"Stand on." The reply was barely a whisper. "Stand on for Jakarta."

Ketalaman's Chief of Staff wondered at the thing clutched so tightly in his Admiral's hand. It looked like a fragment of rock.

*

"What the hell happened?" Arkady exclaimed. Bobbing back above the ridgeline, he regained his situational awareness and was appalled at what he found. The enemy transport line was in flaming chaos, but it wasn't the right kind of chaos.

As per the strike template, the last escort in line behind the two big passenger ferries, the frigate Silas Papare, was falling away behind the formation, dead in the water and burning heavily from multiple missile hits. That was fine; it was everything else that was wrong. The fleet flagship, the Teluk Surabaya, was also showing flames on her deck – but she was still standing on, swinging wide to evade the shapeless inferno that had enveloped the second ship in line, the LSM that wasn't supposed to have been hit at all.

But most critically, the point frigate, the Slamet Riyaid, was still in the fight. Her silhouette was distorted from blast damage and she showed the lingering thermal aura of onboard explosions – but she wasn't burning and she was still maneuvering under control, standing on to the eastward and closing the range with the Shenandoah.

And the Slamet was the stone killer of the rebel task force. While not of the latest mark, the eight American-made Harpoon missiles carried by the frigate were the deadliest and most sophisticated ship-killers available to the Indonesians. Should they lock and launch on the Shenandoah, it was unlikely that the commando carrier's point defenses and countermeasures could stave off the attack.

Arkady's tasking had been to stop that from happening and he was failing!

An urgent electronic warble issued from the SPEED Cobra's threat board, an alarm keyed for just such a contingency. Harpoon fire control radars were activating.

"Shenandoah! Vampire! Vampire! You got missiles coming in!"

Even as he made the warning call, Arkady's mind was racing ahead, patching together a new contingency plan. He squeezed off his last Penguin round, aiming it at the Teluk Surabaya. He had to keep their guns and missile off of him. He had to live at least for a few seconds more.

Then he firewalled the SPEED Cobra's velocity controller, turning the Jeannie II itself into yet another antiship projectile, this one aimed at the Slamet Riyaid.

*

On the bridge of the *Shenandoah*, Amanda heard the vampire call, the warning of an imminent missile attack – but she believed it to be related to the last of the Fatahillah's the Commando carrier was facing. The commander of the single surviving element of the Indonesian battle squadron had gotten a grasp on the tactical situation and was reacting. He'd fired his own countermeasures and was using the gas turbine acceleration and the nimble handling of his smaller ship to bring his own weapons to bear on his larger, clumsier attacker. Given the jittering radar returns on the threat boards, he was trying for radar locks with both his gun and Exocet systems.

It was fast draw time. "CIC," Amanda snapped into her headset, "are we valid with the portside missile bays?"

"We have the angles on target Master 3!" MacIntyre replied, the heat of the battle creeping into his voice. "Portside batteries are hot and standing by!"

"Very well! Take Master Three! Portside missile bays, fire as you clear!"

More concealing panels toppled outward along the *Shenandoah*'s port flank, revealing squat, ominous rhomboid shapes crouching like predatory animals in their hull pockets. Explosive bolts detonated, blowing off launcher cell caps and, one after another, six surface launch variant Penguin missiles roared away into the night, snuffling hungrily for the heat scent of their prey.

Amanda saw the string of hit explosions pulse through the rain like an interconnecting sequence of lightning bolts. The radar emissions of the third Fatahillah disappeared. *Finished! The battle force was down!* Whatever was left out there was no longer a threat.

"Helmsman!" a powerful masculine voice rang behind her. "Hard over! Come left to two eight five."

*Harconan!*

Amanda hesitated only an instant. "Helm, make it so!"

"Aye aye. Coming hard left to two eight zero!"

"My apologies, Captain," Harconan said, turning to her. "But you were running out of channel. The water shoals rapidly into a reef line through here. Your fathometer wouldn't have given you enough warning and, as they say, running aground can ruin your whole day."

"Apologies accepted." Amanda hesitated only a moment more. "Helm, Mr. Harconan is an authorized pilot for these waters. He is cleared to give emergency helm commands."

"Aye aye, Captain."

Amanda blipped her laptop display back from the threat boards to tactical. Leaning into the screen, her eyes narrowing, she assessed the developing situation. The rebel ship formations were disintegrating. The *Shenandoah* had dealt with the battle squadron and Arkady and Stone had done for the light gun and missile forces. Only the primary transport column remained less than four miles off the commando carrier's bow.

Hit flags glowed beside the warships in the column and the tail end charley was falling away behind the transports, apparently dead in the water. But the point ship, the Harpoon-armed Van Speijk was still out there.

"CIC, what's the word from strike lead? What's the status on the transport escorts?"

"Strike lead reports all Penguins expended," MacIntyre fired back. "But Strike Lead is also reporting that the Van Speijk is still a factor. I repeat! It is still a factor and we are picking up Harpoon guidance radars!"

"Damn! Damn! Damn! Helm, maintain your turn to two three zero! Unmask and clear starboard Penguin bays! Countermeasures, fire full patterns! All point defenses, stand by to engage incoming!"

"Strike Lead reports he is continuing the attack!"

Amanda caught herself. "Say again, Elliot? I thought Arkady reported all missiles expended?"

"He did."

Arkady held the Jeannie II just off the treetops as he planed down the ridge slope toward the strait, the SPEED Cobra accelerating swiftly through helicopter to airplane mode. "Vince, do you mind telling me just what the hell we're supposed to be doing?"

"We?" Arkady almost went into a treetop as he twisted around in his harness. A second SPEED Cobra was following him down the slope, angling into his wingman's slot.

"Pink, what in the hell do you think you're doing?" Arkady blurted over the inter-aircraft link.

"Being incredibly stupid, just like my squadron commander?" Pinkerton replied. "What are we doing and how are we going to do it?"

It was useless to argue about it now. They were streaking over the beach line and were still gaining speed. "We're taking out that point frigate!"

"I say again, Lead, how? All we've got left are the 20 millimeters?"

"They'll be enough. Follow me in and target what I target!"

Heavy caliber antiaircraft fire suddenly began to materialize around the two racing aircraft; they were within the firing arc of both the Teluk Surabaya and the Slamet Riyaid.

"Full countermeasures, Pink! Get as low as you can!" Both pilots went to auto-eject on their dispenser racks and edged closer to the wavetops, the chaff streaming behind them glittering in the shell bursts, the anti-IR flares bouncing off the surface of the sea.

The fire streams followed them down, kicking up plumes of spray around the skittering SPEED Cobras. A taller tower of water lanced up behind them as an erratic Crotal missile hit the ocean in their wake.

Arkady grunted his words out in short bursts between jockeying his controls. "Pink ... between the funnel and the aft mast ... hit his missile tubes! Hose the missile tubes!"

It was another tactic salvaged from Arkady's intense study of the old days of naval aviation. During the Second World War, American naval aviators had learned how to sink Imperial Japanese navy destroyers and frigates using machine gun fire alone. It was a matter of strafing the stern of the enemy ship until the depth charge racks on the fantail exploded.

Depth charges were no longer standard on modern men of war, but Arkady presupposed that a Harpoon missile tube packed with high explosives and solid rocket propellant might serve as a reasonable substitute.

"This is nuts!" Pinkerton's mutter triggered his sound-actuated helmet mike. Arkady had to agree.

Flame streaked toward the helicopters from the stern house of the frigate, a Sadral launcher spewing a flight of Mistral missiles. "Evade! Break hard left!" Arkady yelled, instinctively flat skidding the Jeannie II across Pinkerton's flight path, catching and pulling the SAM flight onto himself.

"Vince, watch it!"

Arkady reversed the controls and tried to pitch out of this initial turn, wing and rotor tips almost touching water. Light streaks blazed past the cockpit; then came the single rivet-loosening slam followed by the thwack and whine of shrapnel against the fuselage.

"Vince, you're hit! You're hit!

*No shit, Sherlock!* Arkady thought feverishly. His entire world was shaking into a blur.

It was a rotor strike. One of the Mistrals had caught and blown away a section of blade, fatally unbalancing both the rotor assembly and the entire aircraft. Arkady fought the controls, trying to both climb and kill the wandering gyroscopic precession dragging at the maimed aircraft. The instruments were unreadable – but the surface of the sea and eternity waited a bare fifty feet and a fragment of a second away.

In a conventional helicopter, it would have been technically referred to as a "terminal flight event." But the Jeannie II was not conventional.

Arkady got a hand free from the control stick. Tearing up a sealed switch guard on the side console, he stabbed at the uncovered button.

A muffled explosion followed just behind and above his head. Shaped charges sheered through composites and titanium and the entire rotor hub and blade assembly blew away, forcibly ejected from the airframe. The SPEED crews called it "the Jesus Option." And it was the last resort of all last resorts.

The hammering vibration faded, as did the twisting distortion of the SPEED Cobra's flight path. Arkady hauled back on the stick and, riding its wings alone, his pure airplane lifted back into the safety of the sky.

"Lead, are you okay?"

"Good question! Ask me later!"

The Jesus option wasn't supposed to leave a combat worthy aircraft – it was an emergency measure to get a pilot and a battle-damaged airframe home again – but Arkady found he had valid flight controls; his engine readouts were green and he still had a gun and ammunition.

*Fuck it! Drive on!*

Ahead, the silhouette of the Slamet Riyaid exploded toward them, the slab-sided angularity of British Cold War naval architecture readily apparent. Thank God the Indonesian naval budget had not stretched to include a Goalkeeper or Phalanx Close In Weapons System in the frigate's refit.

Suddenly, a flood of golden light overwhelmed Arkady's night vision system. Arkady tore up his helmet visor to find the target ship starkly outlined in the glare of booster flame. The slender pencil of a Harpoon missile was lifting vertically out of its midships launcher tube. They had designated the *Shenandoah* and they were opening up on her.

"Pink, hit the launcher tubes!" Arkady yelled one last time as he hauled the Jeannie II into a steep zoom after the arcing missile. Crushing the stick trigger under his finger, he hosed cannon shells into the Harpoon's flight path.

Out of the hundreds of rounds he fired, one connected.

A mammoth orange fireball blossomed above the rebel frigate, crumpling and shredding its masts and upperworks. The Jeannie II was swatted helplessly onto her tail by the shockwave. Arkady felt the SPEED Cobra hover on the verge of a non-recoverable stall and groped for the ejector seat handle. Then, a second massive shock wave struck him from below, knocking the compound helo back into level flight.

Something that looked like a ship's funnel sailed past outside the cockpit and Arkady realized he was flying through the flaming debris of the Slamet's superstructure. Against the outline of the frigate's blazing hull, the aviator caught a glimpse of Pink Pinkerton's SPEED Cobra sheering off into the night.

"Is that what I was supposed to be doing, Vince?" Pinkerton inquired.

"Yeah. Pretty much. Form up and let's clear out of here, Pink. Star Child, this is Strike Lead. The last escort is down. I say again – the last escort is down. Strike is out on the side and you are clear."

Ketalaman didn't know how he had made his way to the bridge of the flagship. There had been a shattering blow against the side of the amphib's superstructure that had hurled the Admiral to the deck and the interior lighting had failed, leaving the world lit by the streaks and glares of battery powered battle lanterns.

Choking, Ketalaman had moved, desperately searching for clean air, and somehow he had stumbled into the wheelhouse.

Pebbled glass mixed with blood crunched under his feet. Men yelled into interphones, striving vainly to bring order out of disintegration. Looking out from the bridge over the twisted ruin of the Crotal launcher, all that could be seen of the Teluk Sirabaya was flame and ruin. Massive chunks had been bitten from the amphib's weather decks by missile hits and men moved amid the twisted steel, some few with purpose, the others, the majority, with the convulsions of the dying.

The waters around the flagship were a maritime charnel house of burning ships, burning lakes of fuel, burning dreams reflecting off oil-streaked waters. Life rafts and struggling life-jacketed bodies were illuminated around the peripheries.

And the Teluk Surabaya was driving deeper into the heart of it all.

Beyond this hell there was only the darkness. Ketalaman could not see the mountains.

On the foredeck, the amphibious ship's 76mm twin mount began to fire under local control, blazing futilely at the night beyond the bow, trying to strike at the hantu that waited for them, the devourer of lives and futures that had hunted Merpati Ketalaman and invoked this upon him.

"Turn!" Ketalaman heard a raw croaking voice that he scarcely recognized as his own. "Turn! Turn! Turn!"

The Bridge of the MV Galaxy *Shenandoah*
2324 Hours; Zone Time, November 20, 2008

The squall line was passing and the tropic air stank of picric acid, raw diesel and charred flesh. Amanda Garrett fought down the urge to vomit. She was aware of Makara Harconan standing close beside her in the dimness. She could feel the war weariness in him as it was in her. He too had seen enough of big ship war.

It was time to put an end to it.

Amanda spoke into her headset. "CIC, stand by torpedoes. Get me a firing solution for the Teluk Surabaya, a full four fish salvo."

"Wait!" She felt Harconan's hand on her shoulder. "Save your taxpayers your torpedoes. Ketalaman is doing the job for you. Watch."

Amanda lifted her binoculars. She could see the big Ivan Rogov, fires dotting her decks. The ship was hurt. She was hurt badly. Its bow turret guns were still firing, but the shells were falling nowhere near the *Shenandoah*. The Indonesian vessel was like a battered, defeated boxer lashing out blindly before collapsing.

Then Amanda could see the silhouette lengthen. The Teluk Surabaya was turning away, reversing her course northwestward up the channel. She was trying to run.

"Wait," Harconan repeated softly. "Wait."

MacIntyre's voice was sounding in her headset. "We have a firing solution. Bridge, I repeat – we have a firing solution on the Indonesian flag. Range is closing! Standing by for firing order! Amanda, dammit! Fire!"

"Wait!" came a whisper.

"Wait," she echoed.

Amanda kept her glasses trained. The Teluk Surabaya was halfway through her turn, then three-quarters of the way; then she stopped dead in her own length, her bow lifting and the entire outline of the ship distorting.

Amanda lowered her binoculars. She could imagine the scream of tearing buckling steel and the roar of the inrushing sea. "Combat

511

Information Center, stand down torpedoes and secure the moon pool. We're not going to need them. The target has run aground."

"I told you there was a reef line out there to the north," Harconan said smugly.

The dead ship lay across the reef like a corpse draped across a log. Solidly impaled, she was an artificial island now, the men aboard her no longer crew and passengers but castaways. On the battle-damaged bridge, the sweating radio operator nodded. They had emergency battery power to the Talk-Between-Ships.

The Chief of Staff lifted the hand microphone.

"Attacking force. Attacking force. Hold your fire! Hold your fire! This is Captain Amadari of ... of ... the Indonesian Navy speaking from the Teluk Surabaya. We surrender. We are hard aground and we surrender. All our surviving ships surrender! Hold your fire!"

There was a ship out there. Unidentified and unidentifiable, it held in deep water off the stern of the ruined amphib. Where it had come from, the Chief of Staff didn't know. The only vessel they had detected before the holocaust had been a harmless freighter.

A voice, a woman's voice – firm, decisive and speaking English – replied, "This is the attacking force commander. We are receiving you, Teluk Surabaya. Be advised, your surviving transports have been targeted but we are holding our fire."

"This is Captain Amadari to Attacking Force Commander. What are your terms for surrender?"

"Immediate and unconditional. I repeat, immediate and unconditional. We will guarantee the lives of all rebel faction personnel as Prisoners of War under the Geneva Convention – but only if all orders and instructions are obeyed to the letter. Is that understood, Captain?"

The CoS took a shuddering breath. "Understood. We will comply."

"Very well, Captain. There is a small island off the Lingga coastline approximately six miles astern of your current position. Your two ferry transports will proceed at slow speed to a point in mid-channel directly opposite this island and they will drop anchor. Your ships will shut down their engines and power down all radar and communications systems. They will maintain full illumination on deck at all times.

"You will be kept under continuous observation until the arrival of Government naval forces. If these orders are violated in any way, or if any attempt is made to put boats over the side and land your troop contingents, the attack will be resumed and continued until you have been wiped out. Is that understood?"

The Chief of Staff glanced out into the night. "Attacking Force Commander, we understand and will comply – but we have many people in the water. Very many people. We request permission to conduct rescue operations."

"Permission granted," the woman replied promptly. "Each of your surviving vessels may put one motor lifeboat over the side with a minimum rescue crew aboard. The rescue boats may not land ashore. They must return to your ships after each sweep. We are dropping life rafts to your survivors as well."

"It is understood. We will comply. Thank you."

"We will also be dispatching a boarding party to your vessel. We require that Admiral Ketalaman surrender himself to the authority of the Indonesian government."

The Chief of Staff moistened his lips. "I regret we will not be able to deliver Admiral Ketalaman into your custody."

"Why not, Captain?" the woman's voice demanded.

"Because Admiral Ketalaman is dead." The CoS looked at the dark huddled mass lying in the corner of the wrecked bridge. "We can only hand over his body."

There was a long pause at the other end of the circuit. "Surrendering his body will be satisfactory. How did Admiral Ketalaman die?"

"By self-inflicted gunshot. The Admiral has committed suicide."

"Understood, Captain Amadari. Prepare to receive our boarders. We regret the loss of your ships and personnel."

"As do I." The Chief of Staff returned the microphone to its clip.

Something rasped oddly underfoot as he moved and he looked down into the shadows. Kneeling, he picked up something from the deck.

It was a piece of stone.

This was another of those things you could only practice in the simulator, the glowing blue dots of the runway and approach lights reaching out for the airplane that wasn't really an airplane.

"Easy Vince," Pinkerton chanted over the radio. "Easy ... Easy ... Easy ..." Pink's SPEED Cobra held off his starboard side, monitoring the approach.

Perhaps it would have been more sensible to have simply hit the chicken switch and bail out – but Vince Arkady was the stubborn, unsensible kind of aviator who fought for the aircraft.

They were over the approach lights. Over the tarmac.

The emergency vehicles parked along the edge of the runway flashed past, their blue blinker lights pulsing.

"Down to ten, Vince! Down to five! Keep the damn wings level!"

*Of course, I'm keeping the damn wings level!* Arkady snapped back mentally. *The undercarriage on this thing is about as wide as a goddamn rollerskate!*

Narrow-set wheels buffed the runway. *Let her settle! Feel the load coming off the wings. Come back on the stick! Remember she's a tail dragger! Get her ass down! Down on three points. Power back! Brakes on! Good girl, Jeannie!*

That wasn't so bad.

The tower ground controller interjected, "On behalf of the Singapore Defense Forces, welcome to Singapore, Commander Arkady. We have a hangar and a security team standing by. Do you require a tow vehicle?"

"Thank you, tower. Negative on the tow vehicle. I can taxi in. Standing by for the follow-me truck."

"Star Child reports they have a utility bird launched and inbound for you," Pinkerton said, hovering down beside the taxiway. "I'm taking departure and returning to base."

Arkady popped the canopy, swinging it aside. Humid or not, it felt good. "Roger that, Pink. Tell the ladies I'll be home for breakfast."

At anchor with their decks now brightly lit, the two PELNI ferries lay off the island. The sole survivors of the ill-fated transport force, they had now become floating prison camps for the Muslim militia they carried.

"Targets registered," the Ranger NCO reported. "Ready to engage if we have to."

"Good enough." Stone Quillain leaned back in his tree crotch and propped his boondockers on a convenient branch. "Looks like we got this thing just about wrapped up."

"Yeah, maybe." The ranger sounded dubious. "But we still have about five thousand hostiles just off the beach. Mind if I worry about them a little?"

"Sure, if you fancy." Stone removed a John Wayne bar from a MOLLE harness pouch and began to unwrap it. "But this sort of reminds me of a situation General Pendleton had to handle once ..."

There was a hint of a coming sunrise and the dark of Lingga Island could barely be differentiated from the dark of the sea. The squall line had passed and the day promised to be a beautiful one.

The *Shenandoah* lay hove to, allowing the AAAV platoon to snort and growl its way back into the amphibious vehicle bay. With the approach of the Indonesian Government squadron, the commando carrier had hauled up the strait to the northwest. Neither the surviving rebels, nor the arriving government ships, would ever get a clear look at her.

"Captain Quillain reports recovery complete and the bay secured for sea. All members of the mortar detail are aboard, present and accounted for."

"Very good, Mr. Carstairs." Amanda lifted off her helmet, relieving the strain on her aching neck. "What's the latest sitrep on the Rebel transport force?"

"The ferries and the Teluk Surabaya have all been boarded and secured by the Indonesians, ma'am. Survivor rescue operations are continuing."

"Very good." It was time for the *Shenandoah* to don her civilian identity and get herself elsewhere. "Lee helm, all engines ahead standard, civil power. Make turns for fourteen knots. Helm, steer three double zero.

"Mr. Carstairs, stand down from general quarters and flight stations. Strike all secondary mounts below decks and reconfigure for covert cruise mode. Resume running and deck lighting as soon we're secure."

"Very good, ma'am."

Amanda unpinned her hair and shook it down around her shoulders. The helmsman kicked up the binnacle and control lights to standard setting and, in the green glow, she could make out Harconan leaning back against the chart table, his arms crossed. He was smiling at her. "It was a privilege to see a master at work, Amanda. Thank you."

"It's what I do, Makara, and I am rather good at it, I suppose." She shrugged out of her flak & flotation vest and stacked it on the chart table.

He shook his head. "I can't help but think of what you and I could do with a ship like this. Consider the possibilities! We could make Captain Kidd look like a Sunday school teacher."

Amanda smiled, rather sadly. Nothing would change Makara Harconan, short of a firing squad. "There's no sense in starting that again, Makara." She extended her hand to him. "Thank you for your piloting assistance back there."

The king of the sea straightened and bowed over her hand. "My pleasure, my dear Amanda. And both Lo and I thank you for your assistance. We may both rest now."

"Admiral on the bridge!"

Footsteps sounded in the access passageway and Admiral MacIntyre pushed through the bridge light curtain. Christine Rendino followed him, as did a Marine security team.

"Well, you got to see your sea battle," MacIntyre said ruefully.

"And I wouldn't have missed it for the world," Harconan grinned back.

"Chris, what's the word on Commander Arkady?" Amanda inquired.

She caught the happy flash of the Intel's smile. "He's airborne out of Singapore and should be back aboard in another twenty minutes. His SPEED Cobra is secure and one of our transports will be airlifting it back to the States."

Amanda nodded and shared in Christine's smile.

"The rebel staff officers and Ketalaman's body will also be flown out of Singapore," MacIntyre added. "We'll be taking them to Bali to be handed over to the Indonesian authorities for trial." The Admiral cleared his throat. "We've also received orders from the State Department. Mr. Harconan is to be delivered on the same flight."

The bridge went silent. "Ah well," Harconan said finally. "'All good things', as the saying goes."

"It's not quite that simple, Mr. Harconan," MacIntyre went on.

"You've seen a number of things you weren't supposed to. You're aware of the existence of this ship and of this force and that complicates the equation."

Harconan shook his head soberly. "Not really, Admiral. I am in great debt to you and to this vessel. Would you accept my word that I will not reveal any information about her, or the true status of her captain?"

"Oddly enough, Mr. Harconan, I would," MacIntyre replied with a grim smile. "But that still leaves us with orders to turn you over to the Kediri government. I say again that I will personally see to it that you will receive every possible legal consideration for the assistance you've given NAVSPECFORCE in this campaign."

"And that goes for me as well, Makara," Amanda added quietly. "I promise I won't forget you."

Once more there came that bold and knowing corsair's grin that encompassed her. "And I promise that you won't either, my queen."

Harconan moved before anyone else could even make a start, turning and bolting for the open door to the portside bridge wing. Even as the Marines were fumbling for their sidearms, the taipan vaulted the bridge railing, launching himself into the pre-dawn darkness. By the time Amanda and the others could reach the bridge wing, there was only a pale splash on the surface of the sea, already sweeping aft.

"Stop all engines!" Amanda exclaimed. "Man overboard! Hard left rudder! Mr. Carstairs, start your recovery plot! Whaleboat crews stand to, on the double ..."

"Belay those orders!" Elliot MacIntyre's bellow overrode Amanda's yell. "Helm, hold your course!"

Amanda and Christine stared stunned at the Admiral. "We've loitered around out here for too long already, Captain," he growled. "Our security is at risk. I'm ordering you to get this ship into Malacca Strait and the cover of the shipping channels before full daylight."

"But what about Harconan?" Christine asked.

"Commander, it's an eight-storey drop from this bridge to the ocean's surface," MacIntyre replied, bracing a hand on the rail. "If the fall didn't kill that aggravating bastard outright, then he was probably sucked into the propellers. And, if that didn't finish him, it's a two-mile swim through shark infested waters to reach the nearest land. Any way you look at it, the man's dead and good riddance."

Amanda exchanged glances with MacIntyre and, in the faint but growing predawn light, she could make out a faint, wry smile. "Or at least that's what we can tell the Indonesians."

# Disengagement of Forces

Like a man regaining consciousness from a protracted fever nightmare, Jakarta was awakening. Ravaged, exhausted – but with its temperature broken – the patient had survived. The people who had stayed were back in the streets, rebuilding their lives, jobs and homes – and the people who had fled were returning.

There were no more riots or protests. For the most part, the Indonesian populace had become weary unto death of confrontation, politics and violence. At least for a time, they hungered for peace and order.

Ambassador Randolph Goodyard stood on the wall gangway of the American embassy, looking out across the square. He was back in Jakarta with a skeleton staff, albeit sleeping on a cot in his gutted office. As per expectation, the embassy compound had been well and thoroughly looted – but a platoon of Navy Seabees were hard at work, making preliminary repairs and serving as a temporary security force.

What was important was that the flagpole was still standing and the flag was flying. Everything else would come in time.

Goodyard and his people were not the only ones returning to their duties. Across the square, repairs and refurbishment were also underway at the battered presidential complex and the Ministry of Defense had taken over one of the abandoned business hotels as its ad hoc headquarters. The square itself was still dotted with the burned-out wreckage of military vehicles and one helicopter, but a military band stood by at the base of the smoke-stained MONAS spire, along with a small cluster of government and civil officials.

A Seabee petty officer climbed to the gangway beside the ambassador and saluted smartly. "Sir, communications reports President Kediri's helicopter is inbound at this time."

"Thank you, son. My respects to Lieutenant Culbertson. Could he have my car ready?"

"Right away, sir."

Goodyard turned to the slight, elderly Papuan in the summer weight suit standing at his side. "Mr. Ambassador, would you care to accompany me to greet the President?"

Chief Akima, the Ambassador General of the newborn Papuan Republic of New Guinea, nodded gravely. "I would be most pleased to do so, Mr. Ambassador. My nation wishes to become a good neighbor."

The White House
Washington D.C.
0850 Hours, Zone Time, November 24, 2008

"What do you think, Harry?" the President asked, buttering half of a biscuit.

"I think it's about as favorable an outcome as we could have asked for, sir," Harrison Van Lynden replied from across the table covered with their working breakfast. "At least in the short term. The Ketalaman military coup has collapsed and the Kediri government has regained nominal control over most of the archipelago. Sporadic fighting is continuing on Sumatra, with the Islamic radicalists swearing the usual fight to the death – but they lost their best troops aboard the captured ferries, along with a large number of their senior, most fanatical command cadre. It'll knock the wind out of their sails for a while. The Indonesians won't be able to eliminate the radicals totally, but the previous status quo should be restored."

"What about that nasty situation on Bali?"

"The purge is over and some of the Muslim Balinese are returning. Both sides in the conflict, Hindu and Muslim, are recognizing how they were set up by Ketalaman. There are genuine regrets for how things turned out. If Kediri follows through with his promised semi-autonomy for the Balinese, I think the fences can be mended."

"*If* he follows through," President Childress said pointedly, taking a bite out of his biscuit.

"We control the aid packages the Indonesians are going to need for recovery," the Secretary of State replied. "That will give us a degree of leverage. Beyond that, Kediri had the hell scared out of him. Scared men are sometimes willing to change."

"We can hope."

"It's like the bottom of Pandora's box, sir. There's always hope."

"That's the only thing that keeps me sane in this insanity, Harry." President Childress reached for the other half of his biscuit, wondering if the First Lady might catch him sneaking an illicit spoonful of honey. "What else do we have to worry about?"

527

"The Aegean, Mr. President. Greece and Turkey. This time, I think they mean it."

"I insisted on doing this myself, Major Quillain," Amanda said, deftly pinning the bronze oak leaves to the collar of Stone's khaki uniform shirt. "And this as well." She came up onto her toes and lightly touched the big Marine's cheek with her lips.

The newly promoted commander of the Sea Demon force actually blushed under his tan. "Well, I sure as hell would rather you do it than the Admiral. No disrespect intended, sir."

Laughter rang in the main salon and every officer gathered there – Navy, Marine, Air Force and Army – applauded. So did Amanda as she stepped back, allowing MacIntyre and the others to press close with their barrage of handshakes and shoulder slaps.

More than one mission was ending. The quest to make this radical thing called Phantom Force a cohesive, effective whole had succeeded as well. Bonds had been built over these past few weeks and this evening's wingding in honor of Quillain's cleared promotion would be another brick cemented into place.

A dream that Amanda had committed to paper as an intellectual exercise had suddenly and unexpectedly become reality, sweeping its dreamer into a new adventure.

Dreams have a way of doing that. It had happened to her more than once of late.

Suddenly, Amanda found that she needed a little of that time to herself that she intermittently required. Easing around the perimeter of the group in the salon, she slipped out of the boat deck hatch.

Her ship was chasing the sinking sun into a flame-colored horizon. Weh Island was drifting past to port, the last outrider of the Indonesian archipelago. Ahead lay the open reaches of the Indian Ocean and Diego Garcia.

Within a few days, the commando carrier USS *Shenandoah* would creep back into her cocoon for maintenance and replenishment, and the elements of her air group and Sea Demon force would disperse to their training bases around the world.

As for the merchant ship Galaxy *Shenandoah*, she would cruise the data streams of the world's infonets as a falsified set of shipping documents here or a bribed harbor master there. Like the mythical US navy man of war, the USS *Tuscarora*, she would be the ship that inevitably had just sailed yesterday or that wasn't due in until next week.

Until there was a need.

Captain Amanda Lee Garrett leaned against the rail and found that she was supremely content. Her life had taken a number of radical new turns and, now that she had a moment to contemplate, she found that she approved of them all.

She had a ship to command and she had the promise of the Admiral's stars that had seemed so elusive. An old lover had made the delicate transition to dear friend and an old friend had made the equally delicate transition to dear lover.

She had the rich promise of a new personal life to explore, one that might give her a taste of the roots and the home she had so long been forced to deny herself.

Someone coming to lean beside her brought her back to herself.

"Sherry and soda, correct?" Elliot MacIntyre inquired, passing her a slender glass.

"Correct," she smiled back, taking an appreciative sip. "Mmm, that is good. I know that having a wine mess aboard is hideously decadent and un-navy-like – and that Josephus Daniels is no doubt turning over in his grave – but frankly, I don't give a damn."

MacIntyre took a pull from his own bottle of Tsingtao. "The old Royal Navy fought two World Wars with 'wet' ships and no one ever accused them of being sissies."

"Very true. The world and the Defense Department are just going to have to accept that we do things a little differently aboard the *Shenandoah*."

"Granted." MacIntyre grunted an acknowledgement around another drink of beer. "What are your plans after we dock in Diego?"

"I'm not exactly sure," Amanda replied. "I've got post-mission analysis to do. There's some fine-tuning that needs to be done with the ship, the Sea Demons and the air group. I can see right now we're going to need more long-range anti-shipping capacity aboard. And more area anti-air. I've got some ideas about how we can pull that off without too many structural modifications."

"When's the last time you took a real leave, Amanda?" MacIntyre interrupted.

"Leave?" She had to think about it for a moment. "I suppose it was last year, just before the Sea Fighters went aboard the *Carlson*. Yes, I guess it was a little over a year ago."

"Then you're way past due. When we get back to Diego Garcia, you will stand down and use that accumulated leave time." He cut off her protest. "You may consider that an order, Captain. I do not need a burned-out officer commanding the flag ship of NAVSPECFORCE."

"As you wish, sir," she replied. "And I guess it would be nice to spend Christmas in Norfolk with Dad. He's heard some rather conflicting stories about me lately."

MacIntyre looked toward the darkening horizon astern. "And maybe you could spend a few days in Hawaii on your way back," he said carefully.

"That would be nice too. We could discuss the *Shenandoah*'s modifications package ... among other things."

They exchanged wry looks and Amanda leaned closer, so their shoulders barely brushed. It was going to be very different for both of them. But maybe it was time to be different.

They stood quietly for a time. watching the evening settle over the ever-lengthening wake.

"What do you think, Amanda?" MacIntyre said finally. "You did know him better than any of us. Do you think he really did go into the screws?"

She shook her head. "No, the Old Gods of the East Indies would never allow him to die such a plebian death. He's still out there, Elliot. He's out there somewhere with his sea people and his Morning Stars and his salted away millions. By now, he probably also has a plan. We, the world and President Kediri have not heard the end of Makara Harconan." Amanda looked curiously at her lover. "Does that bother you a little?"

MacIntyre's strong weathered features went thoughtful for a long minute. Then a glint of humor invaded his dark eyes. "No," he said finally. "No, by God, it doesn't. If the seven seas are to stay the seven seas, there's got to be at least one buccaneer left to sail 'on the account'." MacIntyre lifted his drink in salute. "To the Raja Samudra."

Amanda lifted her glass as well. "To the king of the sea."

Far astern, the distant white sails of a Bugi *pinisi* caught and reflected the last green flash of the setting sun.

Printed in Great Britain
by Amazon

44483895R00303